A Summoning of Demons

D1013947

ALSO BY CATE GLASS

An Illusion of Thieves
A Conjuring of Assassins

A
SUMMONING
of
DEMONS

Cate Glass

A TOM DOHERTY ASSOCIATES BOOK

NEW YORK

A SUMMONING OF DEMONS

Copyright © 2021 by Carol Berg

All rights reserved.

Maps by Rhys Davies

A Tor Book
Published by Tom Doherty Associates
120 Broadway
New York, NY 10271

www.tor-forge.com

Tor® is a registered trademark of Macmillan Publishing Group, LLC.

The Library of Congress Cataloging-in-Publication Data
is available upon request.

ISBN 978-1-250-31105-4 (trade paperback)
ISBN 978-1-250-31104-7 (ebook)

Our books may be purchased in bulk for promotional, educational, or business use. Please contact your local bookseller or the Macmillan Corporate and Premium Sales Department at 1–800-221-7945, extension 5442, or by email at MacmillanSpecialMarkets@macmillan.com.

First Edition: February 2021

Printed in the United States of America

0 9 8 7 6 5 4 3 2 1

For booklovers, storytellers, and the world's true heroes

to Eide

Invidia

To Empyria, Lhampur,
and Paolin

Argento

Il Corsia

Kairys

Riccia-by-the-sea

Cantagna

Mare di
Ossa

Cuarona

Tibernia

Varela

Hylides

Mercediare

Mare
di Lacrime

Isles of
Lesh

Rhys Davies

City of CANTAGNA

A. The Heights
B. Merchant Ring
C. Market Ring
D. Asylum Ring
E. Beggars Ring

1. Cambio Gate
2. Piazza Cambio
3. Via Mortua
4. Piazza Livello and Statue of Atladu's Leviathan

5. Palazzo Segnori
6. Gallanos bank
7. Philosophic Academie
8. Palazzo Fermi
9. Palazzo Ignazio

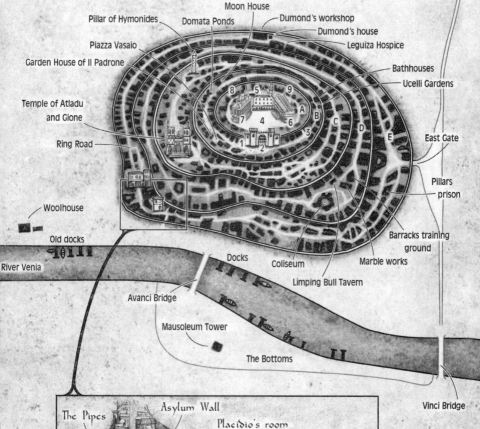

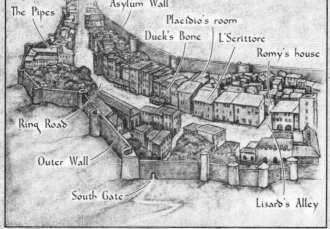

Rhys Davies

A Summoning of Demons

CHIMERA: *A Summoning of Demons*

F ew in the godless world of the Costa Drago prayed. Some
believed that Mother Gione and Father Atladu's abandoned
daughters, Fortune and Virtue, cared what happened to us and
would lift their hands to give advice if we wheedled enough, but
if ever a life was altered by random chance, it was that of Romy of
Lizard's Alley. Mine.

Why was one person born with the taint of the monster
Dragonis—the power for magic—when another was not? No philosophist had ever explained it. Of my parents' thirteen offspring,
I and my young brother Neri were the only ones afflicted. The
taint—the gift, as I had come to understand it—was a death sentence throughout the Costa Drago, and so it remained a secret,
buried deep within the families where it appeared.

What strange fortune decreed that, rather than one of the
myriad lusty fellows who roamed the Beggars Ring of a night, it
happened to be a procurer for the Moon House whose eye fell on
me when I was ten? My mother was delighted to sell me to him
because my demonic secret terrified her. And so was I trained in
both seemly and unseemly ways of pleasing whoever had the good
fortune—and the means—to acquire a very expensive courtesan.

Certain it was chance that the loathsome man who acquired me
at fifteen did not keep me to himself, but gifted me to his nephew,
the wealthiest man in wealthy Cantagna. At twenty, Alessandro
di Gallanos had already come to be known as *il Padroné*, generous
patron of the arts and champion of the rule of law. Fortune's grace
soon revealed him to be a thoughtful teacher and friend. That he
also became known as the Shadow Lord, who did not shy from
whatever was necessary to forward his vision of an enlightened
city, had never frightened me until the day when his suspicions of
my secret made my presence in his house untenable. Nine years
of comfortable companionship had vanished in one hour.

Yet one more random circumstance—a foolish scheme wrought
by a spoiled young woman—forced my brother and me and two

extraordinary men of our acquaintance into a magical intrigue that saved my onetime master's life and prevented a civil war. Our success revealed to *il Padroné* and to the four of us that magic was not fated to cause earthquakes and volcanic eruptions that could free our monstrous ancestor from his prison under the earth. Nor must its sole practical application be to preserve its practitioner's life.

Thus we four became agents of the Shadow Lord, bending our talents to worthy enterprises that his common spies and agents could not accomplish. So far, the exhilaration of using our gifts for good purpose far outweighed the considerable risks of detection. We called ourselves the Chimera.

I

The noisome airs of the lower city always reached their odious peak in the Month of Vines, just before the summer yielded to the ripe sweetness of the harvest. The stink was inescapable, especially when every sticky, sweating citizen of Cantagna crammed the Via Salita, the straightest, thus steepest, road from the Beggars Ring to the Heights. The side lanes were no less crowded and their aroma even worse. *Il Padroné's* Regulations for Good Order forbade chamber pots being emptied in the Ring Roads or the Via Salita.

Of all days to be so unpleasant. I carried a heavy crate packed with wills, contracts, invoices, and letters of charter to deliver to my clients before the proliferation of copied documents burst the walls of my shop. Just one aggravation piled on another.

Almost three months had gone since the Chimera's last venture, and I'd come to think the Shadow Lord had reneged on his assurance that he'd use our services again. Employment as a copyist for the city's lawyers was honorable work and paid better than tavern service. Best of all, it preserved my appearance as yet another resident of the Beggars Ring struggling to keep fed. But after two magical adventures that gave our city and its citizens a chance to flourish, scribing had me near dead from boredom.

I missed Teo. A long conversation with the young man I'd hauled out of the river half drowned three months ago would be the best remedy for the late-summer doldrums. Teo embodied enough mysteries to fill a lifetime's yearning. For one, the ability to make a person believe everything that came out of his mouth. For another, powerful magic, though he lacked any understanding of it. And I believed that Teo's dreams had leaked into mine, hinting at a past . . . and a role in the world . . . that even a year ago, I would have called mythological nonsense.

Every morning I woke hoping he would show up to claim his little bag of silver—his share of the fee for the Chimera's last venture. Last time I'd seen him, he was diving naked into the River Venia in the moonlight. Though I'd watched intently, neither Teo nor the bound captive assassin he had rolled into the river ahead of him had reappeared. Yet I knew in my innermost heart that neither man was drowned, as if a living thread bound Teo and me. Entirely illogical.

Fortunately, this morning I had to climb only as far as the Market Ring, the middlemost of Cantagna's five concentric districts, where my three most prolific customers kept chambers on the same street. Dispute Row housed a number of notaries and lawyers prosperous enough to abandon their old accommodations down in the Asylum Ring, but not yet of such status to afford the more comfortable chambers of the Merchants Ring or the Heights.

I turned into the Market Ring Road, jammed with tradesmen's stalls displaying the wide variety of modest goods Cantagna's growing prosperity could provide. Nothing appealed, except perhaps the baskets of plums—assuming the sun didn't boil them before I got back.

A clot of young men poking, shoving, and hurling the common challenges to true manhood blocked the turn from the Market Ring Road into Dispute Row. The only way around them was an alley, much too long and steep a detour for a hot midday.

"Step aside," I said. "Make way."

A scrawny youth pointed his spiky chin at me while his gaggle of comrades formed up at his sides. "Best watch your step, Damizella Prune Face. The Cavalieri Teschio will scrape you off the street and there'll be none to pay your ransom."

"Though her backside is most fetching . . ." chimed in a pustule-afflicted companion.

". . . and her cheeks have a lusty flush."

Hot and out of patience, I set down my crate, drew my pearl-handled dagger, and brandished it around their closing half circle. "And her knife has a freshly honed blade, Segno *Stronzo* and fellow backside orifices. Her well-trained hand longs to test its keen edge on boy flesh. Maybe cut a hole and let the ignorance out. Any takers? No?"

Though most of the youths backed off, two sidled my way,

shoulder to shoulder as if they thought the width made them more fearsome . . . or attractive . . . or immune to daggers. "We're thinking to join the Cavalieri. They paid our friend a bounty of a silver solet to join up. We could have some fun with the likes of you and earn good coin as well. Don't you think we'd make fine Skull Knights?"

I didn't dignify their posturing with a reply. An abortive lunge with the dagger sent them running. Rolling my eyes, I sheathed my blade, picked up the crate, and climbed Dispute Row.

Cavalieri Teschio. The Skull Knights, or more precisely Death's-head Knights, were a snatch-crew who picked up children from the streets of the Asylum Ring and held them for small ransom. A vicious and effective crew, so I'd heard. The Gardia paid no attention; if a laborer's children disappeared, they could have run off or died of the scourge and who really cared anyway?

New gangs of thieves and scoundrels usually popped up in late winter when food grew scarce, and rain and mud left laborers idle. But this name had been circulating all summer like the smoke and ash from Mount Agguato drifting on the winds from the south. Evil. Out of season.

By the time the bells of the Palazzo Segnori tower rang noontide, I had delivered my work and collected my fees. Relieved of the burdensome load, I debated whether to return home or spend an hour with my friend Vashti, my Chimera partner Dumond's exceptional wife. But I carried three new documents to copy—urgently needed, as always—and had stacks of completed work at home yet to deliver. I should rid myself of one annoyance or the other.

Halfway down the Via Salita, as I neared the arched gateway into the Asylum Ring, my head began to throb. The pain grew swiftly to a pounding worthy of Dumond's forge. Instead of returning home, I considered heading down to the Pipes and standing under the spill of diverted river water. Sadly, five thousand other Beggars Ring residents would be there ahead of me.

A sharp jolt made me stumble, and the hammer behind my eyes became a dagger. Someone must have bumped into me—only I couldn't say where or who.

But then a deep, ominous rumble invaded my body through my ears and feet at the same time, trembling my bones, itching my skin. I staggered as the cobbles began to roll under me. The street . . . the city . . . the world undulated and jiddered.

It wasn't just me. Shouts came from every direction. Men staggered. Women toppled or grabbed hold of the nearest body. Children wailed as parents flailed or clutched them close. Some ran. But there was no escape. Earthquake . . .

A sharp crack like cannon fire split the rumbling, and a stone pediment plummeted from the gate arch, landing with a thud that set dust and stone shards flying and a man screaming in mortal agony.

A swooshing avalanche just behind spun me around to clattering breakage. A woman stared upward, her mouth a perfect *O*, as her market stall awning collapsed on her and her display of pots. On the building above, a balcony creaked and swayed.

Dizzy, unable to hold myself upright, I crouched to the ground and covered my head against the rain of bricks and roof tiles.

The earth heaved again and again, then jerked violently as if to shake humans from its pelt. I fell forward and braced myself on my hands, drawing on all my will as if I could force the world to be still. In that same moment a throaty bellow of soul-searing rage welled up through the lesions inside my skull.

I clapped my hands to my ears before my head could shatter.

That did no good at all. The fury surged inside my skin, poured into me like molten bronze twisting my bones and setting my sinews aflame.

More cracks and snaps and noisy crashes. A toppling timber grazed my hand. I shoved it aside . . . and then everything stopped.

Numb, I took a shaking breath. A taint of such malevolence lingered on my spirit that my stomach emptied itself. My arm blotted bile from my mouth.

A moment of breathless silence. Then voices rose on every side.

"Got to get it off him. Need more hands . . ."

"Mam, wake up! Mam!"

"Over here, here . . . there's folk under this heap."

"'Tis the sign! He's coming . . . Dragonis . . ."

"Can't help. I've got to get home . . . the nursling . . ."

The image of the terrified pottery seller, wide-eyed as the sky fell in on her, was scalded on my vision, a substitute for thought. Shivering as if the quake had inverted the seasons, I scrambled up and ran to the woman's collapsed stall, now buried under the splintered balcony. I dragged away scraps of wood, razor-edged roof tiles, and the rags of the canvas awning. The debris shifted, releasing a thready moan.

"Stay still," I said. "I'll get you out. You'll be all right. Hold on. Here—"

I grabbed the arm of the first person who passed by. "We've got to move this wood. She's trapped underneath."

Together we lifted the twisted plank floor of the fallen balcony and found the woman under a tangle of her awning posts. Though blood streaked her face and bare arms, the tented posts had shielded her from worse injury.

"Virtue's hand," she croaked, and waved me off. I left her sitting dazed in the ruin of her livelihood.

The tower bells had begun a continuous, demanding clangor. Runners would be out already, dispatched from the City Steward's office, diverted from daily duties so they could visit every neighborhood to report fire, damaged water pipes, rescues needed, the injured, the dead. They'd need everyone to help.

My feet moved without purpose. Where to go? Memories of rage echoed inside my skull. Dragonis, people would say, the monster trying to escape his prison under the earth. I didn't believe in myths or monsters, but today . . . The violence had rattled me.

Shaking, I kneaded my temples, wiping my watering eyes to clear them. Home was the only thought I could cling to—the one-room hovel that had once housed my parents and their ever-expanding brood. Though old and ugly, squatting in a filthy alley, it was built of mortared stone—a rarity in the Beggars Ring. We'd be safe there, Neri and I. . . .

Neri! Mother Gione's heart, where was he? Rack my aching head as I tried, I could not remember where my brother was to be today.

My aimless wandering became purposeful. The Via Salita would take me downward. I needed to hurry. To find him. To help. Certain, the Beggars Ring was where the most help would be needed. The dwellings in the Beggars Ring were flimsier than those in the Market Ring . . . poorly built tenements, mud brick, canvas. Such a violent quake could have half the district in ruins.

"Do you think she'll be all right?" Someone fell into step beside me. The fellow who'd helped move the wood—the same spiky-chinned youth who had called me prune face.

I glanced over my shoulder. The pottery woman had gotten to her feet and was placing a clay pitcher, miraculously intact, into my abandoned crate. My client's three rolled documents were nowhere in sight.

"Looks as if," I whispered.

"Are you all right, damizella?"

"Shaken well and good." Blinking away the blur, I inspected my hands . . . the rest of me. Dusty clothes. Scratches and scrapes. My body was numb. Inside, I was a quivering mess. On the other hand, the youth had a gash on his head. Runnels of blood streaked his dirty cheeks. His sleeve was torn at one shoulder and matted to his arm. "Did you know you're bleeding?"

"Crack on the head's left me wiggy," he said. "But I've felt worse shakings."

"Worse? In Cantagna?" This was surely the worst I'd experienced. I'd never felt an earthquake so deep, so harsh and intimate, so violent. And yet . . .

Most permanent structures along the Via Salita stood intact. Stalls were flimsy, and overhangs like balconies, cornices, and decorative pediments often collapsed when the earth shook. But for the most part, the houses were whole. How was that possible when the shaking had been so dreadful as to leak inside me?

Though people yet dug through the mess, the crowd around the fallen pediment had dispersed. The poor man wasn't screaming anymore.

Spirits, Neri . . . please don't be dead. I'll find you.

"Fortune's benefice," I said to the youth. "I need to go."

Shivering, I hurried toward the gate, trying to think where Neri might be. What had he told me this morning? Sword practice with Placidio? Work at the Duck's Bone alehouse? Something. My fogged brain could not catch hold of it.

"Do you think the monster might be free? Is that why you're shaking?" The youth had caught up to me again. "You know . . . Dragonis. My uncle told me there's not been a sorcerer arrested since spring, and some folk back there were saying this is a sign."

"There is no monster under the earth. Dragonis is just a story, and sorcerers don't work to free him. They just—" I bit my idiot tongue. "I need to find my brother."

Leaving the boy behind, I hurried through the gate, dodging past the fallen pediment. Someone had thrown an apron over the dead man. The bells yet clamored the alarm.

The destruction along Via Salita in the Asylum Ring was much the same as what I'd seen. Heaps of debris here and there. But everything else remained standing. Panic had already smoothed to acceptance. People with cuts and scratches were digging out their neighbors or bandaging scrapes. Some were setting up braziers or beds in the streets lest the earth shake again in echo of the first, as so often happened. The streets were mobbed with people shouting out names. Here and there someone sat weeping beside a body much too still.

The thud of hooves emptied the center of the road as a rider careened around the corner from the Asylum Ring Road onto the Via Salita.

"Heed, heed!" shouted the rider. "Cave-in at the coliseum site! Cave-in! Hundreds buried! Heed, heed . . ."

Still crying his message, the horseman vanished up the Via Salita.

A ripple of determined motion threaded the crowd. Anyone who was not already digging moved to join others, many of them bleeding, to form a processional heading east on the Ring Road. Some carried shovels or picks or hatchets; some had naught but a spoon or a stick, anything that might dig. Others pushed barrows or pulled sledges or wagons, or carried bundled sheets or jugs of water.

The coliseum construction was still in its beginnings—deep digging, laying foundation walls. Neri's first paying work had been as a digger . . .

By the Twins! Placidio had a midday match at the old barracks training yard—a common location for refereed challenges that employed professional duelists. Neri might have been there to cheer his swordmaster on. It was only a short walk from the coliseum site.

I joined the throng on the Ring Road. Urgency pushed me between and around and through, leaving them behind when the road took a sharp bend to the southeast toward the coliseum.

The barracks yard was north and east. I'd never visited there, but it was easy to spot. Long, low, derelict buildings of wood upon stone—eight or ten of them—wrapped three sides of a rectangular yard. Several stretches of roof were fallen in, but only one large section at a corner looked freshly broken. The collapse had taken down the walls at that corner, as well.

Once used to house and train Cantagna's small legion, the barracks had been abandoned when the city chose to retain only a small local constabulary and hire condottieri for any real fighting. Besides hosting refereed duels, the yard served as training ground for those mercenaries and some smaller family cohorts, and as a ball court for Cantagnan children.

A steep hillside of sunburnt grass and scrub footed by a low wall formed the fourth side of the rectangle. That would be where onlookers sat.

It appeared as if a giant mole had burrowed a tunnel up the hillside. The section of wall at the foot of the disturbed ground had slumped, spilling dirt and stones onto the hard-packed yard. The sections of wall on either side of the breach were profoundly misaligned.

No one sat on the hillside. The yard was abandoned. Everyone would have run for their homes . . . or to help at the cave-in site. Placidio and Neri would not have ignored the call for help. Neither could I.

2

After two years of labor, the foundation of the coliseum had begun to take shape. The huge oval was dug into Cantagna's steep flank, the uphill side far deeper than the downhill side to leave the floor level for races or jousts or other grand entertainments.

I followed the parade of citizens down a hardened dirt ramp into the works. The dug-out boundaries of the oval had been stabilized with walls of timbers and brick, and around the far western end the floor had started to sprout great stone piers—giant mushrooms that would support the layered arcades of the facade and the banks of seating.

Just where the tighter curve of the oval's west end stretched into the longer, shallower curve of the uphill wall, the hillside had slumped, just as in the barracks yard. But instead of crumbling a short section of rubble wall, the shifting earth had toppled huge timbers, swathes of brick, and two of the massive piers. The mushroom pillars had shattered on the flagstones, crushing everything and everyone within range. Half the hillside had buried the busiest area of the works. And a crowd of Cantagnese citizens were scraping away at it, hoping to free the buried workers with shovels and spoons.

Though I kept my eye out for Neri and Placidio, I could not turn away. A huge crowd dug at the pile. The rest of us carried water, bandages, and sheets to cover the wounded or wrap the dead. I paired with an elderly man to carry a hastily built litter across the oval and up the ramp to add another corpse to the rows of the dead. At least twenty lay under a makeshift tent already.

As we returned to the coliseum to ready another poor soul for that brief journey, a murmur rippled through the crowd. A well-dressed man of middling height moved along one wall, taking a moment with each of the injured and those caring for them, speaking to the workers seated against the wall to rest, laying a hand on the shoulders of those diggers and haulers within reach. Even if I'd not recognized the newcomer's every movement, no matter the distance, I would know the two who flanked him—tall men, white-haired though they were scarce older than I. *Il Padroné* and his twin bodyguards were instantly recognizable. I could have predicted, too, that once he had spoken to each person in the crews, my former master would toss his doublet to his bodyguard Gigo, take up a shovel, and start to dig.

It was impossible to ignore the renewed vigor in every man and woman in the place. Yet what hope could there be? More than two hours had passed since the earthshaking.

"They say there's coves dug into the side wall where a man could shelter," said Benedetto, my litter partner, as if he'd read my thoughts.

"And fallen scaffolding might leave a space for someone to breathe," I said, thinking of the pottery woman.

We touched our latest charge's head and feet in respect, then wrapped him carefully in a patched sheet.

"Aye," said Benedetto. "That fellow over there with the red shirt was one of the first they found alive who hadn't crawled out on his own. He says there's a sizeable shed built down toward the end to keep dry their tools for when the rains come. Could be some sheltered under there."

He pointed to the deepest part of the landslide—surely the height of five men. Someone more optimistic than I had climbed the mound of dirt, rock, and death to attack it from the top. Risky, as huge sharp rocks, brick, and splintered timber poked from the dirt everywhere, and the mound was continually resettling as the diggers removed debris from the bottom. But then—

I squinted against the sun glare. Indeed, the man at the top was not shy of risk. He spent his days fighting other people's battles. Placidio.

My partner's broad, powerful shoulders twisted with strength and fury as he dug, tossing great shovel loads to the side. Those below him waited until the rocks and heavy debris had settled, then raked the dirt aside and hauled it out of the way.

No one else had dared climb so high, which told me Neri wasn't here. He'd never let his swordmaster leave him behind. Spirits, where was he?

Not for the first time, I wished I shared Teo's ability to speak in the mind. I needed to warn Placidio that *il Padroné* was here. Sandro had seen the swordmaster's face on one of our ventures, and glimpsed him masked in the other. He must never learn the identities of my Chimera partners. *Il Padroné's* other self—the Shadow Lord—might someday realize his sorcerer agents posed too great a risk to Cantagna's future.

Climbing up to Placidio could draw the very attention I wished to avoid. I took a moment to tie my woven belt around my forehead, which left my tunic a shapeless bag and me less recognizable, I hoped. When I lifted my end of the litter, Benedetto looked at me curiously.

"Is that who I think it is?" I said, nodding at *il Padroné.*

"No doubt," he said.

"Saw him in a processional once. Who'd imagine he'd be down here digging?"

Benedetto blotted his brow with a dirty rag. "This is his coliseum."

That was true. *Il Padroné* had given the land to the city and persuaded the Sestorale to build the coliseum, thereby attracting builders and artists from all over the Costa Drago and creating respectable work for thousands of Cantagnans. He believed it would become a wonder of the world, benefiting the city for generations. Yet the project was not without its dark side, even before this day. To make way for it, an entire district had to be razed. Three of my brothers had died in riots that had raged for a month. Sandro had shown me the model of the coliseum and told me of his vision, but he'd never mentioned the riots.

Benedetto and I hurried back to the area where the dead awaited tending. There were more dead than wounded so far.

Cheers broke out when two men were dragged from a section of rubble, bleeding and broken, but alive. The grim, grunting silence of effort quickly recaptured the crowd as, one after another, eight more were found crushed by one of the fallen piers. Identifying them would be difficult.

After this flurry of hope and despair, I glanced up at Placidio.

No one had joined him, but a stocky, balding man was climbing the mound with a bundle of rope in his arms and a large pack strapped to his back. Our partner Dumond, the metalsmith. Surely . . .

My gaze scoured the crowd. Standing in the mill of tired, dirty people, not fifteen paces from me, was Neri.

Relief flooded my tired limbs. My hand flew to my mouth to prevent the release of fear in a torrent of weeping.

A twitch of his head in the direction of the remaining piers, a widening of his eyes to make sure I understood, and he turned away, striding purposefully toward the end of the arena.

He wanted to talk to me in private. Before following him, I looked around for my nosy companion. The old man knelt beside our next charge—a terribly mangled young man. Benedetto's fists lay on his knees and his shoulders shook.

"You should rest a moment," I said, laying a hand on his shoulder. "I'll fetch you a cup."

"How can I?" he said, his voice quavering. "Got to keep at it. Laid pipe with this fellow."

I understood. Though the brutal sun had slid from its zenith, there was no relief from the sultry stillness or the rising miasma of death. "Come. He'll be all right to wait a little longer."

With my hand under his elbow, Benedetto rose to shaky legs. He didn't protest as I guided him to a man who'd set up an ale cask and was sharing it out to all comers. Blessing the generous taverner, I accepted one of his cups, took one swallow for myself, and then shoved it into Benedetto's hands. "Sit here and rest, my friend. I'll be back."

Neri waited behind one of the great stone piers that was yet standing. A coil of rope hung from his shoulder. I did my best not to bowl him over with my embrace. "By the Night Eternal, I was so worried, but I couldn't—"

"You all right, sister witch?" He glanced at my trembling hands.

I tightened my fists to still them. "Bruised a bit. You were gone to fetch Dumond."

"Aye. He brought the painted trapdoor we've been using to test his magic. Placidio heard there's a shed buried right below where he's working, and he figures Dumond might be able to open a way to it before the shed collapses. Dumond says that with the three of us joining our magic, maybe he could open a way deep enough, even though it's solid earth. Four will be better."

Certain it was worth a try. But magic . . . here amidst all these people, including the Shadow Lord? The quake had already inflamed the terrors of Dragonis and his sorcerer descendants, so magic sniffers would be everywhere through the city.

"We'll have to be fast," I said. "In and out before anyone climbs up to question what we're doing."

Neri flashed his ever-ready grin. "One of us might have to do some distracting. No question you're the best at that."

I couldn't imagine what I might do.

"Go around behind that next pillar," said Neri, pointing through the dusty sunlight. "It's a steeper path, but most of the way is out of sight."

The first time Placidio had chased me up the steeps of the Boar's Teeth with his sword, yelling at me to "get that blade up" and "block" and "defend" and "don't think I won't draw blood" to teach me that combat was ugly and scary and had nothing in common with tidy dance steps, had been terrifying. Climbing that giant debris pile was worse. The dirt was not half so solid as it looked. My every step caused the surface to shift. Holes yawned beside rocks and timbers, ready to trap a foot or collapse and start the whole mess sliding again, rolling you down the hill to bury you.

I wiped sweat from my brow and pressed between my eyes where my skull still throbbed. A follow-on earthquake, even a mild one, did not bear thinking about.

But my partners and I had learned that rather than just wielding our individual talents with the power pooled inside ourselves, we could open those reservoirs and share our magic with each other. Doing so enabled the one working the magic to stretch far beyond his or her usual limits. We had supported Dumond's portal magic in a few trials, but in no such test as this before us— shifting earth, so very deep, and carefully, so as not to crush any who might be cowering below.

Magical practice sessions were necessarily limited. Magic sniffers could detect the presence of active or residual magic and even follow the tracks of one who'd worked it. But today . . . if we could find someone alive, certain, the risk was worthwhile.

Placidio gave me his enveloping hand as I crawled over the steepest part of the slide and onto a flatter area. "'Tis gladsome to see you arrive here unbroken, lady scribe," he said. "Neri and I were in the open when Dragonis flapped his tail."

Dirt caked his face and beard, masking the cheekbone-to-chin dueling scar and the sun creases around his eyes. His good-humored grin that could buoy the spirits of the dead, rare in the best of times, was nowhere in evidence today.

"I was on the Via Salita," I said, stepping gingerly around a barrier of rocks and packed dirt that I hoped would prevent us slipping down the steeps.

Behind the barrier Placidio had excavated a sizeable crater, deep enough to shield Dumond, who was crouched in its center, from view of anyone but birds—or anyone stupid enough to stand above us on the broken hillside. The metalsmith was setting a square of wood at the lowest point of the crater and packing the earth around it tightly to make a stable boundary. The square was painted with the perfect image of a trapdoor hinged to a wood frame.

Dumond could lay his hands on one of his painted doors, using his magic to convert that flat image into a true door that opened onto another place. If he painted the image on an ordinary wall, we could walk through to the other side. With substantially more effort, he could paint an exactly matching door somewhere else not too far distant, and we could walk from one place to the other. Such a work used everything he had. But thick, dense barriers like masonry and earth, with no matching door waiting, made everything far more difficult. This one? We would see.

"I'm ready," he said. "Didn't bring my paints, but it won't be the failure of the art if this doesn't work."

"Maybe two of us joining in, first," said Placidio. "No need to sap all our reserves if we don't need to. I'll keep shoveling. Watch for sniffers or other busybodies."

"Vashti sent these," said Dumond, pulling a wad of black out of his pack. "In case we're successful."

Masks. Vashti kept a supply of black scarves cut with eyeholes for Chimera business. I tucked mine into a pocket. No one would remark them today.

My brother scooted down into the crater, knelt beside Dumond, and laid a hand on his shoulder. I did the same. As Placidio's shovel took up its rhythmic crunch, Dumond held his hands above the painted door. A deep, quiet, steady heat passed through my hand and into my veins, as if my blood had turned to mead. Magic . . . Dumond's magic.

Dancing blue flames appeared over the metalsmith's open palms, vanishing only when he pressed his palms to his painting. *"Cederé,"* he said. Give way.

On a simple crossing, it would be only moments until the painted door took on the dimension of truth. So deep as this . . .

Time swirled and puddled, going nowhere. Sweat beaded on Dumond's forehead. Wisps of his dun-colored hair were stuck to his head. Neri and I glanced at each other. I spoke with lips, not voice. *You.*

A nod and Neri closed his eyes. Like liquid sunlight, my brother's power joined Dumond's. Strengthened it as well, it seemed, for the painted door wavered, an ever-so-slight shifting of light that gave it bulk and thickness. But in moments it was flat again, and it was my turn.

I focused on the imagining of those who could be trapped in a crowded shed in the pitchy dark. Hot, breathless, feeling the air decay around them. Surely the absence of any sound beyond themselves would speak a certainty that they were already in their graves. *Reach for them, Dumond. Your gift is their hope.*

Bringing all my will to bear, I dipped into my own well of power, bidding it join the river my brother and my friend had made.

"There!" snapped Placidio. "Get the ropes."

Dumond yanked the iron handle. The hinges that had moments before been naught but a mix of powdered pigments and oil on wood opened smoothly to a well of blackness.

The three of us knelt carefully at the edge but could hear nothing.

"Fortune's dam, let the ladder be long enough," said Dumond, unfurling the bundle of rope he'd carried up.

Dumond kept the rope ladder in the single upper room where his family slept, ready to drop out the window and provide a way out if sniffers came hunting in the night. The ladder was fixed to a notched beam of ash just long enough to fit across a window opening—or a trapdoor—and strong enough to support the hanging ladder and whoever was on it.

"Vashti's idea," said Dumond. He pulled a handful of long spikes, a coil of wire, and a hammer from his pack, and proceeded to poke one of the spikes into the rubble here and there, until he found a spot where it encountered solid resistance. Once he'd hammered the spike into the ground, he used a length of wire to anchor one end of the crossbeam to the spike.

"Not so reliable on unsettled ground," he said, as he started poking around with the next spike. "But better than naught."

Meanwhile Neri unfurled his coil of rope and tied one end firmly about his waist. He tossed the coil to Placidio, who knotted the other end about his own waist and pulled on thick leather gloves.

"Wait!" I said, understanding instantly what they were about.

"Somebody's gotta go down," said Neri, tying on Vashti's scarf mask.

But if the earth collapsed again, even Neri's magic wouldn't get him out. My brother could walk through walls of brick or stone if there was an object he wanted badly enough on the other side. But he had to be walking, not buried under half a hillside.

"No discussion," snapped Placidio as I opened my mouth to argue. "You, lady scribe, must help anyone we rescue get down the hill; you're the only one can make sure they don't give us away. Dumond keeps his ladder from getting jerked loose and hauls people out. I hold the safety rope. That leaves Neri to go down. I won't let him fall . . . or get stranded. Certain, I felt the *anticipation* . . . before the quake. Always do."

I didn't ask Placidio how long his magical gift of anticipation gave him before the earth shook. Even for one with his honed reflexes, it was likely just enough to save his own life. In no way would it be long enough to haul Neri up if Dragonis raged again. Perhaps the dreadful pain in my head before the quake actually began was a touch of Placidio's gift of anticipation. Did his linger so long as this one?

Rage . . . The memory of the bawling fury in my head just before the earth shook could make a person believe in the gloriously beautiful monster who had tried to rape Mother Gione so she would beget him children. According to the Canon of the Creation, that crime had set off a millennium of divine warfare that ended only when Atladu, god of sea and sky, had raised a Leviathan from the deeps of Ocean to sweep Dragonis from the sky and imprison him under the lands of the Costa Drago. Exhausted by the war, the gods had retired to the Night Eternal, abandoning their human charges.

I had never believed any of it. But then charming, mysterious Teo had raised questions and imaginings that challenged my whole concept of our god stories. What would he say of this dreadful day?

Neri's black curls vanished below the rim. Placidio sat on the upsloping face of his shallow crater, knees bent, boots dug into packed dirt. He kept a light tension on the coiled rope that lay in front of him, slowly unwinding as Neri climbed down the rope ladder. Dread settled in my gut like a cartload of cannonballs that would not be relieved until my brother returned whole and healthy.

Certain, their plan made sense. I didn't have to like it.

Only a few coils remained when I flattened myself on the rubble and peered down the dark hole.

"Anyone down here?" Neri's quiet call was clear, but scarce hearable. He didn't want to attract attention from those beyond our crater.

A pale, ivory light flared—one of the few magical skills any of us had learned beyond our inborn talent. The darkness in that hole devoured it. Surely Neri wouldn't let anyone see its origin.

"Help's come . . . told you." The shout was muffled. So faint, that voice. So far away. "Breathe, Ista . . ."

A wail rose from below. Spirits, was a child down there?

"Hush," called Neri. "We'll get you."

Placidio tightened his grip on the rope. The taut line jittered, once. Then again.

"A signal?" I said.

"He was to let us know when he reached the bottom of the ladder," said Dumond, joining me beside the hole. "His rope is longer, so he wants the swordmaster to lower him. We just hope it's not too far."

Placidio slowly released the rope. When only a few coils remained, the taut line relaxed.

"He's down," said Dumond. "A gap of almost his height from the bottom of the ladder to wherever his feet are now—the shed roof, we think. Manageable, if there's someone in shape to give folk a boost. Placidio told Neri he was *not* to unrope."

Placidio took up the slack and glanced over at me. "Won't let him get away."

"I'm right on top of you," Neri called. "There's wood here. Gonna kick at this spot. Look for the light. We've got rope and ladder, but only a narrow way out. Doubt you want to dawdle . . ."

Neri's light wavered and it sounded as if he were tearing down a wall, as I suppose he was. Or perhaps it was the desperate people below, knocking a hole in their shelter. There were no screams or fits, only a low surge of voices as wood cracked and tore.

"Whoa! Leave the leftmost rafter," Neri shouted. "That's where I'm standing and where you'll need to stand. That's it, lift her up." A pause, and then he called upward, "One on the way!"

Dumond glanced at me. "You know what you'll need to do once they're up."

"Certain . . ."

Throughout childhood and my years with *il Padroné*, I had believed my only magical talent was the ability to touch another person's flesh and tell a story to replace a memory in that person's head. My parents had first noticed it when my father could no longer recall the hero tales he'd told me, because I'd given him a story more to my liking while sitting in his lap. It was an awful realization, to know I had stolen a piece of another person's life, leaving them with broken connections, confusion, and a new memory that seemed entirely real, yet was somehow wrong. Even though I had discovered that it was only a stunted offshoot of my gift for magical impersonation, there were times when it became necessary, invaluable. I was careful, and replaced the smallest bit I could—less damaging and easier to accomplish.

". . . but I can't do it to a child," I said. "To a mind not yet grown, it's too much of a risk. I won't. But the others, yes."

"I'll not argue," said Dumond, "but give the little ones a different story to hang on to, at least."

The smith turned his attention back to the rope ladder. "Be still; be still," he murmured when the rope ladder began to sway and twist, causing its support beam to tug at the wire-and-stake anchors. "Neri's supposed to tell them not to kick or grab at the sides of the shaft. I just don't know what that would do. . . ."

Magic had opened the passage, but how long would it stay open if someone repeatedly broke the barrier between magic and the shifty earth? Would the hillside collapse?

Though it seemed an eternity, at last a small head sporting multiple dirt-colored braids appeared just below the edge of the trapdoor.

"Reach up and grab my hand." Dumond lay prostrate on the square wood door, stretching both hands forward.

"Mustn't let go." The small voice held back sobs.

"C'mon. Reach. You know, I've got a girl your age. Seven years, are you? Eight?"

"Six, but tall fer it."

"Good. Take one more step up and lean toward me, then let go only one hand and reach. Tall girl like you, strong girl, won't let go till I've got you. Brave girl like you won't stay there holding and block the others from safety. I'll hold you. My girls like to adventure . . . to climb . . ."

Dumond was a gruff, pragmatic man who rarely smiled. But I'd seen him with his girls, and none of the rest of us would have had the patience to coax that child to let go of the ladder and reach for a stranger.

"That's it," he said. "Scooch a little more. What's your name?"

When she let go of the rope at last and grabbed his hand, no god in any universe could have made him let go. After a moment of scrambling, she was in his arms. A small child, dirty and bedraggled. He couldn't hold her long, though, as another child's head came into view.

"'Bout time you got to movin', Ista!" Another child's voice sirened like a trumpet. "My turn to get outta this bunghole. Don't wanna crawl into yours!"

Dumond shoved the little one to me and stretched out for the new arrival. "One more step on the ladder, girl, then let go one hand, lean this way, and reach for me. Your legs'll know what to do . . . and a bit of kindness wouldn't be amiss."

"Shh," I said, patting the first child's shaking back. Great silent sobs racked her. "But it's good to be quiet, so we can hear the others. How many, child? How many are down there?"

She jerked her shoulders.

"Is your da one of them?"

Her grimy braids bobbed, and I felt a moan that seemed likely to break into a screech.

Though I crushed her to my breast, she bent no more than a stick. "We'll try our best to get everyone up, but we must be quiet and still. So good to have a tunnel to crawl through, yes?"

I had to give them a plausible story. A hole from the top of the avalanche was not possible without magic.

"Masks," said Placidio, still in position, gripping Neri's lifeline. "Older ones'll remember."

I tied on the scarf mask. The second girl—a year or two older than the first—knew exactly what to do. As she scrambled out of the hole, she broke into a grin.

"Dandy!" she said and poked the littler one. "See, Ista. Told you some'd come. No demons down there to keep 'em off." She turned her face up to us. "I'm Tacci, bricklayer's daughter."

"How many?" I said. "How many down there?"

"Sixteen? Twenty-ought? Summat like. I get lost past a dozen. Some're hurt bad. Two's dead for sure."

"Can you hold Ista?" I said. "We need you to stay still. Don't want dirt or rocks blocking the crawl. Clever to have a ladder to pull yourself along the way, right?"

Cheerful Tacci lost her smile. "Clever, aye. Why do you folk have masks on?"

"The dust," I said. "Makes us sick, breathing it for these hours. We need to get more out, then we'll take you down and you can go home. You're safe."

A longer lag between. No question why, once the young man collapsed atop Dumond. Dazed and bleeding. Half his face a ruin. He couldn't even crawl. As I helped him away from the hole, his right arm had a death grip on his left. A shard of bone protruded between his dirty fingers. It was all he could do not to scream. How he had climbed that rope ladder was a mystery.

"I should have brought bandages," I said, supporting him so he could sit.

"Please get . . . the rest. Germond made 'em let . . . me follow . . . the littles." The injured young man, sitting curled over his shattered arm, mumbled. "So slow. I just—"

"Of course you were slow," I said. "Would that be Germond the ironmonger?"

"Aye. Got us . . . under. Shed." His every inbreath stuttered with agony. "Saved us. Lifted me . . . to the ladder."

"And Basilio, too?" Germond and Basilio lived on the Beggars Ring Road, around the corner from Neri and me. Both were quiet men and generous to the neighbors with their tools and skills.

"Nay," said the injured man. "Basilio keeps the business, while Germond works here."

Another man was up the ladder. Dumond offered his hand to a grizzled fellow with upper arms like clubs, but the man crawled out on his own—over the dirt, not the trapdoor.

"Mind the edge, goodman," said Placidio. "Don't want to drop dirt on your friends."

The fellow bent over and propped his hands on his knees. "Blessed Gione's sweet tits. I thank—" His face twisted into a frown, when he looked up at the three of us.

"Mask helps keep out the dirt," said Placidio.

"Guess it would," the fellow said. "How the devil did you dig this hole?"

"Tunneled fast as we could," I said. "Maybe you could help this man, goodman, and we can get these children on their way."

"Ah, Fidelio, poor lad," he said, yanking a scarf from around his neck and offering to bind the younger man's arm. "Curse the monster and the demons who feed it!"

The demons bent on freeing Dragonis were, of course, sorcerers. Like the four of us.

"You two should start down," I said, urging the two children to their feet. "The rubble is loose and shifty, so careful steps. I'm warning you, no dawdling or playing until you're down."

As the grizzled man bound Fidelio's arm, I devised the story we needed them to believe. I considered what they had experienced and seen—bravery, fear, pain, and the breathless dark. I envisioned the sizes and shapes of their rescuers. Then, laying my hand on Fidelio's shoulder and the other man's, I summoned my will to the power inside me and whispered a story: *"A clever, big-shouldered man with pale hair dug out a tunnel that came right to the shed roof. He and a robust, foul-mouthed woman companion stretched a rope ladder along the way, and we had to crawl . . ."*

Whatever confusion my magic left behind would be blamed on fear. No one could be buried alive for two hours and not have the mind playing tricks.

I sent the grizzled man after the children. "Could you watch them? There's holes and snags. We'll carry Fidelio later."

He scratched his head "Least I could do. Who'd a thought we could crawl out like that?"

Five . . . six . . . seven . . . One after another, we brought them out, and I replaced the impossible truth of their escape with the lie. Two of the laborers insisted on carrying Fidelio down.

A few people ventured up the rubble heap to see where the straggling parade was coming from. Dumond would toss his pack over the hole, and Placidio would use his shovel to throw dirt into the air. I babbled hysterically and shoved a newly rescued person into their arms, saying, "This one wandered up here instead of down. They say there's a side tunnel. There seems none to be rescued in the rubble up here, but we'll keep trying."

Eighteen . . . nineteen were out. A long wait for the next, a woman with only one leg that could bear weight. Her powerful shoulders had gotten her up the ladder. She lay on her back gazing up at the sky, gulping in great gouts of air. Her whole body quivered, her face bloodless and rigid with pain.

Placidio craned his neck to peer down at the coliseum floor and up at the broken hillside above us. Then he gave three sharp yanks on Neri's rope. "Get them up now!" he snapped. "Can't wait longer."

I scrambled over to the hole, horrified to see a steady rain of dirt clots and pebbles falling down the chute. The earth beneath me shivered. Darts of fire pierced my skull.

Neri was arguing with someone. I couldn't hear all the words, just "Go!"

"Up now!" I yelled down the hole.

Neri called up, "He won't come! We've got to get them—"

Another shiver. Shouts and cries rose from rest of the coliseum crowd. My muscles felt like sand packed beneath my skin, shifting, grating . . .

Placidio held the rope taut and growled through his teeth, "Stop dawdling, boy. Let them choose for themselves."

"Haul him up," I said to Placidio. "Whether he will or no."

Instead, Placidio's rope fell slack. *Spirits, Neri!*

For a moment the rope writhed like a snake, and then drew taut again.

"Now, now, now!" Neri's voice was faint. "Haul it!"

Placidio's thick shoulders were already straining, drawing steadily on the rope.

The earth shuddered. Enough to set rocks rolling down the rubble mound. Enough that the shouts from the crowd below became cacophony.

"Help this lady down," said Dumond to me, ever calm and steady. "We'll see the lad safe. I've got to *close the way* after him."

The trapdoor was resonant with magic and would be for a time even after Dumond shut it down. That magic could be used to trace Dumond through the city. Maybe the rest of us, too, since we'd had a hand in it.

Though I fiercely hated leaving before seeing Neri out safely, the woman had already got herself up to sitting. She must not see Dumond reverse his magic.

"Come," I said, shoving my arm under her shoulders. "That was just a twitch. A caution. What's your name?"

"Gavina," she said, getting her good leg under her.

We hobbled, stumbled, fell a few times. Whenever the rubble slid out from under us, my heart stuttered. I kept watch over my shoulder, willing Neri, Dumond, and Placidio to appear. Near ground level at last, I said, "Hold one moment. Let me catch my breath."

Supporting her weight, I touched her bare wrist, drew on my magic, and whispered the replacement memory.

"What did you say, girl?"

"You are the strongest woman I've ever met, Gavina," I said.

She shook her head as if to clear it. "No. Weak. I let the iron-monger lift me to the ladder, 'stead of going himself. He wouldn't leave me nor Viano, whose back was broke, nor the two others hurt."

Spirits! "Over here," I shouted, beckoning anyone. "Help over here."

When two women took Gavina in hand, I started back up the hill.

"Wait, damizella!" called a commanding male voice from behind me. "Who are you? What's happening up there?"

I glanced over my shoulder. Night Eternal, the demanding questions came from Rinaldo di Bastianni, Sandro's cold, serious friend who had despised *il Padroné's* mistress. Bastianni, a director of the Philosophic Academie, knew my face, and a Confraternity sniffer was just behind him.

"Come back here immediately, young woman!"

I sped upward.

At the top, Neri scrambled away as Placidio wrestled a large, very angry man, covered in blood and tangled in rope, out of the hole. Germond the ironmonger, face to the ground, was fighting to go back down.

Dumond slammed the trapdoor shut.

"Quickly!" Placidio snapped at me.

As the earth shuddered and terrified screams split the air, I touched the back of the writhing Germond's neck, and gave him the story I'd planted in the rest of the survivors. He must not remember it was his neighbors forced him out.

"Sigillaré!" Dumond pressed his hands to the trapdoor. Before he could grab the painted square or the rope ladder, thunderous rumbling set the sides of the crater sliding. Dust rose in a great cloud from the hillside above us. A crack, as of the world's ending, and a booming crash sent us racing and stumbling down the hill.

Placidio shoved the furious Germond into the fleeing crowd and vanished into the mob. Germond staggered.

"Split up," spat Dumond, grabbing Neri before he could go to Germond's aid. "No more to do here."

Yanking off the scarf mask, I let the mob flooding toward the ramps carry me. I was no more than halfway when the frantic ironmonger spotted me.

"Scribe Romy! Did you see those people up the hill?"

"Germond!" I said, forcing myself to face him. He was drenched in blood. Panicked citizens jostled and swirled around us. "Gracious spirits, are you injured?"

"I was buried . . . with others. But some . . . people . . . dragged me out. They had no cause—"

His brow was creased with pain, his eyes clouded in confusion. Grabbing his arm, I urged him toward the ramp. The earth shuddered and rolled. Screams rattled the pounding in my head.

He balked and twisted around, peering behind us. "'Twasn't

righteous. To abandon folk to die alone. Aagh—" He slammed his scarred palms to his head and bent over, as if his skull were cracking. "What's wrong with me?"

My gut twisted. My vision was creased with fire. My body shook with anger. "Get home to your lover, else folk will have risked themselves for a cursed fool. How dare you question fate?"

"No! I just need to—" He shoved my hand away.

Stumbling, I reached for him. But the human flood caught me up and carried me onward.

When I reached the road, I dragged myself homeward, grieving for the ironmonger, a generous man who must live with memories of horror he could not reconcile, and for those living and dead we had forced him to leave behind. My skin burned with shame. How could I have spoken to him so cruelly?

3

A sevenday after the earthquake, the city had begun to heal. The earth had quieted. Rubble heaps were hauled away. Repairs begun. The dead buried. Rumor claimed only two hundred—most of them from the coliseum collapse—had died. A modest toll by history's standard. The grape harvest had begun, always a healthy portent.

But the usual late-summer indolence had been broken. Certain, I had a difficult time shaking off the event. Every night I dreamed of ruin—crumbling walls and crashing roofs in some nameless city or hillside village. I woke in the middle watches filled with rage, shivering as if it were midwinter, and unable to breathe. Rather than improving with the passing days, the nightmares worsened. Now, the cracked pavement, the fallen towers, the crushed houses were always Cantagna.

Guilt forbade me mention my restless sleep to anyone. Many had lost kin or friends or seen their houses crumble or businesses damaged. Parents had children to comfort. I knew it wasn't just me. The signs were everywhere.

As I hurried through the city on an afternoon sticky with late-summer warmth, it was impossible to miss the change. Almost every window and door was hung with a ghiri—a spiky knot of pomegranate leaves supposed to filter out bad luck. In every piazza, red-robed philosophist advocates harangued citizens about the need to renounce the evils of fortunetellers, spiritists, and potion makers, practices they claimed led ordinary folk to accept the supreme deviance of magic. Even people who spoke too enthusiastically about the return of the Unseeable Gods were accused of undermining the Confraternity's teaching that no gods remained to protect us. Only human vigilance would keep the descendants of Dragonis from setting their progenitor free to ravage the world.

Praetorians, the enforcement officers of the Confraternity,

roamed the markets and shops, hunting for evidence of deviance. Worse, like lizards in summer, sniffers scuttled out of every corner and crevice.

A head sheathed in green silk poked out of an alleyway just ahead of me. His chain leash rattling, he dragged his nullifier from the alley into the middle of the Ring Road and spread his silk-clad fingers as if to catch magic flying past like leaves on the smoky breeze.

I ducked my head as I passed but did not alter my pace, and I gripped Dumond's bronze luck charm in my pocket as if to imprint my fingermarks in it. Someday perhaps we'd understand whether sniffers could actually detect the dormant magic in our blood or if the charms truly prevented it. Maybe we were simply lucky. Sniffers were captive sorcerers given the choice to die or to live out their days at the end of a chain. They were gelded and kept naked, sheathed in green silk, their eyes and ears covered. We knew nothing else about them.

The sniffer yipped, animal-like, and dragged his handler down another alley. I breathed easier as I circled the last bend in the road.

We four of the Chimera had stayed apart since the earthquake. Neri slept in the deserted woolhouse outside the walls, coming into the city only to work his shifts at the Duck's Bone alehouse. Even there, where most people knew us, we rarely spoke. Taverner Fesci pursed her lips and tut-tutted whenever I came in; perhaps Neri had told her we had argued. I heard not a word from Dumond or Vashti. Presumably Placidio carried on with his dueling schedule, but he'd not summoned me to our regular sword training, nor had he shown up at the Duck's Bone for his usual post-match refreshment.

As for our neighbor the ironmonger, he no longer called a cheerful greeting to those who passed by. Rather than singing or drinking at the Duck's Bone, or lending his help to someone needing the loan of a tool or a strong arm, good Germond spent his evenings sitting on a bench in his workyard, silent, his hands idle, a subdued Basilio ever at his side.

My writing work had provided me useful distraction . . . until this afternoon when I discovered a folded square of parchment in the sixth message box in the row of them outside my scrivener's shop. It bore a plain seal and the notation Box 6 in a fine, bold, and most familiar script.

A message so soon after the dreadful events at the coliseum threw me off-balance. Was the Shadow Lord offering a new mission? Or was he calling an end to our brief adventures in these fraught days? Unsure of which I wished for, I'd not opened it as yet. Rather I had dispatched Figi, the trustworthy child of a Duck's Bone tap girl, with a message to the other three to meet at our usual place at the Hour of Gathering. Our usual place was Dumond and Vashti's house.

When I reached the end of Cooper's Lane, I nodded politely to the lanky barrel maker, whose business gave the rutted road its designation, and I waved at Dumond's dark-eyed daughter, Cittina. The girl, a year younger than Neri's seventeen, minded her father's covered stall most afternoons. She nodded my way, while showing an elderly woman her father's silver jewelry and small bronze castings.

Off an alley behind the cooper's yard, hidden behind stacks of barrels and a string of ramshackle workshops, stood an ugly blockish stone house. I hurried across the shavings and sawdust of the yard, entering the alley just as my brother hurried in from its far end and my bedraggled swordmaster rapped on the plain door.

"Came soon as I got your message." Neri blotted his forehead with a sodden sleeve, sweeping aside a mop of dark curls dripping with sweat. "Had to dodge three sniffers on my way. What's going?"

Placidio, unshaven, unwashed, and his stained leather jerkin stinking of wine, cast a mournful gaze over his shoulder. "Dumond and Vashti haven't run off and left us to tend their houseful of chittering sparrows, now have they? I was just settled into a most delectable mutton pie at the Limping Bull after a dastardly morning."

"No, it's—"

The gray door swung open with a rush of air that fluttered my limp hair.

"Romy-zha, what's happened?" The web of creases that fanned out from the small woman's dark eyes were tight with concern. Behind her Dumond's bristle-brush eyebrows came together in a near solid line.

"Sorry! I didn't mean my message to fret you all," I said as Dumond and Vashti stepped aside and waved us in.

"Very little new blood on the swordmaster," said Vashti, her
sharp gaze taking in old stains on Placidio's abdomen, limbs, and
backside. "That's reassuring."

Indeed so, and it was a good reminder. Only a half a season
had gone since Neri had hauled Placidio into this house awash in
blood and very near death. Our joined magic had saved him, just
as we'd saved one-and-twenty souls at the coliseum. We were not
demons.

"Couldn't trust this to a messenger." I raised the sealed fold of
fine parchment. "And I couldn't—I thought we should be together
when we opened it."

"It's *his* hand?" asked Placidio, staring at the missive.

"Unmistakably."

Our first adventure had been forced on us by *il Padroné*'s young
wife. The second had been a request from the Shadow Lord's own
mouth as he sat in my scriptorium. But he'd made clear on that
night, and the one time I'd spoken to him since, that we dared not
meet again. My partners and I used magic in his service. He knew
it, intended it, and trusted us to keep that secret as he kept ours.
But if he had recognized any of us at the coliseum and sniffers had
picked up traces of magic there, he might have decided to end our
association. The First Law of Creation allowed no ambiguity. Sub-
orning sorcery, even to good purpose, reaped a death sentence as
inexorably as working the magic . . . even if you were the Shadow
Lord of Cantagna.

"Let's hear it then," said Neri, as we sat on threadbare cushions
around Dumond and Vashti's low table.

I waited for Vashti to reappear with her ever-available teapot
and cups. Vashti would not allow us to count her as a partner of
the Chimera, because she had no gift for magic and did not actively participate in our schemes. But we could not accomplish
anything without her own gifts: a generous anticipation of others'
needs, her impeccable skill with needles and fabric, and a talent
for seeing straight to the knot at the center of a logical tangle.

As she filled our cups, I broke the seal. The missive bore no
greeting or signature, but as I read the words, I could hear Sandro's pleasing baritone. The wry good humor. The intensity of

belief that could push him into such a dangerous undertaking as employing sorcerers. Especially in the fraught aftermath of an earthquake.

> *An urgent matter has arisen of perhaps a less inflammatory nature than our last dealing, but I hope you find the circumstances worthy of your unique skills.*
>
> *A virtuous young woman, my* vicino-figlia, *has just discovered that she is subject to a marriage contract that predates her birth. The young man in question is a stranger to her and familiar to me only by name and family—thus his state of personal virtue is unknown.*
>
> *It has been made known to me that the young woman wishes to refuse the match for* <u>Most Serious Reasons,</u> *unrelated to the young man's state of virtue.*
>
> *Her parents wholly support this contract, which, on its face, seems a most excellent arrangement that will provide their daughter and themselves a comfortable living for the rest of their days. Yesterday, the young man's family claimed the girl and took her to their formidable residence. The wedding is scheduled for the Feast of the Lone Praetorian.*
>
> *My influence—personal or public—wields no merit in this case, and every conventional solution leaves the young woman's parents in devastating forfeit of contract and our independency's governance with dangerous instabilities. If the contract remains unbroken, the particular circumstances of the marriage will most certainly deprive the world of an extraordinary young woman's work. If you choose to take up this cause, the necessary details will be conveyed in the same fashion as before.*

There was no signature.

"A *marriage* contract!" Neri's disappointment could have clouded the sun. Just turned seventeen, he'd only begun to realize how many charming young persons found his thick curls, onyx black eyes, and persistent good humor immensely desirable. He viewed permanent attachments as unpleasant, if not unfathomable, and dealing with one was evidently not near exciting enough for a magical adventure.

"To arrange children's marriage before they are born is a vile custom," said Vashti, flicking her spread fingers in the air in dismissal. "One thing I had no regret for leaving in Paolin. I'd no idea . . . is it widely practiced here?" Her glance at Dumond encompassed every emotion of one with four beloved daughters.

"Old families adhere to old ways like contracted marriage," said Placidio, his brow so clouded in thought he might have been speaking to himself. "And the very rich, like the man who wrote this, often do so. Also those who work the land . . . tenants, say . . . who don't have leave to go round courting partners willing to share such a life. And one more group that I know of; did you notice the day set for the event?"

"The Feast of the Lone Praetorian," I read, trying to piece together a puzzle intended to intrigue us.

"The remembrance of the Lone Praetorian is the most solemn feast day of the Philosophic Confraternity," said Dumond. "And the Confraternity is very particular as to marriage arrangements."

"The Confraternity is involved. . . ." The ancient society of philosophists was dedicated to two objectives: providing rational education for the people of the Costa Drago and protecting humankind from the depredations of sorcery. The Feast of the Lone Praetorian celebrated their victory over a sorcerers' rebellion two centuries past.

The words of Sandro's message might have been standing atop the page, each holding secrets and portents, burdens of significance *il Padroné* did not want to commit to paper.

"Certain, there's more here than a reluctant Confraternity bride," I said, mulling each word for hidden meanings. "For one, Alessandro di Gallanos is the girl's *vicino-padre.*"

Vashti and Neri both looked confused.

"Her *near-father,*" I said. "She is his *vicino-figlia,* his *near-daughter.* At some time her parents asked him to take a benevolent interest in her welfare throughout her life, and he agreed. Or perhaps they asked his family, and he inherited the responsibility when he became the Gallanos segnoré. I didn't know he had that relationship with anyone, which makes the circumstance curious."

"And then there is this bridegroom's *formidable residence,*" said Placidio, holding out his cup for more tea. "If the man's family is attached to the philosophists, as the celebration day suggests, then it's well to note that the Villa Giusti, here in Cantagna, is the only fortified property of the Confraternity. It serves as the residence of their three directors general."

So were more words unpacked, their secrets laid out for us to view. The directors general of the Philosophic Confraternity were three of the most powerful people in the Costa Drago.

I tapped my finger on the page. "Which leads us to the consequences of a broken contract that concern Sandro—these *dangerous instabilities* in our city's governance. Sandro always said that every interaction with the Confraternity Directorate is like dancing on a precipice, because offending them—"

"—can get you falsely accused of sorcery. Drowned. Dead." The dueling scar that creased Placidio's face from brow to chin pulsed red. Normally near invisible, the scar was a measure of his ferocity.

"The consequence might be more direct than that," I said. "For years, the Confraternity has been seeking more influence in official appointments and stricter laws regarding activities they disapprove. The young woman's family would owe a huge debt to the Confraternity for a broken contract. What if she's kin to a member of the Sestorale?"

Nine years of watching the Shadow Lord maneuver through political tangles had taught me certain indisputable truths. One of them was that influence with Cantagna's governing body was a bargaining chip as valuable as coins, especially regarding uncomfortable matters like mysticism and belief.

Placidio rapped a knuckle on the message, much as I had done. "Whatever this woman's *serious reasons*, whatever political entanglements fret the Shadow Lord, this is no trivial matter for the woman herself, either. Atladu's balls, what if she's one of us?"

The bride a sorcerer?

All of us fell quiet for a moment, imagining. Every day I had lived with Sandro—no matter how dear, how joyous they had become—was also a day fraught with terror. One slip, one question demanding my secrets, and I knew I would be undone. Eventually, the unthinkable had happened, but he had neither sent me to the Executioner of the Demon Tainted nor killed me himself. He had kept my secret because he did not wish me dead. A philosophist of the Confraternity, especially a director general or his kin, would have no such compunction.

"Nah! Surely that can't be the case." Neri interrupted the awful visions by shoving the letter across Vashti's table in my direction. "Maybe he's talking of magic, but more likely something else, right? What kind of work would an extraordinary rich girl do? I'm guessing she's rich, if she's wedding a director's son."

"Certain, the phrasing is odd," I said, "but then he'd never dare mention magic in a written message. But even if it's not magic, she's well educated . . . and some men dislike educated women." I'd experienced a bit of that in my years in Sandro's house, though thank the universe Sandro had been just the opposite.

"All serious business," said Dumond. "Difficult for the young woman. Perhaps breaking it off is a worthy endeavor, but I'm leery. For one, the earthquake has made it riskier than ever to use sorcery for anything. For another, if the Shadow Lord can't solve the problem, how in the blighted universe are *we* going to do it? Steal the woman away and everyone will believe it a ploy to break the contract. Feign her death, perhaps, but then how does the world benefit from whatever work she may do any better than if she were married to a philosophist?"

"Assassinating the groom might void the contract," said Neri with a sidewise glance at me. "But the Shadow Lord clearly doesn't think that would work, as he's got henchmen far more suited to assassination than we are."

"The praetorians would never let a killing of one of their own rest anyway," said Dumond. "Seems like the only thing's left is to convince the groom or the families to stop it, and I've not a notion of how one might do that. This message so much as tells us that's the case. And the feast of the Lone Praetorian is . . . what . . . four days hence? Not much time."

"Hmph," Placidio grunted an acknowledgment.

I'd no logic to refute these assessments. The crowds in Cantagna's streets cheering the philosophists' harangues certainly increased the danger of using magic. And sniffers everywhere. And yet . . . the thought of a girl pledged to any man before she was born rankled my every bone.

"No, Basha. You *must* find a way to help this girl. This marriage custom is barbaric." Vashti might have pulled the thought right out of my head, brushing aside our quibbling like the first winter wind sweeps aside the smokes of autumn. Her complexion glowed with a fire the hue of burning sand. "And think . . . a season ago you put yourselves at risk because *il Padroné* had an instinct that the Assassins List posed a danger to Cantagna. He was right, far more than he or any of us imagined. This sounds very like. Something about this young woman—or her work, whatever it is—sparks his belief that she must not be made subordinate to this bridegroom's family. He believes this marriage is wrong, and his own incapacity pushes him to risk using your skills. An intelligent man as he is cannot be unaware of the increased danger so soon after the earthshaking. How will you sleep if you dismiss this, and he's right again?"

Dumond grimaced in wry discomfort and scratched his balding head. Neri pursed his lips as if he'd bitten into an unripe cachi. Placidio blew a long exhale and mumbled, "This wise lady has a point. Would have been nice to be given a bit more time, but certain, I've naught better to be at just now."

I winked at Vashti, and said, "All right, then. I'll send our acceptance to the Shadow Lord's contact tonight and plan to meet him tomorrow. We'll hope his information suggests a workable path. If not, our agreement with the Shadow Lord will hold. He'll bear no ill will if we fail."

Assuming we survived, we would punish ourselves quite enough.

4

I wandered through the shower of dust and grit. Hunting. Listening.
The earth shuddered as if in the last throes of its dying. My arms clung to a slender, toppled pillar until the movement stopped. But even in the stillness that followed I could not move or lift my head. What was the use? There was nowhere to go. The Palazzo Segnori had collapsed in upon itself. The Bank, the Academie—the Cambio Gate—all in fragments. If those sturdy bones of my city were crumbled, what hope was there for the fragile ones—the Beggars Ring shanties, the market stalls. The last cries for help had long died away as my bleeding fingers had scrabbled at broken stones, uncovering my brother's crushed limbs—the hour my heart had died.

My tears had long dried, scorched away by anger. Why was I still living? It wasn't fair. Why could I not find my way out of this maze of destruction?

"Because you have a purpose, O lovely one. You have outlasted all of them—the scholars who condemned you . . . the men who bought and sold you, corrupted you . . . those others who live as leeches on your talents . . ." *The woman's voice rippled through the dry dustfall like spring water, cool and clear. Like a soft finger gliding on my naked skin, caressing my eyelids, my lips . . .*

I shot upright, shaking. Clutching my fists to my chest, I rocked back and forth, whispering, "Just a dream, just a dream, just a dream." My eyes could scarce focus through the clouds of horror and despair. Our scuffed table. The clay brazier. The sturdy stone walls. Intact. Neri's pallet empty but still smelling of him.

Why could I not be rid of the dreams? Why did my insides seethe with fury in the midst of such ruin? The woman was new. So seductive, so dangerous, like poisoned honey.

Sunlight streamed through the cracks around the shutters. Perhaps bathing in its warmth would banish my shivers. It was past time to be up and about. Four . . . now three . . . days until the

Feast of the Lone Praetorian. The Chimera had a mission. Focus on that and maybe I could get over the damnable earthquake.

Information was waiting.

NOONTIDE

The Shadow Lord's consigliere—his advisor in all matters of law—took a stroll every day at the noontide bells, always ending at his favorite tea shop. I trusted he would be watching for me as before, ready to pass on the *necessary details* of this venture—names, locations, and whatever else might help. Details that, I hoped, would give us a hint how to stop a wedding that everyone but the bride and her *vicino-padre* wished to go forward, while leaving all parties satisfied with the outcome, no matter broken contracts, repayment of bride gifts, disappointed grooms, offended philosophists, or whatever specific instabilities in governance the Shadow Lord worried could come of the disruption.

The warm, damp weather had me panting as I hiked up Cantagna's hill through the gates that marked the boundaries of the city's rings. From my home in the Beggars Ring bounded by the outer walls and the River Venia, I ascended through the brothels, artisan workshops, and cheap lodgings of the Asylum Ring, and the Market Ring shops of cobblers, tailors, glovers, spice merchants, and the like. Alehouse wags called the Via Salita "the Road to the Realm of the Blessed," referring to the home of the gods before the war with Dragonis sent them into the Night Eternal.

I kept my eyes open along the way, and not only for sniffers. The Cavalieri Teschio had expanded their crimes to the Market Ring since the earthquake. They stole children from slightly more prosperous families. Asked slightly higher ransoms. The victims might be five years old or seventeen, girl or youth, but always a pretty one who could bring a good price from certain caravans that paused outside Cantagna's walls on their way south to Mercediare or Tibernia, or so the terrified parents believed. The fortunate children—the ones returned home—recalled nothing but black hoods painted with white skulls. How did child-snatchers stay hidden as they went about their foul work?

A third gate passage took me into the Merchants Ring. Only the Heights—the heart of the city—surpassed the Merchants Ring in prestige and elegance, as well as altitude. This was a district of elegant bathhouses, stately guildhalls, luxurious gardens, and fine markets, as well as home to wealthy merchants, commissioners, magistrates, and bankers such as Alessandro di Gallanos. *Il Padroné's* modest childhood home now encompassed an entire neighborhood, housing his aunts, uncles, cousins, and even a few favored friends. Off one of the pleasant Merchants Ring boulevards, tucked away behind a vine-draped lattice, was a fine little shop: Mercurio's Coffee and Teas.

I strolled past the entry, expecting Lawyer Mantegna's clerk to pop out and ambush me in all his doughy pomposity, as on a previous occasion. When that failed to occur, I reversed course and strolled into the shop, happy I'd taken care to don garments slightly more respectable than an ink-stained shirt and leather jerkin. After an unrewarding glance into the shop, I sat myself in a shady corner of the lattice porch where I could see anyone who entered.

A serving man thumped a steaming pot on the tiny table beside me. "Red, flower, straw, or fruit?"

Evidently my dress was too out of fashion to earn courtesy. "Small leaf from southern Paolin, with a hint of dried raspberry—fruit not leaves."

The specialty tea would cost a good deal more, but it was worth the astonishment on the surly man's face. And when it came, every copper was justified.

Certain sensual things—the glissade of true silk across my skin, the scent of hot coffee, and the taste of small-leaf Paolin tea touched by dried raspberry among them—were intensely sharp reminders of the unexpected life I'd once led. Certainly, life as the Shadow Lord's mistress had never been so sweet as memory claimed. Magic had ever weighed on my spirit like the tiny death's-head symbols hidden in great artworks as reminders of mortality. The irony that magic now fueled my *true* life—the one set apart from the drudgery of pen and ink and careful husbandry of coins, bread, and coal—was not lost on me.

A sniff drew me out of my head. "You, girl, a gentleman in the back room asks for your attendance," said the tidy servant, pursing his lips. His disdain had, no doubt, been renewed by an assumption that I occupied a certain lewd position in the ever-shifting order of male and female.

I laughed as he snatched up my teapot as if I might sully it—or him—for future customers. Even as I held firmly to my cup to thwart the twit, my heart skipped a beat. Which gentleman—consigliere or *padroné*?

A full breath, a last swallow to drain the glorious tea, and I followed the twit's pointing finger through an arched brick passage to the back room. A lattice ceiling, open to the sky, spread dappled shade over vine-draped walls, two comfortable chairs, an unlit hearth, a small table set for tea, and, in one of the chairs, Cosimo di Mantegna.

"Lawyer Mantegna, a pleasure," I said as he rose and extended a meaty hand.

Mantegna was a formidable gentleman. Jowls to intimidate the stoutest witness. Heavy black brows over blade-sharp eyes. A trumpet of a nose, large enough to sniff out the sweat of fear. And oversized ears with hairy lobes that had caused endless humorous speculations when I was seventeen and newly confident that Sandro would enjoy my private observations of his friends, no matter how rude or silly.

I accepted his proffered hand, laden with ornate rings that were his only vanity.

"*Damizella*." He smiled and his warm grip firmed. "It is a great pleasure to see you. Well, it appears. Flourishing, I think."

"And you, segno. I hope your good wife and children flourish."

"Indeed they do."

His expression sobered, and he did not offer me a chair. "I profoundly apologize for the nature of my dismissal a few moments from now. A diversion, you understand. Execrable."

Ah, so there was a reason the tidy servant had assumed my unsavory status. Mantegna wanted to make sure none would view me as his friend, acquaintance, or client.

"I understand completely, segno. Life drags us in strange directions, imposing necessities we might wish other."

"Indeed. I have been instructed to deliver these few pieces of information without committing them to paper, else I'd have spared you such ignominy."

"No matter. Go on." I didn't remind him that I had actually been *living* as a whore for most of our acquaintance.

"The woman in question is Livia di Nardo, age nineteen years." His voice had dropped to a volume only I and the nearby chair might hear. "The only child of Piero and Andreana di Nardo—yes, *that* Piero di Nardo whom you've certainly met. Livia is a studious young woman of incisive mind and strong opinions who has traveled widely with her uncle, Marco di Nardo, now deceased. She has written a treatise on the formation of mountains."

He raised his formidable brows in question.

Clearly I'd no time to fully assimilate the range of astonishments he presented. The girl was a traveling scholar with a historical . . . or perhaps scientific . . . bent. That was curious. But my earlier misgivings about the debt the bride's parents would owe a Confraternity director for a broken contract had burst into appalling life.

Piero di Nardo, an honorable man, was the steward of Cantagna. The steward appointed and controlled the magistrates, constables, architects, street cleaners, street builders . . . all the functionaries who kept the city running. A steward deeply indebted to a member of the Directorate would be a certain impetus for more Confraternity influence in the city. Magistrates would punish fortunetellers and any others whose professions bordered on the mystic . . . and clamp down on artists, writers, and scholars whose works challenged the Confraternity's views of the Creation stories . . . and hound anyone who cherished hopes that the Unseeable Gods might return to succor the world. A most definite *instability* in Cantagna's current governance.

Mantegna continued. "The young gentleman involved is Donato di Bastianni, called Dono, aged one-and-twenty, eldest son of Rinaldo and Diani. Dono has completed a course of philosophy and rhetoric at the Academie. He spent one year at the Philosophic Academie of Tibernia, but otherwise he has not traveled, and never beyond the Costa Drago. As Donato is in his twenty-second year, he will be assuming his red robe as an initiated philosophist with a position of responsibility on the Feast of the Lone Praetorian—the same day he is to be wed. His area of responsibility is unknown, though we can be sure it is a prestigious position, as his father, Rinaldo, as you know . . ."

". . . is a director of the Philosophic Confraternity, and both friend and philosophical sparring partner of your client," I said, my dismay overflowing.

Another reason *il Padroné* could not interfere. I'd heard many a friendly debate between the two from behind the painted screen in Sandro's house. Without question, Rinaldo di Bastianni had most definite ideas about how Cantagna should be run. Even if the marriage contract remained unbroken and the young couple wed, he would wield influence with the steward. Piero was getting old and would be grooming a successor. Who better than a devoted son-in-law of impeccable pedigree? The whole business was fraught with risk for Cantagna.

"I understand your client's concerns," I said. "Most definitely."

With a nod of somber approval, the lawyer moved on. "The Bastianni family claimed young Livia two days ago on the basis of a marriage contract made two years before her birth. In that year, Piero's only daughter by his first wife was murdered by the girl's new husband—a soldier of unsavory origins. A tragic story that affected the gentleman deeply."

I could guess a finish to that story. "It created the desire for an unbreakable marriage contract with an ultimately respectable family for any daughter he might sire in the future. Most likely it also encouraged him to see that child become *il Padrone's vicino-figlia.*"

"That appears to be so. Piero himself claims not to recall the exact circumstance, but admits that he was so ensnarled in rage and grief in that year he certainly could have made such a contract. He and the contract witnesses have verified his signature on the agreement. My *client's* relationship to the girl actually commenced in her twelfth year when she embarked on her travels with her uncle."

His eyes darted to the passage doorway, as if he suspected someone might be eavesdropping on our meeting. "Livia is now in residence, properly chaperoned, at Villa Giusti. As required by the contract, the groom's family has verified her . . . maiden status."

"Fortune's ever-blessed dam," I spluttered in disgust. Knowing that Sandro's family had done the same for his contracted wife made the practice no more palatable. Courtesans were endlessly inspected for signs of disease all their years in the Moon House, and there was no circumstance which made it anything but degrading. Certain, those who purchased courtesans or wed virginal young women were *not* inspected.

"Indeed so. Once certified, this status is not revocable by claim or *purposeful* incident without breaking the contract. Even a *lamentable event* is not a contractual impediment, unless Dono refuses her as too damaged. That is unlikely, as the contract does not specify that this marriage ever be consummated."

So we could not contrive a sham assault or offer Livia a willing partner to alter her *maiden status*.

Thus we advanced to the only relevant question. "So how in the cursed world can this contract be dissolved without invoking penalties or unpalatable consequences?"

Mantegna sighed. "As I've told my client repeatedly, there are only four provisions that could apply. First, if the two parties are discovered to be brother and sister. Not even with Mother Gione's help is this going to happen. Second, if the bride is proved to be dead, which does not help the dilemma of her future work whatsoever. Third, if both sets of parents agree to dissolve the contract. Fourth, if the two young people are both come of age and *freely*—in front of their families and impartial witnesses and entirely without coercion—agree to dissolve it. As to the likelihood of three or four, I would sooner lay a wager on the moon being hung from my bedpost when I retire this night."

Mantegna fidgeted with one of his multitude of rings—a measure of his agitation, especially as its bulky design, topped by an arrow of gold and a shield of a single emerald, suggested it was a poison ring. Mayhap the kind that opened up to dispense a few toxic droplets in a cup of wine. Or the little arrow might rotate upward with a flick of a thumb and inject poison when plunged into an enemy's vein.

I sympathized.

"When is the girl's birthday?"

"Four days hence. The day *after* the wedding."

"Which likely inspired the rushed timing." Livia would come of age at twenty. "Would they enforce this brutal contract with a *dead* groom?"

Mantegna did not even bother to huff at my despairing cynicism. "Indeed, a dead Donato would not interfere. With some gift of foresight, these contract writers included a provision that if the eldest son is deceased, the next would be party, and so on. Dono has three healthy younger brothers—ages eighteen, fifteen, and twelve."

Two decades past, the Confraternity had judged the possibility of such a union an opportunity and locked it up securely. Piero was already the steward, but had not yet married Diani, the girl's mother. That was odd. Odder still, neither family had enforced the contract when the girl was fifteen or sixteen—the more usual timing of arranged marriages. Why now?

A last effort. "I know you've gone over it word by word, Cosimo, but could you provide me a copy of the contract?"

A shake of the lawyer's formidable head told the answer before he spoke it. "As the agent of the girl's *vicino-padre,* I was permitted to review the document. Under supervision. I was *not* permitted to bring a copyist with me. Both families view this as a sacred match, meant to heal wounds of a generation of misunderstanding and disregard between the Confraternity and Cantagna's civil authorities. Now, damizella, we must call an end. Too much time together could be suspect . . ."

I nodded.

He guided me gently through the passage into the tea house, still whispering in my ear. "I cannot emphasize how concerned my client is. We just received word this morning that the Bastiannis plan the ceremony of betrothal—the *giuntura*—tomorrow at half-morn. You see the urgency. . . ."

Before I could fully comprehend his whispered message, Mantegna shouted, "Get this impertinent female out of my sight," and shoved me into the tea shop.

Much too gentlemanly a shove. I tugged my hair over my face and stumbled forward.

"You are neither witness nor claimant, but only a charlatan," he called after me. "Back to the stews where you belong!"

This awkward performance would not enhance his reputation as a ferocious, incisive legal adversary, but I scurried away, head bent as if properly chastised. His last message provided fire under my feet.

Giuntura . . . *tomorrow half-morn.* Throughout the Costa Drago, the hour of the *giuntura* was considered the official interweaving of the two families, no matter when or if a public wedding celebration occurred. Most commonly the two were done together. We didn't have three days to stop the marriage. We had twenty hours.

5

As the afternoon shadows lengthened, my brother and I strode across the Piazza Livello, the heart of Cantagna. Before us stood the harmonious architecture of the Palazzo Segnori, where Cantagna's citizen-elected Sestorale met to shape the rule of law, and the High Magistrate held court to uphold it. To our right sat the imposing Gallanos Bank, the engine that had made Cantagna the wealthiest of the nine independencies of the Costa Drago. And to the left were the wide steps and twisting columns of the venerable temple of learning known as the Philosophic Academie.

Just behind the Academie, out of sight from our position, sat the Villa Giusti, the fortified residence of the Confraternity Directorate—the three directors responsible for all Confraternity activities in Cantagna. Our destination.

The squeeze of time had left our immediate objective clear. Stop the *giuntura* ceremony. Our choice of strategy was similarly limited. A subtle infiltration of the household to discover a flaw in the ironbound contract or some other malleability in the situation would take days at the least—with no promise of success. Incinerating Villa Giusti to force everyone out, as Neri preferred, was physically impossible. To thwart the implementation of the contract, we had to remove one of the principals.

Clearly Donato was our proper target. Abducting Livia alone, or even both of them together, risked exposing our purpose as disrupting the betrothal. We could demand ransom for Donato as if we were an ordinary snatch-crew like the Skull Knights, albeit one that could successfully break into a fortified dwelling. Once we had Donato safely hidden away, we would have to persuade him to disavow the marriage contract in the face of his family's express wishes. Threats, gentle persuasion, logic? We'd no idea what might work.

Strategizing the snatch was simple. We must steal him from his own bed in the middle of the night. We knew too little of the young man to lure him into our clutches.

It was the *doing* seemed an unscalable cliff. The Villa Giusti not only housed three important, well-guarded families, but served as the headquarters of the most dedicated and efficient military cohort in Cantagna. It also appeared very near impregnable.

Before coming to the piazza, Neri and I had assessed the Villa Giusti's main—and only—public gate. The massive walls were protected at four corners by stout hexagonal towers; a fifth tower topped the gate itself. A queue of delivery carts and visitors proceeded slowly through the gates. A second queue waited to pass back outward. Both ingoing and outgoing carts were searched, and all visitors presented documents on both entry and exit. The grand duc of Riccia himself could have no more secure a residence.

The assessment was discouraging. Portraying ourselves as visitors, attaching ourselves to deliveries, or even smuggling a captive out of the compound once we got inside would be impossible. Placidio, whose talent for anticipating danger made him near invincible in a fight, could no doubt handle the six praetorians standing post outside the portcullis, but who knew how many more occupied the towers or stood at ready in the courtyard beyond. We needed stealth.

No doubt Dumond could provide us a passage through the masonry at some other position. But a cursory scout revealed no easily accessible stretch of the wall where he could paint unobserved.

One possible entry had presented itself during our inspection. High above the valley of stone that separated the villa's encircling walls and the Philosophic Academie stretched a covered footbridge. The directors and Confraternity philosophists who had business at the villa or the Academie would not like negotiating the delays and confusions of common business at the main gate while moving between the two buildings. Perhaps entry from the footbridge would be less daunting.

So here we were, scouting. While Placidio searched for a place to stash our hostage, Dumond was hiring transport to carry us there. Vashti stitched capes and hoods bearing the death's-head emblem of the Cavalieri Teschio for the snatch, while assembling supplies needed to sustain our hostage and the Chimera long enough to convince the young man to do as we wished.

Neri's steps slowed. He didn't remove his eyes from the formidable Academie entrance. "So we're just going to march in there like we belong?"

"We are wearing the costumes of acceptance," I said, brushing the sleeveless gray academic gown Vashti had hastily concocted for me. Its lappets and hem were trimmed with the white border designating senior Academie students—*anzioni;* Neri's was trimmed with the green of new students—*allievi.* "I'll talk our way through the halls, and you observe. No one's going to ask you to write an essay on Floriatto's theory of drama."

"So you say."

In his seventeen years, danger had never deterred Neri. He'd grown up wild, angry, and illiterate in the squalor of a family with too many children and no use for the tainted one who could get them all murdered. Over the year since my return to the Beggars Ring, my brother had grown immensely in discipline, skills, and judgment, thanks mostly to Placidio, but he'd made very little progress in academics. More fearsome to Neri than the magic sniffers who might lurk in the marble halls were students and tutors who spoke the language of the intellect.

The hot breeze tugged at the papers I carried—a few documents from my legal clients and a rolled map I'd stolen from the City Architect's office for our last adventure. A flurry of pigeons swooped past as we quickened our pace, Neri one step behind me. My experience with Academie tutors told me that academic rank and protocol were of inordinate importance.

Spirits, a little more time to plan would be useful!

As we ascended the last few steps, one of the tall carved doors flew open. A red-gowned philosophist and a student, engaged in lively conversation, swept across the portico and past Neri and me.

Neri darted up and caught the door before it fell shut in front of me. Nerves, I guessed, certainly not some sudden blossoming of manners.

"Be confident," I whispered as I passed him. "We belong here as much as they."

Yet my own assurance flagged once we entered the Academie rotunda. The ceiling rose at least three stories to a dome circled with a base of windows. Light poured in from above, illuminating chaos below.

On the upper gallery that overlooked the rotunda, a tutor rang a handbell as if the universe were afire and she the fire warden. An arched doorway to our left disgorged a chattering mass of *allievi* in their green-trimmed gray, while other *allievi* and *anzioni* crowded past them to enter the hall they'd just abandoned. More students, with here and there a red-gowned philosophist intermingled, scurried into other halls. Pairs and trios of students and tutors ascended or descended the curved branches of a split staircase that led up to the gallery and more arched doorways. Hundreds of people on the move—and every one of them talking. Those not traveling up, down, in, or out stood in clumps of three or five or more—talking, listening, arguing. I'd assumed the Academie would be somber and strict, not a hive of bees, all of whom had something to say.

No one stood gawking at the somber portraits of studious men and women that adorned the pale walls. No one dawdled beside the statuary scattered like game pieces on the rectangular tiles. Only Neri and I stood idle . . . and one other pairing.

At the foot of the split stair, in a niche between its branches, a grizzled man in a bilious green-and-yellow tabard sat watching the comings and goings. Crouched on the floor at his side, linked to his belt by a length of chain, was a human-like figure sheathed head to toe in a skin of green silk.

The sniffer's head swayed slowly side to side like that of a restive hound. We needed to keep moving.

"Come, Nico," I said, choosing the rightmost branch of the stair. "Let's find a study room to review our map."

Somewhere on that upper gallery, we should find a route to the footbridge and Villa Giusti.

"Look *interested* in whatever I babble," I said quietly as we joined the throng on the shallow steps.

As we climbed, I rattled on about the military history of Cantagna. Neri cocked his head as if listening carefully. None but I could see his eyes roaming the people on the opposite arm of the stair, those on the floor below, those behind or above us. We knew to note doorways, alcoves, artworks, lamps that might remain lit after sunset, whatever there was to be seen. Placidio had taught us to be observant.

Neri paused when we reached the top of the stair—the center point of the U-shaped gallery. "I have a question, *anziana* . . ."

As he posed a question about tunnels used for plague victims, we stepped out of the way of those ascending behind us. Three clusters of students and tutors passed us, dispersing when they reached the top. Neri only moved again when a lone woman who trailed behind the three groups passed us. The woman wore a red cloak trimmed in gold—a senior philosophist.

I nodded, understanding his move. Senior philosophists were more likely than lower-ranked scholars to visit Villa Giusti.

As we strolled along the gallery behind the woman, I spoke of a ten-year war with Tibernia, and an attack that had scorched the eastern half of the upper city and brought the plague to Cantagna a century ago.

The drone of lecturing spilled from one arched doorway, the back-and-forth of sharp questions and answers from another. When the woman philosophist turned into one of the archways, we continued past the opening. A glance showed a chamber filled with lamplit tables. Students sat poring over books or pages, alone or together, some writing, some whispering. A study room, not a passage to Villa Giusti. From there to the gallery's end at the front wall of the rotunda, we saw no sign of any passage or any bridge.

We retraced our steps.

"*Anziana!* What are you doing?" The high-pitched challenge came from behind me just as we passed the head of the stair into the unexplored half of the gallery. "This *allievo* belongs in tutorial at this hour. As do you most likely."

An icy wash crossed my skin.

With all I knew of philosophist hauteur, I pointed an autocratic finger at Neri to hold position and then pivoted slowly toward the man behind me.

The man had a massive forehead. His tiny eyebrows looked like bits of juniper scrub embedded halfway up a cliff. The lack of gold or silver trim on his red gown named him an ordinary tutor or administrator. The lappets of his gown were sewn with pockets, bulging with an interesting variety of shapes, as if his duties included a great deal of fetching and carrying.

"Excuse me, Master—?"

"Tano," he announced, as if only an idiot would not know it. "You are out of—"

"I am Eliani di Corso, Master Tano," I said, bowing my head

smartly, "a mentor from the Invidian Academie assigned to this student. You've likely heard of Captain Vito di Savene, brought to Cantagna at the behest of Segnoré Rodrigo di Fermi to retrain his House cohort after some lamentable failure in the spring. Captain di Savene has brought his family here from Invidia, and this is his son, Nico."

Neri gave a stiff bow, as I had taught him. Passing students and tutors glanced at us in curiosity.

I plunged ahead, not waiting for the philosophist to take control of our exchange. "The captain hopes that the famed Cantagna Academie can provide his son better prospects than—excuse my disparagement—the inadequate resources of the Invidian Academie. Director Meucci appointed me to accompany Nico and mentor him until his proficiency is up to Cantagnese standards."

Tano pruned his lips and wrinkled his mighty brow, clearly unsure whether to preen, reprove, or investigate. Questioning would expose his ignorance of matters regarding Fermi, a notable member of the Sestorale, and Meucci, a Confraternity director he'd never heard of. Tano didn't look like a man who enjoyed displaying ignorance on any matter.

"Seems a very odd situation to me," he snapped. "The youth should have a mentor from *this* Academie."

I leaned my head toward Tano, as if sharing a confidence, and dropped my voice. "Well, of course, it is the problematic dialect, Master. Invidians are as like to be mistaken for tribesmen of Empyria as citizens of a Costa Drago independency. I myself was born in Varela and received most of my education there. But I am as new to your Academie as Nico, so perhaps you could direct me to your map library? Nico is most excellent at maps, and I was thinking that's where we might start in smoothing out his language skills."

"Maps and other documents are found just there." He pointed a well-manicured finger at a doorway arch ahead of us. "But you'll need the documentarian, who is currently engaged downstairs, to unlock the bookpresses and chests. Students are forbidden to rummage among valuable documents as their whims take them."

"The Varela Academie is similarly disciplined, Master. We will examine the map I've brought as we await the return of the documentarian." I tapped the scroll I'd managed not to crush in a fit of nerves. "Fortune's benefice for the coming evening, Master Tano."

Without waiting for his reply, I signaled Neri to proceed down the gallery. Tano's mouth dropped open.

My back burned as I took up our discussion of plagues and crypts—adding a touch of Invidian inflection. It was all I could do not to look backward.

Determined not to hurry, Neri and I strolled past an arch that opened to a lecture hall. The next one opened into a cluster of smaller chambers populated with individual students and tutors working together.

An elaborate cornice shaped as a lion's head marked each of the opposing corners where the gallery spanning the back wall of the rotunda joined the shorter side galleries. We were approaching the corner when two red-robed men emerged from an archway directly under the lion's head. One of them wore a crimson toque, trimmed in gold; the spare planes of his cheek were deadly familiar.

". . . an uproar. Honestly, Rinaldo, it's short notice for such a celebration." Engrossed in conversation, the two deigned us only a glance.

"Indeed. But the world is ripe for certainty," said the man in the toque. Rinaldo di Bastianni, Director of the Philosophic Academie. Father of the man we planned to abduct. Friend of *il Padroné*, thus a man who could recognize *il Padroné*'s whore.

"In here, Nico." Heart thumping, I shoved Neri through the doorway Tano had indicated and near stepped on his heels as I followed. "Sit. You must attend your lessons else appear eternally ignorant!"

Orderly arrangements of book presses and scroll cases surrounded four long tables. The chamber was dim, only a lamp set in a bracket by the doorway was lit. No one occupied the neatly ordered stools. I spread the map on the table in front of Neri and kept my back to the doorway, babbling of Cantagna's history.

A shadow blocked the light from the gallery. Bastianni. "Who are you? What are you doing here unsupervised?"

Head bowed, I gave him the same story I'd told earlier, adding, "Master Tano ordered us to wait here for the documentarian."

"Hmph." It seemed an eternal pause until he moved on.

I sagged to the stool beside Neri.

The sniffer at the bottom of the stair and Master Tano at the top had unsettled me more than they should. Then to encounter Bastianni himself . . .

"You don't need me to—to let you out, do you?" said Neri, staring at my face. "You look mostly like yourself, but you sound just like one of these pinchy folk."

I smothered a laugh. "I'm myself. Just need to take a breath."

Neri knew very well that I wasn't planning on using my impersonation magic on this occasion, not in the very heart of the Confraternity, but he was understandably nervous about any sudden change in that plan. My very useful talent was still hampered by its most inconvenient flaw. I was unable to shake off the magic and become Romy again on my own—a terrifying result, as I had learned through hard experience. To trigger this relinquishing, someone had to touch my skin and speak my name aloud. Only our friend Teo had managed it elsewhere, a direct manifestation of the connection—the thread—that bound us together.

"Good," Neri said. He positioned himself behind a cupboard where he could see into the gallery. "There's no sign of action behind us."

"The one in the toque was Director Bastianni."

"Bastianni. The same—?" He swallowed hard and took another quick glance through the doorway.

"That's right. The groom's father."

"Makes sense. Since we came up the stair, there's been a regular processional through that door under the lion's head, where he came out. Mostly folk in red, not gray. I'll lay you a silver solet that's our bridge. Let's go see."

Neri had recovered from the shock faster than I. And he was right. We needed more than a *likely* location for the bridge entry. "Let's take a quick stroll and see what we're facing," I said. "Then we'll beat an orderly retreat."

"We need to get a look inside the villa walls, too. The place could have a thousand rooms for all we know. Just give me a distraction. You know the kind of thing will work. You draw them out, and I'll get through whatever opens onto that bridge."

I, too, hated the thought of us going in blind. The high walls had prevented even a glimpse of the house, and none of us had ever been inside Villa Giusti. If we had a hint of where Donato was housed, our night's gambit would go much faster. But using magic to get past a guarded doorway merely for a scouting expedition was a terrible risk with sniffers about, especially when Placidio and Dumond weren't with us.

"We *cannot* put them on alert," I whispered. "And you've nothing to aim for, so your magic wouldn't work to get you in anyway, and we're so far from home . . . could you even get out?"

"There's a cutler out on the piazza who's displaying some fine daggers on his cart. He's got one I'd give a month's eating to have. I could walk to it from most anywhere."

To trigger his magic, Neri needed a destination he could visualize and an object he desired. As long as the destination object was reasonably close, his magic could get him through walls even so thick as Villa Giusti's. He claimed the real spark was the *wanting*—sometimes for the object, sometimes for what he could do with it.

"What if he's sold the dagger?"

Neri grinned. "The one I want's hanging from his belt. I've tried to buy it off him before."

"You'd have to be fast." No doubt there were more sniffers lurking in the villa.

"Quick as lightning. We need a better look."

His excitement was infectious. Though we dared not risk too much, the hours until the *giuntura* were expiring quickly.

"If there's a clear path for you to get in, and a reasonable way to distract a praetorian or a philosophist so you can learn something, I'll do it. But you follow *my* lead."

"I will."

"Let's go, then," I said, "and see what's to be seen."

The Academie had changed in our brief retreat. The bell had stopped ringing. The gallery and stairs were almost deserted. We marched out of the document room, turned left toward the lion's head cornice and then left again through the doorway arch underneath the lion.

"Ha!" Neri murmured in triumph.

The bare-walled corridor plunged deep into the Academie. Two women in red gowns approached. I kept lecturing, and we walked briskly and paid them no mind as if we knew exactly where we were going. Engaged in their own conversation, they passed without slowing. Good. It must not be unknown for students to go this way.

A zig and a zag in the corridor brought us to an upward ramp and into a new section. Easy to see that the corridor had become the covered bridge. Arrow loops slotted the walls on both sides. The right-side loops gave us a view of the flat, creneled roof of the Academie and a cityscape of rooftops beyond. The left-side loops looked over the barren gulf of stonemasonry between the Academie building and the thick Villa Giusti wall.

The damnably narrow arrow loops yielded no view of any structure behind the wall, so we still had no view of the villa itself. Its courts could hold a sea of praetorians and sniffers.

"Why is a house full of philosophists locked up so tight?" asked Neri as we walked purposefully onward.

"No idea," I said. "The directors and their families live there. I suppose there's a praetorian barracks."

Public officials or wealthy merchants were more likely targets for assassination or abduction than Confraternity directors. God-believers, charm sellers, and fortunetellers were not exactly formidable enemies, nor could individual sorcerers storm the thick walls hunting vengeance unless they were a great deal more skilled than the four of us.

Fifty or sixty paces ahead, the bridge ended in a dark alcove that penetrated a wall of milled stone. Blocking any closer look at the alcove was a gaggle of ten or more older students following a red-robed tutor heading straight for it.

Eyeing Neri, I dipped my head to the gaggle and we drifted forward to join them.

A few steps farther and I could make out a door set deep inside the alcove and the two praetorians who guarded it. I'd wager that the door opened into one of the Villa's hexagonal towers. Excitement heated my cheeks.

Certain, when we came back tonight, Placidio and Neri could take down these two praetorians, and the others who surely waited on the other side. In half an hour or so of meticulous painting and an instant's application of magic, Dumond could get us through the door, whether it was iron or wood.

We followed as the group entered the alcove.

"Students to provide assistance in setting up for tomorrow's rites," announced our guide in a pompous tenor. Master Tano.

Damnation! But we couldn't miss the chance. With only a quick nod, Neri and I ducked our heads and stayed close to the back of the group.

"Hold right there." One of the praetorians rapped an iron ring.

The students murmured to each other as we waited. A chain rattled against the stone. The students at the front edged closer to one side of the alcove. A human-shaped creature sheathed in green silk crawled between the alcove wall and our group.

The sniffer's long chain was not linked to a nullifier's belt, but to an eyebolt embedded in the masonry. I shifted with the group, but elsewise did not move, did not breathe. Neri pressed his shoulder to mine. I felt his hand move to the knife sheathed under his gown.

The sniffer slunk closer to our feet, tilting his head side to side as if listening to sounds we could not hear. The green silk shroud he wore—a second skin that obscured every part of him including eyes, ears, and mouth—made it easy to believe him some kind of prescient worm crawled out from a crack in the earth. The inhuman terror of a sniffer's pointing finger and wordless howl was all consuming, demanding you run . . . and reveal your fear to all.

Neri and I had grown up assuming a sniffer could detect the stain of magic on our souls, even if we weren't using it right then, even if we hadn't used it in years. Dumond had given us little bronze luck charms that supposedly protected us. And certain, none of us four could detect the dormant gift in each other. But then, none of us could follow the tracks of a sorcerer who had used magic recently, either, or detect the residue of a magical working. We couldn't even detect active magic unless we touched that sorcerer's skin. Sniffers could do all of those things; I'd witnessed it for myself. Perhaps if one was close enough, they could detect the dormant magic, too.

What enabled such skills? Was it their particular talent? Or the severe limitations on their senses? Or the lack of any purpose in life beyond detecting magic? We'd no way to know. There were no books of magical lore for the demon-tainted to study. No schools of magic. Nor did we know other magical practitioners we could consult. Random chance had brought the four of us together.

"Naddi!" The praetorian rapped the iron ring again. "Gah! He must be off to piss."

He pulled out a ring of keys and after sufficient rattling for four or five locks, the ironbound door swung open.

"Come on. Move on through," snapped the irritated guard. "Halt on the other side."

The sniffer slunk back into the shadows. The group moved forward, avoiding him.

The door opened to a dimly lit guardroom. The praetorian who held the heavy door grumbled quietly of extra long shifts and "every breathing body in the Academie demanding entry."

Neri and I crowded through the opening with the rest. The door slammed shut, and the sniffer did not howl.

By Lady Fortune's whispers, we were in.

6

*N*ow observe. *What's normal? What's out of order? What's unex-pected?* Placidio's teaching was embedded in my bones.

This would be the northeast hexagonal tower of Villa Giusti. One wall was the door we'd just entered. One wall opened onto a spiral stair. Arrow loops penetrated the other four walls.

The praetorian shot five bolts in the door behind us—well-made steel bolts to supplement the thick oak bar that stood upright at this hour. Before Master Tano could lead us across the cramped room to the stair, the guard stepped in front of him. "Visitors needs must wait for the usher to proceed farther. Directors' orders."

"But I'm urgently expected. I've the official Order of the Rite with me and these students to assist, and we are needed *now*." Tano snatched a loosely folded page from one of his lappet pockets.

"Even you, Master. Directors' orders 'til further notice."

Were they worried about an invasion to prevent the *giuntura*? Perhaps Sandro had let his disapproval be known.

Two other praetorians sat at a small table. They slapped down grubby cards and snatched up cards or coins in a game of Joust. No sniffer lurked on this side of the door.

After a nervous wait, accompanied by Master Tano's elabo-rate sighs, a thumping of boots on stone brought a well-groomed white-haired gentleman in black brocade from the tower stair. His face pulsed red with heat and hurry. After a glancing scowl at Tano, he turned his scrutiny to the rest of us.

"We're much too busy to deal with student researchers today."

Tano explained again about his duties and the Order of the Rite and the urgent need for assistants to prepare candles and robes and chairs and cleansing basins.

"Come on then," said the gentleman usher. "This whole busi-ness is annoying."

Student researchers—was there a library here?

Scarce believing our luck, Neri and I followed the troop of stu-

dents down the corkscrew stair into a courtyard awash in gold
light. Two rows of stately cypress trees, one fountain centered by
three spikes of bronze of staggered height, and a few square plant-
ings bordered by neatly raked gravel paths did little to soften the
areas between the stout walls, the great house, and a number of
outbuildings behind the great house.

"Anziana di Corso!"

I was so absorbed in memorizing landmarks and relative positions that Master Tano's bark near popped me out of my skin. He
had stepped to the side to inspect his troop, and his manicured
fingers gripped Neri by his collar.

"What kind of indiscipline prevails in the Invidian Academie
that you believe you are allowed to wander so freely?" His round
cheeks were flushed. "I'll have the two of you out on your ears."

"Please, Master," I said, grasping at words. "We—we found the
document room, but no one came to help us, so we thought we'd
gone into the wrong place. By the time we saw you and your most
well-disciplined students, we were entirely lost. We planned to
beg your guidance as soon as possible. We mustn't begin our stay
here with discipline infractions. They would be reported to our
sponsor, Segnoré di Fermi, and Nico's father, Captain di Savene,
who would be so disappointed. The segnoré assured us that we
would find exceptional tutors here and never feel lost."

"Aye, did he so." Neri chimed in. "The gentleman grand supe-
rior *fista splendi* ist. Director Meucci furious angert *neichi*?"

Neri's great black eyes, so solemn and innocent, and his fractured version of the Invidian dialect, which he'd likely never heard
spoken, were near perfect.

"I've no time—but you mustn't—and I cannot allow you—"
Master Tano spluttered and his gaze flicked continually toward
the great house. He loosed his grip and shoved Neri toward me.

"By Majestic Reason, you people have no sense, no manners, no
discipline. I must write to this Director Meucci." He waved at our
white-haired escort. "Usher Gacci, I've two miscreants here who
must be returned to their tutors."

"Why would you choose miscreants to assist in the rites?"

"I didn't choose them." Tano sighed, flapping his parchment at
us. "These two are *foreign* students who got themselves lost. I don't
trust them not to tumble off the gallery, and wouldn't care if they

did so were they not under the patronage of Segnoré Rodrigo di Fermi. But Director Bastianni said he'd have my hide did I not get the Order of the Rite to him snip-snap. Once I'm delivered of that charge and have set these others to work, I'm dragging these two back to the tutorial office and recommending they have bells tied on them, so *everyone* can herd them where they need to go. Either nursemaid them here or take them back to the Academie."

Usher Gacci waved a hand. "I cannot leave the villa. I've duties at dinner. Send one of these other gawking imbeciles."

The rest of the students were indeed taking an uncomfortable interest in Neri and me.

"But I need all ten! Please, Gacci. My errand will take only a few moments. The urgency . . ."

The usher's nose wrinkled as he examined us. "Certain, you cannot drag two foreigners into the director's chambers."

"Director Bastianni is waiting for me *now*."

I didn't speak up to mention I'd just seen the man in the Academie.

"Oh, don't combust. I'll mind them for you," said the weary usher. "Won't mind a quiet moment. House is all in a fever with this new development."

A *new* development? The *giuntura* or something else?

Had the Confraternity got wind of the girl's disapproval? Or perhaps her father, the steward, was having second thoughts . . . or someone had discovered a loophole in the contract . . . Spirits, so much we didn't know!

The annoyed Usher Gacci pointed Neri and me to a stone bench beside the gravel path. "Sit there and be quiet," he said. "Be quick, Tano. Director Bastianni has me supervising the chit's quarters once they've dined."

The *chit*? Livia? Not exactly a respectful address for the young woman marrying into a director's family.

"Many thanks. My apologies. If I'd known . . ." He'd have done nothing different. That was clear. Tano jogged across the courtyard to the great house, his gaggle of students trotting behind.

Despite the impressive fortifications, the house was no fortress keep, but a large, comfortable family home as one might see in the rolling hills north and east of the city. A harmonious symmetry marked the rose-hued stone facade and the two protruding wings, each with two ranks of windows. Each window was topped with a curved pediment of darker stone like an inquisitive eyebrow. The narrow third level of the main house was centered with a sculpted medallion, displaying the emblem of the Confraternity—an open book flanked by a lance and a flaming torch. Atop all stood a many-windowed cupola.

Interesting that Tano didn't enter the house through the main house doors, but through a door halfway down the left or western wing. A procession of carts like those we'd seen at the main gate rolled slowly on a graveled road around the east wing to the rear of the house. Two men on tall ladders hung Confraternity banners above the main entry. I would have expected more visible signs of preparation for the rushed celebration.

"So you're foreigners, eh?" said the usher, turning his glare toward us, hands on his hips. "Where from?"

"Invidia, segno. My name is—"

"Never the mind. Never met anyone from Invidia worth knowing."

Eliani di Corso would have retorted indignantly that the new captain of House Fermi's cohort was from Invidia, and that her companion was the captain's son, and that a house servant such as an usher had no business making such insulting judgments. If I had still been Mistress Cataline, companion to Cantagna's Shadow Lord, I would have slapped the man. But for today, I didn't need Gacci's respect, only information.

The usher had mentioned research. All books were valuable, but Neri was right. To merit such thick walls and guard towers, there had to be something here worth defending. So I made a guess.

"When are *anzioni* to be allowed to do research here again, Usher Gacci? I was sent here as this youth's language mentor, but my masters at both the Varelan and the Invidian Academies encouraged me to take advantage of all the Cantagnan Academie research opportunities. Books, artifacts . . . everything."

"Depends on whether you speak of research in the Athenaeum or the *pérasma*."

"Athenaeum, naturally. My ambition is to be a philosophist advocate." I'd no idea what the *pérasma* was, though I was fairly certain it had nothing to do with books.

Philosophists were divided into three branches, each with its own badge, each led by its own director. Those who taught in the Academies—by far the majority of them—were designated philosophist academicians and wore the badge of the Book.

Philosophist enforcers wore the badge of the Lance and commanded the praetorians. A separate arm of the enforcers dealt with nullifiers and the arcane depravity of creating sniffers.

Philosophist advocates promulgated the Canon of the Creation—the stories of Dragonis and his war with the gods, his defeat by Atladu's raising of Leviathan, his imprisonment under the drowned city of Sysaline—and also with the prosecution of magic users. As Cantagna's director advocate, Donato di Bastianni's father, Rinaldo, was responsible for rooting out all deviance from the Canon in artworks, scholarship, and teaching throughout Cantagna.

"An advocate, indeed?" said Gacci, disbelieving. "You aim high, girl. Very few are selected to wear the red. Fewer yet to wear the badge of the Flame."

"My tutors have kindly commended my diligence and approved my course of study."

"Then I assume they have written recommendations to appropriate tutors here who will arrange for you to visit whatever section of the Athenaeum is appropriate to your studies when they see fit. *Not* at your whim."

So the Athenaeum was indeed a library. With books that needed protecting behind this massive wall . . .

"Certain, I'm to meet with my mentor tomorrow morning. This delay"—I waved my hand at the line of carts—"will it be long? I am eager to resume my studies."

"'Tis only a day's hullaballoo for now. Books and pages aren't going to run off before you get there."

"Is it a Cantagnan feast day? We weren't told anything of celebrations."

Gacci glanced at me sharply. "'Tis none of students' concern."

"Of course. Excuse my boldness, Usher." His glare unsettled me, so I turned to Neri. "Now, Nico, where were we with the history of Cantagna?"

I precluded any nosiness on Usher Gacci's part by returning to my previous lecturing—and a bit of language practice. The man soon turned his back on us, clasping his hands behind him in the age-old position of waiting servants. Neri made a prune face at the fellow's back, but his own posture was that of a hound who scented warm meat. I gave him a raised brow, and then composed myself so as not to appear the same.

Master Tano must have had to pantomime the Order of the Rite or translate it into the archaic tongue of Typhon. The bells from the Palazzo Segnori tower rang the Hour of Gathering.

I continued my lecture and questioning.

The bells struck a single chime. A quarter hour had passed. When the next quarter struck, my tongue had run out of words.

Gacci was pacing in aggravation. Our urgency was at least equal to his. I risked his attention. "Should we not return to the Academie, Usher Gacci?"

"Of course you should," he said, snarling. "But I could be summoned at any moment, and undisciplined foreigners cannot be trusted. I hope you're both dismissed for this inconvenience."

Almost an hour had passed since we'd emerged from the tower door, just ten steps behind us. There had been a constant trickle of philosophists, students, and praetorians back and forth, an especial surge around the Hour of Gathering. Gacci accosted everyone coming from the house to the tower, asking if they'd seen Master Tano. And anyone of tutor's rank or lower who emerged from the tower was dispatched to the house bearing the same message: *Usher Gacci has urgent duties and cannot wet-nurse Tano's stray students a quarter hour longer.*

Soon the flurry of gate crossers died away.

My nerves were as threadbare as Gacci's. What a waste this had been for such paltry information. The time until our mission was speeding past. And the longer we sat here and the more people who heard a story of stray foreign students, the more likely someone would take a closer look at us or ask a few simple questions and discover we didn't belong. I tried to form more inquiries—to learn something to make use of the time—but my every movement elicited another glare from Gacci.

When the next hour bell rang—seven strikes—Gacci burst into a most foul malediction. I near jumped out of my skin. His waving fist might have been a hammer nailing us to the bench. "I cannot stay longer. You will sit here. You will not move a toe. Someone will return immediately to take you back to the Academie."

I rose, motioning Neri to the same. "We can return on our own, segno. We'll ask for direction. No need to trouble yourself."

"You cannot pass the gate without escort. Tano, may the *daemoni discordia* gorge on his bowels, knows that. Now sit."

"Certain," I said. And we did.

His strides devoured the courtyard. As Tano had, Gacci headed for the west wing of the house. Perhaps that was the location of Director Bastianni's household. Three directors. Two wings and the main house. A reasonable place to start a hunt for Donato. Maybe we'd learned *something* in this tedium.

Neri leapt from the bench and circled it twice, spluttering in exasperation. "I suppose we daren't go exploring."

"No," I said. "Though it sounds like there might be things besides unhappy brides and wedding preparations that are worth a look. Like what books do they hold so close in this Athenaeum—whatever it is? But someone's going to burst out of that house at any moment, ready to scoop us up. I'm hoping it's only an usher."

But we didn't have to wait for that. Halfway across the yard, Gacci encountered a serving girl carrying a great bundle over one shoulder. His gesticulations in our direction made the conversation clear.

"I think we're about to be scooped up," I said, turning to see Neri examining the flared base of the hexagonal tower. "Get back over here."

Neri flopped onto the bench, drew his feet up under his gown, and hugged his knees. "At least I've a clear image of that fountain, so's I can come back to scout later if need be. And there's a dandy hiding place between the tower foot and the wall."

"It would have to be late, if you came back. Any one of those windows could hide prying eyes."

We stood as the maidservant approached. A green rag tied up her tangle of rust-colored hair, and she squinted in annoyance as she pointed us to the tower.

"Sorry if escorting us intrudes on your work," I said. "Usher Gacci said students weren't allowed to pass the gate on our own, which seems strange for a walkway between the Academie and this lovely house."

"I got to take this clean laundering tae the 'sophists' closet, doan

I, damizella student? Just another task fer the high and mighties. Mustn't see them wrinkled or spilt on while tending brightness the likes of you."

"We thank you," I said, as we trailed after her up the twisting stair. "We're new to the Academie and got ourselves lost on our first day."

She snorted. "Missed supper. Poor little hungered sheep, they are."

I was happy she had her own grievances and cared naught for us.

We were soon back to the guardroom. Naturally, the guard had changed. When they challenged us, the maidservant waved her hand at us. "Explain yerselfs, young studentfolk. Usher Gacci was not so clear as he might have been."

We told our story, referencing Master Tano and Usher Gacci, and the maidservant told her own. ". . . and all on us are gettin' feathered inta tasks unfamiliar because of the hurly-burly, and I've got to be back in time to serve the dinner."

One of the guards pulled open her bag, pulled up a fistful of nicely ironed red fabric. He grinned at the girl as he shoved it back into the bag in a wad.

"Prick." She spat on the floor, just missing his boots.

The guard—one of only two on this shift—raised a warning hand. But he glanced at Neri and me, raised the beam, and un-latched the door. "Be on your way, then."

I stepped aside so the maidservant could lead us through, but the sniffer blocked the way.

The praetorian kicked him aside. He was the same sniffer as earlier, and he crawled back to our feet, head wagging. A low grat-ing burr came from him, tightening the stretch of my nerves.

I focused on his feet. As with so many of his kind, his feet were crusted with dried blood. Rough cobbles and dirt and filth tore the silk fabric and the naked skin underneath. Human feet. Not pads or hooves or claws. Sniffers were human men. Perhaps wicked. Perhaps mad. His breath wheezed, and a white crust stained the silk over his mouth.

"Spirits, how could you choose this?" I murmured.

His attention jerked my way, and my skin shriveled.

The maidservant led Neri and me onto the bridge. The sniffer did not howl. Every step away from the tower left my spirit ten times lighter.

"So some wedding rite has caused all this confusion?" I said, catching up with Neri and the red-haired girl.

"'Tis a merging more like," she said. "Two planets colliding in the bowl of the sky."

The comment struck me as odd, but no matter how I prodded or wheedled, the girl refused to say more. Odder yet, once down the stair she marched straight through the rotunda. Every step lengthened her stride. We had to dodge statuary and straggling students to keep up. By the time we realized she wasn't delivering us to anyone, her determined tread had taken her through the front doors and down the steps, where she plunged into the evening maelstrom of the Piazza Livello.

"Wait!" I called after her, but she had vanished in a stream of costumed dancers trying to lure the pleasure-minded to some kind of festival.

Neri stood on tiptoes, peering through the dancers' giant masks, swirling ribbons, and twining chains of flowers. "Over to the fountain," he shouted over the skirling pipes.

We shoved through what seemed like half of Cantagna's population to reach the great bronze of Atladu and his Leviathan, but the girl was nowhere in sight.

Neri crouched down and pulled a gray bag, sodden and empty, from the fountain pool. Then a few wet red robes and a soggy knot of bedsheets.

He glanced up, stunned. "Is it possible?"

"Spirits of the ancients," I said. "I think we just met our unhappy bride. After her!"

7

We scoured every lane that branched off the Piazza Livello. Neri left a dozen vine-draped walls ragged from his scramble to the top to get a wider look. I dashed into alleys and through colonnades, then back down again to the next street. If Livia ran away, the marriage contract was broken, bringing all its consequences down on her father the steward, the city he had served so faithfully, and whoever gave her refuge. Did she understand that?

If we could grab her before anyone suspected she'd left on her own, we could alter our plan—put our Cavalieri snatch on her instead of the groom. Then we could find out what in the universe was so special about her, and whether she understood the situation she was creating. But first we had to find her.

Ladies and gentlemen in feathered hats and tall, starched ruffs scowled as we barged through the press to peer around a corner. More than one threatened to report our rude behavior to the Academie before we had the sense to pull off the instantly recognizable Academie gowns. A doubly wise move, as we began to see praetorians everywhere, knocking on doors, in conversation with market sellers and watchmen posted at private homes and businesses. At least half an hour had gone. They'd surely discovered the girl missing.

Neri and I met back near the Cambio Gate, empty-handed.

"Where do we look next?" I said, yanking at my hair as if it might sharpen my wits. "Perhaps the bathhouses or the Cat's Eyes. I can't imagine she'd have gone to her family or anyone known to her family; they'd be marching her up the steps of the Academie right now. Perhaps she knows someone else . . . or plans to get away on her own. She's traveled widely. In truth, she could be anywhere in the city by this time, which means we've likely lost her . . ."

". . . and our mission's done," said Neri.

Though discouraged, I wasn't ready to declare us failed. "Then again, she could be lurking in a coal bin, waiting for full night and thinner traffic to find her refuge, as there are so many damnable praetorians about."

"I don't think she's left the Heights," said Neri, catching my arm. He nodded at the towered gate.

Except for the Shadow Lord's secret way through the Street of the Coffinmakers that no one but he, his bodyguards, and the Chimera knew of, the Cambio Gate was the only way in or out of the Heights. Unlike most of Cantagna's inner gates, it was patrolled at all hours by wardens of the Gardia Sestorale—the city's own guard. Tonight, two alert praetorians stood post just inside the shadowed gate tunnel as well.

"They've been there since we started searching," Neri said.

"You're sure of that?" Silly that I'd not thought to look.

"Aye. Certain, she'd not risk them spotting her."

A spark kindled my hopes. "Truly. If she thinks to get out of the city tonight, whether on her own or with help, we may still have a chance to grab her. If we dawdle here in the piazza long enough, we might spot her play."

Neri grinned. "Throw one of these student's robes over her, and we could bundle her off to the Via Mortua passage and away." Sandro's passage.

Thus, instead of trying to outguess a young woman we didn't know, Neri and I strolled arm-in-arm around the grand piazza. Along with the hundreds of others taking the evening air in the heart of the city, we bought tea and sat beside the Leviathan fountain. We stood alongside gawkers as three adults and five children juggled fire at one end of the piazza and costumed players enacted a lewd farce on the other. But instead of the entertainers, we watched the watchers, observing every person who might be our quarry, whether walking, hurrying, or lingering. Though we poked our noses into stray nooks and crannies where someone might hide, we kept our closest watch on the Cambio Gate.

When the bells told us an hour had passed, Neri grumbled that we were wasting time again.

"A little while longer," I said. The bustle of evening had slowed. Torches yet brightened the open areas, but the shadows in empty corners and side streets grew deeper. "Certain, she can't wait until everyone's abed or she'll stand out like one of these mummers on stilts. If we've lost this gamble, there's no business left to rush us."

We began yet another circuit of the fountain.

We were no more than halfway round when two praetorians stepped smartly through the Academie doors, down the wide steps, and across the piazza. They whistled at the two on post and met them just outside the gate tunnel, joining in animated conversation.

I tugged Neri toward them. If we could hear what they were saying . . .

Neri squeezed my arm sharply. A dark figure darted from behind a shuttered flower stall and into the gate tunnel right behind the four men. The woman wore servant's drab gray; a green turban wrapped her hair.

Hurrying into the tunnel, we closed in behind just as she slipped between the wall and an oncoming horseman. The portly merchant guided his oversized mount slowly through the passage. As linkboys flared the torches flanking the exit into life, the nervous beast jinked, reducing the already cramped passage to nothing safe. Were we not desperate, I'd never have risked a trampling to squeeze past.

"You're loony," breathed Neri as we emerged unscathed into the Piazza Cambio.

"There," I said, pointing. The girl was vanishing into the Street of the Cloth Merchants. If she got away again, our mission was over.

Using every skill Placidio had taught us, we shadowed our quarry through the Merchant Ring evening market. A flat leather bag over her shoulder, she made a pretense of examining the fine woven linens and richly dyed woolens—better than anything one would see in the Market Ring, unimaginable to those who had never shopped anywhere but the rag shops of the Beggars Ring. She would drift to a new stall, hold a length up to the lamplight, shielding her eyes so that her face was shaded, and turn just enough to glance back the way she'd come. Someone had taught her how to spot a spy on her tail.

"Do you think she's noticed us?" I whispered to Neri, tucked behind a pillar carved with the emblems and noble promises of the Cantagnan Wool Guild.

"Don't think so," said Neri. "She's not running."

The girl moved on to a lacemaker's stall, let her hand trail through the hanging samples until one slipped off the stretched cord. Then she ducked down out of sight as if to pick it up.

Neri jerked as if to run after. But I grabbed his arm.

"Watch!" I snapped softly. "She'll pop up somewhere else."

And indeed the next time she came into view, she was disappearing into a side lane farther along the street.

As soon as she vanished into the lane, Neri and I raced through the shadows behind the market stalls. The Street of the Bookbinders. One of my customers lived about halfway down the row. There was no way out besides the way she'd gone in.

"Do we go after or wait to snag her when she comes back?"

"Wait here," I said. "If she comes back, follow her as before and I'll join you. If she's gone to ground, I'll fetch you and we'll decide how to take her."

"Right."

Lamplight from the glazed windows of my customer Falzi's fine house and those of his prosperous neighbors softened the growing darkness. Wafting smokes smelled of roasting meat and candles instead of the ever-present stink of city streets. Muted conversation, the clanking of dishes, an occasional shout only emphasized the quiet. In the third house down the lane, someone was arguing.

Livia had visited here before. Without hesitation she hurried up the light-dappled street. I scuttled from shadow to shadow, flattening myself to a wall when she raced up a steep stair on the side of a small house tucked into the far end of the lane. Her urgent knock on the upper door carried easily through the quiet.

A splash of dim light outlined the doorway where Livia waited. I crouched low, not daring to move.

She glanced around behind as if she sensed my presence.

Another knock and a third. I imagined I could hear her heartbeat racing, feel her disappointment. Her fear. Or maybe those were my own. I shrank into a squeeze between two walls, wishing some magic could make me invisible.

A door creaked open, spilling light on the stair landing. Livia vanished inside. I gave thought to creeping closer, at least as far as

the front of the house where I might see a signboard such as Lawyer Falzi displayed, or a plaque bearing the name of the house—
anything that might help me identify it.

But at my first move, the door opened again. A moment of muffled voices and steps hurried down the stair. I sank deeper into the
squeeze. Livia darted past. The house wasn't a refuge, then.

When Livia was almost out of sight in the murk, I pelted down
the street after her. Delayed by a boisterous party of men, women,
and children just rounding the corner, I scurried into the Street of
the Cloth Merchants well behind. The girl had vanished.

Neri crouched behind a notary's signboard where the Via Salita opened into the piazza fronting the Cambio Gate.

"I've lost her," I said, frantically scanning the downward road.
"Did you see her pass?"

"See the queue up to the Cambio? Third from the end."

And there she was.

"The *Cambio* Gate? She's returning to the Heights? Why would
she?" Such a risk to return to the neighborhood of the Confraternity.

"Looks as if. She dodged out of the rank when a troop of praetorians came through, but then scooted right back into line."

"She spoke to someone in a house at the end of the Street of the
Bookbinders," I said. "Perhaps she was turned away and hopes
someone in the Heights will take her in."

But who? Avoiding detection would be much more difficult in
the Heights with more people, more Gardia wardens, more praetorians about.

Cautious, we sauntered toward the gate just as our quarry disappeared into the gate tunnel. We joined the queue behind her,
chafing at every slow step. No praetorians stood watch inside.
Once through, a bronze of Sandro's grandfather on his favored
horse served as our observation post. From my perch overlooking
the milling crowds of the Piazza Livello, it was not difficult to
find her. A red-haired woman, dressed in a slim, elegant gown,
climbed the steps of the Philosophic Academie in company with
other well-dressed folk on their way to a lecture or a musicale or
a poetry reading as often happened this time of the evening. A
green scarf was looped about her neck and tucked modestly in
her bodice.

The world twisted in a new direction. "She's going back!"

"That's her? How did she change—?" Neri jumped down from the plinth and ran. When I joined him beside Atladu's fountain, I wasn't at all surprised to see a shabby gray servant's dress awash in the water. A flat leather bag had sunk to the bottom. It was empty.

Instead of escaping from her incipient betrothal, Livia had returned to the Academie. Instead of seeking refuge with a friend—I fingered the sodden leather bag—had she delivered something to a person in the Street of the Bookbinders? Something she could not entrust to a Confraternity messenger?

What exactly was the "treatise on the formation of mountains" Mantegna had mentioned? I'd thought it might be a history of mountain life or mountain warfare, or perhaps a work of natural philosophy, like those which described alchemical reactions or the causes of seasonal weather patterns. But *formation* meant origins, so maybe she'd written some overview of the Creation Wars, how the monster Dragonis's tail had shattered our coastline into rocky islands and crumpled the land's midsection into a spine of craggy mountains. Had she written of volcanoes or . . . by the Twins . . . the earthquakes which often accompanied them?

The thought shifted my perspective. The Confraternity had ignored this marriage contract for nineteen years. In the ordinary, this would mean they had little interest in fulfilling it. Perhaps the young man had objected or the family decided the match was unsuitable in other ways. But now they rushed to fulfill it before Livia came of age and could publicly assert her own refusal, risky and useless though that might be. Something had changed. Was it significant that only a few days had passed since the worst earthquake in decades?

"I'm going back there," I blurted.

"Into the Academie?" Neri spat. "Are you bats?"

"No. To the Street of the Bookbinders." I tossed the empty bag back into the fountain pool. "Livia must have left something in that house, and we need to understand what it is. You head for the woolhouse. Tell the others everything we observed this afternoon about the Academie, the footbridge entry, and the villa. Plan how we're going to get around that sniffer. Prepare for the snatch, just as we talked of. I'll join you there quick as may be. But I suspect the key to this mission is whatever Livia delivered to the person in that house."

• • •

I was exceedingly mindful as I retraced my steps to the Street of the Bookbinders. The evening was waning and the gate wardens were more attentive to those of us in attire unusual for a woman in the Heights. I'd worn slim trousers, tunic, and jerkin under my Academie gown—the best garments for sword training ... and sneaking ... and other Chimera activities. The guards' interest waned quickly when I told them I was a bodyguard for Vivienne di Agnesi—a reclusive and notoriously vengeful painter, who employed only women.

The Street of the Bookbinders had settled. Soft lamp glow from upper rooms had already replaced the more boisterous brilliance of early evening. Few besides the Shadow Lord and his kind could afford to squander oil or candles to hold off the night's darkness, especially as the autumn days grew shorter. I sauntered down the lane to Lawyer Falzi's house and around to the tradesmen's entry at a small side gate, as I did when bringing him copied documents. There I paused and waited, watching the street. No one passed. No untoward noise interrupted the quiet.

Relieved, I sped through the shadows to the house at the end of the lane. On the corner was a tidy brass signboard, listing two names. The lower read FILIPPI—SEED IMPORTER. The upper name read MARSILIA DI BIANCHI—STITCHED FOLIOS, PAMPHLETS, MISCELLANEA.

Gleaming lamplight outlined a shuttered window and the age-darkened plank door at the top of the stair. A rap brought no reply.

I knocked again. Still no reply. So I gripped the handle and slid my dagger blade through the gap between door and frame in search of a latch, only to feel the heavy slab shift at my first pressure. The door was unlocked.

"Dama Bianchi?" I called as I stepped inside and closed the door behind me.

The cluttered, lamplit room smelled of old paper and dust and ... perhaps a chamber pot too long unemptied? Careless heaps of folded pages littered the plank floor and a workbench that spanned most of the room. Pens, ink bottles, awls, boxes of needles, large spools of linen string, and an array of small, sharp knives lay in a clutter. Finished pamphlets looked to have been tossed one upon the other against the front wall of the house. An off-kilter doorway led into another room.

If I needed someone to bind a document, I doubted I'd choose anyone so careless with her work, unless— Had someone else come here searching?

In one corner, a pot with spout and lid hissed and spat atop a brazier, far from the precious pages, but enough to make the lingering warmth of the day unpleasantly damp.

My hand touched my dagger. With the other I rapped hard on the worktable.

"Hello, Marsilia di Bianchi! I'm a law scribe come to inquire about stitching some of my clients' documents. A friend recommended you. Your door is unlocked, and your pot is about to boil dry."

A soft scratching from the other room was accompanied by a sucking sound—very like the noise Teo had made when he was drowning.

"Dama Bianchi?" My skin shivered and I crept through the clutter to the crooked doorway. The second room was no more tidy—with clothes chest and sling bed upended; the gray wool stuffing of the mattress coated the room like early snow. This was no careless clutter. And there was blood. . . .

Halfway between the upended bed and a washing cabinet, a gray-haired woman sprawled on the floor. She was scratching the planks with her fingernails and choking on the blood oozing from her broken nose. Myriad cuts and bruises scarred her arms, face, and legs. Her ripped garments were sodden.

I dropped to my knees at her side, grabbing the ripped bed sheet to blot the blood from her battered cheek. The pulse at her wrist was faint. My attempt to roll her to her back elicited a thready cry, so I left her be and bent down so she might see my face.

"Dama, who's done this? That girl who came here . . . she didn't . . ."

"Red devils." The harsh sucking noise was her attempt at breathing. More difficult with each one. "Won't silence her. Ever."

Red *devils*? Philosophists!

"Did they find what she left?" I said, the story clear as sunlight.

Certain, this was about Livia's writings. "Brave woman, you tried. I can see that."

"None'll find it, save one we trust." Her clenched teeth could have bitten holes in her pamphlets. A shudder racked her bony frame.

"The devils . . . you mean philosophists, yes?"

Her head twitched in assent as she struggled for another breath. She didn't have many more in her, so it was no time to play with secrets.

"Please believe me. I'm a friend, trying to protect Livia. Her *vicino-padre* asked me to keep her and her work safe if you could not. When the philosophists can't make her tell what she left here, they'll come back—perhaps before the one you trust comes to help. They'll tear this place apart and they'll find it for sure. If we're to preserve it, we must do it now. I'll keep it safe."

Her eyes glared at me, warning of a death curse. "Name. *Vicino-padre.*"

"Alessandro di Gallanos. *Il Padroné.* He wants Livia's work to continue."

Her hand, slick with warm blood, grabbed my wrist. "Swear it. Mean it."

"By the grace of this universe, by the womb of the Great Mother and the spear of the Lord of Sea and Sky, by words or books or whatever you and I both hold sacred, I swear to keep Livia and her work safe at peril of my life."

"Don't believe in Mother. Nor Sea Lord." She squeezed her eyes closed and grinned—blood outlining her broken teeth. "But the universe, yes. And *il Padroné . . .*"

"Marsilia, please tell me."

Her grip on my wrist fell slack; her half-curled fist tapped weakly on the floor. "Last place . . . any . . . sophist—"

Her grin faded. The tapping stopped.

Helpless, I shook her gently. "The last place any philosophist . . . what? Would go? Would look? Dama?"

But it was no use. Laying a hand on her forehead, I bade her good journeying to wherever the universe might take her, and promised to make the villains who'd murdered her pay for their crime. Then I stood and looked helplessly at the mess the searchers had left.

Her ravaged body and this upheaval smacked of fury—of certainty that there was something here to find. I doubted they would treat Livia so brutally. Surely she'd never have gone back if she feared that. But they would search her, question her. And they'd return here.

What was the last place any philosophist would look?

Begging the dead woman's pardon, I checked under her skirts and down her bodice. The beasts had searched those already. Her fist had tapped the floor. So under it?

I hunted for loose planks in the floor and then the walls, to no avail. There were no loose sections of her bedposts. No entry to the attic in her stained ceilings. Back in the workroom, I peered under the worktable and inside every vessel of ink, every thread spool, every box, and bin. Every stack of pages. The searchers had been thorough.

Stepping back through the crooked doorway, I tried to observe with a newcomer's eyes. And the hiding place was clearly visible. Marsilia had tried to tell me. A finger of her half-curled fist pointed across the room, where only one item sat undisturbed, serenely filthy in its cubbyhole, pretending innocence even while exuding a stink no priggish philosophist would ever think to search. The last thing *anyone* would wish to touch.

I knelt in front of the washing cabinet and removed the ornate ceramic chamber pot, hoping I wouldn't need to rummage inside it. Modeled on a Typhonese amphora, painted with figures of athletes and jugglers, its rounded base fit into a matching depression in a rectangular holder of polished wood. One could not set the pot aside without spilling its overabundant contents.

Believing she would approve, I made a nest from Marsilia's body and her torn and bloody sheets to hold the pot upright. Examining the holder revealed that its wooden bottom would slide away and expose a very private little space—clean and dry—where a leather pouch and a set of rolled pages wrapped in oiled leather awaited me.

The pouch held a small book with a red-dyed cover. The worn lettering of the title read *Canonical Teachings of the Creation Wars and the Shaping of the Earth*. The cover displayed the open book, lance, and flaming torch crest of the Philosophic Confraternity.

But my first glance at Livia's pages explained all. Her document was titled, "Exposing the False Mythology of Creation Stories Using Observations of Natural Phenomena."

Though I'd no time to read the texts, the significance of the pairing was not lost on me. *False* mythology. Spirits!

With apologies for disrespect, I placed Marsilia, the vile chamber pot, and its now empty holder into the exact positions in which I'd found them. I left the shambles of her home little changed, and though it was difficult to contravene years of cautions about fire, I even left the brazier burning.

I crammed the pouch containing the book inside my jerkin. The document, I rewrapped in its oiled skin, retied into as thin a scroll as I could make it, and slipped it into the knife sheath in my boot. The upper end stuck out a bit under my trousers. That would have to do.

With all the care and mindfulness Placidio had battered into my head, I ventured into the night, speeding downward through the city to meet with the Chimera. For now, we had to stop a marriage. But Marsilia di Bianchi was dead and Livia di Nardo was in danger of arrest. We were going to save the girl, and then someday she was going to tell me why she had entrusted a brave old woman with what could be among the most dangerous items in all of the Costa Drago. The canonical teachings of the creation were the foundation of the sorcery laws.

8

Dumond studied Placidio's sketched map in the dusty lantern light of the woolhouse.

"Is this refuge defensible?" said Dumond. "Wouldn't need to worry about a siege, as long as I've time to paint us a way out. But praetorians are fierce. And they don't stop."

"Aye," said Placidio. "The path to the top of the bluff is steep and narrow, easy to defend. The rest is cliffs around. A skillful, determined man who knows the country well might find a way up with ropes and picks, but the place is out of the way."

I stood beside the map with the others, yet I could not force myself to take in all the details of Placidio's inartistic efforts. Shortly before I'd arrived from the Street of the Bookbinders with a tale of murder and sedition and how sorely we had underestimated the significance of this mission, Neri had gone back to scout the Villa Giusti.

"This Perdition's Brink is close to the city, you say, but no one lives there?" Vashti sat on the pounded earth floor, her needle flying along a seam of black cloth.

"It's mostly a ruin, deserted since long before I came to Cantagna," said Placidio. He tossed his stick of plummet onto the scrap of parchment spread on the upended barrel. "I heard of it through a bit of dueling lore. It lies north and easterly, a quick back and forth with Dumond's friend's horses. No more than two hours by foot, should need arise. We can get the horse cart to the bottom of the hill easy, and though the path's a bit steep for carrying supplies the rest of the way, that's all the better for staying hid."

Placidio and Dumond had agreed we had no choice but to abduct Livia as well. We needed to tell her about Marsilia and find out what in all the universe she thought she was doing. It was no good to persuade Donato to void the contract, only to have Livia insist on the marriage after all.

"But why has no one rebuilt such a place so near the city?" said Vashti. "So much land in the countryside of vineyards . . ."

"Same reason this place, solid as ever, sits available for us to practice our skills whenever we please." Placidio waved his hand at the sturdy brick walls and mostly intact roof of the riverside warehouse. "Superstition. Instead of lingering plague ghosts, it's a sorcerer's curse scares folk away. After three years of blighted grapes, Conte Fumigari, the landholder, accused the neighboring landowner, Draco di Benetti, of hiring a sorcerer to curse his vineyards. To Fumigari's delight, the Confraternity judiciar agreed. To Fumigari's *dismay*, not only did the judiciar burn Benetti at a stake set in the middle of the blighted vineyard, the conte's own overseer was the person accused of the doing the magic! Though Conte Fumigari—and a succession of buyers—tried to revive the field, the vineyard never bore another grape, and the Fumigari line died out in one generation."

"Thus the name," said Dumond.

"Aye. The place looks a blight, but the keep has a solid roof and the spring tastes sweet. Unless anyone here's squeamish, it'll do fine for us to hole up and figure out how to convince this Confraternity stripling to void his marriage contract."

"All right, then," said Dumond, scratching his thinning hair as he settled to the ground at Vashti's side. "We'd best spend these few hours before we breach the philosophic fortress hauling supplies up there. I'll work on an escape door once we're settled, assuming we're successful in extracting the bride and groom."

"Perhaps Neri will bring good news on that." Vashti reached over to pat my foot. "Unknot yourself, Romy-zha. Truly, he's not been gone so long. And before he left, he and the swordmaster went over exactly what he needed to learn and how to be so very careful."

I stilled my drumming fingers and ceased chewing my lips. "Certain, he proved himself thrice over at Palazzo Ignazio."

My brother's skill at darting in and out of a stranger's lair without being seen had been the twine that bound our mad scheme regarding the document known as the Assassins List into a successful whole. But he always tried to do too much on his scouting excursions. Over and again Lady Fortune had dealt him a lucky hand. Someday the payment would come due.

Thus I could not tear my eyes from the largest of the three leather bolsters hanging from the woolhouse rafters. Most days, we used it for developing our skills at punching and kicking with authority. Tonight, so they'd told me, it was the spot where Neri's magic had enabled him to walk straight from the woolhouse to the three-spike fountain in the Villa Giusti courtyard. If all went well, he would reappear in the same spot with information enough to abduct Donato and Livia from their beds.

"He remembers there's sniffers about the villa," said Placidio, with his own attempt to soothe my agitation. "I reminded him what they do first, once they decide to offer a captive sorcerer the opportunity to stay undrowned. I think he'll be well-focused."

The reminder did not help my nerves. Only a young male sorcerer was even given the choice to remain living as a sniffer, and the first thing the Confraternity did was geld him.

"Such risks we're taking," I said, staring down at the book and manuscript in my hands. "And now we don't even know if Livia truly wants this done. Why would she go back to that house, knowing the Confraternity would consider this writing and this book together—a pilfered book, it would appear—blasphemous? She should have run as far and fast as her feet would take her. Does she think submitting to the marriage will somehow save her?"

"It might be the *only* way to save her," said Dumond. "The Confraternity would never risk a public arrest and trial, as they'd have to admit her true offense. Even if every word she's writ is drivel, they could never allow such arguments to be exposed. She's an otherwise virtuous young woman, the steward's daughter, embroiled in a draconian marriage contract, but accepting its terms. Very sympathetic."

Lacking time to read the whole treatise, we'd shared the first few paragraphs which laid out Livia's thesis quite clearly: For millennia the Confraternity had chosen to assert the infallibility of the Creation Story—in particular the drowning of the city of Sysaline and imprisonment of Dragonis beneath the lands of the Costa Drago—for the sole purpose of eradicating sorcery. Earthquakes and volcanoes that shattered mountains and fractured the landscape were their evidence. Livia asserted that, in her travels throughout the world, she had gathered evidence from multiple locations and sources that led her to conclude that mountains and earthquakes arose from perfectly natural processes, not divinities warring with a monster. She believed evidence could be gathered in the Costa Drago to prove the same.

It was no wonder *il Padroné*, besides any personal concern for the girl, would be both fascinated by her theories and concerned for her well-being. If no raging monster existed beneath the earth waiting to be set free by his magical kin, then the underpinning of the Confraternity's two-thousand-year campaign to exterminate sorcery collapsed. Eventually, the balance of authority through-out the Costa Drago might change in reason's favor—and sorcery could be studied in a more rational light. The stakes of this mission had become deeply personal for each of us.

Abruptly, Placidio glanced up from his map. His sword appeared in his hand as if by conjuring.

The air crackled as in the moments before a lightning strike. I brushed at my face as stray hairs, escaped from my braid, tickled my cheeks and eyelashes.

Footsteps pounded in the distance. Impossible to tell whether they approached from outside the woolhouse or somewhere else . . .

Dumond leapt to his feet in front of Vashti.

And then Neri charged into the middle of the room, breathing hard . . . and grinning.

"Job done!" he said. "I'm parched!"

He pounced on the cask of Placidio's dreadful restorative con-coction of salt-and-ginger tea, always available for swordmaster and exhausted students. While he filled a cup, my heart and gut slowly untwisted, weapons were sheathed, and a smiling Vashti tied off another seam. Moments passed with only the sounds of pouring and drinking.

"Enough preening," said Placidio with a dry edge. "We've suf-ficiently admired your unscathed backside. Now report."

"Where's our sketch?" Neri spun around to face us. His grin had vanished, but the glow of accomplishment had not. "I've learned a deal. . . ."

Pride colored his eager report. On the reverse of Placidio's map of Perdition's Brink was a tidier drawing of Villa Giusti, the walls, the tower, and the bridge to the Academie. Neri sketched in entrances and exits from the west wing—confirmed as Director

Bastianni's residential wing—and guard posts atop the walls, and he reported what he had observed of the watch schedules.

"There's no guards to speak of in the house, just ushers scooting hither and yon to open doors and let in maids to tidy when the great folk leave a room. The sentries out on the walls—looked like two for each span—don't seem too nosy. They only snap to when the captain comes round. By the city bell strikes, I'd say that's something like twice an hour. You mustn't assume any spot in the center courtyard is safe, but near the base of the wall it would take a sentry with a spyglass and a torch in hand to take note of you."

"You arrived back where you started, so I'm assuming sniffers aren't a problem," said Placidio.

Neri's greatest vulnerability when he was on one of his magical excursions was his need to keep his magic active in order to preserve his retreat. Cutting it off once he'd arrived meant he had to fix on a different object of his desire and call up his power a second time when he was ready to leave. A time when he could well be depleted or immobilized.

Did I imagine I saw him swallow hard?

"I kept on the move, never still for more than a blink, even while I was watching the walls. And not a single green slinker did I see in the house. Nor in the outer precincts when I went looking for somewhere could Dumond paint us out. But amidst the outbuildings . . ."

He hesitated and folded his arms across his chest, excitement and satisfaction faded. "A rectangular blockish building behind the kitchens is certain the barracks; praetorians were in and out every watch change. There are stables built up along the walls behind the barracks, as well as the armorers and such. But another building—one built in a dome shape atop four square walls—is set apart from all the rest across a cobble yard. It's made of rough and rubble, not smooth-cut stone like the rest. I couldn't see in, as the only openings are narrow holes high up the walls more than a man's height. I couldn't even get close, as there was a deep trough filled with oily water like a sleugh, and it wasn't just across the entry but around the whole damnable place."

"A sleugh!" I said. Sleughs were oil-and-water-filled troughs built across doorways, supposedly to prevent demons from entering. Most houses in Cantagna had one. Mine did. I'd never heard of a sleugh *surrounding* anything, but then the Confraternity encouraged people to think of sorcerers as demons.

Neri continued, "Two different nullifiers dragged their sniffers into that place. They laid a plank over the sleugh. Pulled it up when they came back out without the sniffers. There was a rotten smell about the place, and some noises—mewling, I'd call it, begging without words—that made my skin crawl." His gaze darted from one to the other of us. "It wasn't big, but maybe that's where they keep 'em."

"Sniffers didn't detect you while you were scouting? Set up a howling? Your magic was still active." Placidio's question snapped like a dry stick.

"Didn't hear any hunting noises." He returned to the tea cask and spoke over his shoulder. "Didn't see any hunting parties out, neither. Maybe they just believe sorcerers can't get inside the walls. Because . . . why would we?"

"You didn't answer the question," I said. "Did a sniffer detect you? One in the yard, maybe?" Neri was skilled at dodging unpleasant details. "You were running."

"Maybe there was one there at the end caught a whiff of me. Pointed my way as I crossed the courtyard. But I didn't hear a howl. Honest. And he couldn't have seen me vanish. That fountain pumps a lot of water."

"But you didn't think it worthwhile to mention?" said Placidio, smoldering. "If they've detected magic in the yard, it's more risky for all of us."

"Just wanted to get to the useful bits first," said Neri. "Wouldn't have let us go in without saying. But we're going in, no matter, right?"

"Tell us everything," I said. "Then we'll tell you how I found the bookbinder murdered and why any hint of sorcery could put them on the alert."

Neri lost color for a moment, then returned to his map, more sober. "They've a cesspool out near the northwest tower. It drains through pipes stuck through the walls and washes down the steeps. Nobody was out there, and the guards atop the walls hustle past that corner as the stink's so foul. There's other refuse littered about in the shadow of that tower, as well—bricks and wood, and broken stone like it might be the ruins of older buildings. And,

Dumond, it's dark as the Night Eternal out there. If you were to have a canvas propped over you to mask your light, I'm sure you could find a decent bit of wall to paint us a hole."

"In the cesspool? Under a canvas?" Dumond was near choking. "By the Great Anvil, boy, couldn't you find me a venue a bit *less* pleasant to spend an hour?"

"Not *in* the cesspool. More like beside it. Truth be told, it's the only likely spot. And if we go in over the bridge, they'll assume we'll go out the same way. I figured it would be clever, you know, to work in such a place where fine folk would stay away." Neri's shoulders lifted as if to shift that particular burden to Dumond.

"Clever, indeed so." Vashti pressed two fingers to her mouth, but they could not hide her smile. "Perhaps the spring in this new hiding place may not stay so sweet, Basha, after you've spent the night in a cesspool!"

Dumond was a tidy man. Though he worked in a foundry and made his home in an alley, his workshop, house, and children were always meticulously clean. Vashti forever teased that if Dumond were a better cook, he would make someone a fine housekeeper.

"Where will we find the husband-to-be?" asked Placidio. The rough edge to his words promised that Neri would hear more of his incomplete reporting when there was time to emphasize the lesson.

Neri pointed out details on the sketch. Scurrying servants and a buzz of conversation had led him to believe that Director Bastianni's chambers lay about halfway down the upper floor of western wing and the four Bastianni sons' accommodations were those farthest from the main house.

"Servants come and go by a stair at that farthest end past the sons' bedchambers," he said. "It goes all the way down to cellars and a decent way out of the house. If you can keep the fellow quiet, we can manage this easy."

Easy was not my estimate of what he'd told us; we still had to get in through the bridge, past guards and at least one sniffer. And then there was Livia.

"Did you get any notion of where Livia's sleeping?" I said.

"There was way too many servants busying around to stay long," he said. "But some of 'em were back and forth from the north end of that upper passage, closer to the main house. Lots of rooms there."

"We've decided we must take her, too."

"Cripes! Taking them both will stretch us. Keeping them both will be worse."

No one contradicted him.

"Come," said Vashti, rising from the straw with red and black garments draped over her arms and shoulders. "Time for last alterations if any be needful."

Vashti had brushed our student gowns, and all we had to do was make sure they hid the black hooded capes of the Skull Knights underneath. Placidio and Dumond's guises were a bit more difficult. Neither could pass for a student, so they had to wear philosophist red to enter the Academie so late in the night—and the style had to be well-finished to pass muster.

While the men grumbled, Vashti fussed, and Neri gorged himself on the contents of the supper basket Vashti had brought to the woolhouse, I wandered over to the leather bolster where Neri had reappeared. I ran my fingers over the bolster and the hard-packed dirt and straw floor on every side of it, curious if I could detect any sign of my brother's passage.

Reaching for magic, I held out my spread hands as the sniffer had done the previous day on my way to Coopers Lane. Then I knelt and lowered my face to the ground, closing my eyes, blocking out the chatter from the others, and tilting my head from side to side as the sniffer in the bridge alcove had done. I sensed nothing.

Our mystical friend Teo had spoken of turning inward. He could slow his own heart and make his breathing scarce detectable, getting out of the way so his body could heal, as he put it. He was in that state when he'd first told me his name—our first connection—and again when I shared his dream of a magnificent city of art and learning, threatened by cracks that leaked molten rock. Was his method something others could learn? Maybe sniffers were taught to get out of the way so their inborn reservoir of power could enable them to follow traces of magic.

One breath . . . pause . . . another . . . pause. Slow. Even. Focus. Such a long, fraught day it had been. I sat on my heels and cupped my hands, letting them rest on my knees. Breathe. Focus. Drift . . .

The murals depicted sweeping vistas of hill and meadow. Young trees nestled in the soft folds of the land, colors and shape deepened by the steep angles of orange-red sunset. The grass rippled as if pleasured by the light.

At the horizon, great Ocean itself peeped between hillocks. Even so distant I felt its thunderous power and smelled the faint hint of salt in the breeze. I checked my imaginings . . . this was paint on stone walls . . . immense walls that surrounded me.

"Do my artworks please, lovely one?" The woman's voice, so close behind, brushed me like the breeze. Her fingers stroked and twined my hair, firm and sure as ever pleasured me best.

"They're magnificent," I said. "Living art. Is it magic?"

Laughter, the music of innocence, turned me around. She was not behind me but high on a scaffold, painting a deep forest—ancient, virginal trees kissed by moonlight. The light flowed from her brushes as she added more leaves. . . .

"Lady scribe, we're ready to go. Sleep must wait."

Dirt and straw ground into my cheek. I lay on the floor of our woolhouse training ground. Placidio crouched beside me, cinder-gray eyes picking at my thoughts, reflecting a bit of worry and a bit of puzzlement. "Are you all right?"

My hand flew to my hair, half loose from my braid, my scalp still tingling from . . . what?

"Ready? Yes, of course. Has it gone winter while you two dressed?"

Shivering, I pushed up from the ground, snatching up my hands gingerly. They felt as if they lay in a pile of feathers. The sensation faded as I got to my feet.

Neri stood by the door, poised like an owl ready to pounce on a distracted mouse. The lantern was dimmed. Vashti and Dumond held each others' hands, bringing them first to her forehead, then his.

"My swordmaster taught me to nap at any opportunity," I said. "I'm quite refreshed. Onward."

Our plans could not wait; I could not afford to distract my partners. But these were not ordinary dreams. When we had a moment to breathe, I had to tell them.

9

Assurance was the touchstone of any deception. Our earlier Chimera ventures had proved the point. If you act as if you belong in the role you play, others have far less reason to doubt. Assurance—conviction—played an enormous part in the efficacy of my impersonation magic as well. In effect, I created my role in so deeply believable a fashion that I succumbed to the deception too. But tonight it was Placidio and Dumond who carried the weight of our plan.

As they swept up the steps of the Philosophic Academie in the quiet hours of the night in red robes and face-shadowing toques, stated their names and business, and motioned for the two praetorians to unlock the doors, the soldiers found no reason to doubt the rightness of the command. I, the female student who trailed behind, arms loaded with pages and scrolls, likely did not even register on the two guards' senses.

"Stupid girl!" announced Placidio, after I had conveniently tripped and scattered my burden all over the floor tiles. I had also conveniently observed that no one else occupied the Academie rotunda at such an hour. "Step inside here, praetorians, and help this chit clean up her mess. We've urgent preparations to make for this morning's rites and cannot wait for her to bumble about. Director Bastianni will have her head!"

Well-attuned to the directives of their superiors, the two praetorians did as ordered, though increasingly anxious as I let even more scraps fly.

"We need to get back to our posts, Excellency."

"Hmmph, I suppose." Placidio waved a dismissal and went on to lambaste me for my clumsiness. The guards retreated to their posts and locked the door behind us.

I quickly reclaimed my pages. My habit of collecting scraps of used parchment from every junk seller in the Beggars Ring—a scribe always had need for a place to test a new pen, new ink, or a questionable wording—had been fortunate for our ruse.

"One obstacle cleared," said Placidio.

We sped up the split stair and into the corridor under the lion's head. As we made the zigzag turn onto the footbridge and spotted the two praetorians on post in the shadowed gateway arch, Dumond berated me. "Come girl, speed your steps, or we'll send you to wake Director Bastianni and explain how you miscopied the Order of the Rite. Tano was a fool to trust you."

"Please, masters, I'll do whatever's necessary," I said, loud enough for the guards to hear. "There's hours yet, and it's all a matter of the corrected anointing and adding the extra pledges. I've the proper documents to validate every change. No need to wake anyone."

"A minor confusion of steps is not so minor when it could invalidate his son's betrothal," Placidio said. "By Reason's Light, you'll be fortunate to escape with mere expulsion."

"Who goes there?" The sharp query came from one of the praetorians.

Placidio spun around and walked backward for a moment. "Two swords," he whispered. "A third person—the sniffer?—on the ground but moving. I'll take the leftmost."

Then he waved his arm majestically to beckon us onward, reversed himself, and bellowed, "Advocate Uglino and Advocate Sensi with the damnedest fool of an *anziana* this Academie has ever produced. One who wakes her tutors in the midwatches to inform them that she has bungled the single most important duty she has even been assigned and that we must take her to the Villa Giusti to make things right before it is discovered and someone finds reason to chuck her over the wall."

I shifted the pages to my left arm. My right hand unsheathed my dagger, masking it under the drooping sheaf.

"I thought I had seen everything. . . ." Placidio's diatribe continued without cease, as did our steady march into the alcove. By the time we crossed into the dark little tunnel, I had identified the shadowed outline of the guard on the right.

"Wait! Hold on there," he said.

Three more steps and I threw the sheaf of scraps into his puzzled face. As he spluttered and fumbled, I blocked his sword with my dagger, backed him to the wall, and pressed my hastily drawn main gauche to his throat.

Two massive thuds on my left and a toppling body told me that Placidio had taken care of one guard. A moment later he relieved me of my own burden and laid him out beside his fellow.

"Bindo?" A knocking from inside the iron-banded door accompanied the query. "What's doing?"

Growls and choking moans came from the squirming sniffer Dumond had pinned to the floor. A rag jammed into the silk-covered mouth kept the sniffer's noise to a minimum while I administered Vashti's mysenthe tincture to the guards—a few drops inside their cheeks.

Daughter of a mysenthe trader, Vashti knew exactly how to concoct a potion strong enough to keep the recipient in a silent stupor for several hours, while using little enough of the vile mysenthe that it would not drive the recipient into the devilish hunger.

While Placidio held the sniffer's wrists and feet, Dumond yanked the rag aside and slit a hole in the stretched silk mouth covering.

"Swallow this," he said quietly, holding the dropper where the captive could see it, "and you may have a few hours of peace."

But the growling sniffer writhed and twisted, until we had to force the drops into him and hold his mouth shut until he calmed and fell limp. It seemed a cruelty upon cruelty.

"He chose," whispered Dumond. "Don't forget that."

He pulled out his paints, wiped the door's surface, and began his work.

"Bindo?" A louder rap on the door. "Status?"

Placidio coughed loudly and growled. "Post silence, praetorian. Snag time."

Not another sound came from beyond the door. I glanced a question at the swordmaster, who stood at the ready beside Dumond.

"I told him to shut his mouth and be alert, as a commander was planning an inspection."

We spoke softly so as not to undo his good work.

"But the specific words were so odd. How did you—?"

"Might have been a praetorian once. Briefly. Pay was good." Placidio's past was a sporadically unspooling mystery.

As Dumond's swift brushes shaped a simple oak and iron door in the center of the actual one, Placidio kept watch through the arrow loops in the passage walls.

The scuffle on the floor had torn the green silk on the sniffer's cheek, exposing what appeared to be red paint on the pale skin underneath. Only . . . My finger caught a frayed edge of the silk and pulled it away. Not paint. Ink. I wrenched away more of the tight sheathing to reveal half the man's face. As with Teo, symbols were inked into the sniffer's skin. But unlike the pleasing variety of Teo's black or silver designs, these marks were all the same. Each blood-red mark comprised two concentric ovals, the centermost halved by a sawtooth line—like a horrid mouth. On his cheeks, his shaven head, his neck. I tugged at the torn wrapping of his feet, exposing foot, ankle, leg . . . More of the same. Even if a sniffer got free of his captors, he could never hide what he was.

"Is it the library they're hiding with all this defense?" I said, joining Placidio at the arrow loops. "Or is it the structure with the sleugh around it?"

"Both, I'd say," Placidio murmured, staring at what I'd revealed. "Whatever mustn't see the daylight. As folk don't think making sorcerers into chained slaves is all so terrible, I don't like imagining what anyone thinks *would* offend. Never imagined that."

"So in your brief time, you didn't . . ."

"Praetorians don't know aught of sniffers. The two are different arms of the enforcers."

It was impossible to tell whether the sniffer was twenty or fifty, whether he had once been plain or pleasing to the eye, whether he had ever laughed or sung or kissed a lover. The marks took on a life of their own, as if they pulsed or crawled around the bare flesh.

"Almost done," said Dumond, dabbing at details that gave his painted wood its grain and bulk. Even before he invoked his magic, his fingers and eye worked marvels with his paints. "Be ready."

Placidio and I shed our Confraternity gowns and stuffed them in a cloth bag. Our black tunics and hooded capes would help obscure us in the villa courtyard. We would wait until later to expose the white death's-heads of the Cavalieri.

Dumond wiped and stowed his brushes, then jumped to his

feet and shed his philosophist robe. Meanwhile, I strapped the lids on his paint pots and replaced them in their case. The paint case went on Dumond's back, the garment bag on mine. Placidio's sword and my dagger were in our hands.

"*Sien vah*," Dumond murmured when he glimpsed the sniffer. Only a few times had I heard him utter the Shadhi malediction, calling down the fate of *soul's death* on the one responsible for a deed. I could not disagree.

But we had business to attend. "You'll signal Neri from the tower if I can't," I said to Dumond. Neri had taken his own route into Villa Giusti.

He nodded. "And the reverse. Long life to us all!"

As one, the three of us nodded. Dumond raised his hands, closed his eyes, and in moments blue flames flared from his hands. The wonder of it never got stale.

"*Cederé*," he said, and pressed his palms to the painted door, extinguishing the fire and transforming art into the reality of a smaller door in the middle of the existing one. "Go!"

We pulled up the black scarves that served as masks and Placidio laid his boot to Dumond's door. The explosive entry wasn't necessary to open it, but rather to distract and surprise those on the other side who might notice a very odd change in the gate they guarded.

We swarmed through the opening.

One man, sitting dazed on the floor of the tower guardroom with blood dribbling down his face, appeared to have been slammed in the head by the opening door. I added the insult of my dagger's hilt to the blow and he collapsed. Placidio engaged the fellow's two companions. They dodged, ducked, and slashed with short swords in the tight quarters of the tower guard room. I planted a boot in one man's backside, throwing him off-balance, which gave Placidio respite enough to crack his elbow into his other opponent's ear. Once that one was down, he plowed his ham fist into my staggering victim's chin.

With all three down and groaning, Dumond pressed his hands to the now closed false door and whispered, "*Sigillaré*."

All evidence of the magical portal vanished, leaving both sides of the iron-banded door intact. More importantly, Dumond's magic was no longer active. Like Neri's, Dumond's magic was a living tether. As long as the painted portal existed, providing us a way back and forth, a sniffer could detect it. How long it took for the invisible residue to fade once he had closed the way, we had no idea.

I pulled the tincture bottle from my pocket, ready to dose the three before they regained their wits. In a moment's quiet, we heard stealthy footsteps descending the spiral stair. A fourth person must have been in the guardroom when we burst in. Someone who might have seen Dumond closing off the breach in the gate. Placidio took out after, his boots thudding on the stair.

Be ready, little brother. Neri's task was just this—to be waiting in the courtyard to prevent anyone leaving the tower guardroom but the three of us.

Dumond held each stunned guard still while I shoved the dropper into his mouth. The third man, the one with the bleeding forehead, scuttled crablike away from us. His hand flailed, trying to capture one of the dropped swords.

"Who are you?" he croaked, glancing from the solid door to our masked faces. "How—?"

Realization drained his face of blood just as I knelt on his flapping hand. He hissed in pain, still managing to squeeze out, "Magic."

"Not magic," I said, as Dumond held him, and I forced the drops into his mouth. As I kept a firm grip to prevent him spitting out the potion, I drew on my own power. *The Cavalieri Teschio broke through our iron-bound gate. What picklocks they must be! Such stealth. Only two of them it took to defeat our three . . .*

I planted a description of two Skull Knights who looked nothing like any of us. Then I released my magic. I'd no opportunity to do the same for the other two. They were already out of mind asleep. Their stories should be confused enough. More worrisome were the grunts and curses now coming from the bottom of the tower stair.

Dumond and I hurried quietly down the steps and peered out.

A body lay uncomfortably still, sprawled on the grass near the base of the tower. Not Neri. Even in the courtyard's dimness, a praetorian's yellow badge glared from the man's tabard.

A few paces away, a ferocious Placidio grappled with a hulking opponent, muzzling him and shoving him inexorably backward toward the protruding bulk of the tower. With a release and a twist, he slammed the brute to the ground and threw his full weight on the man's back. This one wore the yellow shoulder stripe of a guard captain.

"Give the proper reassurance to all within hearing," Placidio growled through his teeth. "And tell them to hold positions. If I've the slightest doubt as to your accuracy, I'll snap your neck as if 'twere your daughter's stick dolly." He lowered his mouth to the struggling man's ear. "I'll know if it's false. It's grind time, praetorian. By the Lone. You can survive it or not."

The victim stilled. "Give me a breath . . . bastard traitor."

Placidio let up slightly, and the man yelled, "Status—virgin night. All stand."

From high atop the defense wall, the call echoed, "Virgin night. Clear and clear."

As soon as the words were out, Placidio grabbed the captain's hair, yanked his head back, and set his knife to his throat. "Now where's the lad?"

My heart lurched.

The man grinned, blood oozing through his teeth. "What lad would that be? The one what appeared out of nowhere and shone a light into the guardpost, though he'd no lamp, no lantern, nothing natural to make it? Such a fine specimen, he is. He'll have a long career on the chain. Sniffing."

Placidio pressed the knife harder. "Best tell me, else my blade'll decide you're no use."

The captain laughed through clenched teeth. "You'll never— get—out. Already—more—on the way."

"Witch." The call was not from the bleeding guard captain, and it was so soft that Placidio with the fury of battle raging in him would never hear it. Nor would anyone five steps farther away. Only Neri ever called me witch.

Frantic, I abandoned the tower doorway and spun around. Where would he be? What was it he'd found when we'd sat here for an hour waiting? *A dandy hiding place . . . the tower foot.*

Each corner of the hexagonal tower was supported by a buttress that flared outward at its base. I examined one, the next, the next. Ensconced in a dark little nest of weeds grown up between the flaring buttress of one tower corner and the thick footing of the wall, I found Neri. His left arm clutched his right tight to his chest.

"I'm all right," he said, preempting my question when I touched his black tunic and found it warm and soggy. "Didn't ought to shout. Are we still on?"

"For the moment," I said, holding him down. "Let me see it."

"Just needs tying up."

"Hold on." I darted around the pier to signal Placidio and Dumond that I'd found him.

Placidio landed a blow to his captive's head that would blur his vision for a year and climbed off the man's back. "Do we abort?"

"Wounded, but awake . . . and himself."

Dumond blew a relieved exhale.

Placidio glared down at the unconscious brute. "Can you adjust this man's perceptions?"

"Not when he's unconscious," I said. "You'll have to make sure he can't get away."

A flick of Dumond's knife provided strips of gray student's gown to bind the gouting slash in Neri's upper arm and bind the arm itself to his chest. He had lost a great deal of blood.

"You'll enjoy the cesspool with me, lad," said Dumond, helping him to his feet. "You can hold my paints."

"But I can—"

"No. You're done for the night," I said, slipping my arm under his left shoulder to hold him up. He was quivering. "We'll make do."

"Does that one need the tincture?" I said, as Placidio dragged the captain past us and crammed him into the weedy niche.

"No. What of that other one?"

The sprawled praetorian had not moved since we'd arrived. Dumond had his cheek to the man's mouth. He sat up and shook his head. Dead, then.

"Didn't mean to kill him," said Neri. "But he was right there when I walked in—bad luck—and he ran for the tower. He'd have warned them. I chased him, muzzled him, but then the captain came out the tower, and I just . . . demons . . . wasn't anything else to do . . . but I didn't mean—"

"It's done," said Placidio, laying his solid hand on Neri's unwounded shoulder. "Isn't the first. Won't be the last. It's the way of the world. The way of spies. We'll talk of it later." He hauled the body around and stuffed it atop the captain. I suspected the captain was dead, too.

With a somber touch of hands all around, Dumond grabbed our bag of robes and Neri. They vanished into the shadows, heading for the cesspool to make us a way out.

"Hard part's done," said Placidio. "We've got till the captain fails to show for rounds. Less if someone discovers the tower gate's not manned. Half hour at most."

10

The bell tower of the Palazzo Segnori might have been perched atop the Villa Giusti. When the bells rang the Hour of the Spirits, their clamor masked our entry to the cellar at the outer end of the west wing. Neri hadn't mentioned the creaking metal doors with hinges older than the Confraternity itself.

How could anyone in the house stay asleep?

The outside torches gave us a bit of light, filtered down the stair. A convenient shelf of small oil lamps, candlesticks, and firepots, ready for servants' use, offered a chance to do a quick scout of the cellar before setting out to find Donato and Livia. We might need a bolt-hole.

We found storerooms. Linen cupboards. Candle rooms. Bathing tubs and shelves of towels. Buckets and mops and baskets of rags. Everything you might expect for a very large house with plenty of servants. An L-shaped turning led into a long hallway.

A bump and a clang, quickly silenced, drew my attention to a row of bells mounted on the low ceiling. Placidio grimaced and rubbed his head. Summoning bells. This was the servants' quarters.

We retreated to the stair and doused the lamp, holding our breath to make sure the cellar remained quiet. We couldn't wait long.

Then it was up the stair . . . ground floor . . . second floor . . . and a door that took us from the plain, cramped utility of the servants' stair into a long hall. On our right was the orderly row of windows so harmonious on the house facade. And even in the dimness of night lamps, one could have spent a year examining the beautiful tapestries and artworks hanging on our left, in-between the elegant doorways. Instead, we pulled up our hoods and checked our masks.

I pressed my ear to the first door. Hearing no hint of movement, we quietly peeked inside. A skinny boy in slops sprawled atop his rumpled sheets. Without doubt the twelve-year-old. The youngest Bastianni brother.

We backed out and hurried to the next, creeping inside to get a closer look. The chamber stank of boy and horse. Riding clothes were scattered everywhere. This youth was slightly older, but no hair on his chin and only a scattering anywhere else that we could see. Fifteen, he was. The same age my brother was when he saw his father's hand lopped off for Neri's own crime. As we backed away, the boy turned over and mumbled in his sleep.

The third room was quiet as well—or perhaps I wasn't listening carefully enough. When I opened the door, a faint light filtered through bed-curtains, a youthful male giggle along with it. "Silvio, wait . . . 's too quick!" A gray tunic and breeches lay in a heap on the floor.

Heart pounding, I shut the door softly. The bridegroom was not named Silvio.

We moved to the next. A plain, leather-padded bench sat outside the door. The leather was slightly worn, slightly dented, and slightly warm. Recently occupied, then. This occupant's status merited a night usher. Placidio and I both pressed an ear to the door before opening it. All was quiet. We slipped in soundlessly, and were grateful for a nightlamp beside the bed that revealed no attendant lurking. Maybe he was the one sharing a romp with Silvio. . . .

Donato di Bastianni slept sitting up and wore a linen night-shirt. Unlike his brothers' rooms, his bedchamber was orderly. Clothes chest shut. Dressing table bare. Chairs set in perfect symmetry on either side of a small hearth. A writing table with clean parchment and bottles of ink that showed no evidence of having ever been opened. No books. No art. No anything of a personal nature. His finery for the next day—brocades, ruffs, lace-trimmed sleeves, plenty of wool for stuffing his trousses—had been laid out in perfect order on a velvet divan. He must be the dullest, tidiest young man in Cantagna.

I remained by the door, dagger at the ready.

Quick as a cat, Placidio climbed onto the high bed, reached across the slim body, and rolled Donato onto his chest. Then he sat on him.

The young man squirmed, moaned, scrabbled his arms, kicked his feet, and yelled. But one of Placidio's huge hands crushed the rising protests into the pillows as their owner spoke in the fellow's ear. "I can press a bit harder and cut off your air, and then you'll stay quiet. Or you can shut your mouth and I'll let you breathe a little whilst we prepare you for a little adventure. Which is your choice?"

Donato kicked harder and tried to reach backward, but Placidio just pushed his face deeper into the pillows until the young man's trembling hands flew upward in surrender. I bound his ankles, wrists, and elbows with leather straps, while Placidio gagged him with a scarf. Once done, we rolled him to his back and let him see our masks and hoods and the death's-heads Vashti had painted on them.

His eyes—deep set and black as burnt coals—grew to roughly the size of Placidio's outsized palms. Though his mouth opened around the gag, he didn't even squeak. Instead, he fainted.

"Well, I'll kiss a toad." After this quiet expression of astonishment, Placidio checked Donato's blood pulse and shrugged. "He's alive."

To be sure he wasn't playing us, I chose a most sensitive part of his anatomy and pinched it. Hard. His body twitched, but no sense returned, and he remained limp as a dead fish. We rolled him in a sheet. After making sure the missing attendant had not returned, we carried him down to the cellar and left him in the candle room.

Now Livia. Would that her capture could be so easy. Would that the house might stay quiet and the halls deserted. We had assumed Neri would be with us to create a diversion if need be.

Back upstairs and grateful for the strip of carpet that silenced our steps, we sped past an ornately outfitted vestibule that Neri had told us led to Director Bastianni's own chambers. Two gray-clad ushers snored on a bench just like the one outside Dono's chamber. Farther down the corridor, the north end where Neri had said we'd surely find the bride, doorways opened to vacant rooms. At the farthest end of the hall, four pillars marked the right turn from the west wing to the main house. Just round the corner was a pair of painted double doors. No usher or maidservant, but a praetorian stood post outside them.

Placidio and I made a soundless retreat into one of the empty chambers. I felt a bit breathless and greatly disappointed.

"New plan?" I whispered.

Placidio tilted his head. "Mmm . . . Mistress Cataline?"

Perfectly clear. Perfectly clever. Romy of Lizard's Alley, dressed in scuffed black trousers and tunic, could certainly distract a praetorian. But Mistress Cataline of the Moon House, a courtesan who could assume any attire and any role her master desired and still be alluring, had been trained to melt the resolve of a stone pillar. Over the past year and a half, the distance between Romy and Cataline had grown wide. Reclaiming that self, that conviction, required an impersonation, magic . . . wherein lay the ever-present risk.

"You'll be here? With my name and a friendly hand?"

Placidio nodded soberly, and then broke into the brilliant, dashing, world-embracing grin that could illuminate a winter midnight. He would have to bring me back to myself.

I shed the hooded cape and my boots, and unpinned and unbraided my hair. Closing my eyes, I reached deep for magic and let its heat flood my veins. Then I stepped into the corridor and into that other life, so particular and remote. *I am beauty itself . . . my every movement is grace . . . enticement . . . promise. My skin is silken and radiant; my eyes gleam and suggest pleasure without boundaries. My tutors crushed the child I was into dust and splinters and rebuilt her into the embodiment of sensuality and strength, obedience and resilience, for what delight is to be found in mastering a weakling? I am able to leave myself entirely open to the one who has chosen me. His desires are my guide and my law, my fulfillment and my truth. Tonight he wishes me to draw a third into our games.*

"*Use your finest allurements, my beauteous Cataline,*" he'd said, "*and we shall break this dull soldier's discipline for our amusement. . . .*"

I crept through the hall and around the corner. He was there, the stalwart my master wished to see naked on his knees, begging for our indulgence. We'd played our spy game all night. My master found it thrilling to sneak around a stranger's house and take our pleasures where we would and of the sort he most enjoyed. Now something even bolder, he'd told me.

"Ssst, praetorian!" My beckoning was just low enough, he had to break posture to hear.

"What's that? Damizella?" He had turned round and squinted at me, but did not approach.

I glanced both ways along the hall, then darted toward him

on bare feet, my hair teased into a cloud, my disheveled tunic un-
laced.

Folded hands on my breasts, I gazed up at him. Tears welled at
my command. "Oh please come, good sir. I need help desperately."

"I mustn't . . ." He tried to look away. His gaze flicked back
once. Then a second time. "Who *are* you? By the Night Eternal,
you are so—"

"Good segno, I beg you. I've been so wicked." Another flick of
his eyes—away and then back to me.

"Wicked? Surely not. I shouldn't even listen— All right, what is
it?" Hooked.

Rejecting the urge to smile, I dipped my head in submission.
"I must show you. You'll be well rewarded. It's *the director* asking."

The man nearly choked. My master had said that title would
draw the fellow sure. *The director* owned this fine house.

I tiptoed lightly back toward the bedchamber, glancing back
only once. Though the soldier's sword remained at his side, his
lance stood propped against the wall. Eager curiosity shaped
his goodly face.

I beckoned him through the doorway. "I've fetched the handsome fellow as you said, Master."

My master drew him into the shadows in a chokehold and
quickly had him bound, blindfolded, and on his knees.

I had closed the door and knelt gracefully. "Shall I remove his
garments, Master?"

He cleared his throat. "I think that's a fine idea. Capo would
certainly approve such a play."

Alarmed, the soldier shook his head, twisting and protesting
with squeaks and grunts. He was not so clean as I might like, but
he showed fire, which would please my master and make the taking all the sweeter.

When done, I waited for Master to take the lead. It was not my
place to initiate. Hands behind his back, he circled the soldier.
Then, as the fellow whined and shuddered, Master took my hand
and drew me into a shadowed corner. He bent to whisper in my
ear. "Well done, *Romy*."

As Cataline's persona vanished, Placidio stepped briskly aside.
The blindfolded soldier twisted this way and that as if to discover
where we'd gone.

"Did you enjoy that?" I murmured as the world readjusted it-self. I pulled on my boots, laced my tunic, and twisted my hair into a knot.

"Part of the job," whispered Placidio cheerily. "I've found a hidey-hole where he can stew. I figure he's less likely to break free and run for help this way. And we need to be on our way."

He strode back to our captive, lifted him bodily, and stuffed the struggling man into an empty clothes chest.

Indeed, our window of time was rapidly closing.

"We shall have to play another day," I said, and kissed the top of the guard's head. As Placidio pushed it down and closed the lid of the lovely enameled chest, I replaced my cape, hood, and mask.

In three breaths, we were opening one of the painted double doors and slipping into an enormous, high-ceilinged bedchamber. Nicely quiet. Lacking maidservants or nannies. A night lamp on a low table laid a dim path across the Paolin carpet. Velvet bed-curtains were tied back, but the mounded bedclothes were still.

Avoiding the lampglow, we crept swiftly to the bedside only to come up short. Where was the bride?

"Who in this household of cretins and sycophants are you two?" The sharp question originated from a window seat half ob-scured by draperies. If she'd not spoken, we'd never have known she was there. She was sitting sideways, her knees drawn up close.

"We could ask the same," said Placidio. I remained quiet at his side in the shadows. "We've been told the person in this room has value to this household. Is that so?"

"I'd not have phrased it so bluntly, but yes. I do." She was not at all afraid. Curious, certainly, but steady.

I'd first thought to frighten the girl with Marsilia's murder and persuade her to come with us, but with the stakes grown larger, Placidio had insisted we maintain our roles as a Cavalieri snatch-crew. There was no time just now for persuasion, and once we revealed that we were not the Cavalieri, there was no going back. Time enough for truth once we reached Perdition's Brink.

"Why does my value interest a man and his . . . companion"—she ducked and tilted her head as if to see more clearly—"in the middle of the night in a fortress of philosophists? Is this a seduc-tion? If so, I must inform you that I take no physical interest in men, especially skulkers, cowards, or bombastic bullies. Women, when one can find one with a mind more developed than an olive pit, are much more amiable in *all* ways."

I swallowed a veritable knot of words.

Placidio hesitated a moment, as if he, too, were digesting surprises, but he took up smoothly. "My intentions are pure in those intimate regards, damizella. What I would appreciate is permission to approach you with a proposition of a more businesslike nature."

"Though I am intrigued at your mannerly approach, this is the Hour of the Spirits on the night before my betrothal. Your proposition cannot be *entirely* honorable."

"Ah, clever damizella, there is truth in what you say."

If we weren't so pressed for time, and Neri wasn't out there bleeding in a cesspit with the trace of magic on him and sniffers nearby, I could have pulled up a chair and watched this joust continue into morning. Instead, I poked Placidio in the ribs.

"Honestly, it doesn't matter whether or not you give me permission," said Placidio, regretfully. "You are required to accompany my friend and me on a brief journey. The purpose will be explained in due time. Could I provide you a gown—or a cloak—to make you more comfortable traveling in the night?"

"So I'm guessing that the praetorian has been removed from my door. Or bribed to look away. Come as you will." She did not sit up, stand up, or shrink away.

I recognized the sound of Placidio's dagger slipping from its leather home. That surprised me. But then this woman had traveled in wild lands for years, and our appearance evoked no fear in her. I drew my own dagger.

"Masks!" she said as we moved into the lampglow. "How dashing! And your companion . . . a youth? Or a woman? I am intri—"

Placidio jerked and let fly his dagger. It struck the window glass right beside Livia's head, some ten paces from our position.

With reflexes well matched to my swordmaster's, Livia rolled from the window seat to the floor and into a crouch. But Placidio was already airborne and landed square on top of her, one huge paw gripping her fist that held a short, curved blade.

"Assistance, partner mine," he said, his voice just strained enough to tell me that Livia di Nardo was strong, determined, and very likely had a second weapon threatening his anatomy some-where I couldn't see.

I snatched the wicked little dagger, freeing Placidio to wrestle a stiletto from her alter hand. More leather bindings hung at my waist.

She craned her neck to look at us. "Death's-heads? Truly? I've seen naked cannibals lunching on human flesh. Thugs do not frighten me."

"Your fear is yours to manage, damizella," said Placidio, snug-ging her ankles, "but your future is up for bidding. We'll see who values you, and who can produce the funds to buy you back."

"You'll never get out of—"

I crammed the gag in her mouth before she could finish her re-tort and decide to let fly a scream. Placidio grasped the wriggling girl and laid her on the bed. She was modest enough in a plain chemise and a bedgown of thin wool.

Scrabbling through the bed coverings, I found a blanket thin enough to roll her in while yet allowing her to breathe. But first, I pulled out the tincture bottle, stuck my finger in the side of her mouth to pull the gag away, and dribbled three droplets at the back of her cheek.

She bit me. Drew blood. But I held her still and breathless long enough she could not refrain from swallowing. It took the two of us to roll her, but by the time Placidio threw her over his shoulder, she had gone limp.

"Mercy!" he said. "Are you sure we're supposed to save this one? I think the fainting groom is the one needs rescuing."

"Beware of women with minds more developed than an olive pit."

He snorted in good humor. "I've already learned *that* lesson. I hope you can carry one of these two. Honestly, I think the groom is lighter."

The city bells were ringing again, and in the midst of the clan-gor rose another noise that erased all good humor and set my hair on end. Howling.

"Fortune's dam," I whispered, "let that not be for Neri and Dumond." Placidio's gaze met mine through the eyeholes of our masks. For, of course, both of us had used magic, too. My imper-sonation. His anticipation of danger that had granted him the mo-ment to distract the lady before she could gut him.

"We go separate to Dumond," he snapped. "Me behind the kitchen buildings; you along the defense wall. And if one—"

"If one of us gets there and the other is not yet, get out and away."

"Aye, well, give or take a few breaths."

. . .

Assurance. Placidio would not have let me carry Livia—indeed he'd admitted Livia was the lighter—if he wasn't certain I could do it. He would have found another way. Carried them both himself. Made a second trip to the villa for one or the other. Something. He was the one who had transformed me from an agile former courtesan, who had developed an unfortunate habit of drinking too much wine to assuage her melancholy, into a confidential agent who could run up the Boar's Teeth scarp three times in a day and still use strength and good technique to upend a full-grown man. So if he believed I could carry a woman's dead weight around the peripheries of the Villa Giusti, I could.

Only I thought I might die on the endless route, rough with weeds, stones, and broken masonry, and much too near the guards atop the wall who might spy movements in the murk. The pounding of my heart and the rasp of my breathing must surely be audible to every resident of the infernal fortress.

I leaned against a rectangular wall buttress and pressed the rolled bundle that was Livia di Nardo to the dressed stones to rest my aching shoulders. The northwest tower, lit only by one small watchfire in its guardroom, loomed in the distance ahead of me. In the dark corner beyond it lay the cesspool.

Much too soon for my agonized back, I pulled away and slogged northward again. It was easy to be confident and magnanimous, telling Placidio that he and the others should leave me behind if I didn't get to them soon enough, but I dearly hoped they wouldn't. Certain, if I glimpsed Dumond's blue fire opening the portal, I would throw the troublesome Livia in the midden and charge through the magical gap.

Immediately in front of me a black jumble of small outbuildings that smelled of hay and leather hugged the wall. Not the main stable, but tack sheds and hay stores, likely deserted so late. I chose to go around them, lest a stable hand be sleeping inside. But the moment's pause quieted the pounding of blood in my ears just enough I could hear a soft, burring moan and quiet clink behind me. A sniffer. Very close.

I staggered into a half-collapsed hay store that stank of horse dung and mold. Sinking to my knees, I unloaded Livia, then burrowed both of us into the fouled, matted heap.

The stinking, stifling dark enfolded me. I held still, fighting to calm my harsh breath and roiling gut. My ears played tricks. Were those whispers or a night breeze . . . scurrying feet . . . or soft breathing? Was that hay tickling my cheeks or a rat's whiskers . . . or a finger caressing the line of my jaw . . . my lips . . . *lovely one* . . .

Shivering, tired beyond bearing, aching, frightened, it took an age to decide when to move on. But I dug out the sleeping Livia, hoisted her onto my shoulders yet again, and took up my journey. The yips and howls were far behind now—back toward the main gate and the tower we'd breached to get inside. Please the universe they were not on Placidio's tail. The guard captain's reference to Neri living out his life at the end of a chain had iced my blood.

Another step. And another.

Never had I thought the scent of excrement could be enticing, but on this wretched journey, the first wafting tendrils raised my spirits.

"Ssst. Sister witch."

I warned my feet to take another step. Surely it was my fear of being late that roused imaginings of Neri's whisper.

"Almost there. Can't share the load, but I'll guide you in." An icy hand touched my arm, then gripped hard as I stumbled— startled out of my exhausted fog of night and fear.

Great Ocean, his face shone like a moon in the dark. Not a splotch of color in it.

"You should be in bed," I croaked softly, touching his cheek just to be sure he was real.

"You're the one feels fevered," he said. "Gods' balls, your skin's like burning paper."

His hold was reassuring, but his feet dragged worse than mine.

"You've no blood left in you, and you've no business out here. . . ."

"Got to get you out first. Swordmaster told me you were coming this route."

My mind took hold of the situation. "So he's there but not gone? Not taken you through? I'll kill him!"

The moon face crinkled as if I were a lunatic. "Went through almost an hour since. Took his bundle of groom off to fetch the cart and horses. He's bringing them up for us. We convinced him that was better than going back into the villa for you. We knew you'd make it through."

Impossible. And the sniffers . . . My mind refused to grasp this. "Dumond wouldn't dare leave the portal open so long. Live magic . . ."

"Dumond's painted a second exit for us. Once he shut the first behind Placidio, he ran around the whole cursed villa painting little bird-sized holes, opening them, then shutting them to cut off the magic. Chalked the sigil of the Skull Knights at each spot. Said he did about twenty. Now he's just waiting for you. It's been near two hours that the swordmaster left you at the cellar door."

"That can't be right. I had to hole up in a hay store, but not for so long. . . ."

"We figured you might have had to go to ground. But we didn't hear any hullaballoo saying you'd been caught, and he figured you'd show up when it was safe enough."

Two hours. Even with the seeming eternity of drudgery, two hours could not possibly have passed. I wasn't a snail. Placidio had given me the shorter route, and yes, Livia was a weight across my shoulders, but I'd carried heavy loads through the streets of Cantagna.

Neri and I kept silent and breathed shallow as we passed beneath the northwest tower and into the full aura of the cesspool. Moments later, blessed Dumond's strong arms relieved me of Livia and laid her beside a painted piece of wall the size of a trapdoor. A surge of blue fire and he crawled through his portal, dragging Livia after him. Between us, we helped Neri scoot through on his backside. Then me. A cacophony of sniffer howls surged in our direction. Blue fire blazing, Dumond slammed his door. I imagined green bodies slamming against the bare masonry in search of sorcerers who weren't there.

Dumond carried Livia, and Neri and I supported each other

as we climbed a short, rough berm and dodged through an abandoned fullers' manufactury, refuse heaps, and other remnants of the past to a pitch-dark lane. A shaded lantern hung above a waiting cart.

"Atladu's holy, blessed balls, lady scribe," said Placidio, helping Dumond shift Livia into the cart. "Where in this confounded universe have you been?"

"Walking . . ."

It took my last spoonful of strength to climb into the cart beside the bundled captives and a collapsed Neri. Dumond took the reins of the two cart horses, while Placidio mounted the third beast. I brushed away straw that prickled my back, neck, and arms.

". . . a hay store . . . I stopped to hide . . . Maybe I fell asleep."

"How could you fall asleep?"

The cart lurched forward, leaving Placidio's startled question unanswered.

But it roused a fleeting memory that glanced across my mind's horizon—of smoking ruins, collapsed houses, decaying corpses . . . and a man's deep, melodious voice . . .

Come, my lovely one, he'd said, his warm fingers stroking my cheek. That voice . . . it had shivered my bones, enfolded me in his pleasure, his admiration, his understanding. *Walk with me awhile. Leave off your burdens. . . .*

I'd done so, for he was so gloriously beautiful—long and lithe, hair of deep red-brown that floated on the smoky wind like strands of silk, skin of golden bronze, eyes kissed by the sun. His voice had threaded my veins with fire like magic itself as he told me of his hopes and dreams.

I wrapped my arms about my chest. Beneath my clothes, my skin burned. What were his hopes? Though I had comprehended his words in perfect clarity, they escaped me now, for they were formed in a language I did not know.

The cart jogged down the cobbles toward the Beggars Ring and the city's North Gate and the next stage of our venture. Placidio's strong back on the horse and Dumond's broad shoulders on the driving seat of the cart made me feel safe. So why could I not let go and sleep? Anger simmered in my gut. My clenched hands trembled. What was wrong with me?

A hard bump jostled Neri and he rolled onto my legs. Rage

blistered me; to resist shoving him over the side required all my remaining strength.

Horrified, I huddled deeper into the corner of the cart, crushing my hands beneath my arms. *I must tell the others about the dreams.*

II

Sunlight through a slot of broken stone pried my eyes open. I brushed dirt and grit from my cheek, meanwhile noting the unyielding jags and bumps beneath the blanket that separated me from bare ground. I was not outdoors. High above me thick trusses supported a square, mostly intact roof and some dangling floor timbers, most of which held only remnants of actual floor. Yet *inside* hardly applied either. A crow squawked and landed on one of the walls' numerous gaps and holes open to the wakening sky.

Down on my level beside a broken stone staircase, one of those wall gaps opened onto a wasteland of scrub, dry cedars, and more broken walls. Perdition's Brink. Exactly as Placidio had described it.

Neri!

In the same moment I realized the name of the place where I was and why I was there, I also realized the source of the boulder-sized heaviness inside my chest—Neri's awful wound. All that blood. The morning was quiet, save for the complaints of the birds, and neither brother nor partners were anywhere in sight.

As I scrambled to my feet amid a jumble of blankets, the rest of my reasons for concern pummeled my sore shoulders as if the dangling timbers had decided to release themselves all at once. Our captives. The strange gap in time while I hid in the hay store. The dreams . . .

The jostle of the cart over city cobbles and rutted lanes had left me numb and unobservant upon our arrival in the last pitchy hours of the night. My partners had guided me up a steep path and through a forest of sharp pinnacles and tree skeletons. When they'd pointed at a blanket spread on the ground, I'd dropped and fled into restless, tangled sleep. No dreams that I could recall . . . but remembering dreams upon waking didn't seem to be the usual way of things anymore.

So where was everyone?

An ale cask, a hammer, bundles of blankets, rope, and pots, and bags of fruit and other foodstuffs had been piled against one wall of the square tower. This must be the old fortress keep. Its identity was confirmed the moment I stepped outside to search for the others. Despite the gaping holes, the thick side walls yet supported the tower's slate roof. Likely it would take Dragonis himself to flatten the squat structure.

Leery of shouting, I wandered through broken remnants and courtyards of a more expansive house, more decrepit, though not quite so old as the keep. Just outside the keep, a courtyard that might once have been pleasant was now a rubble of broken planters, columns, benches, and a stair that plunged steeply downward into the dark heart of the rock beneath the ruins.

A string of curses and a muffled groan of effort burst out just behind me. Turning back, I met Neri just as he staggered up the last step of that plunging stair. He carried a bucket of water with his non-wounded arm, and he looked like death itself.

He mustered a weak grin. "You're awa—"

I caught the pail just as it slipped from his grasp and him just before he collapsed on top of it.

"What are you doing, idiot child?" I said, guiding him, stumbling, back into the keep to the jumble of blankets. Some of them were bloody. "And what are our damnable partners thinking to let you haul water?"

"Just knackered," he mumbled. "Don't fuss. Let me sit."

Once he pressed his back to the wall and slid to the ground, I reached to untie his dirty bandages. They were still damp.

"Ow! Stop." He sucked his teeth and batted my hand away. "Jus' give me a bit."

"Looks like you're still bleeding," I said, annoyed at his dismissal. "I need to see—"

"Not now. Hurts like the devil, and there's naught to do till Dumond's back."

"I need to look at the wound. Don't be a fool." Every word he spoke was like a thorn pushed under my skin.

"Stop calling me that." Angry, he shoved my hand away again.

"I'll stop when you show some sense."

"You're not Da nor Mam. And you don't know everything. Leave me be!"

"Sleep then. Let it fester. I'll come back and see to it when you're out of your head."

I stormed out to fetch his water bucket from the courtyard.

Half of a broken stone bench provided a seat while I scooped a handful of the water to cool my overheated face. Naught could soothe the sour taste of my hateful words.

A shadow blocked the streaming sunlight for a moment. Placidio had come around the corner of the keep carrying a good-sized metal chest.

"Fortune's benefice this fine morn, lady scribe." His thick fingers tapped the chest. "Dumond says this box is for anything birds, vermin, or other creepy-crawlers might find tasty."

He disappeared into the keep long enough to set it down.

"Where have you been?" I demanded when he returned. "Napping again?"

"Only one's had any sleep is you. But I'm on my way to do just that. I'll confess I'm like to carry something off the cliff if I don't take an hour. Dumond's just come from the city with more supplies and thinks to head straight back soon as the cart's emptied. Now you're awake, maybe you could help him unload. Leave the casks for me to fetch later. Our captives are both yet dozing."

He wouldn't get off so easy. "I found Neri hauling water up this stair. His arm is still seeping, and he was near collapse. How could you allow—?"

"Told him to give it some rest. But being wounded's extra hard when you're young and had a rough night, and certain, he's got wounds beyond the arm, if one gives a *thought* to what happened last night. Dumond's brought some kind of healing salve for the wound. Maybe it will still your frets as well. I doubt anything but keeping busy's going to soothe the boy's other hurt." He threw a blanket over his shoulder and headed into the skeletal forest of chimneys and archways and broken columns.

Spirits . . . Neri had killed a man last night. His first. No wonder he was unable to sit still or sleep easy or believe his own hurts were of any importance. And no sleep for Placidio and Dumond . . . and on the night before the snatch, while I had dozed for a few hours, they had come up here to prepare accommodations for our captives. They'd been two overlong days without rest.

Halfway repentant, I called after Placidio, "After you sleep . . . I've things I need to tell you."

Certain, it wasn't just worries about Neri or the mission had me so snappish. It was the dreams.

• • •

It took two trips up and down the path for me to shake off that tempestuous waking. By my third visit to the foot of the path, I could fully appreciate the placement of Perdition's Brink. Silhouetted against the morning sky, the squat, square outline of the tower keep provided the only clue that human hands had played a role in shaping the jagged granite prominence. Someone had wanted limited access and an unobstructed view of the rolling landscape. The only path up was steep and one person wide, and the view was excellent in every direction.

It was easy to imagine the folded land skirting Perdition's Brink was cursed. The morning light that streaked the nearby hillsides highlighted the ranks of brown, curled scrub and the skeletons of grapevines. Everywhere else was pale, sorry dirt and spiky grass that stank of tar and lacked any semblance of moisture. Yet beyond the relics of stone walls and rowed cypress trees so often used as estate boundaries, the angled light crossed hills mantled in healthy greens, autumn golds, and the orderly dark green patches of precious vineyards.

With multiple bags hung from arms and shoulders, I grasped a crate of bread, sausage, and cheese with one hand and a tied bundle of shirts in the other. Dumond was checking harness and promising the horses that this next would be their last trip to the city for a while.

"When are *you* going to sleep?" I said, shamed at my lingering annoyance when I considered all Dumond and Placidio had done to get us settled.

"I'll doze for a while at the woolhouse, then take a stroll about town listening for news before I head back out. Back here early afternoon, I'm thinking." He nudged a small brown bag dangling from the crook of my elbow. "This is the honey salve Vash sent for

Neri's wound, and some clean linen to bind it. She says get it on right away, and check it every morning and evening."

"Maybe he'll heed Vashti's advice better than mine." Just because I felt guilty at weakness and spooked by nightmares didn't mean I wasn't right to be upset with everyone.

Dumond hefted the last small cask from the cart and set it at the bottom of the path with two others for Placidio to haul up. "Neri's a good lad. And you and the swordmaster have done well by him. But he's got a canker in his gut drives him. It's healed some, but still bites. Likely will forever."

"The canker is our da's hand," I said. The lopsman's blow, the spurting blood, and Da's terrible cry would certainly live in *my* mind forever. "And not knowing whether Da or the rest of the family survived it. Exiled who knows where. . . . they could have starved to death by now."

Spirits, this world was a cruel and terrible place. And now my little brother had a dead man weighing on him, too.

Dumond climbed onto the cart seat. "Boy *shouldn't* forget things like that, but you want them built into his bones, not left open to poison."

"So how do I make that happen?"

"That's the mystery with tending young ones, yeh? *Keep steady* is my way."

A good way, seeing how he was with his daughters—strong, calm, constant. I'd never heard him yell at or argue with them. "Maybe I'll try that."

The cart rolled away. As circling hawks mocked me, I trudged up the steep path with my load, this new worry about Neri, and our present dilemma. How were we going to deal with our two captives, currently sleeping off the last of Vashti's powerful potion?

Certain, Donato's bedchamber could not have given us less of a clue about what the man might value or fear enough to cross his parents' wishes and forgo the marriage. Before we could present any proposal, we had to know him better.

And Livia? I had met her father, the city steward, numerous times. A good man, fair and honest. Not the most adventurous or imaginative mind, but excellent at balancing the needs of the city, the deployment of workers and funds, and the imperious demands of important people—including *il Padroné* and his dangerous, ever-present shadow self. I'd been vaguely aware the steward had a daughter. Ever jealous of happy families, I had assumed he doted on her. But perhaps not.

Certain, she seemed difficult. Perhaps that's why Piero had sent her traveling with her uncle. Should we tell her that we were allies right away or keep our secrets and try to learn more of her plans while she felt threatened? I could argue either way. Dumond would say we should tell her all. Placidio wouldn't trust her; he was the one nursing a knife cut on one hip.

"He's waked up." Neri, wan and hollow-eyed, met me at the top of the path, a narrow strip of level ground that skirted the fallen gatehouse.

"Placidio? Already?"

"No, the bridegroom." Neri relieved me of the bundled shirts, wincing as the firm bundle pressed on the wounded arm strapped to his chest. His black tunic clung in the way that suggested more seepage. "I went to see where he was."

For the moment, I attempted to *keep steady*. Calm. No reprimand. No smothering. "Did you speak to him? We agreed not for a while at first."

"Nah. Maybe he's not actually awake. He's sitting up, but his eyes are closed."

We threaded the fallen stones and the charred, rotting timbers of the gatehouse and crossed what remained of the old bailey.

"When we took him, he was sitting up in his bed," I said. "Maybe he has some illness like brittle lung or gut churn that makes him sleep sitting up. Sisters, I hope he doesn't die out here." Though Neri's own condition was much more worrisome.

Neri fumbled the bundle and dropped the shirts on the weedy flat. "Sorry."

He squatted to gather them again, favoring his wounded side and wobbling a little as he stood.

"Soon as I stow these things and set them to rights, we'll rebandage your arm," I said, stripping out any hint of lingering argument. "Vashti sent some clean linen, a salve, and another Cavalieri tunic that won't stink so bad as the one you're wearing. Placidio believes we should let our captives sweat a bit in their confines."

"Sweating should be no problem."

Indeed, the autumn sun was already baking this pile of rock. At least being up so high with the soaring hawks, we caught a goodly breeze. The sheen of moisture on Neri's forehead unsettled me.

"Where in all the bowels of the universe are we, you infernal scum?" The complaint sirened from the southern end of the bluff, accompanied by the raucous clatter of a chain on stone.

We had put Livia in an old cellar room at the southern extremity of the ruin and Donato in a similar one at the northern extremity of the ruin on purpose. We didn't want them to be able to speak to each other or even to know the other was captive.

"Sounds as if the lady is awake, too," I said, tossing the bags of food into the metal chest. "But first things first. Let's pile these blankets over here where I slept. And we'll make this crate our medical store. Now, sit."

This time, Neri didn't argue. To the music of Livia's extensive vocabulary of complaints, I peeled away the blood-soaked tunic and the unrecognizable remnant of my Academie student's gown we'd used to bandage the wound. Keeping steady, I told him about Donato's bedchamber and the contrast with those of his three brothers while I blotted the very ugly gash in his upper arm and shoulder. Still seeping blood, it could surely use a stitching, but we'd no implements. The flesh around it was red and tender.

"This will help. Truly," I said as, despite his best efforts, he flinched at my every touch. "I've always heard a honey salve was best for preventing sepsis, and Vashti knows how to make it, which I do not. It's like cooking, I suppose. My biggest failing."

"Ow!"

"Oh *Sisters*, Neri, I'm sorry."

I'd not thought Neri's deep-hued complexion could get any paler. Besides the usual dirt and blood from his fight with the villa guard, every bruise and scrape glared at me.

By the time I had the wound bound and a glass of wine poured down his throat, he was drowsing. "Sorry," he said, slurring a bit. "Useless brute. Oughta throw me in a pit, too."

He curled up atop the pile of blankets, even as I sat up straighter. He'd given me a fine idea.

Carefully, I set aside the bucket of water he'd hauled from the spring, and the rag I'd thought to use to clean the dirt from his face.

"Not useless," I said dragging a thin blanket around his bare shoulders. "Not ever. Hear this and believe it. This mission is *worthy*. If we give this girl a future, her ideas could change everything for people like us. Set us free. Save countless lives. You're helping us make that happen."

Likely he'd not heard me. I wished him dreamless sleep and hurried off to find Placidio in the warren of broken rooms beyond the tower. I wanted to share my new idea.

He was sitting upright in a shady corner, his chin dropped to his chest. The hot breeze ruffled his tangled hair as he snored, slow and relaxed. Like Donato, Placidio often slept sitting up or slouched in corners. Placidio said it kept him alert. Easy to wake. But I doubted the incurious son of a Confraternity director had the same reasons to wake easily as a professional duelist who had been the target of multiple vendettas over his career. I left him be.

Meanwhile, Livia had grown quiet. That worried me more than the noise. We had never decided whether to reveal our true purposes once we had her away from the villa. But I tended to agree with Placidio. She had returned to the Bastianni household and we didn't know why. It would take some certainty of her reasons and her plans going forward before I trusted her with any hint of our identities, our magic, or our partnership with her *vicino-padre*.

Not wishing to give notice of my coming, I moved stealthily along the scuff of bootprints leading to the old cellar. When I neared the spike of an ancient chimney, I crept forward on my belly and peered over the edge of Livia's dungeon—four stone walls the height of three tall men, a floor of dirt and broken flagstones, and a fallen slab of stone that provided half a roof. Her accommodation was roughly twice the size of my Lizard's Alley hovel.

The young woman had somehow got loose of the shackle that had been locked about one ankle. Her long bedgown shed in favor of her chemise, she had piled every flat shard of rubble from that pit into a perfectly balanced pile at the base of one wall. She was now approximately halfway up the wall, clinging to the mottled stone with bare toes and fingertips like a great lizard with a mop of unruly red hair.

In an instant's blur, she missed a fingerhold and slipped, landing on the dirt floor with naught but a quiet expulsion of air. She reset a few rocks that had been knocked aside, tested the steadiness of her stepstool, climbed up, and started up the wall again.

Fascinating. Twice more, I watched her tumble. The last time, she'd made it two-thirds of the way to the top, but had been unable to find a next fingerhold. She had pushed away and jumped down apurpose. Hefting a jagged rock shard, she began prying and beating at the shackle, muffling the sound with her wadded bedgown.

I puzzled over it, until she tried scraping at the stone with the twisted chunk of metal. Lady Virtue's whispers, she was making herself a tool. If we didn't do something, our bride would be free before we'd spoken to her. Footsteps approached from the keep. Livia's head popped up. I ducked and retreated, waving at Placidio to stay back.

"We've got ourselves a lizard," I whispered when I joined him. "A very determined one, who makes tools." I told him what I'd seen.

"How'd she get out of the shackle? It wasn't close fitting but I'd bent it so she couldn't slip her foot out."

"You bent it . . . with your hands?"

"Aye, but—" He scratched his beard. "Well, all right, I suppose . . . with the right tool or rock, she could pry it open. No doubt she's strong enough. I didn't exactly have time to clean up the place yesterday. Are you ready to tell her about her friend's murder?"

"Not to start. First, I'm going to see if I can make her talk with *me*—or rather with someone who might help her get away from her kidnappers. Neri gave me an idea. . . ."

A short time later, Placidio, his black hood raised, made a noisy approach and glared over the rim of Livia's prison. I stood silently at his right hand in my own hood and cape.

"Enjoying your stay, damizella?" he called down. "A bit of a comedown from Villa Giusti?"

"I'll survive."

She sat half in, half out of the shaded portion of her prison, where we couldn't notice that she was free of her shackle. I'd wager there were several sharp rocks beside her hidden hand.

"We all survive as we can," said Placidio. "That's how we came to our choice of business. And certain, you will survive. Though it might not be a life you'd enjoy. Might involve men—most assuredly thugs and bullies."

"So you're a slaver."

"Nay, not us."

"A snatcher then, who deals with slavers?" A brave front she put on. Her voice did not quaver, but it was close.

"Mayhap. But we think you have some value to those in Villa Giusti. We've put them and your father on notice that they'll receive our price before midnight. Any assistance you can offer to sharpen our bargaining would be to your advantage. I'll leave you to think on that."

"My father . . ." She lifted her chin sharply. "So if I die from thirst, you'll reap *nothing* for all your trouble."

Her challenge rang like that of a pitcher half-filled instead of empty. Was it the notion of ransom or the mention of her father had spiked her hopes?

"Dying of thirst takes a while," said Placidio, snarling in devilish pleasure. "A traveler of the wild like you will likely know just how long. Nis, when you water the rest of our stock, be sure to skip this one."

"But, Capo, she—" Placidio backhanded me.

I staggered and dropped to my knees. Uninjured. A man like Placidio, who found it needful to lose as many duels as he won, was a master at false moves and had taught Neri and me a few.

"But stop by here on your rounds," said Placidio. "Make sure she sees you have a flask . . . just in case the stubborn lady changes her mind."

I touched my head to the ground, and then slunk after him until we were out of Livia's sight and earshot. I hoped she had taken note.

"Well played," I said. "We'll let that simmer a bit, along with the afternoon heat. We'd best keep a close watch until you replace the shackle, though. Wouldn't want her loose. I'd wager *il Padrone*'s treasury she could find her way back to the city using the stars."

Placidio grunted. "Likely."

"But she'll be wary for a bit. We likely have time to visit her contracted husband."

"You are a hard taskmaster, lady scribe."

"Did you notice any kind of hook we could use to persuade young Donato to contravene his parents' wishes? I didn't."

"Perhaps the lady's expressed preference for women. But if politics is driving the marriage, likely not even that."

"The Canon of the Creation is far more than politics."

Donato's chamber was similar to Livia's, but only about half the size and it lacked any sheltering roof. To my astonishment, the man was still asleep. Sitting upright in a corner. Eyes closed. One ankle was shackled to a bolt halfway along the wall.

"How can he stay so still?" I whispered. "And why?"

"Not *entirely* still," Placidio said softly, after stepping back from the rim of the hole. "Before you woke this morning, he was in the adjacent corner. He likes the shade. I doubt he's asleep."

Placidio picked up a pebble, stepped round the rim until he was just above and to one side of Donato, and flung the pebble hard and straight. It struck just beside Donato di Bastianni's ear.

The man did not jump, flinch, or twitch.

"Spirits!" I said, joining him well away from the rim. "Clearly you were wrong."

"That's not sleep," said Placidio. "That's discipline."

"But why?"

"That's the question, I'd say. Certain, it changes things a bit. Let's see if he'll talk."

We adjusted our masks and hoods. A fixed rope and a pail served to lower sausage, cheese, and a flask of ale into Donato's hole. Dumond had supplied us a rope ladder like the one we'd used in the coliseum rescue, driving iron spikes into the rock to hold it and the supply rope.

Placidio descended first, and sat cross-legged in front of our prisoner. I followed suit, placing the refreshments within Donato's reach before taking a seat beside Placidio.

"Segno di Bastianni," I began. "We've come to introduce ourselves. The food and drink should display our good intentions."

He didn't move or even look.

"Honestly, we've no reason to harm you, despite my partner's rude rock throwing and the abrupt nature of our introduction last night. We are engaged in a simple business transaction."

"The rock-throwing was only a test," said Placidio. "You are a most disciplined young man. I commend you. We've no ill intent."

Donato's eyes blinked open. His was a narrow, well-proportioned face, with a nicely sculpted indentation of his cheeks, a shelf of black brows shading deep-set eyes, and a night's scruff of black on his chin. His hands trembled slightly.

Glancing from one of us to the other, he pressed his hands into his lap and breathed deeply, as one does when embarking on a perilous venture. Just as I did every time I released my soul and became someone else.

"I don't believe you," he said. "Not any of it." Precise. Even. As if he had used a hot flatiron to remove every inflection—and every fearful quaver. Discipline, indeed.

"Why is that?" I said. "Because of our garb? Masks and symbols are but distractions."

He dropped his gaze to his folded hands. They were still now. "Perhaps because you tried to smother me, and then hauled me into the wilderness and chained me in a hole. No honest business relationship involves such tactics."

His plain logic was scarce audible, even at a short distance away. Somehow that only added to its offense.

"Spoken by a privileged son of the Philosophic Confraternity," I spat, "whose *honest business* involves stripping young men naked, gelding them, and forcing them to live forever in a skin of silk at the end of a chain."

His gaze snapped to mine—alarmed—only to drop just as quickly. Discipline, again? His knotted fingers stilled. "Sniffers are not men. They are servants of evil who have chosen their fate— demons who have accepted their true nature. Why would the Cavalieri Teschio care? Is this a test?"

The young coward's blank face begged for a slap.

"I care about hypocrisy," I blurted . . . and immediately wanted to tear out my tongue. A stupid reply. An inept exchange and entirely out of character for a hardened kidnapper. Entirely *not* where I wished this interview to go. It was the Confraternity speaking through his mouth. I doubted he'd even considered the words before spitting them out.

"This is certainly a test," said Placidio, salvaging the moment. "We test the value of those who populate our city. Our business has thrived on young persons with limited prospects whose families seem to approve our modest estimates of their value. But you, segno, a young man of unlimited prospects, mark a significant change in our merchandise. We have some disagreements in our ranks as to the price you'll bring. What would you say is your worth to your family? Ten thousand silver solets? A hundred gold? A thousand? Where will they balk and say, 'Too expensive for a dull, incurious lump; find another buyer'?"

Placidio leaned forward as if to speak in confidence. "And be sure, for a well-formed young fellow like you with healthy skin and good teeth, even one with an empty head, we have other buyers at the ready."

Donato's complexion took on a rosy cast. "You will never get the opportunity. Whatever you think you know, you chose the wrong family to test. My father—"

"Truly, are you going to invoke your father?" I snapped. "Does he groom his precious boy to succeed him? To be a Confraternity director is a mighty aspiration. But I suppose a director would insist on proper placement for his eldest son."

"My father shall serve nobly for the full span of his life, as will his deputies, may their seasons be long and fruitful"—one would think his father was listening—"while I do as— While I proudly become a defender of truth." His mouth worked, but nothing more came out.

No practiced or prescribed answer for this one? After a few moments, I feared he might faint again. "In other words, you will do as you are told to defend the truth as the Philosophic Confraternity proclaims it."

"Yes. That. Certainly."

Defend. Was he to be a praetorian, then? Could there ever have been a young man less suited to a soldier's life? And no matter family, one did not arrive at the post of *director* enforcer without serving as a praetorian. Perhaps the defense he spoke of was scholarship. . . .

"If not to succeed him as director advocate, perhaps your noble father has some other advocacy position in mind for you. He is an authority on ancient artifacts, I've heard." Indeed, Rinaldo di Bastianni had validated the antiquity of the Antigonean bronze, the statue that now sat in the grand duc of Riccia's treasury, the statue that had brought Teo to Cantagna. "Do you study antiquities or myths?"

"The undying truth of the ancient is a proper study for all."

Another standard philosophist recitation, invoking the Canon. How I wished I had Livia's pages and the stolen book there with me to challenge him, but we'd come directly from the villa. In no way had I dared risk the precious documents on our foray into the heart of the Confraternity.

"But he's also chosen you a wife," said Placidio. "Perhaps *she* is to be your preoccupation. Will she not persuade your family to buy you back?"

"Perhaps she finds him a dullard and will rejoice if he vanishes," I said. "Perhaps we should apply to her and see what she will pay for her preferred outcome."

"The match is a business arrangement. Agreed to by her, her family, and my own. There is no need for persuasion." No hint of doubt shadowed this declaration.

Snarling, I poked at Placidio's shoulder. "You see, Capo, he's naught but a token in his betters' game. I think we should strip him and send him straight to Tregawny before I find need to blemish his sweet balls myself. Boys like him raise the wolf in me."

"Aye, that's quite clear on this fine morning. But I'm sure this fellow was not the one dragged your lover away in chains for claiming visions of the Unseeable Gods. Was that you, boy?"

Donato opened his mouth, but this time he snapped it shut and averted his gaze. Did he not trust the answer that came to mind? Or his ability to speak it without revealing more than he wished?

"So is there anything you wish us to tell your family?" asked Placidio. "Mayhap we should report that you are spewing the Confraternity's deepest secrets. Or shivering in your boots. Or pissing yourself—"

"No!" Donato's breath had quickened, his posture grown stiff. Was it fear? Anger? Perhaps he had some difficulty like the falling sickness; some believed that disease was infestation by demons. Or perhaps he suffered some shameful incapacity; the very intelligent daughter of one of Sandro's friends had been word-blind, incapable of reading words on a page. Perhaps Donato had been trained or even beaten to hide his limitations. That might explain this combination of confidence, discipline, and terror. But I would wager good coin that it was more.

From above and behind us screeches and the beat of feathered wings broke the quiet as the entire colony of hawks rose together and swooped westward.

In the momentary interruption, Donato had closed his eyes again. His limbs had relaxed. Discipline? Perhaps so. Either that or he had fainted again. Perhaps there was a *fainting* sickness, less violent but just as debilitating as the falling sickness.

Enough. We were getting nowhere. Even the birds were bored.

"Eat your dinner and contemplate your worth," I said, rising smoothly to my feet. "We will dispatch our offer to your family by midnight. I hope they *don't* pay."

Placidio rose as well. "Never mind this scold, young gentleman. Certain, we'll listen if you've a suggestion as to the amount to ask, but we've a sense about these things and will know if you aim too low. As I said, we've other markets."

Donato gave no sign of hearing us. I resisted the temptation to kick him to ensure he was breathing.

We left the food within his reach. I clambered up the rope ladder and over the rim, ready to be shed of the hot black cloak. As I hauled up the empty food bucket, Placidio climbed the ladder.

Just as I coiled the bucket rope, a clink of metal and a harsh gasp popped my head up.

"Gods' balls!" Placidio lay sprawled over the rim of the wall, arms outstretched and clawing at the rock and scrub. One foot was tangled in the ladder which now hung from only one spike. The remaining loop of rope threatened to pop off its spike at any moment.

I flung myself to the ground and grasped Placidio's wrists, locking my legs around the splintered trunk of a long-dead cedar. Lacking the muscle to haul him up, I could only provide him purchase.

Forearms planted, shoulders straining, he dragged a knee over the rim. In moments he was sitting on solid ground, chest heaving.

"Well done," he said when he had settled. "Don't know how—" He snatched something from the rock beside him. "Boundless Night, Dumond. I've words for you."

He tossed me an iron spike as long as my fingertip to wrist. Unbroken. Unbent.

"Did he hammer it into dirt?" I said. "Or just not deep enough in the rock? I can't believe Dumond would make a mistake like that. Even so late, without sleep." And after having worked not one, but two magical portals and his twenty teaser holes. He'd fought beside us, as well. "We all pushed ourselves past our limits last night. I know I've not slept well since the earthquake."

Placidio had pulled up the ladder and was now examining the two anchor points. "The damnable rock is cracked around that hole," he said, uncertain. "Difficult to notice when working in bad light after a very long two days. Guess I won't kill him."

He left the spike and the bundled ladder on the rim of the roof-less cellar.

Before we withdrew to consider our next moves, I peeked into the cellar. Donato had slumped over his knees, his hands wrapped over his head. A head full of empty words and seething fears. Livia was annoying, but, spirits, at least she was alive.

12

Placidio, Dumond, and I pulled out bread, cheese, figs, and ale from blessed Vashti's provisioning. As Neri slept on in the keep, we spread our meal in the shade of a broken arch. The two of them had just reported that the spikes at the rim of Donato's den were reset and would not pull out were Atladu himself to attempt it. Livia's ladder supports were verified as well set.

"Still don't understand how I could have missed that," said Dumond, staring at his fingers. "When I set them, I used magelight—brighter than I've ever managed before. My eyes must have been crossed."

Dumond had been appalled when he heard of our near disaster. A fall from the cellar rim would have broken bones—the one injury Placidio's self-healing magic could not address. As soon as we had unloaded the cart, they'd gone off to see to the problem.

I sliced off a Neri-sized chunk of cheese for myself. For the first time since escaping the Villa Giusti, I was ravenous. "You checked that Livia's not gotten out of the new shackle?"

"Seems to be sleeping," Placidio said. "Mayhap she's human after all and not one of the *daemoni discordia* crawled out of the Great Abyss. We'd best deliver the Cavalieri ransom demands soon. Elsewise we might be paying her parents to take her back."

Placidio's grumbling was understandable. The shallow cut in his hip Livia had inflicted during the snatch yet stung. And when he had ventured into Livia's cellar to replace her broken tether, fully expecting her to attack, she had still managed to scratch his cheek with her chipping tool.

"Aye, sooner is better," said Dumond. "Gossip says the city steward has joined the Confraternity in demanding the Sestorale convene immediately. Everyone assumes they'll ask for the Gardia to join the praetorians in the hunt. The philosophists have already put half a legion in the streets. Setting a time and place for the exchange might well change the focus of their hunt. They'll assume we're in-side the city."

I agreed. "That could buy us more time to understand Livia and pry Donato's secrets out of him. He near collapsed when Placidio suggested we might tell his family that he was pissing himself."

"There's more going on with him than cowardice," said Pla-cidio. "Why did he ask us if 'this is a test'—*this* being the snatch? And what did he mean by 'whatever you think you know' when you challenged him about making sorcerers into sniffers, or 'you picked the wrong family to test'? That was more than preening his feathers to scare us. His words are very well-considered. He knew exactly who the Cavalieri Teschio are. Why would he think they were testing him?"

Lost in hatred of Donato's people—and fear for Neri—I had seen the whole fabric of the conversation but missed the most in-teresting threads.

"You also warned we might tell his father he was revealing Confraternity secrets," I said. "Just before he removed himself."

"Aye. That I did. Maybe it's not just his da he's afraid of. Maybe he knows something he shouldn't. He's got to be wondering how the Cavalieri got into the villa to snatch him."

"Which leaves us interesting speculations," said Dumond, "but no more information to persuade him to forgo his coming marriage. The young man isn't a fool, but perhaps is not quite sure what's happening to him. So you two should keep watching, while I deliver our ransom demands."

I disagreed. "I was thinking that someone else should go."

"It's clear Neri can't do it," said Dumond, cutting off a hunk of sausage. "Nor provide a sword here in case someone finds us while Placidio's off to the city. And a woman traveling alone at night will invite too many questions."

Neri, of course, could have used his magic to dart in and out of the Academie to deliver ransom demands. But Dumond . . .

"You can't," I said. "A stranger showing up to deliver a message is going to be detained, if not immediately arrested. Making a por-tal to get inside leaves you exposed for too long, especially if you leave it open for a quick escape; the Academie and Villa Giusti and likely the steward's house, as well, will be on high alert for any magic. But I know some ways to deliver messages without getting personally or magically involved, and I can talk my way through the gates if I need to."

"And having *you* here fixing us an escape route will be a boon, my friend," said Placidio.

Dumond conceded our points. A rocky grotto, down the stair where I'd found Neri, housed the ruin's spring. Dumond planned to paint a door down in the grotto and a matching one somewhere near the base of the bluff, allowing us to bypass the narrow path if we needed to escape an assault. But the spanning distance through solid rock would be greater than any he had ever attempted. He wasn't sure he could make it work.

I downed a last fig. "Before I set out, I think it's time for my first venture as Nis, the unhappy cavaliera. See if I can worm anything useful out of Livia."

"You'll think out your questioning this time, yes?" said Placidio.

I swallowed all retorts that came to mind. No question I'd been stupid with Dono. "His Confraternity prattling just got under my skin. Maybe Neri can do better, if he ever wakes—"

"He's awake, and for any who's worried, he's quite recovered." My shirtless brother sat himself between Dumond and me, engulfing us in the scent of overripe youth. "And I'm hoping most of this feast is left for me. I think my last week's meals leaked out with all that blood."

Despite the brave words, Neri's lips were colorless, and his grin forced. He reached for the cheese, but instantly aborted the move and grabbed his bandaged shoulder. "Demonscat!"

He eased himself backward until he could lean on a broken column. His limp black curls dangled over his eyes. "Maybe not entirely recovered."

I set the bag of figs where he could reach it and took the opportunity to feel his hand and his cheek. "You're not fevered. You're walking. Certain, you were not useless last night." Easy to see the guilt reddening his face. "And maybe not even so useless today, if you're willing to be a bit more uncomfortable. Before you dozed off this morning, you said we ought to throw you in a pit . . ."

I told him how he'd given me the idea to impersonate an unwilling member of the Cavalieri in hopes of getting some answers out of Livia. "And Placidio and I thought that maybe, while your wound still so clearly pains you, and before you wash . . ."

"You could throw me in with Dono the Groom." Though his eyes were yet squeezed as he breathed through the pain, he managed the shadow of a grin. "I could do that. Certain, no playacting's required to act uncomfortable."

"Things are getting complicated in the city," I said, "and the sooner we can make a plan for these two, the better. While I beard the she-wolf in her den, Placidio can stash you in the cellar with Donato. We'll say we've acquired a new captive and had to rough him up. Then you can observe what he does when his captors aren't looking, see if you can poke him into giving us a clue as to what he's about . . . what scares him besides his father."

"Are you sure the woman's stewed long enough for you to question her again?" said Placidio. "She's tough as a buck's hindquarters and will take some softening."

"Three days from now she comes of age. The philosophists want her wed before that, so every hour that passes makes this riskier. With the Gardia joining in the search, I'm not sure we're safe to hide them very long. I need for her to trust me."

We made sure Neri consumed enough ale and figs to keep him going. In truth he couldn't stomach much. Once we'd told him of our conversation with Donato, I dosed his horrid, seeping wound with Vashti's salve, somewhat comforted that the redness and swelling had not worsened. After wrapping it with fresh bandage, I dampened the filthy, blood-stiffened rags we'd used to bind the wound at the villa.

"I hate doing this," I said, rewrapping the nasty strips over the fresh. "But it's only for a few hours. Then we'll clean everything again and use the salve—"

"Stop fretting," said Neri. He lurched to his feet. "It's a good plan. Smart. And I won't have to loll around here with naught to do but feel sorry for myself."

"I'm off to Livia," I said. "I've decided to do a *real* impersonation for her. This girl is smart and observant. If she suspects I'm pretending, she'll not tell me anything."

"Makes sense. Are we ready?" Placidio had donned his black hood and cape.

When Neri nodded, Placidio heaved him as gently as possible over his shoulder. "You'll follow my lead, eh?"

"Will," said Neri, gulping repeatedly, as if ready to spew down

Placidio's back. "Make him believe this, swordmaster. Don't know as I could fight a suckling just now."

I smeared a little extra dirt on his face with my bloody fingers. "Put all you know about Donato right out of your head. He's got to be a stranger to you. Forget all you know of Placidio, too. He's your cruel captor, who's cut you and doesn't care if you die."

Dangling upside down, Neri could produce only a finger wag.

"And you, lady scribe," said Placidio, "be wary of this Livia. She's stronger than you'll believe."

"I will."

Placidio drew up his hood and marched down the path. Soon we heard him bellowing curses, and complaints that this new fellow would be the death of us all. "No ransom for you, little pustule! It's off to the skin traders."

Spirits, Neri . . .

"The swordsman will keep watch on him," said Dumond, at my side, "and I'll do the same for you, soon as I've taken care of the beasts."

"I'll be fine," I said.

"Certain, you will."

Dumond headed for the downward path. The borrowed mare and cart horses had been left on a ground tether between two outcropping bastions of the bluff. The grazing was so poor, he'd brought hay and oats in his last cartload.

Time to go. I bit my lip hard to make it bleed and swell. Then I pricked my finger with my knife and smeared a bit of blood on my forehead and a fringe of hair. It would be dry by the time I got to Livia. After the rough night, I'd no fear that my appearance might belie my impersonation of an abused partisan of the Cavalieri Teschio.

Breathing away my immediate concerns, I considered who I needed to become. Nis would be daughter of the nameless man who founded the Cavalieri. She had been horrified to learn what her father and his capos really did. When an attempt to run away—her first and only—failed, her father threatened to sell her to the Cavalieri's sordid partners. Since then she had served as a minder for the snatch-crew's young victims, ensuring that were the Cavalieri ever caught, she would hang alongside them.

I pocketed a small flask of ale, hung a cup and a sturdy stick at my belt, and wiped more dirt on my face and neck—likely unnecessary by this point. Surely I was as filthy and ripe as Neri. As I walked down the path, I considered all I knew of Livia, including the slip she had made; certain, it was the mention of her father had boosted her confidence.

When I reached for magic, it flooded into me with such raw, convulsive power, it almost knocked me to the ground. As soon as I could breathe again, I abandoned myself . . .

This new girl captive is so bold. Capo wants to repay her attempt to stab him, so he thinks to tame her with thirst. Certain, she's no beauty. Her arms are sinewy, more like a man's. Her chest is flat and her complexion sun-blotched. But her red hair has a pretty wave, were it tamed and brushed, and her overlarge lips and light, fierce eyes could be an advantage if she gave half a try. But if she's starved and withered, the traders will declare her a drab—and a troublesome one at that. She'd bring a wretched price. Then Capo would blame me for not tending her, and Da, who ever believes Capo's word over mine, will have me beaten again.

Peering over the rim of the cellar, I saw the girl's still form under the slab half-roof. I threw the rope ladder down and descended quickly. Stick at the ready, I stepped under the slab, keeping as far from her as I could. Capo had made her new shackle shorter than the one she broke and tighter around her ankle, but she was tall and had long arms.

I knew she was someone important. The house where we snatched her was huge and fine, but a guard had been posted at her bedchamber door. So was she a captive *there* as well as here? That seemed unlikely; she'd had two weapons at hand, ready to use. We'd never taken a captive girl near my own age. They'd always been whiny youngers.

"Sssst. Girl!"

She didn't move.

Like always I could hear Mam's warning in my head: *Don't trust the wolf that lies still when you go near. Its muscles are ready to spring.*

"I've brought ale for you, girl. Move to hurt me and I'll take it away and not come back. And if you think Capo will relent and feed you, I'll tell stories about how much he hates females who defy him."

"Your very presence here makes all you say a lie. The big bully's probably just out of sight up there, ready to laugh as you torment me. But I won't play. I don't care what you've brought."

She already sounded dry, ready to snap like a dead twig.

"The rasp in your throat makes *that* a lie," I said, spitting on the ground. "The day's hot. I'm not stupid. And Capo is off on another snatch. Once he gets back here, we'll deliver news of your price to that house where we found you."

You'd think she was bit by a wasp, she sat up so sharp. "To the *Confraternity*? He said he was delivering it to my father."

"It's going to the people in the house where you were. You claimed you were to be betrothed today. Capo may be a brute, but he's smart, too. He looked around and he got thinking the people in that big house valued you more than your family does. They'd likely paid good money for you already. Had a guard on you. He said perhaps they don't know you as well as your own folks."

"They don't." She said this to herself, not to me. "Not yet."

My eyes were getting accustomed to the shade, so I could see her face. She believed I was nothing. Stupid as one of the rocks.

Easing close as I dared, I set down the cup, opened the flask, and poured a swallow of ale into the cup so she could smell it. I kept the flask and sat down, farther away.

She eyed me and the ale cup, one and then the other, but made no move to get it. Likely she didn't know she was rubbing her dry lips together or how frequently she blinked, trying to dampen her gritty eyes. I knew what thirst looked like.

"So why are you here?" she said. "Won't your capo beat you for bringing me that?"

"If your people won't pay, then Capo don't care how much you bring from the skin traders. He'd rather watch you shrivel to nothing—maybe die—cause you knifed him. Though the fault would lie with your people and with him, I'm the one'll get blamed." I touched the bloody spot on my head where Capo had cuffed me. "So I'll bring you a drink when I can. But a favor's not cheap. You have to pay before I give it to you. I want to know why."

Her eyebrows raised up so her light-colored eyes looked like a beacon in the shade. "Why *what*? You people are the felons. Not me. I hope you hang."

I squirmed a little. Capo said he'd left her without any rocks to throw, but she was clever, and I'd never done this kind of thing.

"Never had a chance to talk to a rich girl before. Why did you carry two knives in a house where you were going to marry? Do all girls like you do that? And why did they have a guard at your door—to keep you in or to keep somebody out? And was it the lord or one of those boys to be your husband?"

"Pssh. I owe you no answers." She propped her wrists on her knees, letting her hands dangle, as if naught in the world bothered. How was she not scared?

Well, we'd see. I emptied the cup into the dirt. Then poured another swallow into the cup and moved backward again.

"You're a brassy one," I said. "I'm scared all the time. Asleep. Awake. In my dreams. I want to know how you got brave. Or maybe it's just you're too stupid to be scared."

She snorted and didn't move. So I did it again—another drink poured into the dirt. A third bit in the cup. She'd understand sooner or later. When the flask was empty, I'd leave.

I waited. The broken pavement throbbed with heat, even in the shade. The breezes of the heights didn't reach down here. My own tongue was already parched.

"Oh, all right." She had to stretch out full length to reach, but she emptied that cup in one swallow and held it out for more.

"Answer first."

She rolled her eyes. "I carry knives because I've learned that there are very few people in this world one can trust. I've no idea if other rich girls carry knives. I never thought of myself as a rich girl, but I suppose you'd see it that way. They had a guard on me because I ran away. You'd think they'd reason that since I came back of my own will, I wasn't planning to leave again, but then Confraternity people are either blind fools or conniving liars. All they care about is ordering the world in their own way. And I'm contracted to Director Bastianni's eldest son. I had no say in the business. Evidently it was done before I was even born."

"You said you were one as liked women. Was that why you run off?"

"Partly. And also why I went back. Sometimes you have to choose unpleasant paths to get what you want. That's why I decided to accept the contract. It would have worked if you cretins hadn't dragged me off. Now they'll think I arranged this to get out of it."

If she weren't such a shrew, I might've felt a bit sorry for her, strange as that seemed. "Maybe we've done you a favor. The fellow likely won't want you back once you've been in the hands of scum like Capo. You're likely well shed of him. He was havin' a romp with some other fellow when we was looking to find you."

"That would be Silvio, Dono's brother, who's entirely a creature of flesh and impulse. Dono would never in the world commit a human act. He has an attendant who probably pisses for him and chews his food. Had I been asked my preference, I would have chosen Silvio a hundred times over Dono. But like me, Silvio wasn't even born when they made this damnable contract."

Something about that nicked at me—about the brothers.

"So was it the milksop you was to wed? Two were just childer, but the other woke up, saw our skull marks, and fainted dead away."

"Dono doesn't faint, he . . . leaves. Don't know how he does it. Some whisper that he's sickly or a half-wit, but I think he's just—"

Curiosity got the better of me. "Just what?"

She smirked and held out the cup.

"Set it down and move back where you were."

She tried to stay close enough to grab me, but I wasn't having any. When she was back to the wall, I poured another swallow and scooted back to my place.

The girl sipped, savoring it. "Aren't you satisfied yet?" she said.

I wasn't. Her story didn't make sense once I gave it a thought. "So if he's not sickly, then what was he doing? And why did you run away, if you had already decided to wed him?"

"You wouldn't understand."

"Why? Because I'm stupid and you're a high-and-mighty?" I scrambled to my feet and shoved the flask into my pocket. I'd had enough of her sharp tongue. "Who's gonna end up a drab for skin traders, yeah? Because *I'm* the one gonna deliver the ransom message tonight, and maybe it'll just get lost along the way. All I want is to hear a story what's different from mine. Not a favor. Not even a copper solet or a pretty ribbon. Not nothin' that it would cost you to give."

I was halfway to the ladder when she called me back.

"Nis—is that your proper name? Come back. Please. I . . . beg you."

Never thought I'd hear a rich girl say *please*. Or *beg* . . .

Be careful, daughter. She thinks to play you. Mam was wise. Always warning me.

"Aye, I'm Nis." I sauntered back her way. "Thirst don't quit, does it?"

Even though she was in the shade and I stood in the sun, that girl was staring at me as if trying to peel my skin away and see my insides. "*You're* carrying the ransom message?"

"Aye. If I'm kilt or arrested, 'tis no great loss. That's the way Capo sees it. He don't let me know where his crew are quartered. They don't let me know their true names—just Lizard and Vole and such, and Capo, of course. I don't even know where *this* place is to tell the constables or wardens nothing."

"That's awful, Nis. Truly. Maybe we could make a bargain."

"I won't set you free. Can't."

"I understand that. All I want is for you to deliver that message to my father instead of the Confraternity."

"Why?"

She was sitting up now, as if to make sure I understood she meant it. "Because my father will pay the ransom, even if he has to sell his house or his honor. The Confraternity, on the other hand . . . I think they would be very happy if I vanished. Dead . . . a slave . . . they won't care which. '*Poor Livia, abducted by slavers,*' they'll say. Your capo will have solved their problem."

"Them as want you married to the lackwit would *do* that? That's crazy. . . ."

"If I marry him, they believe they can control me—what I say and what I write. And they will for a while. There are reasons why it suits me to live in that house, and you can be sure I'll take advantage. But, all in all, they'd rather me be out of the way with no hint of scandal on their part. They're likely thanking Lady Fortune for you every moment."

I looked at what she'd said from every direction. Dangerous, sure, to go to one house instead of the other. Capo would go loony if he found out. But if the ransom truly got paid, Da would forgive most anything. Maybe he'd even believe what I said about Capo.

"Risky," I said. "What would I get for it?"

"I'll tell you whatever you want to know. And maybe—if we can make it work, and I know that's no sure thing—maybe I could get you out of this." Her hand waved around the cellar. "I could use a maidservant who was loyal to me. Who was brave enough to try."

You've nothing to lose, daughter. And perhaps everything to gain.

Even Mam thought it sounded fair, though neither of us believed this girl could get me away from Da. Mam had tried it. That's why she was dead.

A glance at the sun and I sidled back under the roof. We had maybe an hour till Capo was back. She had put the cup back where I'd first set it and moved back to the wall. I poured another mouthful and retreated to my seat.

"It's a deal," I said. "So why did you run away?"

"I had to leave off some important pages with a secret friend who would keep them safe. And I had her send a message for me."

"To your lover?"

"Yes. I had to tell her not to wait for me."

"I can see that. But *pages*? Like writing work? *That's* the reason they'd as soon see you dead as married?"

"Yes."

"What writing work could make them leave you for dead?"

"It started when my father sent me to the Academie to study. . . ."

I'd never heard such an adventure as she told me . . . Strict schoolmasters. Exasperated parents. A scoundrel uncle who relished birds, beasts, and mountains, and talking to tribesmen, priests, and scholars while stealing their books and treasures. Traveling in caravans, on donkeys, on foot. Forbidden books. A secret library . . .

Everything was bottled up inside her, so that once she started talking, she almost couldn't stop. Seemed like she forgot who she was talking to. But the sun shifted, and I had to stop her. I took the cup and flask, and promised more when I could do it safely. She told me exactly where and how I needed to deliver the ransom message, and I swore to keep my word.

"You never told me what was wrong with the milksop," I said.

"He's a coward. A paralyzed mind. He memorizes all the right things to say, but doesn't dare put two thoughts together for himself. We were at the Academie together for a few years when we were children. Other boys hated him for being a director's son and accused him of getting the best placements and having special tutors. They called him *tartaruga* and threatened to crack his shell. Sometimes they did, and he would scream at them that they were beggars or thieves or half-wits until proctors came. But always Dono the turtle would crawl back into his shell, deeper every time.

When he was about fourteen, an older boy named Guillam de Fere
flew into a rage when Dono trounced him in a debate. He and a
few special friends dragged Dono off to a study room and beat
him. The fight was so vicious a heavy shelf collapsed and knocked
Dono and a younger boy insensible. The younger boy died of a
cracked skull, and Dono woke with a broken arm. Dono accused
Guillam of using sorcery to collapse the shelf."

"Demon sorcerers! In the philosophists' school!" I couldn't
imagine such a thing.

"Sorcery is nonsense," she said. "The *tartaruga* retreated into
his shell. Students hated him more than ever. Papa said they kept
Dono out of school for a whole year. You know, like some families
hide their ugly or deformed children. Or their disgusting cowardly ones."

That made some sense to me. I'd have to think on it. "And now
you've got to marry him."

She folded her arms across her chest and her eyes flared like a
solstice fire. "Papa failed to mention that little circumstance at the
time."

"One last question," I said, as I got up to go. "What's her name?
Your lover?"

She looked at me hard, then shook her head. "No. She's no part
of this bargain."

"That's righteous," I said, grinning. "Maybe I can trust you."

I climbed the rope ladder, pulled it up, and made sure to leave
it just the way Capo did.

Footsteps scuffed the dirt behind me.

My heart near exploded. Before I could turn, a hard hand covered my mouth, and an arm wrapped around and dragged me
back from the rim of the cellar. A grizzled cheek brushed my ear.

"You're safe, *Romy*. You must have had an interesting time."

13

Interesting wasn't the half of it," I said, still breathless as Dumond and I walked briskly across the bluff in the growing twilight. "She believes the Confraternity wants her dead! She begged me to take the ransom demand to her father, not the Confraternity. And I know why she ran and why she risked going back despite that belief. It's the library. The Athenaeum. Evidently they have every sort of writing there—books, scrolls, clay tablets, rubbings from gravestones and cave walls. They've collected them from all over the world. That's what her traveling uncle did; he worked for the Confraternity, gathering, buying, stealing evidence of the Creation stories or alternative beliefs. The director advocates—most recently Bastianni—buried all of it in the Athenaeum where they can limit access. Where they can study it. Where they can control what's taught, what's known, and what's forgotten."

"So she wants to know what's hidden," said Dumond.

"Yes. That's everything to her. The knowing. She doesn't care what use people make of it. Purposeful ignorance and limits on learning infuriate her. But she showed no interest in the consequences of her actions on the city or even her family."

My mind felt like a boulder-sized knot. I couldn't just drop Nis like a soiled gown, as I had my impersonation of Mistress Cataline. I had to keep the words Nis had heard in a semblance of order and separate her interpretations from my own.

Dumond knew not to push, though I could feel him ready to burst with questions.

"There was another small thing, about the contract. Mantegna said Piero didn't entirely recall signing the contract, but believed it true because he'd been so consumed by anger and grief at the time."

"And the signature was his. . . ."

"Yes, and the two witnesses were called in to confirm the

event. But the contract specified that if Donato was dead, then the girl would marry the next younger brother and then the next. But even Silvio, the second eldest, wasn't born twenty-one years ago. If the Confraternity was trying to ensure future influence over the steward, why wouldn't Bastianni have made the just-in-case groom one of his nephews or cousins? And Livia told a story about Donato from when they were both students at the Cantagnan Academie; she would have been something like twelve years old. The story is fascinating in itself. But at the time, when she and her father talked about the incident, her father didn't mention that Donato was her contracted husband. That seems very odd."

"Certain, if the contract was forged, that would be a fine outcome," said Dumond. "Maybe when you get back to the city, you could inquire who were those witnesses . . ."

". . . and we could figure out how they might be persuaded to recant." Any glimmer of possibility that did not involve convincing Donato to refuse his father's wishes seemed worth pursuing.

"Where's Placidio?" I said.

"Watching over Neri. We've been alternating keeping an eye on the two of you and ensuring no praetorians are sneaking up on us. Last time he looked, Donato had eaten the food you left and returned to his state of . . . whatever you call it."

"Departure?" I offered. "Livia says he just *leaves*."

"So she thinks of it as purposeful discipline, the way the swordmaster does."

"In a way. She doesn't think him as devious, just entirely lacking in imagination or courage. The story she told involved a bitter fight with an older boy and his friends that got one child killed and Donato's arm badly broken. Donato accused the older boy of using magic to bring down the shelf that injured them. . . ."

I paused, wishing Nis had asked Livia what had become of that older boy—Guillam de Fere. Had the directors believed Donato's accusation?

"Anyway, since then Donato's been so afraid of violating his father's rules or displeasing him in any way that he'll not read, eat, think, or believe anything that's not prescribed for him. When she spoke of the library, she said that after a few years of obedient marriage—while having full access to the Athenaeum—she would find a way to publish what she wants."

"Changing the young man's loyalties certainly doesn't sound likely."

"True. But she deems Dono so infinitely predictable that she can work around him to learn what she wants to know—which is everything about everything."

"Hmm. Not an easy life. So what did you do to get all this out of her?"

"I promised to keep her alive."

We paused in a little stand of spindle-shaped cypress trees. Just beyond it lay a field of boulders and building rubble, dotted with more of the small belowground chambers like Donato's. Placidio had surmised they were used to cache jars of oil, grain, and other stores in case of a siege.

"Are you steady?" said Dumond. "I should make rounds and then get back to make sure the lady doesn't get out of the new shackle. We should meet at moonrise to decide how we proceed. I can hear the rest of this interesting conversation then."

"Yes to all that. I've got my own legs back." I waved him on his way and approached Donato's cell quietly.

A rhythmic clattering noise grew louder as I drew near.

"Where are you, devil? Left me here with a dead man." Neri's croaking bravado echoed in the night's quiet. "Is that what this is? A grave? Din't do nothing to you or yours."

Placidio was stretched out flat between a scrubby thicket and a rubble wall. His chin rested on his hands as he observed the scene below. I stretched out beside him. He nodded in satisfaction when I pressed palms to my head and spread them as if my skull had swollen with information.

Another clatter. "Told you my da's hanged and my mam threw me out years ago. Are you up there watching, you gods-cursed prick?"

Neri sat back to the wall to our right, a thin blanket wrapped about his shoulders. He was launching pebbles at the stone wall directly across from him, where Donato sat in the same posture I'd seen hours ago.

His finger signing me to stay put, Placidio rose, picked up our provision bucket, and walked around to the path, only making noise when he was well away from me. He marched toward the rope ladder, singing in his robust baritone.

Damizella, damizella, come and have a feast with me.
No fish nor fowl nor pig will tell the landlord what they see.
We can roast them in the firepit, while we wrestle in the hay.
With bellies full and pleasure sate, we'll laugh the night away.

"Are you ready to grovel, new boy?" he said, tying the bucket to the rope. "I reckon it's been a day since you stuffed that belly of yours. Maybe two, if you can count that high."

The bucket bumped the stone wall as Placidio lowered it into the cellar.

Neri aimed his next rock at Placidio. With only his left hand to throw, it fell far short. He curled over his knees, not quite muzzling a groan.

Placidio snorted. "Ah, poor lad with a tender slice out of him. Tell me who'll pay to see you home again, and I'll send you some tasties and a flask—maybe even a needle and thread for the hole in your shoulder. I ween you've a gammy or an uncle still thinks you're better'n dog meat, even if them as spawned you don't. My partner said you had a good knife on you. Too bad his was quicker in the using."

He swung the bucket like a fisherman dangles a worm.

"My kin got nothing you would want," snapped Neri.

"Well then, it's a waste feeding ye." The bucket clattered against the wall as it rose. "That other fellow down there ain't dead, by the bye. He enjoyed the tidbits I sent down earlier. You'll enjoy watching him eat whilst you starve."

From the rim above the rope ladder, Placido let fly a small dark bundle. It landed on a sandy spot in the middle of the pit. A waterskin. Neri threw off the blanket and scrambled toward it as best he could with one arm and two legs. It lay just out of reach.

"Wake up, you friggin' corpse!" he said, gripping his arm and panting with unfeigned agony. "Maybe you can reach it."

Be strong, little brother. If he doesn't speak by morning, we'll have you out of there.

As night wiped away the lingering twilight and filled the cellar with blackness, Placidio whispered that he was going to walk the cramps out of his legs. Before too long an almost full moon would be rising in the east. I was counting on the moonlight to guide me back to the city.

After a pause of quiet, Neri began spewing such an unceasing and inventive stream of curses that even I, who knew him best, was astounded. It went on and on with no signs of abating.

A stirring of clothes and limbs and the clinking rattle of a shackle signaled movement . . . and the unmistakable sound of someone relieving himself. No grunts of effort. No change in the profane litany. So it wasn't Neri. Good to know *something* could draw Dono out from behind his screen.

The movements quieted. Neri's fetid commentary continued.

"Would you mind stilling your foul tongue?" A polite, well-modulated request. Tones not at all fearful or tremulous. Donato di Bastianni might have been asking his manservant for an extra pillow. "No need to make this ridiculous situation worse."

"Maybe your arm's not half sliced off. Your righteous arm. Feels like the blade's still in there. A little ditty helps get my mind to a different place."

"I can appreciate that. Just would prefer you do it at a lower volume. Unless our gentleman jailer put you down here as an additional insult. Or to spy on me. You can tell him that I move, speak, eat, and relieve myself, and will take exceptional pleasure when I see him and his masters hanged for this. You alongside him, if you're his instrument."

"None could pay me enough for this," Neri grumbled. "It'd be a fair stupid *instrument* who let his partner slice his arm off to diddle a prisoner."

"Maybe not that. But I'm beginning to think the bombastic fool and his needle-tongued woman are not what I believed."

Still cool and even. Thinking. Logical. Showing no anger or fear. Showing no emotion at all, though I knew he was afraid. I had seen his hands trembling both here and at the villa. Who had he thought we were? Someone testing him, someone who knew his secrets? Nis hadn't paid enough attention to Livia's tale. Something connected all these glimpses, fragments, dropped words, and furtive glances. They were like splotches of ink on a page that would flow one into the other and create a story that made sense.

"These villains pinched me in the middle of a memorial processional down by the coliseum. You know . . . from the earthquake. Best day in months for a fellow with clever fingers to make a good day's living, if you know what I mean. Blackguards figured I had kin amongst the crowd. So where did they snatch you?"

"Not thieving."

Not human, Livia had said. One might easily believe that. *Discipline,* Placidio had called it. But to what purpose? How in the name of sense were we going to persuade this person to forgo the marriage his parents demanded?

"Night's already freezing cold. Cripes, if I had two arms working, I'd climb out of here. Rocks will break the shackle. Why don't you?"

Donato didn't answer, and soon both of them fell quiet. When growing moonshine faded the stars in the eastern sky, it was time for me to go. I hated leaving. Placidio and Dumond would have to take turns sleeping, watching for marauders, and watching over our prisoners.

The moon seemed to leap from the horizon. As its light reached into the cellar, I took one last glance and slithered backward. Only to stop and creep back again. Had something changed?

Neri lay huddled in his blanket. Donato was still sitting, but he had curled up over his knees, his short cloak wrapped over his head. The waterskin yet lay between them.

I couldn't figure it out.

TWO DAYS BEFORE THE WEDDING
LATE EVENING

Quicksilver and I had a fine understanding. The aging mare carried me along the moonlit road, and I let her take her own time about it. Though urgency knotted my gut—about Neri's wound, about my brother and my partners sitting atop a bluff with two captives that could get us all hanged—it would not benefit anyone were I to ruin the horse or break my neck. My partners and I had agreed that I would compose and deliver the ransom message to Villa Giusti. I'd send another message to Lawyer Mantegna, asking who were the witnesses to the marriage contract and pointing out the oddities— the brothers unborn and Livia's testimony that her father said nothing of any marriage agreement when Dono was involved with a boy's death.

Nis's promise to Livia would remain unfulfilled. I wanted to know if she was right that the Confraternity would not pay for her return.

The watchfires on Cantagna's walls gleamed in the distance. Not long till home. A little time to write out our demands, an hour or so to see them delivered, and then sleep. Dreamless sleep, I hoped.

Before leaving Perdition's Brink, I'd detailed my conversation with Livia for Placidio and Dumond. Dumond was of a mind that we should tell Livia about her friend's murder right away, but I still chose not. Not yet. Clearly the girl realized the dangers of the Confraternity—perhaps more starkly than we had—yet I could not help but believe her terribly naïve. She assumed she had outwitted her captors, yet her bookbinder friend lay dead. She assumed her father would compromise his honor for her, which he very well might, but she showed no grasp of how a compromised steward could harm the city. She believed she could survive being married to Donato while actively working to expose truths that would undermine his beliefs. I had lived a deception for nine years in much easier circumstances, and events had still conspired to end it. Determined as she was to have her own way about her future, with no sense of the consequences, I wasn't easy with entrusting her with Chimera secrets.

And yet, I had no reservations about our mission. Never had I imagined that a challenge to the First Law of Creation might arise from a prickly girl of nineteen with a bent for natural philosophy. The origins of mountains . . . mountains that had once been seas. Who could imagine that? But she'd seen mountain rocks containing the bones of sea creatures. And matching layers at various heights in differing locales, and some pressed into rock like that found around volcanoes. Only bits and pieces of her theories had been sprinkled through her tales, but enough to illuminate the brilliance of her intellect and the breadth of her vision. I could understand her hunger for the secrets hidden in the Athenaeum. There could be secrets of sorcery there as well— truths that the four of us could not even imagine. Livia could be the key to *knowing.* So how did we keep her alive and free to learn more?

Unmasking Donato's oddities might benefit her more than anything else we could do. Despite Livia's intelligence, I was beginning to think her estimate of him much too simplistic.

As Quicksilver plodded onward, I tried to parse some sense of the person beneath Donato's exchange with Neri. Most of it was a playscript: *This is what I ought to say in this situation; no emotion required, nothing revealing.* His uncertainty about us, his captors, fit with his questions about testing. Not until he'd made the "not thieving" comment had I heard something new. Was there a touch of irony in his response to Neri's question? Something like, *You were being wicked, stealing from mourners' pockets, while I was sitting in my bed being invisible to the world, and yet here we are sharing the same fate.* Irony, perhaps, and despair.

Two words. Ridiculous. Here I was trying to fill an empty shell—a purposefully empty shell—with unsupported theories. We needed to raise the pressure on our *tartaruga*. Crack his shell so we could convince him that he did not want to marry Livia. Scare him, maybe. Would true magic do that?

My mind wandered off into possibilities as Quicksilver's steady walk lulled me . . .

. . . *into memories of wonder. A fiery sunset in the ice-clad mountains, a palace of sculpted ice, glittering with reflected starlight. I followed trails of light in the sky made of colors I could not name . . . feeling my muscles lengthen and my shape smooth as I plunged into the sea . . . a forest of color and life and darting creatures and below it the mystery of cold and beckoning darkness . . . until I leapt upward, shedding the salty mantle, and took wing on the airs of autumn . . .*

"State your name and business."

The hail startled me and I clung to Quicksilver's neck. My musings fled, leaving me bereft . . . or had I been asleep? Another dream? Yet I felt no anger. No unsettling lust. Only longing.

Torches glared from just ahead of me. Cantagna's North Gate, manned by two gate wardens and two praetorians, as well as the warden leaning out of the gatehouse window shouting at me to dismount. I gathered my wits and sat up straight.

"I am Gwynnever di Fortissi, returning home from my mistress's errand." The four circled and closed in like vultures to a dead sheep.

"A woman!" crowed one. "What kind of woman appears in such unwomanly attire?"

Another warden bawled, "What errand takes a woman out in

the night watches? And armed? Do you know how to wield that sword or did you steal it?"

More serious questions than usual. Less lusty banter.

"Who is your mistress, Damizella Gwynnever?"

My hand rested on the sword hilt. "I know very well how to wield my weapons, praetorian. But only in good service to my mistress. She has various requirements for those in her employ. Protection from . . . predators . . . of all kinds. And alas"—I proffered a cloth bag stuffed with madder, bedstraw, and plenty of the tar-smelling grass of Perdition's Brink—"plants which must be gathered at midnight to provide the certain efficacy useful in making inks and washes and implements for use in her artworks."

"You're talking of Segnora di Agnesi, the paint slinger," said one of the Gardia wardens through clenched teeth. "You're one of her harridans."

Doing my courtesan's best work to provide a smile of mystery, I made a shallow bow of acknowledgment. "Vivienne di Agnesi refuses such appellations as *segnora* or *damizella* and resents those such as *harridan* or *paint slinger*. The women in her service do the same. May I pass or must I protest to your superiors that you are hampering a weary servant of the renowned muralist whose works celebrate our city's grandeur?"

"Does this Agnesi woman believe these plants are somehow imbued with supernatural properties at midnight?" The questioner stepped from the gate tunnel. His red robes bore the badge of the flame. A philosophist advocate, then. Bastianni's man.

"Nay, I understand 'tis the natural cooling of the plant in the night is the need," I said, my tongue spewing the first nonsense it could find. "Think of flowers and herbs which spread their aroma when heated by the sun. These same will often curl their petals at night, withholding those vital essences and developing more to be spread on the morrow. So too with certain grasses and leaves. I am but a bodyguard, honorable philosophist, a fighter, no botanist or natural philosopher to explain the workings of plants. Are weedy matters of concern to the Confraternity these days?"

"We are concerned with seditious rogues who skulk about in the night. Did you meet other travelers on your road?"

"Only a few shy bucks. Are those of interest?"

He didn't appreciate the humor. "Tell your mistress that even the celebrated are not immune to the ravages of rogues. Or the demands of good order."

A jerk of his head had the others stepping aside to let me pass. A metallic chink from the gate tunnel had my ears straining. It could have been many things—harness, weapons. Or it could be a chain leash. I urged Quicksilver through the dark passage at a steady pace, and did not examine the inky niches or recesses to learn if a sniffer lurked there.

A sleepy boy at a hostelry just inside the gate took charge of Quicksilver, and I did my best to vanish into the narrowest, dankest alleys of the Beggars Ring, pausing, backtracking, climbing stairs to cross rooftops. No reason they should follow. Vivienne di Agnesi was well-known as an eccentric recluse. But my nerves didn't settle until I was well around the Beggars Ring Road without being accosted.

Not just praetorians, but a philosophist advocate at a city gate. I'd never seen that. Their sniffers must have confirmed the residue of our magic inside the villa as well as Dumond's fleeting traces on the walls.

I stopped first at my shop. Did I glimpse my pallet and pillow, I'd never get this done. The Confraternity must believe that Livia and Donato's disappearance was merely a snatch, lest they look for deeper motives. We needed time to find our way with the two of them, thus we had to behave as a snatch-crew would.

So, a ransom message.

I doubted the Cavalieri Teschio extended their extortion demands by way of wax-sealed folds of inked parchment. But then, they had been selecting victims from a population where maybe one in seven could read. Rumor said the Cavalieri intruded on the parents of the abducted child, told them the amount and method of payment along with the dire consequences of non-payment, and left. Certain, I was not going to deliver my demands to the director advocate of the Confraternity in person.

My years living in the Shadow Lord's house had taught me many things and allowed me to meet many interesting people. One of those people, Agoston saz Rumos, provided exactly the service I needed. Agoston, a most charming Invidian gentleman with moustaches so elaborate and so abundant he kept a barber on call solely dedicated to their maintenance, provided a secure, discreet, and neutral messenger service to the elite of Cantagna. No disagreement, no feud, not even a vendetta interfered with the prompt delivery of messages between members of his prized circle of customers. That circle most assuredly included members of the Sestorale, *il Padroné,* the steward of the city, the directors of the Philosophic Confraternity, and most of the city's elite. It also included a few wealthy but less savory persons whose enterprises were so embedded in the city's finances that even the Shadow Lord's best efforts had not rid the city of them. Those names were rarely spoken in company. Not only did I know Agoston, I knew a few of those unsavory names.

I pulled out some scraps of parchment, a pen long past good use, and an inkpot with only the dregs remaining. Even the Cavalieri would know that any ordinary messenger dispatched with a ransom demand would be arrested for collaboration with the snatch-crew. But if they worked for one of Agoston's less savory customers, they would have access to his services.

We didn't have much leeway for the ransom exchange. We needed time to persuade our captives to our will, but if we set the exchange too far in the future, the Confraternity might assume we were giving ourselves time to run with our captives. The second day from this was the Feast of the Lone Praetorian, Livia and Donato's wedding day. On the following day, Livia would come of age. Set the exchange for the last hour of the feast day, and they might wait to hunt us down. Set it any later and certain they would be after us. So the message was simple:

> To get back the missing items set 6000 silver solets divvyed in 6 small sized millers' bags half crost the Avanci brige before Midnite on Ninth Day. Two nites hence.
>
> If wardin or prayturyan or sniffer is seen in the Bottoms or along the River path or on the Brige tower or in any botes strayd on the river in that Midnite hour, the missing items will stay missing. For ever.
>
> The Cavalieri Teschio

And, of course, I sketched the death's-head emblem. Around this crude missive, I wrapped a piece of fine parchment and set a blank seal to the wax. It was addressed to Director Advocate Rinaldo di Bastianni at Villa Giusti.

I donned a respectable mantle I kept in the shop for meeting clients and set out for the Merchants Ring and House Rumos.

Never had I seen so many soldiers patrolling the streets. Both Gardia and praetorians. Like ants around dropped crumbs, they gathered around anyone abroad in the night.

To my relief they cared little for a woman alone. Those who stopped me to ask my business were easily satisfied with my identity as a wet nurse summoned to care for a colicky new infant at House Gianelli. The segnoré of the Gianelli Leather Importers and his wife presided over an exceptionally fecund household. Some of their uncountable offspring were producing their own by now. Scarce a month went by without an announcement of a new arrival.

Several of the solicitous city guard warned me to be alert. "There's a vicious snatch-crew taking young persons from their beds, both male and female, and even such as you could be a target for them. They've suborned sorcerers to their work, so's it's doubly evil."

Dumond would be pleased to hear that his death's-head symbols on the walls of Villa Giusti had worked in multiple ways. The Cavalieri would never again be ignored, even if their targets were children none but their families cared about.

The protocol at House Rumos had been set in stone for at least a decade, so Sandro had told me on a night when I accompanied him on one of his anonymous walks about the city. "Follow the flower arbor to its end and you'll find a simple door of dark blue. Ring the bell beside it. Be prepared to offer a gift of at least two silvers to the woman who answers the door in addition to the twenty-silver fee for each message. She will give you a wooden chip with a number on it. . . ."

The blue door, the bell, and the ever-burning lamp were exactly where they were supposed to be. When the sleepy woman answered the bell, I almost burst out laughing. She was exactly as Sandro had described her, right down to the extremely pointed toes of her shoes and the waxed curl in the middle of her forehead. I whispered an unsavory sponsor's name in her ear, and she accepted my message and the substantial fee in exchange for the wooden chip that I could exchange for replies to my missive. She could now afford several new pairs of pointed-toe shoes.

As I returned home by a different route, I considered that woman and wondered if she—and not the public gentleman with the moustaches—was the actual Agoston di Rumos. When I tried to recall *her* face, all I could see was the waxed curl, the odd shoes, and the extended palm. What better disguise than a few oddities?

Night in the city was breathless. The heat of the day lingered in the damp air. Banners hung limp over shops. Laundry hung out to dry would feel wetter come morning. Both my muscles and my head weighed like mud and functioned no better. Perhaps, back in my own bed, I could sleep without dreaming.

My feet moved faster at the thought of it.

Though the moon was still high enough to light the way, I could have found my way home no matter how dark. I knew every rut, every stone, every stink of Lizards Alley. Were I stone blind, my hand could locate the door latch in one try.

Yet on this night a surprise did await me, and if not for the moon I would have missed it. Under the aged bench just outside our door stood a small stone crock sealed with wax. Curious, I carried it inside and left it on the table as I grabbed the tinderbox and made a fire in our brazier. Once a lamp was lit and a pot filled and set on to boil, I took another look. No markings on the crock or scribed in the wax seal. No message attached. Lamp in hand, I examined the bench in the alley and the space below it.

In the end, I pried up the wax, assuming that the contents had to be the message. And so they were. A distinctive aroma rose from the jar where small silvery fish were packed tightly in oil and herbs.

No matter every other happening of the previous days, the sight and smell had me laughing. Only one friend did I have who had ever worked down at Cantagna's docks helping to pack pilchards.

Teo.

It was a measure of my exhaustion that I fell on my bed, rather than racing to the docks to roust Teo and present all the questions I had ready for him. A few hours' sleep might ensure that I could comprehend his answers.

14

Fish. Lemon. A clean-smelling bulk close by. Breathing.

My eyes blinked open to sunlight and Teo, sitting cross-legged on the floor beside my pallet.

"Friend Romy," he said, his head tilted slightly as always when he smiled. A smile that could light a winter solstice midnight. "Gladsome it is to see thee again, *kyria*."

I scrambled to sitting, happy I'd not bothered to strip off my garments when collapsing on my pallet.

"And you, fair traveler from the Isles of Lesh," I said. "Your greeting—packed I assume with your grandmother's favored herbs—gladdened my heart as well. Had it not been very late, and me dead on my feet, I would have met you at the docks as soon as I found it."

"Wise, as ever. When I saw the jar was moved this morning, I assumed your invitation to return here yet held . . . and I very much need to speak with you."

"Always," I said. "But I'll be much more sensible if I make tea before we talk."

"I'd never presume to hinder your waking."

I laughed and shoved a mug into his hand. "You may help yourself to Neri's cask, if you want."

Teo cared little for tea or wine, preferring Placidio's salt, ginger, and lemon brew. Fortunately Neri kept a small cask of the horrid stuff in the house.

"Not this morning."

Barefoot, his lean frame clad in loose tunic, slops, and leggings that covered the inked symbols marking his skin from throat to ankles and wrists, Teo was assuredly the same man I'd seen dive naked into the river three months ago. And yet the daylight was revelatory.

In moonlight, I would have noticed that his pale hair had been cropped short, and how a patch covered one of his iridescent eyes, and that his once-torn earlobes now bore dangling slips of engraved brass. But I might have missed the more subtle changes.

In the days after I dragged Teo from the River Venia at the brink of death, he had been charming and generous, filled with a childlike whimsy. His emotions had shown through his skin, making it impossible to disbelieve him. He had expressed humble gratitude for my help and astonishment that I called the marvels of his talents magic. Laying open his heart, he confessed how he was struggling to reclaim the part of his life that lay beyond what he called *the glaring lens of the world*. He had a duty, he'd said, to find something he could sense but could not name, and feared that his brokenness risked failure that could endanger his people.

On this morning, my friend was neither lost nor uncertain. His courtesy was bound with threads of urgency. His back and shoulders were tense, the shifting colors of his eye more intense than I remembered. Nothing about him spoke of whimsy.

"Your brother is well?" he said, as I filled the pot with water and set it on the reawakened fire of the brazier. "And your noble friends of the Chimera?"

"Indeed so. Everyone will be delighted to hear you've come back to Cantagna. Dumond's wife, Vashti, our quiet sage, has felt cheated that she had no chance to meet our *other friend from distant shores.*"

"Someday." His smile was fleeting.

At my invitation, he moved to one of the stools beside my table. I offered him a biscuit and some grapes left from our last market foray. He declined.

"Not eating or drinking this morning?" I said. "Is it your eye? I hope the problem is only a passing thing."

"It is not so much a problem as an inconvenience," he said, slipping the patch from his face. "The covering is protection until new ink is properly set. What do you think?"

A new mark encircled his left eye. A delicate lacework of small spirals in silver that glinted in the light. Impossible to make out more details of the design without moving too close to be polite.

"Beautiful and mysterious. It suits you."

And it demanded attention. The patch would remain beyond

the setting of the ink, I guessed, as long as he was among strangers. I could not help but contrast it with the horrid red mouths that marked the sniffer on the Academie footbridge.

"A new mark means you've learned something new," I said. He had told me that the inked symbols were reminders of joys or sorrows, of stories, people, beliefs, or lessons learned. It just happened that the particular symbols his people used were only seen on fading mosaics and painted urns from centuries past.

"Indeed, I've remembered many things, though not all. I'm confident, however. I found Domenika."

"Your mother's servant!" As far as he had been able to tell us, Teo had been sent by his family to meet this woman in Cuarona. But on his journey from the distant isles of his home, he had been waylaid by thieves who had beaten him to the brink of death and thrown him in the river. I had blamed the beating for Teo's faulty memory, though Placidio, ever the frustrating well of privacies, believed there was more significance to the gaps in Teo than a bruised head.

"Aye. She took charge of me—and my education—which was my family's intent all along. We will continue with that until I return home to Lesh. She also took custody of your captive assassin. He lives, and in time will be given opportunities to learn and improve himself. As I promised, he will harm no one else."

But had Teo recalled what he'd been sent here to find? Placidio and I had concluded that the object of his search was a mysterious antiquity—a small bronze statue of the god Atladu, the monster Dragonis, and a third, mostly missing figure, that I had come to believe was Leviathan, the mythical sea creature who had enabled the gods to imprison Dragonis. The statue had not depicted the three as combatants, as was usual, but rather as companions in a hunt or a footrace. We had chosen not to tell Teo of our conclusion until his faulty memory was improved. Thus the statue remained safely in the possession of the devout and scholarly grand duc of Riccia-by-the-sea. Unless . . .

"Have you come back to Cantagna to take up your search?"

"No." Though yet sitting, he stretched taller. He'd been waiting for my question. "Romy, you are in terrible danger."

I scooped crushed leaves and herbs into my cup, added the steaming water, and set it on the table to steep. Then I sat across from Teo. "I've lived with danger all my life."

He leaned forward, his somber demeanor demanding that I heed. "This is not the danger you know—from your own kind—but something far worse. You must come with me to Domenika. Today."

"Today? Certainly not." The air shifted, as if a crack had opened between the seasons, mingling shards of winter with the warm smokes of autumn. But I could pay no heed. Two young people sat at Perdition's Brink—their futures and our city's in the balance, and our knowledge as yet incomplete. And even afterward . . . "My life is in Cantagna. My family . . . my friends . . . our work is here."

"Were you dreaming, friend Romy, just now before you woke?"

All warmth vanished from the sunlight. "No, I—"

Denial died on my tongue. Attention to the matter raised the memory, as if I'd opened a drapery obscuring a window. The man with golden skin and sun-blazed eyes had led me from the ruins into a vineyard, stealing grapes to pop in my mouth as he whispered secrets in my ear. Each fruit, plump and ripe, had burst with tart sweetness that lingered on my tongue even now. *You and I, my lovely, shall reclaim my birthright,* he'd said. Or had it been the woman again? Her voice like a river of honey. Her lips brushing mine to taste the juice of the grape . . .

"Feel my hand." Teo's words yanked me back. His slender hand held steady in the center of the table, and as if drawn by invisible strings my fingers touched his.

"Cold," I murmured, shuddering. "You're cold as the night I pulled you from the river."

He shook his head. "But I'm not. Not this time. Let me show you."

He held my finger and plunged it into my steaming tea. It felt no more than tepid. Teo's gaze did not leave my face, though a part of my seeing yet beheld that other face, smiling indulgently and setting my blood and flesh on fire. In truth?

I jerked my hand from Teo's grasp and clutched my unscalded finger to my chest. Squeezing my eyes shut, I willed the dream away and reopened them to his somber visage.

"Spirits of the Night Eternal, Teo! How did you know I was dreaming?"

"When I arrived here this morning, you were trembling in

your sleep, flushed . . . as you are now. As anyone would be when encountering the Enemy."

The Enemy! I would not speak the name that came to mind, lest it shatter the structures of logic and reason. "It was only a dream!"

"I doubt that."

Rueful, he was, and firm, and gentle. He gathered my hands and cupped them in his. Not so cold now. Or was it my own flesh had cooled down.

"The important question is— Please tell me that this morning was the first time you dreamed like this."

"No," I murmured. Resentment and anger simmered in my gut. "And certain, I know it's no ordinary dream. But it isn't always the same. Not even the same person in the dream every time. I see no . . . monster."

"The Enemy is many manifestations bound into one being. This one learns what draws your interest. That one speaks words that have meaning to you. In dreams they discover your weaknesses, your strengths, your pleasures, your guilts. But it is only the one being."

I reclaimed my hands, planting my elbows on the table and my chin on their folded knot.

How dare this man tell me I was a tool of his Enemy? Though he'd not actually said the word *tool*, the implication was clear. But the stories he referred to were myth. There was no Enemy imprisoned beneath the earth or the sea. No gods had ever manifested themselves outside of tales, so how could the other stories be true? No Gione returned to bless the harvests—bountiful or lean as it might be. No Atladu responded to prayers to make the Venia recede when it flooded half the Beggars Ring or opened his mighty hand to grant us rain in the years the vines withered. So how could there be a Dragonis? Or Leviathan . . .

And there I stumbled. Only three months since, I had installed Teo into the myth of Leviathan. He bore an abiding love for the sea, and could swim impossible distances against the current of the Venia. He believed his duty was to prevent monsters from hurting others. He refused to lie. He wore these ancient markings on his skin, and the language that came to him most naturally was Typhonese, which had not been spoken for uncounted centuries.

In hours, he had healed himself of injuries that would kill an ordinary man.

Placidio claimed that Leviathan, the mythic sea creature who lay dormant waiting for the world's need, was sometimes portrayed as a human, naked like Atladu. Naked, as I had seen Teo on the night he dove into the river with a vicious assassin—a captive human monster. And Placidio, a man of secrets who was not one to be swayed by lies or storytelling, had bowed to Teo and said his people and their secrets and customs were worthy of respect. . . .

"All right, these dreams are not ordinary," I said. "They're terrible and unusually vivid . . ." Neri's crushed bones. The painted walls of a prison. The touch on my hair that tingled long after waking. The simmering resentments and the anger that gnawed at me even now.

"Tell me, friend Romy." Teo's voice was soft. Apologetic, as if my growing fear was his fault. Unyielding, though. "By the bright universe, you must tell me everything."

My gaze met his. In the fathomless iridescence of those eyes was his change most vivid. So much knowledge. So much worry. Curiosity and wonder had fled along with his confusion. In the span of three months, he had aged years.

I lurched to my feet to ensure I kept them solidly on the floor. "This is about the earthquake, isn't it?" I said. "Everything started after the earthquake. No—just before. That was the first time, though not a dream. On that day it was only rage. . . ."

Pacing, circling the confines of my house, I told him everything. About the pain in my head on the day of the earthquake. About the continual, worsening dreams of ruination and death. Of the first where the woman appeared and told me I had a purpose. Of the man who whispered of hopes and longings that I understood but could not recall, for they were in a language I didn't know outside the dream. Of the vision in the woolhouse—perhaps not a dream because I was searching for magic and had tried his own technique of turning inward. That was where the woman had been painting the landscapes on the walls of her prison. I told him of her lingering, seductive touch on my hair.

"My skin burns after the dreams," I said, "and I think— No, I can't think. I'm always exhausted. Certain, I know they aren't

simple dreams. They leave my soul twisted in anger, and . . . oh
blessed Sisters . . . my body aroused. Even now, I resent your waking me and forcing me to tell you these things, and yet I know I
have to tell and *want* to tell. Spirits, Teo, what's happening to me?"

He caught my hand in his cool ones again and drew me back
to my stool.

"The walls that imprison the Enemy are ancient and many,
built with power no longer within our reach. Think of concentric
rings much like these that shape your city. I could tell you of some
of them, but not all. Not yet. Domenika is not yet finished with
me."

"So Domenika the historian is also a teacher." I said.

He had told me a historian was one who unraveled the winds
of time. My skin prickled with the wonder and mystery of those
words, just as on that starry night when Teo had first spoken them.
Was the mother she served the woman who had birthed Teo or was
it *Theía Mitéra* whom Teo had invoked when he lay dying? The god-
dess mother—the Unseeable Gione. I wasn't sure I wanted to hear
that answer.

"Taskmaster is perhaps a more accurate description. One might
think of *Teacher* Domenika as a kind and gracious mentor. One
would be wrong."

For a moment, I glimpsed the whimsical humor of the traveler
I'd introduced to noodles and tomato broth, to demon dancers and
other Cantagnese customs. To sniffers and to the ramifications of
the First Law of Creation.

But clouds reclaimed that moment's glimpse of the sun. Sober,
he continued, "The lawmakers of the world claim that descendants
of the Enemy—sorcerers—plot to break those encircling walls, but
it is doubtful anyone living could set out to break them *all*, even if
they knew how, even if they had reason to do such a thing. Time
and the workings of nature are more like to erode them. But there
is another way the Enemy can escape captivity. In every human
soul, gifted with magic or not, there exists a barrier between truth
and lies, between the woven fabric of the world and . . . chaos. We
call it the Singular Wall."

"Placidio says your people never lie," I said.

"We dare not. Perceptions of untruth that take on the mantle of
truth weaken the Singular Wall, much in the way a tossed pebble

can nick this stone that surrounds us here. No single blow is fatal to its existence, nor even ten at once, but over time . . ."

". . . could wear it away." Logic whispered must come next, rousing a dread that stifled every other sensation.

A dip of his head acknowledged my point. "The more immediate danger arises when the talents we share with the Enemy—the very power that enables us to protect ourselves and do whatever work nature calls us to—are of the kind that dissolve the Singular Wall."

"Like mine," I said, my dread confirmed. "Because when I become someone else, I pour all the power I have into the impersonation . . . the lie . . . until I believe it myself. Are you saying that this Enemy—assuming such a person does exist, which I am not accepting as yet—can somehow creep through a door I've created into my own soul? And then, what? I become the Enemy or release that Enemy into the world?"

By the Unseeable, what did I believe? For my entire life, I had skated between belief in the gods as they were taught to me and skepticism born of logic and reason. And here was Teo, himself a singular wall between belief and non-belief, telling me that I'd been wrong to doubt.

"We don't know what form the Enemy will take or the nature of the inevitable attack," he said. "I wish I could tell you. But there is so much knowledge that has been lost, so much that even Domenika cannot revive in herself or in me, but from what you've described—that you experience the Enemy's anger and resentments and desires and find them influencing your actions—I believe we have ample reason to worry. Unlike the talents of your brother and friends, your magic separates your soul from this world. The world is altered. In that fragment of time, *Romy* is not here, only the other person of your creation. And yes, I believe this recent earthquake was the Enemy's first move in a new attempt to get free."

The Enemy . . . Dragonis. Beloved eldest of the gods whose loneliness had drawn him to lie with human women and men and seed them with magic. The monster who raged at his imprisonment. "Night Eternal, Teo, did I cause—?"

"No!" Teo enfolded my hands to reclaim my attention. "Here is what Domenika believes. There has been a confluence of events that have their root in the hours I lay in this room so near death that in order to maintain my existence, I had to lower every protection I had ever learned, every barrier I'd been taught to hold. You later told me of your belief that you had shared my dreams in those hours. I told Domenika of this, for I am required to be entirely open with her that she might guide me in my learning and my duties. And I told her of your talents as your friends explained them to me, and of what I perceived on that night of your adventure, when you became someone else."

The night we'd gone after the Assassins List.

"She was concerned. Was it you or I who enabled the transfer of dreams? Does your talent necessarily mean your Singular Wall is fragile or did I somehow damage you while I was so weak? She was still searching for answers until this tenday ago when the earth shook. Domenika and I both perceived that it was not the shiftings of nature, but the Enemy who raged that day. And she knew that if your Singular Wall was compromised, it might have been further damaged by that assault. What you've told me suggests that possibility. That you are slipping into dream even when you're not abed affirms it. Clearly it's getting worse."

Dragonis had caused the earthquake . . . and I, one of the demon-tainted . . . was at least a witness to it. Just as the Confraternity claimed. A part of me rebelled at that hateful conclusion. But only a part.

I rose and, without intending it, backed away from Teo. Was this what had dimmed his good humor, believing I was a danger that had to be eliminated?

"So Domenika wants me brought to her for what? Examination? Confinement? Execution? That would be a certain way to prevent whatever you fear."

"Oh, my friend Romy, never harm!" His brow had creased so deeply his new mark near vanished. "Domenika will teach you to strengthen your Singular Wall. To recognize the wiles of the Enemy. To protect yourself on the occasions you use your power. The frequency of your encounters tells me we have no time to waste. I can help as we travel—stand watch, so to speak. Keep you as safe as I am able. But every hour is critical. We must go now."

I turned my back on him. His very presence—those eyes that testified to truths beyond those I knew, the honesty and generosity still genuine despite his changes—made it impossible to dismiss the story he told.

But once released from the sight of him, lingering skepticism scoffed at my overwhelming relief. Stories. Myths. Certain, to rid myself of the dreams, whatever their true cause, would be a gift, and the idea that I might learn more of Teo and his people, their magic, and why they believed as they did was most enticing. But the Chimera had two young people trapped in holes in the ground—and Neri with them, suffering an untreated wound that could cost him his arm, if not his life—because we wanted to protect Livia di Nardo's future and prevent the Confraternity gaining a chokehold on our city.

Even such brief exposure to Livia's mind as I'd had, filtered as it was through Nis's perceptions, justified Sandro's determination to protect her. And everything Livia had told me argued against Teo's tale of a monster under the earth. The triumph of reason could mean freeing those with magic to live without fear, to openly explore the wonders of our gifts. In the best case, Livia and Donato's decisions over the next days could change the world for the better. And the worst? Teo couldn't tell me.

No matter what came of it all, I had just delivered a message that would bring matters to a head two days from this. My partners were waiting for me to help unravel the mystery of our captives. I certainly could not abandon them to reap the consequences of risks we had already taken.

"I cannot go with you today," I said, pivoting back to my friend. "We're in the middle of a new venture. A young woman's life, and likely many more, depend on us getting it right. Surely two more days won't make that much difference. By then our work will be done for good or ill."

"But, Romy, if the Enemy should—"

"Should *what*? You said you don't know what would happen or when. And we would spend those two same days traveling to Cuarona with me still unprepared. Could *you* not begin this teaching? At the least you could *stand watch,* as you put it."

"Teaching is not my duty or my skill, I fear. And I'm as yet unready for—anything else." He scuffed his hair and blew a note of resignation. "Is there no way your partners can finish the task without you?"

"Our new mission is worthy and has consequences we *can* foresee. We might fail in the end, but I *won't* abandon it and leave Neri and Dumond and Placidio at risk." At the very least, they needed me to ensure Livia and Donato could not identify the three of them. But there was something else I couldn't forget. "Two days ago a woman gave her life for this girl. As she lay dying, I swore to her that I'd do the same. I don't regret that oath."

"Then I suppose I've no choice but to go with you."

"You will be welcome. Indeed, a man of skills, who is interested in earthquakes, might find the circumstances quite interesting."

Though he smiled, his brow was creased with worry.

On my feet now, I set my mind to business. "Before I leave the city I've got to gather a few things, write a few messages, and check for a response to another."

I quickly wrote out a brief message for Lawyer Mantegna, asking who were the witnesses to the marriage contract. I had him reply directly to Vashti and Dumond's message box. The other message was to Vashti herself, reassuring her that all was well, and asking her to prepare just as if we were to go through with the ransom. To carry the messages, I enlisted my faithful Figi.

Figi spoke only to her mother and trusted no one other than her mother, Taverner Fesci, and Neri—and by association with Neri, me. She spent a great deal of her time stacking pebbles in orderly patterns in an alley, and then unstacking them again. Most people believed her witless. But Figi paid attention to things no one else did—like the exact number of threads in a spiderweb—and she had a map of every street, alley, and structure in Cantagna engraved upon her memory. Unlike Teo, she was a perfect messenger. No one paid her any mind.

Teo hadn't mentioned what he was not ready for. He had once told me that he was "not meant for killing." But one who protected the world from monsters must surely have some way to do what was necessary if my nightmares loosed one on the world or if I became one.

• • •

Teo and I left my house within the hour.

I wore a brown cloak and wide hat, and presented my numbered token at the House Rumos blue door. It was returned with a check mark indicating the message had been delivered, but no response awaited me. The director advocate had not countered the terms.

Leaving the city was not so easy as getting in. Every cart, wagon, carriage, and barrow was being searched by praetorians or Gardia wardens. Every rider or passenger had to dismount, and every bag, bucket, and parcel was examined. Nullifiers with their sniffers patrolled each queue of those waiting—riders, pedestrians, carts.

Two rowdy youths ahead of Teo in the queue of pedestrians were dragged out of line for questioning. I doubted that their noisy complaints at the delay marked them; everyone was complaining. More likely their youth and their ragged, dark-colored tunics. They reminded me of the boys who had stopped me on the day of the earthquake, posturing and bragging that they wanted to be Cavalieri Teschio initiates. These two fools tried to resist and ended up battered and groveling in front of a praetorian captain. I didn't see what happened to them after that. I stepped forward, eyes down, leading Quicksilver.

Only a few places more until I would be first in line and then through the tunnel. I glanced quickly across at Teo in the pedestrian queue. A sniffer touched a terrified woman a few places in front of him. The woman shrank away and yelled at the Gardia wardens looking on.

"What did that one do?" she demanded, pointing off to her right. "Already this morn, I saw praetorians stop two men because they were wearing black cloaks. When the men resisted, they were cut down. For nothing. That fellow's in black, too. If the Shadow Lord wore black, would he be—?"

One of her neighbors in the line grabbed hold of her and pressed her hand across the woman's mouth. She was right, though. In the shadows beyond their queue, a man lay crumpled in the shadow of the gate tower. He had no more life in him than the abandoned bags and boxes littering the gate approaches.

Teo stood motionless and silent, eyes averted, as the sniffer pawed at him.

A metallic rattle and a yip of pain at my side signaled my turn had come. I did not look directly at them. Green-clad fingers stroked my arm—shoulder to fingertip. The sniffer paused, cocked his head, passed his hand before his featureless face. I shuddered as he moved on.

The man just behind me, whose wide-brimmed hat sported the red-and-gray badge of a post messenger, tried to shove the green fingers from his shirt. "What's this nastiness?" he blurted. "Letting d-demons grope honest folk."

"Got summat to hide, do yeh?" said the nullifier. "Maybe you should step out the line. We've evil doings afoot in this city— snatch-crews working sorcery."

"'Tis against the law to interfere with a licensed post messenger without cause," said the nervous man.

"Take your complaint to the Sestorale." The nullifier bashed his axe handle on the man's thigh. The man yelled, staggered, and went down right in front of his mount. The startled horse neighed and sidestepped. The groaning man rolled aside just in time to avoid being kicked in the head. By the time I had calmed Quicksilver, a group of soldiers and travelers had gathered around the yelling messenger, the queue had closed up the gap, and the sniffer was nosing around the next person in line behind me. His master stood an arm's length from me.

The nullifier was a wiry, heavy-browed man, with hollow, pockmarked cheeks. His green tabard was clean and new, the black broidery of his yellow badge crisp and hard-edged. Had his wife stitched it and sent him off proudly that morning to chain a slave to his belt and terrorize good citizens? His badge . . .

I whirled around. "Your honor."

The nullifier turned and raked his eyes over me. "What?"

"I just wanted to thank you . . . for *defending* us . . . from demons."

"'Tis my duty and my pleasure," he said, grinning as he puffed out his chest where the badge was pinned and yanked the chain at his belt. The sniffer staggered and fell to his knees.

Nauseated, I bobbed my head and turned back to Quicksilver. The words stitched on the nullifier's badge were blazoned in my head: DEFENDER OF TRUTH.

Donato di Bastianni had claimed that his future was to serve as a "defender of truth." After dismissing any possibility of such an odd weakling becoming a praetorian, I had assumed he meant to pursue some academic specialty to root out deviance.

But Confraternity enforcers were more than just praetorians.

And if their badge bore that exact phrase . . . maybe that was exactly what he meant. Certain, it would explain why he had been surprised when I accused him of forcing young sorcerers to live forever at the end of a chain. No director's son would become a brutish nullifier. Which left only one possibility. In some way—either directing the work or doing it himself—Donato was going to make men into sniffers.

15

Teo didn't rejoin me until we were in the open on the riverside path, past the Avanci Bridge. Two hours it had taken us to get through the city gate. Neither of us spoke until we were past the River Gate and the city's southern wall.

If I needed any warning that this was no game the Chimera played, I'd just seen it. I didn't know why that man at the gate was dead or whether two others were slain because they wore black cloaks. But the hunt for Livia and Donato had caused the happenings at the city gate. People were getting hurt, their belongings broken or confiscated. Yet the sight of praetorians brutalizing Cantagnese citizens was also a reminder of why the Confraternity must not expand its influence over our city.

"We go this way," I said, guiding Quicksilver from the riverside path onto the northward track that ran parallel to the city walls.

"A moment's indulgence, friend Romy."

Without explanation, and without waiting for questions or agreement either one, Teo darted toward the river. He slipped and slid down the steep bank and, to my astonishment, dived into the swift-flowing water, clothes and all.

Uncertain as to whether I should go on without him, I mumbled my resentments to Quicksilver and fidgeted. Sitting still in the open on a sunny midmorning was on Placidio's list of Very Bad Ideas for those trying to avoid scrutiny.

Indeed, it was only moments until Teo emerged, slightly upstream from where I waited. Water droplets flew from his clothes and hair as he ran to rejoin me.

"Better," he said, as we continued on the narrow path. "You can pick up the pace if you wish. I've spent too much time with schooling of late. I need a good trot."

"And a good bathe?"

"Waiting there at the gate so near that pitiful slave, I sensed—I don't know." He glanced up at me and grimaced. "Sometimes a dunking gives me clarity. Sometimes not."

He said no more as I encouraged Quicksilver to a fast walk, and he jogged alongside.

A caravan of mule-drawn carts skirled the dust on the distant road to the north. The high road emerged from Cantagna's North Gate and wriggled its way north through the Cantagnan hills toward Argento. But we'd not stay with it so far. A side road would lead us into the rolling countryside and Perdition's Brink.

Now the opportunity had come to ask some of my questions, I wasn't sure how to begin. In appreciation for my saving his life, Teo had once pledged to do anything I asked of him. But just this morning, he had also just reiterated that he could not and would not lie. If I truly believed that, then pressing him for information he had not offered could squeeze him into a very difficult position. So I waited for him to offer more of what he had learned of himself and the reasons he'd been sent to the Costa Drago with his memory broken.

He didn't offer. That was another change in him.

Maybe I could start by revealing something I had kept hidden when I was unsure whether to trust him. I pulled a slip of bronze from my waist pocket and passed it to Teo.

"Many years ago, Dumond met an old woman down on the coast of Varela," I said. "She caught him working magic and gave him a luck charm, saying to wear it always as it was the *surest protection for one of the demon-tainted*. Years later, when he caught Neri using magic to rob him, he gave him a copy of his charm. Now Placidio and I carry them, too. Dumond believes it might prevent sniffers from detecting the magic we carry. Indeed that cursed sniffer passed me by at the gate. And you, as well."

Teo stopped to examine the charm, while Quicksilver and I continued on our way.

The charm carried only a single design—a triangle of three equal sides enclosing a tight-wound spiral. One side of the triangle was a sinuous curve. One side was bowed inward. One side bowed outward. Dumond's wife Vashti said the three curves represented water, earth, and magic. I'd never see the design anywhere else until Teo lay dying on my pallet three months ago. It was inked in the flesh over his heart.

A few moments and Teo was back jogging along beside me. He neither smiled nor frowned nor exhibited any other revelatory expression as he passed me the charm. "When I was here before, you asked me about that mark. I remember wondering why that one and not any of the others, as if you recognized its import. Especially as it was on the same day you spoke your fear that I might be of demonkind."

Curious. I'd not associated the two—my query and my mostly unserious accusation of his demonic origins on that day. But I did recall the true horror in Teo's face at that moment—and the sensation of spider feet on my skin in response. *Demons*. That was a word I and everyone in the Costa Drago tossed about as we did the names of gods and heroes we no longer believed in.

"You said it was the mark of your family."

"That was exactly the truth as I knew it then. And 'tis still true, though in a larger sense. May I defer the answer a short while longer? Rather than yes or no, it is a story. I could share it with the others at the same time—when I'm not chuffing along to keep up with this fine beast."

"Certain." But I wasn't sure how many opportunities would come for questions, so I took another turn. "Are there truly such things as demons?"

"Yes."

As on the day I had accused him of being one, my skin prickled at his surety. "Do I have a demon inside that fires my magic?"

"Certainly not. Your magic is an inborn aspect of you just as is the shape of your nose. Just as the curl of Neri's hair. Placidio's strength and agility. Dumond's skill at painting."

For a moment, I thought that would be all.

"Demons are . . . beings . . . a part of the story that explains the triangle mark"—he touched his chest over his heart—"but for now think of them as faulty scraps left over from the Enemy's attempt to create worthy companions. That attempt failed. Because they have no bodies of flesh and blood to warm them, they lurk in the deeps of the world where the earth's fires are hot."

"The Great Abyss," I murmured, recalling another childhood tale that was now taking on uncomfortable truth. "Where the *daemoni discordia* wait to torment the unvirtuous."

Teo crinkled his brow. "Humans—virtuous or unvirtuous— cannot live in a volcano's heart. And demons are not purposeful evildoers. They cannot manipulate material objects. Bred for obedience, they have no minds but instinct and a longing to be complete. Is that sufficient to your question?"

Almost. "So demons don't live in the human world?"

His eyes closed for a moment, as if searching his memory—or deciding what to tell. "If humans built cities in the maw of a volcano, perhaps. If a volcano erupts or an earthquake fractures the land deeply, demons may drift into occupied lands and linger wherever they find warmth. But of themselves, demons have no ability to cross the barrier of the flesh. That's when they could cause trouble, being creations of the Enemy and taking on the fullness of human life."

"So when I suggested you might be of demonkind . . ."

"I believed you meant that I was somehow evil, and though I did not consider myself evil, I also knew that I was not entirely myself. I worried that you might believe I was broken and lost—which I was—and a companion of the Enemy—which I was not—though I could not have articulated it so clearly then. It might reassure you to know that the barriers that confine the Enemy are also impermeable to demons. They cannot find their way back to their creator, which would also be problematic. He eats them. They are his creation, a part of his being that he expended to shape them, thus devouring them makes him stronger."

"And yet, you protect yourself from them?"

"I do."

"And water . . . does what?"

"If the water is cool enough, deep enough, powerful enough, the demon becomes dormant and can be dealt with." A moment's flick of his gaze and the slightest defensive twitch of his shoulder warned me that one of his barriers had snapped into place. Spirits, I wanted to *know*. But I had pushed him as far as he was willing to go. And I couldn't recapture how Dono had phrased a mention of demons that set me on edge.

"Thank you." I held up the luck charm before slipping it back into my jerkin. "Just to be clear . . . we should keep the charms in our pockets?"

"Ah, my determined friend, indeed so," he said, a fleeting smile breaking through. "Though against the skin might be even better."

"And *in* the skin better yet?" Though I cringed at imagining what skin-inking felt like.

He smiled. "For *you and your friends* that would not be necessary. So, our route changes just ahead?"

Indeed it did. Which was a momentary throttle on my curiosity, now swollen like risen bread. I needed to change the subject before I exploded with more questions.

Before we made the turn onto the wider, more beaten road, I pointed back to the city, where Villa Giusti perched at the northwestern edge of the Heights, emptying its cesspool down the steep slopes toward the poorer quarters of the lower rings. "My partners and I were hired to prevent a marriage. . . ."

PERDITION'S BRINK
AFTERNOON

"That's where we've stashed them." I pointed at Perdition's Brink, crowning the bluffs, and waved to whichever of my partners might be standing watch. We had made excellent time; Teo was tireless, and Quicksilver had eagerly kept pace with him.

As I dismounted, Teo took a long pull from a flask and surveyed the desiccated landscape. "What's happened here?"

He'd said little as I'd told him of our mission. Only a few requests for clarification had told me he was listening.

"Another legend of magic and human folly," I said. As we led Quicksilver around to the bluff to join the cart horses, I told him of the Conte Fumigari and the sorcerer's curse.

Story and horse coddling done, saddle stowed in the cart bed and covered with canvas, Teo shouldered the saddle packs. "It's been a very long time since a mage's work could blight the land so sorely."

I gave Quicksilver a last pat and started back around to the upward path. "Teo, when you say things like that, you set moths fluttering in my gut."

He broke into robust laughter, sounding for that moment like the Teo I remembered. The sound of it lightened my own foreboding.

"Much of what you've told me on this journey affects me much the same," he said as we started the climb. "This is just . . . the practice of sorcery has declined since some chose to exterminate sorcerers. You've said it before. No books. No mentors. Tell me, do you believe that the kind of magic you, your brother, and your friends do could be considered *natural phenomena* to which this intelligent young woman refers?"

Such a simple question to tie my mind in knots. "I've never considered magic at all natural."

"And yet, you and your friends are most certainly born of nature, are you not?"

"Certain, though the Philosophic Confraternity would argue it."

It was a curious question. Teo himself gave no hint of how I might reconcile a young woman's *observations of natural phenomena* with his own claims about an imprisoned Enemy who could cause the earth to fracture and shudder.

Dumond met us at the top of the climb. "A welcome surprise, knight of the isles," he said when Teo joined us. "Romy insisted you'd come back. The swordmaster never believed it."

Dumond relieved Teo of the saddle packs and led us through the warren of broken walls. I'd never thought of Teo as a knight— but somehow it fit. A knight in an armor of ink.

"And you, wise maker of portals, did *you* think I would renege on my swearing?" said Teo.

"Duty can oft interfere with intent," said Dumond.

"Indeed so. And yet sometimes one informs the other, so that both can be satisfied." Teo brushed his fingers on a carved doorpost, then a broken gargoyle, and then fallen lintels, foundation stones, and standing hearths, moving quickly from one to the other as if reading lines on a page.

Dumond halted me with a hand on my arm and spoke under his breath. "Have you told him what's going on here?"

"Yes," I said aloud. "Though he's come with me for a somewhat singular purpose that has naught to do with our scheme."

Out here in the daylight world, as we pursued a venture to protect the balance of power in Cantagna and the future of a very real young woman, the menace of an imprisoned monster using a disgraced courtesan to escape retreated into the realms of improbable legend. Surely someone else in the history of the world had possessed talent like mine, and surely our very existence in a prosperous city of a fortunate land like the Costa Drago proved that this Enemy of Teo's had never gotten free. The dreams were real, and

I believed Teo spoke truth . . . but he had admitted he didn't know how the danger might play out.

Dumond deposited my saddle packs inside the keep.

I pulled out a kerchief, dampened it from our water cask, and swiped the road dust from my face. "How's Neri?"

"Hungry. Though we've slipped him a bite or two, he's ready to eat his breeks. The arm pains him."

"I promised we'd pull him out this morning."

"This place is fascinating. And sorrowful," said Teo, rejoining us inside the keep. He spun as he took in the high roof and broken interior of the ruin. "Such a mingling of ancient and new. Romy spoke of its history. I think I would have known something of it even without her telling. Good Dumond, do you find your magics flow stronger here?"

Dumond's brushy brows lifted. "When I tested our escape route, the effort did seem a deal less than expected."

"Yes, now you mention it," I said, recalling the convulsive energy when I became Nis. "You're saying it has something to do with Perdition's Brink?"

Teo folded his arms and paused as if searching for words. "At some time, someone or some happening infused this piece of the earth with the influence of"—he glanced at us from under his long lashes—"the ancients. Power, energy, or whatever you might call it that's neither good nor ill, but simply . . . influence. Anyone, whether with the gifts you carry or not, might find something similar in sites they name holy. Or haunted. Or frightening. It is a sympathetic influence, thus could enhance natural power whether for good or ill. Is that meaningful?"

Dumond and I mumbled an affirmation in unison.

"Some people say such things about changes of the season or certain times of day," I added, "that the winter solstice or sunset hour are luckier or closer to the divine."

"Not *luck* so much," said Teo, with a smile. Which left a gap in the flimsy explanation that I could not fill.

Dumond blew a sharp exhale and shook his head. "Certain, you've tickled my imaginings."

"I'm guessing *the ancients* and their *influence* are a part of your elusive story," I said, as I unpacked the stores I'd brought. Shirts to a canvas bag. Apples, honey, bread, and pilchard crock to our supply chest.

"Aye, that's so. I could—"

"Not sure what your elusive story is, my friend, but 'tis a grace to share your company again." Placidio stood in the doorway from the outer courtyard. As at his first meeting with Teo, Placidio made a modest bow. I had seen him show such genuine respect to only one other person—the grand duc of Riccia-by-the-sea.

"It's a fine pleasure to greet you again, swordmaster." Unlike at their previous meeting, Teo returned the respectful gesture. My mouth fell open in astonishment . . . quickly subsumed by annoyance.

This unspoken understanding between them grated on me, knowing that Placidio would not explain and certain that asking Teo would put him in that squeeze between oathswearing and his inability to lie about information he had not offered.

"Teo invited himself along," I snapped. "You'll find his generous gift of pilchards in our larder."

"Ahh, so tempting." Placidio rolled his eyes in pleasure. He relished the salty little fish. "But our captives await."

"Might there be a few moments before you proceed?" said Teo. "Romy asked me to tell about the mark on your luck charms and on me. I would share what I can."

One might have thought time itself stopped.

"Certain," I said, and Dumond and Placidio quickly agreed.

We sat on our bags and chests of supplies, passed Teo a mug of salt-and-ginger tea, and he began.

"As I've told Romy, I have lived these past few months in the embrace of my family. My faulty memory has been repaired for the most part, but as a result, I now have constraints I did not have then. While my duties and my preparation must remain private, it seems only right to speak a little of history after your generosity of those days, sharing your own secrets and your friendship, and allowing me to contribute to your adventure."

"*Allowing* was not so much the case as begging, as I recall," said Dumond.

"*Coercing* would be a good description," said Placidio.

Teo laughed, his demeanor not so grim as it had seemed.

"You've all heard a variant of the Creation story—how Father At-ladu and Mother Gione gave birth to the world in all the rich and wondrous variety of sea and land. How they treasured all their flying, creeping, running, and upright creatures, sentient and non-sentient. And how the most beautiful of all their creatures was Dragonis, a sexless being who could take varied shapes, but preferred a winged form of shimmering fire. These stories say that the heart of Dragonis grew sour because he had no match among the other creatures, no worthy companions, no worthy opponents. She wanted to be worshipped and brought gifts as was her due. He—for Dragonis was male and female, both and neither—lurked in the mountains and tried to create his own companions. Unsatis-fied, Dragonis mated with human men and women, seducing and seeding them with strange gifts to set them above the others of their kind. Thus came the Creation Wars that fractured the world and forced the gods into the Night Eternal."

"Myths," said Dumond. "Every village, city, tribe, or clan has them."

"'Tis true. But the story told in my homeland, the story that shapes my life—and yours, it is fair to say—parallels this grand tale of jealous gods and uncompromising war. It tells of two clans whose extraordinary talents and long lives appeared to ancient peoples as godlike. Mages we would name them—beings of ex-traordinary magic. They were of two kinds. Mages of the waves took their power from water. Mages of the flame took their power from the fire spawned in the earth's heart. Together they nurtured the peoples who rapidly spread across the world, teaching them to tend the earth and tame its waters, and to shape clay and metal with fire. It was a grand harmony."

As he paused for a swallow of tea, my mind snapped to the duc of Riccia's statue, and its depiction of Atladu running in peace with Dragonis and the other—the missing image I had named Le-viathan. Fire and water. I yet firmly believed that recovery of that statue was at least a part of Teo's mysterious *duties*.

He set the flask aside. "One of the most skilled of all mages, a mage of the fire, was named Macheon. Macheon worked tirelessly to protect humans from the devastation of volcanoes and earthquakes. The lands that later became the Costa Drago were a particular prob-lem because of how close the fires were to the surface. The circumstance left the soil rich and fertile, but the people lived in constant danger. When Mount Cazzotto became restless, belching rock and ash, threatening several fledgling cities, Macheon persuaded other mages of the fire to join their power to contain it. Now called the Dragoni, they joined in a circle around that mountain to create a great spellworking intended to suppress its fury.

"The mages of the waters warned Macheon that pouring so much magic into the earth in a small region could cause a terrible backlash. But Macheon replied that they surely cared only for themselves and not his beloved people. His fury at their judgment incited his believers to take vengeance on all who spoke against him—especially those mages who took power from waters."

"Your family," I said. Those of the water. So much made sense.

"Aye. My people who survived the slaughter withdrew to their home far out to sea to attend their own studies of hurricanes, tidal waves, and floods. In the very next season came the great destruction. Mount Cazzotto indeed stayed quiet, as Macheon intended, but instead a whole chain of volcanoes erupted, shattering the southern reaches of the Costa Drago into a thousand islands, showering fiery ash over half the world, burying or drowning tens of thousands, including every one of Macheon's fellow Dragoni. Much of my own people's land was inundated, and nine of every ten died. Macheon blamed the sea mages for the disaster, because of the scalding rain and the walls of searing mud that had raced down mountainsides and through cities faster than people could outrun it. The conflagration darkened the skies for a generation."

Nothing in my experience reached the scale of such devastation. To imagine the scene at the coliseum after the earthquake a thousand times over . . . and with fire and ash and landslides of molten rock and boiling mud added to the horror of mangled bodies, the trapped living, and evil skies . . . wrung my soul.

Teo continued, solemn. "Frenzied with hatred and guilt, Macheon swore to rebuild his power. He drew on the power of the destruction he had wrought and attempted to create loyal companions—a new army—by separating human spirits from the limitations of their physical bodies. Even the earlier slaughter did not match this one."

"Demons," I said. "Macheon created fragments of human souls. Bound to obedience. Hungering for the warmth of life."

Teo signaled agreement as the story flowed from him. "So came the Second War. Lacking physical sensations and power of their own, the demons had no magic to help their maker work spells. Even so, the remnants of my family were the only ones left with the power to face Macheon. They defeated the Enemy in all its manifestations, but were not strong enough to destroy them. Instead, they built a prison, locked Macheon away, and offered the world their own future to maintain it . . ."

". . . with the power of earth, sea, and magic," said Dumond. "The mark on my luck charm. The symbol of your family."

Teo acknowledged it.

Macheon the Dragoni . . . the imprisoned Enemy . . . Dragonis.

"Thank you for sharing the story," said Dumond.

Placidio stood in the doorway, listening, but did not speak. I wondered if he knew the story already. I still had questions.

"You told me that time and the workings of nature conspired to weaken the protections around the Enemy's prison," I said, "and that your people do not increase as they once did. When you lay dying back in the spring, I shared your dream of a graceful city falling to ruin from cracks of molten fire. Is that what you're working to remedy? And Domenika—"

"We work to recover all we have lost. Please, I cannot say more. I just needed all of you to know I won't be much help with other tasks. Indeed, I am not permitted—" He scrunched his features as if his bare feet had just encountered broken glass. "My family—my mentors—insist I not engage in . . . local matters. Please believe that I would not change the choices I made when I was here before. And it's not to say that these matters you address are unimportant, but only that my duties require . . . other choices."

No mistaking the weight of responsibility that had replaced Teo's confusion.

"Your safety cannot be risked," said Placidio.

"So I am told." His pale complexion flushed like summer sunrise. "I am here to keep watch for the moves of the Enemy, prevent them if I can. Nothing else."

"Stay close, then," I said. "*We* must do what we can to protect the independence of our city and its steward and his daughter, and then get these two young people home."

The fear that had faded in glaring daylight wafted into the

shady keep like smoky fingers, ready to shred my resolve. I could not allow that. We had bought this time, believing the Confraternity's hunt might be moderated by the prospect of catching us at the ransom exchange. But seeing the harassment at the gates . . . the praetorians' violence . . . I didn't like to think how matters might get worse.

16

I pointed Teo to the water cask and the courtyard doorway. "This is good water from the spring down the stair on the far side of that courtyard. Make free of it and anything else here. Our rations are a bit limited, but you're welcome to share. For now, we must move our plan forward. We're running short of time."

"Aye," said Dumond. "We've an angry bride, a stubborn bridegroom, and a very hungry partner to see to. Without Romy, it's been a stretch to ensure our prisoners are not in true distress—and keep watch for unwelcome visitors at the same time."

"So Donato still won't talk."

"To be clear," said Placidio. "It's going to take at least a lightning strike to rouse him. I've never seen such a disciplined demeanor. Yet he does nothing with it. He doesn't try to fight me; twice I've left him a clear opening."

Dumond joined in. "Nothing moves him. Swordmaster warned Neri he'd get hauled out for a beating did he not tell us who'll pay for him, and told Dono that neither of them would eat till Neri spoke. I went down after. Gave them each a couple of plums and told him we didn't really want either of them dead. All I got was more Confraternity codswallop. The threats had Dono shaking, though. He's hungry, thirsty, and scared to his boots."

"It's about us," I said. "He was so confident at first, because he thought he knew what this snatch was about. But by last night, he was questioning his assumptions. Maybe he's come to believe we really *are* planning to sell him off."

Placidio looked skeptical. "I'm not sure he thinks at all. He neither pleads, argues, reasons, or attempts escape. His shackle is no stronger than Livia's first one but remains unbroken. And last night the wind laid an opportunity in his lap. It blew the ladder into a tangle halfway down the wall. If he'd had a long branch, he might've hooked it down. Neri tried to persuade Donato to give him a boost . . . see if he could reach it . . . but the fool wouldn't even try. He said it would *jeopardize the ransom bargain*."

Something in Placidio's story pricked at a memory . . . moonlight rising . . . something important . . .

"*Is* there a ransom bargain, Romy?" Dumond rummaged in the bag of apples I'd brought and quickly devoured two.

The thread of memory slipped away before I could find what was at its end.

"The ransom message was delivered anonymously," I said, annoyed with myself. "As of this morning there were no replies."

I told them about the sniffers, wardens, and praetorians plaguing the city, and my query about the contract witnesses.

"Between all that and having a somewhat terrifying talk about dreams with our friend here—which *he* will tell you about at some time—I gave some thought to our next steps. I think it's time Nis tells Livia about her friend's murder. Perhaps the shock will get her thinking more carefully about this marriage."

"You're not revealing the Chimera?" said ever-cautious Dumond.

"No. I'd not trust her so far as that as yet. I'm not sure I ever will. She's far more confident of her own judgment than I am. As for Donato, I've a notion about him. He was startled when I yelled at him that his holy Confraternity was gelding young men, and when Placidio spoke of *Confraternity secrets*, he started shaking. Back at the beginning, Mantegna said that on the same day he was to be married, Donato would receive the red philosophist's robe and be elevated to a prestigious position in the Confraternity. Donato himself told us that his future was to become a *defender of truth*. But I don't think he meant defending it as a praetorian— he's clearly unsuited—or with some scholarly pursuit. *Defender of Truth* is the motto on nullifier badges. I think our groom is going to create sniffers."

"That would perhaps explain the fellow's concern about testing," said Dumond. "Many in the Confraternity might think such an awkward person unsuitable for so important and secret a task."

"Then again, perhaps that sort of elevation requires a particular test of loyalty and commitment to their principles—however grotesque those might be," mused Placidio. "Perhaps we'll be fortunate and have occasion to kill the little worm."

"I think Donato needs a shock, too," I said. "The Confraternity and the city have inextricably linked the Cavalieri Teschio with magic. So let's use that connection to give the Confraternity boy a scare."

"Show him some magic . . ." said Dumond, thoughtful, deliberate. "I like that."

"I know it's a risk." I pulled my Cavalieri garb from the canvas bag. "But we've always worn these masks in front of him, so he shouldn't be able to identify us. While I go and let Nis speak with Livia, you two figure out how we can spook Donato into telling us what's got him so nervous; then perhaps we'll know how to scare him out of his wedding."

"Aye, an interesting approach," said Placidio. "And one of us will be there when you finish with Livia—and Nis."

Yes, the flaw in my impersonation magic. "Even if Teo can't get involved with our business," I said, "I'm guessing he can at least fetch one of you when I'm ready to be myself again."

"You intend to use your magic? Romy, you must not." Teo's quiet horror chilled me more than any shouting could.

Dumond and Placidio looked bewildered. I finished lacing my black tunic and fastened the black cloak at my shoulders.

"You confessed that you don't know whether I'm weak or damaged or what the Enemy might do if I am. But our mission here, Teo . . . we see the dangers and possibilities of the situation clearly. The future of sorcerers and many others living in Cantagna. A young woman's life. The contributions she might make to human knowledge. We don't have days or even hours for me to sit aside and learn to protect myself. If a monster comes crawling out of my head, do what's needed to protect us. Tell these two what you told me, while I go and try to speed things up a little."

I stuffed a small bag with a flask of ale, a cup, and a roll of thin bread spread with olive paste and headed for Livia.

Neither lady nor gentlemen were at all like I'd imagined. Yet I felt more determined than ever to prevent them being forced into the Confraternity's scheme—Director Bastianni's scheme. He, not his cowering son, was the manipulator.

Insects rasped and darted as I strode through the scrub and ruin. One of the others could show Teo the way, once they'd heard him out.

By the time I had quieted my irritations and prepared myself for what Nis needed to do, Teo had joined me. He remained a few steps away in the sparse shade of a slender cypress. He sat on his haunches, silent and watchful, like gargoyles carved over lintels or under the eaves to discourage demons.

Demons . . . *Faulty scraps left over from the creation,* so Teo had said. *Lurking in the deeps, searching for warmth.*

I shivered. Without speaking, I acknowledged Teo's presence—grateful for it, no matter what he could or could not do. Then turned my back and turned inward. Magic filled me like a fiery flood tide. *My name is Nis. . . .*

• • •

Like a spider on a web, I crept down the rope ladder. The girl Livia lay under the stone roof, curled atop the blanket Capo had allowed me to bring her. The nights were chill on this cursed rock. Innocent she looked. But I knew better.

"I've brought food," I said as I scurried under the slab roof. "Capo's off to the caravans to tell them all about you and his other new *merchandise.*"

"But the ransom!" She popped up like mushrooms after a rain. "Did you tell Papa? He didn't *refuse.* He wouldn't. How—how much was asked?"

I set the bread roll and a cup of ale where she could reach it. Still better for me if she wasn't a skeleton and could bring a good price.

Soon as I sat back in my usual place, she scrambled up there and wolfed the goods. I glared at her and believed that's what she was. A wolf. Just like all the other rich folk, playing us unders to their own uses.

"Last night I delivered the ransom message. Your price is six thousand silvers by tomorrow midnight. Got no answer by this morning afore we come back here. And every hour is more danger. The city's awash with praetorians and wardens and constables."

She jumped to her feet. "Six thousand! So much . . . and in two days!" She weren't brassy no more. "How can anyone possibly do that?"

"Someone better do. You're the one said it should be your da. But from what I heard in the city, I'm wondering if he'll think he's better off without you, just like your man's folks. I just don't know what to believe from a *gods-cursed liar.*"

"I do not lie," she snapped, moving close as she could like she might catch me in her jaws. Her shackle rattled with every step. "Everything I told you was the truth."

"Except that when you ran away from the philosophists, you didn't leave your 'important pages' with your 'secret friend'—your friend in the Street of the Bookbinders. You killed her."

"What?" She stopped dead, spluttering.

"It was talked of everywhere in the city. A woman was found dead two nights ago in the Street of the *Bookbinders.* They're hunting everywhere for the one that done it—someone that tried to force the woman to make a wrongful pamplit. I wonder if they know it's the same sad rich girl they're hunting as was snatched from that big house—you."

"No, no, no! Oh, blighted universe!" She clapped her hand over her mouth and sagged back to the wall. "That's not possible. I made sure no one followed me. And only two people in the world know that Marsilia publishes my pamphlets. Every other book or pamphlet she works on is for the Academie or the Sestorale Library—all perfectly acceptable."

"Maybe you're not so clever as you think. Or maybe you're the one killed her because she didn't want to publish wickedness no more."

"Nis, I swear to you, everything I told you was the truth. Because you were brave enough to believe me and help save my life. Brave enough to come down here and feed me in the first place."

I didn't want to think she'd done it. I'd got to like the notion of being her maidservant, thinking maybe I'd be wearing a fine gray dress like those in the house where we snatched her. I didn't like hearing I was as stupid as people thought.

"Then who killed her?"

She crouched down and spoke low, as if the birds might carry word of her talking to her enemies. "I told you yesterday. What I write is natural philosophy—science and reason, everything that the Philosophic Confraternity hates. They won't allow anything to be published that suggests their teachings are wrong, much less purposefully wrong."

"The *philosophists*. The very people you plan to go live with. You're saying *they* killed the bookbinder?"

"For four years, Marsilia published my writing because she believed in my ideas. She never told anyone that it was she who did the binding. Nor did I. And the only ones who knew she worked with me were my uncle, who's three years dead, and one other who would never in the world betray—" She near swallowed her tongue.

"Ahhh . . . your lover?"

She didn't answer, only crouched there staring into nothing. Like she was dead. "Tirza," she whispered, as if the person she talked to was dead, too. "You knew what Marsilia meant to me . . ."

She looked back at me as if I might make some sense out of what she was saying. But it wasn't me she was talking to.

". . . but they found the lever, didn't they? The Mardi lawsuit that could mean your father's ruin."

"You're saying they knew about the bookbinder because your *lover* told them how to find her."

"It's my fault. They asked if I'd ever been intimate with anyone. I don't lie. So I told them I had and that she was a woman. They didn't care as long as . . . as I'd not had a man inside me, though I'm not sure even that would have stopped anything. I refused to tell them her name. But Mama knew of Tirza, and Mama will do anything a man tells her. And Tirza loves her father, who is on the verge of ruin, and she knew about Marsilia. So when they found me missing, they must have questioned her . . . and found Marsilia . . . stars and stones . . ."

I thought she might collapse and cry and show me she was not so brave after all. But she didn't.

"You should go, Nis, and you should run away from these horrible men who make your life such a misery. Don't trust anyone. Ever. Not kin. Not friend. Not lover. Not anyone."

"Capo still don't know I delivered the message to the different house. If I run, I'll be dead sure. Wouldn't even know where to go. But hearing you tell about all your traveling . . . you're the one should run away instead of marrying someone so wicked. His people killed your friend, the bookbinder, and who knows what awful things they said—or did—to your lover made her give up the bookbinder's name. Did *he* know of the murder, do you think? Your man. He's one of them, right? Works for them?"

She stared at me like I were a mouldering corpse raised up from a grave. "Dono? I don't— He's a nothing. Of course he's to wear the red, but only because he's a director's son. I'm not even sure he knows about my writings. He never asked about my travels or what I studied or why I wrote such *lies*, as he would deem them. Certain, his father knows—no guessing there—why else would he insist on this wedding? But Dono himself? In those two days before this happened, we met several times. He does speak, but it's all pretty manners and Academie prattle. He doesn't attend any lectures or musicales. He's no interest in why some stars stay in fixed patterns and why some change position every night. He claimed never to have heard of the opticum which reveals the tiny creatures our eyes cannot see, but is concerned that such a thing could easily be demonic. He said he read history at the Academie and sometimes reviewed historical papers—boring things about improvements in weaving and the construction of aqueducts. He mentioned that he would assume an official post on the same day as we were to be wed—a Confraternity feast day. Something about working with people new to the Confraternity. So he's to be a tutor or mentor, I assume, but he never said what subjects. I can't imagine him in a position of authority. He has an attendant with him at all times, like he needs someone to tell him where to sit and which knife to use. He said not one single thing of interest or import, enough that I knew he was just as dull and thickheaded as when he was a boy."

How could one person have so many words in her as this?

"He didn't touch me even once—when any other man would have kissed my hand." She rolled her eyes and yanked at her hair. "Not that I want his touch. Worse, he wouldn't even look at me like I might be a human person. The idiot talked about what apartments we might be given in the villa. About whether I would wish to have a lapdog. Stars . . . a lapdog . . . as if I had no mind to put to sensible use. And that was on that same evening after I'd gone and come back—the night they put a guard on my door—and he didn't even mention that, as if it were the most ordinary thing in the world to have a soldier at his bride's door. That was the night they killed her. Could he have been showing me his dull good manners while his people murdered an old woman because of *me*?"

She near spewed sparks as she talked. If that Dono were with us, she'd've strangled him right there.

What would she do if her people paid to get her home? She didn't need me to tell her that marrying a man who conspired with his da and approved her friend's murder was not so simple as marrying a cowardly dullwit. What a strange girl she was to be so smart and so ignorant all at once.

"I've been thinking on that story you told me about him," I said, "that boy he ratted out as a sorcerer. What happened to him? Was he really a demon?"

"There are no sorcerers, Nis. No demons. Reason . . . scientific thought . . . can explain everything, even if we don't understand it all as yet. The philosophists know this, but they want people to be superstitious and afraid. As for Guillam, Papa said they brought in their horrid sniffers and *claimed* they found evidence of magic on the collapsed shelf. Praetorians came for Guillam that night at supper, anyway, and dragged him away screaming. His family was arrested, too, but Papa said they were eventually released and told that Guillam was dead. They moved away from Cantagna. Papa supposed that it came out that no magic was involved, that the shelf fell because of the fight, and Guillam was blamed because he was the eldest there. A boy had died, after all, and another was injured. Someone had to pay for it."

"Maybe they made a sniffer out of him." Sometimes I had wicked dreams about sniffers.

Livia hunched her shoulders, not caring. "I suppose they might have. They say they only make sniffers out of sorcerers, but certain, they might have told themselves that doing it was as just a punishment as hanging for a boy of fourteen. At least he would get to stay alive."

I shivered. To be one of those green monsters on a chain—going around naked, but for the silk, whether it was raining or cold or blistering hot. Blinded. Ears plugged. Their talk nothing but howls and moans. Maybe their tongues were cut. Made me want to puke.

She rubbed her forehead, smudging it with her fingers sticky from the olive paste. "You should go, Nis. Before your capo gets back."

I couldn't let the story go. My trip to the city had scared me. "Sniffers were everywhere in the city last night. Where do they all come from? We don't hear about that many sorcerers being arrested, and lots of those are old folks or broken ones who think

they're Lady Fortune's favored. But people in the street were saying the Cavalieri who snatched the girl from that big house were
magic users, which we're not. What if they catch me?"

This time Livia looked straight at me. "They wouldn't make
you a sniffer, Nis. They claim sorcery gets passed through the
blood, so they don't want women, because they might bear children. So it's only men—cut men—they make into sniffers. They'd
just hang you or drown you. I swear if I get out of this mess alive,
I'll try to do right by you. But likely it would be better if you would
run away from me as far and as fast as you can."

She dragged herself over to her blanket and curled up on it, her
hands over her face. Maybe she was crying then—losing her friend
and discovering awful things about her lover and her gonna-be
husband—but I didn't wait to see. I scrambled up the rope ladder
in a hurry, as I needed to get . . . something . . . done before Capo
came back. Something to do with the other prisoner. Feared as
I was of hanging or drowning, I didn't want Capo to throw me
out, though if I stayed with him, I was like to be dead before I was
one-and-twenty anyways. Certain, my imagining of being maidservant to Livia didn't look at all promising with her married to
a murderer. It was hard to keep my own weeps from leaking out.

Once close to the top of the ladder, I held still for a goodly while
listening, remembering that lurkers could be nearby. After a bit,
I shimmied quiet over the rim but I wasn't so sure which way to
go next. The scrubby trees and rock spires all looked the same in
every direction. The sky was milk and silver, and I was tired as if
I'd not slept in a year. I wanted to curl up like Livia and sleep for
a month.

A rustling from a shrub off to one side struck a spark inside
me that burst into full flame. Someone was hiding in there who
was not Capo nor Lizard. I swallowed a scream and ran—crazy,
lunatic, leaping over rocks, dragging through thorn bushes, scraping my arms on broken walls, slapped in the face by dry limbs,
then down a gully, darting through shadows till my feet skidded
and stumbled to keep up lest I lose my balance and tumble down
the endless steeps. A man with a familiar face perched on a rock
nearby. He reached out for me. So elegant he was, so handsome.
Eyes the colors of fire and sunset, shimmering blood and molten
rock. Skin the rich red-brown of copper. Long, graceful fingers.

"Do not fear, my lovely. I'll not let you fall. So precious you are to me." His voice was low and sweet, caressing my ears and soaking into my skin until it burned my heart. *"Our time approaches. Let us whisper of pleasures to be found in the domes of sky and sea, of our future where you shall reclaim your proper place among your kind. My consort . . . my completion . . . perfect. I've waited so long."* He stretched out his hand . . . and I reached for it . . . almost touching . . .

"Romy, no!"

I blinked and looked out over nothing. Five fingers of ice-glazed iron around my wrist were all that prevented me plummeting down a cliff of red rock and gullied grit to the wasteland far below. Nis was fled, and by Lady Fortune's whim, a granite-faced Teo gathered me into his imprisoning embrace and dragged me away from the brink of Perdition's Brink.

17

She needs to come with me to Domenika."

"Our lady scribe needs to do as she chooses. She is a woman of her own mind."

"As long as her mind is her own. Today . . . I'm not sure that was the case. You saw her fight me."

"The swordsman's right. She chose to return here this morning, knowing full well the risks. That is, I presume you presented the risks to her as starkly as you've presented them to us."

"It's why I came. Domenika does not travel, and though she has assistants who could explain more than I can, I believed Romy would listen to me. Yes, the timing is awkward; clearly the same event has set all of these conflicts in motion at once. But I fear for my friend, and for the unknowns of power beyond all of our experience—yours, mine, and that of my elders."

No matter that my arms covered my eyes and ears, I could not escape the argument. Teo. Placidio. Dumond. Good friends who cared about me. Not lovers. Not . . . seducers, like the one in my dreams. That one was so angry, yet so passionate and so very, very beautiful. Her touch was the kiss of lightning; his gaze was magic itself. My body quivered at the memory of it. Spirits, what would their *kiss* be like?

Why should I be afraid? The Moon House had taught me how to manage demanding, passionate, angry masters. Even beautiful ones.

Keep aware of your true surroundings, Romy. Don't drift. Teo had been clear about that. *Keep all of your senses well-grounded in the place where you are. And let your own voice be the one to command your actions, your choices, your feelings.*

So . . . the stone was smooth and cool under my cheek. Pleasantly so. And wet. They had brought me to this shady grotto and doused me with scoops of water from the spring because the heat of flesh and fury had driven me to madness. Bruises on my arms pulsed with my heartbeat.

Faint light and fresh air that smelled of warmed cedar filtered in from a distant hole in the cliff. Supposedly, you could walk from this grotto of the spring and its upward stair to that hole and look out on the wide world. Yet the opening was impossible to access from the flats below, and reachable only with ropes, spikes, hammers, and skilled climbing from above.

A most unnatural odor of oils and pigments intruded on the scent of cedar and wet stone, reminding me that the odd streaks on the shadowed stone beyond the pool was a painted door awaiting Dumond's magic.

Had either of my partners slept while I was gone to the city? My alert, focused senses insisted both of them needed a wash, despite all the water I had splashed on them when they had at last dipped my entire body in the spring.

I'd lain here wallowing in these normal sensations much longer than I needed, enjoying the moment's release from responsibility, while Teo explained to the others about the Singular Wall and my dangerous dreaming. Dumond had asked the questions I had refrained from about the prison and his mysterious duties—and Teo regretfully refused answers, as I'd known he would, saying that we lived in the world where the Enemy had eyes and ears, and no, he could not say exactly what those were, but to please be cautious with every mention of these mysteries . . . and him. Poor Teo hated to ask that of them. To protect *him*.

"I cannot interfere with what goes on here. It grieves me, but my duties—and my work to become capable of them—demand that I remain apart. Certain, I'll do whatever's possible to prevent the Enemy from prevailing . . . but naught else."

Placidio, no surprise, accepted Teo's strictures, though he said it was a damnable nuisance that the lady scribe had not seen fit to trust them with her terrifying dreams.

Dumond grumbled and said Teo might as well not have bothered coming or warning us if he couldn't tell us what to expect or what to do about it save to keep watch so Romy doesn't wander off a cliff.

"I'm going back up top," said Dumond. "This delay will not have settled either Neri or our bridegroom."

"I'll scout the perimeter while the light is good," said Placidio. "The first night after the ransom demand is riskiest. Will the praetorians wait for the exchange or will they spread over the countryside, knowing we can't be too far away? We must be vigilant."

Dumond squatted beside me. "We'll see you when you're ready to move ahead, Romy. Give yourself what time you need."

I patted his boot—scuffed leather, droplets of once-molten metal stuck here and there, currently very damp. He seemed to take the pat as reassurance and followed Placidio up the stairs.

Teo made no move to go with them. Nor did I. I wanted to start with simple.

Once their footsteps had faded, I lifted my boulder of a head and supported it with an arm abuzz with scrapes from Nis's race to perdition. "Thank you, my friend. Again."

"Are you feeling entirely yourself, Romy?" Teo slipped from the rock where he was perched and dropped onto his knees at my side. "Such a fright you gave us. Another waking dream, yes? Or more of a—visitation? You understand, this Enemy who intrudes upon your dreams is the same Macheon I told of. Her power increases; his prison weakens. We don't know how or why. The last Dragoni yearns to be free."

I pushed up and curled my legs under me, feeling the delicate pressure of his gaze. "Visitation. Yes. Though similar to the dreams. The male ... manifestation ... this time. Spewing flattery. Promises. He said, '*Our time approaches.*' All very unspecific. All with the same ... sensations. Spirits, Teo, when you told the others what was going on with me, you didn't miss a single intimate detail of my dreams. Your recollection is astonishing and somewhat disconcerting."

He didn't smile, but his worry lines smoothed a bit. He'd removed his eye patch down here in the mottled glow of four torches and remote daylight. The mark around his eye was a lacework of silver. "Recollection is my existence of late."

"I see it in you," I said. "So much change in the span of three months. This teaching ... but not just teaching, I think. *Recollection* encompasses more than merely listening to someone speak of history."

"You are a perceptive woman."

I touched the intricate marking about his eye, knowing he

would rather I didn't, but hoping I could convince him to trust me. The tracing was cool; my finger could have followed the design even were my eyes closed. But I would not ask its meaning or if, like Dumond's painting, it could be roused to some sort of purpose with a touch of magic.

"I cannot speak of—"

My fingers touched his mouth to shush him. Then I returned my hand to my knee. "Here are my conclusions about your situation. Some I gleaned three months ago, some today. Domenika drives you to be ready for what's coming—whether either of you know what's coming or not. Those dreams we shared told me that. Someone apologized for sending you *beforetime* because they needed you to search for something that had been lost and found again. And your own people broke your memory before they sent you, because you didn't know enough to hide what you are."

His lashes were lowered. "Romy, please . . ."

"I'm *not* going to pry. I'm not going to push to know if I'm correct or to ask for more. Please understand that you can trust me. You don't have to apologize for your reticence. Spirits know—and *you* know—that I am damnably curious, and that I already must honor one of my partner's privacies far more than I like. But I do so because I respect him. I respect you as well."

He tried to start again, but again I stopped him.

"The two of them are right. I believe what you say about the danger. But I choose to *not* think about it, and to accept the risk that comes with the choice. The attack you fear may or may not come today or tomorrow, but the consequences that we are working to avert will most certainly happen if we fail. So I am grateful beyond words for your coming, but I have to continue. I trust that you will pull me back from the brink when I need pulling."

"I don't know if I can."

"I don't know if we can persuade this *tartaruga* Donato to come out of his shell before tomorrow night either, but we'll give it our damnedest. That's what the world—through the voice of the Shadow Lord—asks of us. Though still a bit damp, I'm quite well. I promise to remember the rules you repeated a thousand times over as I lay here, and I've no more need to use my magic just now. Before I do it again, I'll warn you. Indeed, I think I made progress with Livia today. She has grave misgivings about the marriage.

Now we have to do the same with Donato—find some way to learn enough about him that we can persuade him to cross his parents' wishes. He is so strange—so closed—I'm not sure we can do it, but we have to try."

"Another lesson learned," he said, slipping his eye patch back over his mark. "I shall watch, not push. And I'll hope that you are successful very soon."

"Thank you. Now I must to business."

"I'll be close by."

"I'm depending on it. But first we're going to haul Neri out of the cellar. He'll be pleased to see you."

* * *

Neri's third cup of ale was almost emptied after washing down a fist-sized lump of cheese, all of our figs, and half a loaf of bread. He could have eaten more, but we needed to talk before venturing our visit to Dono's cellar. And as soon as I finished dressing his shoulder, we needed him to do some screaming. We didn't want Donato to think Neri had been coddled and fed while he was out of his shackle.

"This could look much worse," I said as I smeared more of Vashti's salve over the ugly black crease where the praetorian's blade had sliced him. Certain, it looked bad enough. His chest, shoulder, and upper arm displayed fifty hues of purple, green, and black. The wound itself was yet swollen and seeping, and he squirmed when I pressed on the flesh next to it. But I saw no obvious pockets of pus. His putrid stink was to be expected of any young man after three harrowing days. I had to remind myself it had only been a day and a half since the fight in the Villa Giusti courtyard.

"Is there something here inside the keep that you can fix on . . . in case you need to magic yourself out of the cellar?" I said.

Neri glanced around. "That box that has all the food in it. Easy to see it in my head—the nail heads, the dents, the latch. Those scratches along the side. And certain, there's no lack of the wanting. One decent feed is not near enough for two whole days starving."

"Good. Be sure of it and maybe a few other destinations." Knowing that his magic could get him free on his own was reassuring. Placidio would make sure he could shed his shackle.

"Blood for now, meat for later." Placidio strode in from the courtyard with a dead hare in one hand and a bowl of blood in the other. "Has he told you anything useful about the Confraternity, boy?"

Neri took advantage of the interruption to tear another fistful of bread from the shrinking loaf, and answered between bites. "He don't like to talk. He walks around in the dark. Sits. Walks again. I guess that's why he's not turned to stone or something. I yelled at him once for getting up so often. It's so damnably quiet out here, his chain wakes me."

I'd not even thought . . . Neri had never slept anywhere farther from the city than the woolhouse. The first time Sandro had taken me to his country villa, the quiet had been unnerving. "What did he say to your yelling?"

"Said he 'didn't mean to bother.' " Neri snorted. "Never thought I'd have a Confraternity man come that close to apologizing."

I tied a strip of clean linen over his shoulder. "Did he stop getting up?"

"No."

Dumond had followed Placido inside. "Did you ask him why he sat up to sleep?"

"Didn't." My brother's face registered nothing but bliss as he sucked on a plum. "Thought that would sound too interested in him. But then he told me anyway."

My hands fell still, holding the damp, filthy, sour wrapping I was ready to layer over the fresh bandage. "Yes?"

"Sometime in the night, I guess, I started yelling."

"I heard that," said Placidio. "By the time I got there everything looked all right. Thought maybe I'd dropped asleep and dreamed it."

"I woke myself up. After you walked away—your big feet can't be quiet no matter how you try—Dono asked me what was wrong, calm as could be, like he says everything. Was it my arm? I said it was just a nightmare. And, gods' truth, he laughed."

"Laughed?" Placidio and I said it at the same time, with the same tone of disbelief.

"OK, snorted maybe, but it was as close to a laugh as I ever thought to hear from him. And then he said, 'Sit up when you sleep, and you can stop them before they get serious.' I told him I mostly slept like one of these dead trees and that maybe my problem was being stuck in a hole with ugly devils and she-witches threatening to skin me."

Neri flashed a grin that made me feel better about his healing than any peering or sniffing at his wound.

"Then he said he hadn't slept a full night since he was a nub, but there came a time when his arm got broke and he had wicked nightmares and someone taught him to sit up and it helped. That was it. I didn't sit up, but I didn't wake until Placidio started bawling at us this morning."

"I wonder if it was his broken arm gave him wicked dreams or guilt at accusing his attacker of sorcery," I said. "Maybe that's where we start our assault on Dono the *tartaruga*—something about this boy Guillam. If he's wondering if we're real Cavalieri anyway . . ." I quickly recounted Livia's tale of the childhood fight and this day's addendum. "We could let him think we're taking revenge for Guillam. Then maybe bring the magic into play."

"Might work," said Placidio. "But no more talk for now. We need to get one of us back on watch and get this shirker back in the hole lest our mark get suspicious when we suddenly start talking about the day his arm was broken." He flexed a nasty-looking bundle of smoothed limbs he'd cut from a lonely birch sapling and tied together with lengths of twine.

Neri's hand slowed as he lowered the polished pit of his plum. "Wait. You're not really going to . . ."

Placidio grunted. "Want to make the playacting easy, don't we? Dumond can saddle you over his back while I give a stripe or ten on your hind end. Did it in my Gardia training days."

"But the arm," said Dumond, sadly. "Romy'd likely have her dagger in your craw if we risked tearing that slice open." Unable to hold sobriety for the moment, the two of them started snickering.

Neri took aim and the plum pit found its mark in Placidio's scruff of a beard. The three of them burst into quiet laughter, and I joined in.

"Maybe you don't have to worry about the boy's health," said Dumond. "That throw was with his wounded arm. A finger's breadth higher and we'd be fishing that pit from the swordmaster's gullet."

Placidio flexed the switch. "Time to scream, student."

We all moved into the courtyard outside the keep, where Placidio had bundled blankets and canvas around a dead trunk. He'd not really imagined the prisoners would hear the blows as he flailed the birch switch, but the rhythm gave Neri a cue to let fly a series of increasingly tormented screams and curses.

Meanwhile Dumond ripped Neri's already ragged shirt a little more and his artist's hand skillfully added fresh streaks of hare's blood with a birch twig. Once the flailing and screaming were done, he added more streaks and splotches to Neri's slops and I dribbled some of the hare's gift on my brother's bandaged arm and bare skin. Dumond delivered the finishing touch by flicking one of his paint brushes loaded with blood, thereby delivering a fine spray on Placidio's face and hands. Anyone would believe he and Neri had been involved in a session of purest torment.

"One thing before you go back," I said. "You've observed Donato more than the rest of us together. What do you *think* of him?"

Unlike his usual, Neri considered before speaking. "Different than I expected. If I didn't know he was from the philosophists . . . just a fellow in the nick with me . . . I'd've guessed he was brought up rich, educated, been taught manners. Nothing else special. But he's got something off with his da. I said something about cutting my foot off to get out of the shackle, and how it would make me a match for my wicked da who had his hand lopped for thieving. He said I 'don't know anything about wicked fathers.' He's strange no doubt, scared to his boots like Dumond says it, and more cursed private even than"—he jerked his head at Placidio—"certain people we know. But he's no lunatic. I think his strangeness and his privacy is just how he keeps his frights from making him into one."

"That's useful," I said. And more than I'd expected.

"I'd agree," said Dumond. "Well-considered. We'll make a spy of you yet."

"All right. Last time for this, lad." Placidio loaded Neri on his shoulder again. "Certain, I'll be glad when I'm done hauling your carcass up and down that blighted ladder. Dumond?"

"I examined the spikes after you brought him up," said Dumond, as he cleaned his blood-laden brush. "Tight as your warlike ass."

"One more thing, sister witch," croaked Neri, convincingly hoarse from all the screaming. "Dono wears summat round his neck—a pendant or the like under his shirt. He checks for it time to time, even when he's sleeping, like to make sure it's still there. Not sure he even knows he does it."

I'd never imagined Dono might have worn jewelry to bed.

"Well done, little brother. We'll need to check on that." I put the bucket that contained Donato's water flask and evening food ration into Neri's hand. "As soon as I've cleaned up and changed back to Cavalieri garb, I'll be over to watch."

Placidio marched Neri off to Donato's cellar. Dumond put his cleaned brush with his paint case and set off to patrol the perimeter of the ridgetop while there was still plenty of light. I pulled open the canvas clothing bag and stared into the dark jumble inside.

Darkness swallowed me. I could not move, could not think at all what I was doing.

"Neri is a brave fellow," said Teo.

My attention snapped to the doorway to the keep. I'd almost forgotten Teo was with us. But in that same instant the events of two hours previous engulfed me—a torrent of sensations, of terror, of the view from the cliff where I'd come a hair's breadth from plunging to my death.

"Breathe, Romy."

My waking in the grotto of the spring had been a charmed time, as if the water had not only cooled the rage that lingered under my skin, but veiled the horror of the event. Only now, inhaling the heavy airs of late afternoon, hearing the clicks and rasps of beetles and spiders and other lively denizens of the rocks, and seeing blood under my fingernails . . .

"Spirits," I said, clamping a trembling hand over my mouth before a wail could rouse the settling hawks to flight again. I sank to the broken, blood-splotched paving suffering a fit of the shakes that rattled my bones and a certainty that collapsed my every belief.

"I can't unsee his eyes, Teo. They were fire, sunset, shimmering blood, molten rock. It was him, wasn't it? Dragonis. The beauteous monster is real. His voice . . . reached inside, as if to grab the heart right out of me. And I wanted— Spirits of Night and Day, of Moon and Stars and the Unseeable Gods lost in the Night Eternal, I *wanted* him to do it."

Teo knelt in front of me, his lean, ageless form so reminiscent of the marble divinities in our ruined temples, sculpted at a time when the popular style rejected natural muscle and bone in favor of the sublime. The shifting hues of his eyes—blues and purples, violets and greens so different from those other eyes—soothed the lancing terror. I inhaled his peace in great gulping sobs, but it did not stop my shaking.

"Did you perceive the wonder that I just beheld?" he said, taking my hands in his slim, cool ones. "The four of you . . . laughing in the face of your dangers, bearing each other upon your shoulders as you prepared for the good work you've chosen. Cling to that. That echo of human life—courage, friendship, respect, pain—all of those will give you power."

Ferocious now, he squeezed my hands, reminding me of the strength in those lean sinews. "When the monster speaks, use that power to mask her gaze, to drown his seductive lies. Know the true name of your Enemy. Macheon. Anything else is but myth. Certain, the being who bears that name is your ancestor, but neither he nor she nor it is at all like you."

18

Clouds pregnant with moisture had built over the eastern horizon while I lay fevered with visions in the grotto. The air was heavy and uncomfortably warm and carried the first grumbles of thunder. Teo waited in the courtyard as I returned to the keep long enough to don my Cavalieri disguise.

Teo's reassurance had to be enough. Placidio would have Neri back in the pit by now, and I needed to be there. By this time on the morrow, we needed a plan in place for returning our two captives unharmed . . . and unmarried. Yet Dono remained an enigma. Neither weather nor my horrors could be allowed to interfere.

"You'll stay close?" I said, ashamed of my collapse, as we hurried across the rocks and ruin toward Donato's hole.

"I cannot . . . *must* not . . . interfere in your ordinary magics in the way I did before. Until my preparation—my learning and all that it encompasses—is complete, such activities can leave me vulnerable. But in the matter of *your* vulnerability, my hand is at your service until you can hold on your own."

I wasn't sure that would ever be possible.

Teo inserted himself into a jumble of rock spires and fallen blocks of masonry where he could observe what was going on—with me in particular—while remaining out of sight to those below. I stood at the top of the rope ladder.

Neri lay unmoving in a bloody heap. Placidio had set Donato's provision bucket aside and was busy reattaching the shackle to Neri's ankle—without locking it, of course.

Donato stood at the limit of his own chain looking on, arms crossed as if observing the delivery of a new furnishing. "You're just going to leave him like that?"

"Looks worse'n it is." Placidio rose and nudged Neri with his boot. "He's a bleeder as well as a screamer. Jackleg like him don't need a nursemaid, but maybe he'll give a thought next time he flaps that sassy tongue."

"And doing this to your captives profits you in some way? Who'll pay for him now?"

Placidio grinned. Dumond's blood spatter had stained his teeth. "Sometimes the richest pay comes from putting down a frisky whelp like him. Might could come from doing the same to a rich boy thinks he's better'n everyone else." He spit on the ground in Donato's direction.

"If I'm damaged, my father will see the Cavalieri Teschio wiped out. Tell your master this is beyond lunacy."

"My master . . ." Placidio strolled slowly toward Donato. "Cavalieri got no masters. Even if we did, what would a *stronzo* like you know of them?"

Dono returned to the wall and sat. He glanced up to where I stood, took a deep breath, and again became a shapeless lump in a bedraggled shirt long past help from laundering. His bare feet were filthy; his face smudged; his abundant dark hair an oily mat.

Placidio looked up at me and shrugged, waiting for me to join him.

For a moment I held still, examining the scene, trying to explain to myself what I had just seen and heard. Truly, Donato was the strangest—no, the most complicated—person I'd ever observed. Why would he bait Placidio who, no matter threats and bombast, had fed him and otherwise done him no harm? He'd taken note of Neri's beating, but hadn't asked Placidio that he be cared for—

My gaze whipped back to Neri. The bucket with Donato's evening food and water sat abandoned where Placidio had set it aside. I knew he'd not meant to leave it there. Was it possible the *nothing* had just done a kindness?

Oh, smartly done, young man. And not so cold as you try to appear, providing your beaten cellmate with a drink and a bite. Subtle.

Yet I could not forget my guess about the post Donato would assume on the morrow—or whenever his life took up its assigned course. Defender of Truth. Slavemaster? Would he have ventured this little act of compassion had he known of Neri's gift?

And that consideration sent me into the fray angry. Perhaps not the best way to begin what was, after all, a negotiation. As Donato slept, or whatever it was he did, I waited for Placidio to join me. Our plan needed to change. No clever magics—but a different kind of shock.

"Are you sure?" said Placidio when I told him what I wanted. "No going back once it's done."

"There's nothing to go back to," I said. "We've gotten nowhere up to now. But there's a great deal more going on behind his shell than a scared Confraternity boy."

Placidio acknowledged the point and was off before I could blink.

Once down the ladder, I strolled over to Neri and bent over him, as if to make sure he was still breathing. Then I wandered over to stand just outside Donato's range of freedom—not that I expected violence from him, but then I was risking a lot on my sketchy interpretation of his character. I sat, trying to appear as if I was ready to wait him out.

A short time later, Placidio appeared on the rim just above Donato's position. He raised one hand. All was ready.

I began, "I think it is time for you to stop hiding from the world, Segno di Bastianni. Fail to do so on your own, and I'll set my brutish partner to whipping your bare feet until you acknowledge us. It's time you answered for crimes being done in your name."

Donato breathed a soft exhale. "You, who have wide experience in crimes, dare accuse me? My ears are open."

As were his eyes. Hands and voice seemed firmly under his control. Our position reminded me of Placidio opening a duel. Were we standing, we now should each make a bow and wait for the scarf to drop in between us. Instead, I began with a feint. "Tell me of your contracted bride, segno."

"My—?" I thought for a moment he was going to choke, something like when a horse takes off in a new direction and the rider is wholly unprepared. Or when the opposing duelist suddenly sheathes his blade and pulls out a bird.

"Discussing a virtuous lady with the agents of slavers seems inappropriate." A decent recovery for a student recitation.

Back to swords. "But setting her up to be accused of murder is gentlemanlike?"

"Murder?" He sat up straight.

Another feint. "Perhaps if you answer a few questions, it might set your mind to thinking instead of reciting your Confraternity lessons. Have you even met this virtuous lady?"

"Yes, certain. What murder?"

"Describe her appearance."

"So you can snatch her, too?"

Well done, Dono. Respond to an attack with an attack.

My turn again. "Answer my questions—"

"—or I'll end up like that fellow over there? Excuse me, but tell me the reason for all this or I'll waste no more breath, no matter your crude threats."

He was certainly engaged. And not terrified. That was good. Our purpose, after all, was to persuade him to forgo the marriage, not leave him a bloody wreck. My submerged anger suggested that might come after.

"Young man with all the blood," I said, "will you please demonstrate that all is not as it seems . . . uh . . . with your state of health?" I daren't have Neri misconstrue my meaning and vanish. "Then you can make free of the provisions in the bucket that was *inadvertently* left beside you."

"Certain. Best pleasure I'll have had in a while."

While Neri's shackle clinked behind me, I kept my eyes on our quarry. Donato's lips parted, and his eyes locked to Neri. On my periphery Neri's bloody shirt flew into the air and settled to the broken flagstones.

"You were a spy after all!" Donato shook his head in disgust. "Who are you people? *Not* the Cavalieri Teschio, but amateurs who didn't even notice that Cavalieri emblems are most often on the left side of the tunic—not centered."

Night Eternal! How did a Confraternity man who'd never been anywhere know that? We would revisit that question later.

"Expound upon your lady's virtues, and I will enlighten you as to both actual and possible murders, and the reasons we asked this stalwart young man to spend some time with you."

"This makes no sense. Why are you even interested in her? Why are you interested in my opinions? My family will either pay the ransom or hound you to your hanging. Perhaps both."

"Because if this is to be my last adventure, I would like to understand the people involved. You've nothing more pressing to do, am I correct? You have a mind. Presumably you bring it out for exercise now and then. And you have matters to answer for. Since I am interested and available, I must task you with thinking."

Our flurry of attacks and parries felt like a testing round, as my swordmaster referred to such back-and-forth with no intent to wound.

"You don't even sound like a Skull Knight," he said, his gaze firmly fixed in the area of his feet.

"How would you know that?"

"I—have heard. Everyone's heard. Brutes. Ignorant. Not conversational."

"Masks hide all sorts of things. But then, you know that very well, having used one—a very odd one—for much of your life. Tell me of your unfortunate bride."

"If the unfortunate circumstance you refer to is that ours will be a contracted marriage, that is *good* fortune, not ill. Certainly not murderous." The note of impatience was rewarding. A true reaction, not playacting. "The lady's parents and my own believe that a joining of our two families will benefit all. The practice is not uncommon among families of influence."

"So she is deemed suitable for a man of your breeding and position in life, a man soon to be granted the red—the mark of a philosophist—and a responsible appointment in the noble Confraternity."

My verbal sword must have pricked him. *This* parry required a moment's thought.

"Certain, she is—suitable," he said, not so smoothly. "Educated. Healthy. Of excellent family."

"Educated! How modern of your family to embrace that. What are her intellectual interests?"

His gaze lifted. His lips parted. But the world waited one moment and then another. Good. I wanted him to work at this. Thunder rumbled more forcefully. The sun slid behind a canopy of gray.

"Travel," he said at last, examining the rope ladder as if analyzing its construction. "I understand she has seen a great deal of the world, which I have not."

But my press did not slow. "Will she teach your children of what she has observed on her travels?"

"I—I deem"—only a slight stumble—"that to speak of children

before we are wed is presumptuous. And a matter of privacy. But of course, if we are so gifted, we would share in the education of our children." Back to Confraternity rote.

"Very delicate of you." I leaned forward as if to whisper secrets, yet I continued to speak so that those observing the conversation from the rim of the cellar might hear. "To assure that gift, you might have to alter your habits of retreat both before and after the child's arrival. Quite an adjustment for a *tartaruga*."

The clouded evening light was quite sufficient to see the childhood insult drive the color from Donato's complexion.

The testing round was over. Any attack was a gamble, yet I had to believe that he was more than the facade he had constructed, else there was no hope of persuasion. It was time for thrust and slash.

"I'm delighted to hear that you would share in the blessed children's enlightenment. Would you teach them of their mother's friend, the bookbinder and pamphleteer, who was brutally murdered on the eve of your betrothal and slandered with the labels *unholy* and *blasphemous*? And if your bride were captive here alongside you, would you be so certain that your father would pay her ransom as you are that your own will be paid? Or might *that* ransom demand get lost along the way and conveniently leave you a grieving widower before you are even a bridegroom?"

He leapt to his feet and shouted, "Who *are* you?"

"Tell me why your father picked Livia di Nardo to wed his dull, retiring eldest son. If she was not born yet, then how could it be because of her health and education? Perhaps it was all family connection, linking the Confraternity with the steward of Cantagna. Quite opportunistic. Then again, now that I consider it, two-and-twenty years ago Piero di Nardo had only been steward for two years. No one yet understood what honor he would bring to his office or what a force for reason he would become in our city."

Bewilderment had replaced dismay on Donato's well-proportioned face.

I could not relent. "But then, perhaps you could tell me why your prospective father-in-law cannot quite recall the day he signed that contract, and why it refers to younger Bastianni brothers who were not yet born, rather than ensuring such a fortunate merging of families with some living male of House Bastianni.

I've sent an inquiry, seeking to learn who witnessed the document when you were but a babe-in-arms and your bride-to-be not yet born. Will I discover that those witnesses are dead? Or happen to be loyal Confraternity brethren presently residing in Paolin or Empyria?"

"This is slander . . . gossip . . . unrighteous." Dono struggled to find his voice. "I know naught of bookbinders or murder. Nothing of the contract but what I was told. And naturally, the ransom— The lady was in our custod—in our care. My family would take responsibility."

With every phrase, he took a step away from me. I did not want him to get so far as the wall, where he would slide down and back into his stupor. I raised two fingers, signaling to Placidio that it was time to engage our next weapon. Then I thrust again.

"Surely your father informs you of matters that so profoundly affect your future. Tell me of your bride, Donato. Why would she believe your father would prefer her lost to slavers than in your bed?"

"You don't know that. How could you possibly guess at my father's reasoning or know what the woman thinks? She speaks of lands I will never see and people I will never meet, yet she is a child. She writes of fish skeletons and rock strata, yet there are truths in this world—"

He cut himself off, scraping his fingers through his matted hair.

So he *had* read her work. Though curious, I dared not relent. "Do you ever think beyond yourself, Donato? Have you done so even once since Guillam died?"

And here did my slash go wide of the mark. He charged to the full extent of the chain, his pleasant features a knot of rage. "You know nothing of Guillam di Fere, the insufferable little prick. No one ever knew the truth of him. No one would believe ill of him except those who suffered under his unceasing foulness. It's no one's fault who they were born."

An ironic claim for one who mutilated sorcerers, but I wasn't ready to let him know I suspected where his future lay within the Confraternity. "Did a youth of sixteen deserve to die for a schoolboy fight? Or did he suffer worse than death?"

Then did I fear I'd gone too far, for rage, bewilderment, and every other scrap of human feeling vanished from Donato's body. He pivoted sharply and dragged his chain toward the wall.

Thank Lady Fortune that Livia jumped down from the last rung of the rope ladder just then. She came to stand beside me, regal in her dusty white bedgown and crowned with an exuberant whorl of red curls. Placidio, who had climbed down after her, joined Neri behind me.

"Fortune's benefice, Segno di Bastianni," Livia said to Donato's back. "It seems we are both embroiled in a great deception."

He swung around as if the distant lightning had struck him.

"Child as I am," she continued with a bitter edge, "I've not yet unraveled all this. This morning I had come to the conclusion that this farce we find ourselves party to was your family's work. But like you, I have been played. Tell me, Dono, what do you make of these Skull Knights?"

Her glance in my direction had an edge so keen, a noonday sun would likely have set it glittering.

It took Donato a moment to comprehend her presence. Her disarray. Her feet, bare and filthy. "They abducted you, too, these impostors? From your bed in the villa? Brought you to this awful place?"

"I would have preferred a setting more lively," said Livia, cold as a frost moon. "Yet if this were a masquerade of my devising and I'd known *you* were to be a part of it, I would have chosen the Dungeons of Kulbaer, barren isles northerly of Eide, the coldest, bleakest pits of iron and cruelty in all the known world. The tides leak into the cells and it is impossible to keep one's feet from rotting in the cold, salty damp."

She stepped closer, as if daring Donato to challenge her.

"Marsilia di Bianchi was her name. She produced books of poetry, histories, pamphlets containing essays by the brightest philosophers of this bright era. She did it for love of the word. Of the mind. Of *truth*. And because of one five-page treatise on what an observant girl with a decent mind noticed on her travels, she had to be slaughtered in her home?"

"I do not condone murder, even for serious matters. This woman"—he jerked his head at me—"whoever she is, mentioned blasphemy which can endanger us all, but I—I've no idea what that might mean in this case. My responsibilities lie elsewhere, and I cannot live normally or keep straight ordinary matters."

He was trying, at least. He rubbed his forehead and began

again. "The Philosophic Confraternity has taken on the responsibility for the world's safety. I am committed entirely to that work. My own . . . ineptitude . . . with words and people cannot convey the seriousness of my belief. Sometimes, it's true, our work is tainted . . . mistakes . . . overreaching . . . even wrong, but we cannot, dare not, relent."

In essence he repeated standard Confraternity preachings against sorcery. Yet I'd never heard them delivered with such raw sincerity or any admission of mistakes.

One would have thought he had just ascended a mountain. Perhaps he had. He was trembling. Pale. Exhausted. Harrowed. In any other circumstance, he would surely have closed his eyes and left, as Livia described it. What had convinced him that even while marching forward in the beliefs he had been taught, he had to create a way to abandon his own life so completely? Against all expectation, I was fascinated. Frustrated, too, at my inability to decide where to go next.

As I dithered, Livia shifted her attention to me. "What is the purpose of this farce? Did I need to be snatched from my bed, dragged here in my undergarments, starved, and deceived only to stand here and hear more Confraternity babble?"

"Damizella, do you wish to marry this man?" I snapped. "You told a young friend of mine that you had *reasons* for acceptance of this marriage, despite your—despite an outlandish contract you'd no reason to approve." Spirits, I'd come near revealing she had expressed her disdain for it, but I'd no idea whether she had mentioned her desires to anyone save her *vicino-padre*.

"*Wish* to?" She sneered. "I would sooner wed a *tartaruga*. Yes, I had resigned myself to it, before . . . these events. Before I knew of murder and betrayal. *Will* I do it? Get me out of this place and ask me again. Oh yes, and tell me that my answer will carry any weight whatsoever."

She could be no clearer.

"Segno, do you *wish* to marry this woman who despises you and everything you stand for? Would you force her to marry into a family she believes murdered her friend and wishes her—under your name—either dead or forever silenced about the things she learns?"

"I am a loyal s-son." He could almost not speak for the shaking.

"I have d-duties that others cannot— I bear you no ill will, Damizella Livia, but your theories are wrong and dangerous. Believe me. Please."

"But your father commands we wed. And you, of course, do whatever your father commands."

"You know nothing of my father," snapped Donato, roused to some semblance of life.

"And I *wish* to know noth—"

"Ware!" snapped Placido. "Set him loose." He tossed Neri a ring of keys, sped to the rope ladder, and scrambled up deftly as a spider.

"Is this more playacting?" said Livia, shaking off my grip.

"No," I said. "Something's coming. Danger. *Real* danger." Something Placido's magic had warned of.

I reasserted my hold and shoved Livia into the corner farthest from the ladder. Banked by rock spires and dry cedars, it was the dimmest corner in the gray evening light. I drew my own short sword.

Neri got Donato's shackle off and herded him into the corner alongside Livia. I tossed him my pearl-handled dagger. He caught it with his left hand, unable to hide a grimace and a clutch at his wounded shoulder.

"Get behind these two and stay low," I said. "Out of sight."

Holding my sword at ready, I set myself in front of the three— and hoped Livia wouldn't try to strangle me.

Placido approached the rim. I could feel his listening. Carefully, silently he reached over the rim and gripped Dumond's well-set spike with one hand, drawing his main gauche with the other. He was ready to heave himself up, roll over the rim, and strike all at one. I'd never managed to get even halfway through that move.

But the next movement occurred halfway round the cellar, where a black-clad figure emerged from the stand of cedars from which I'd observed Dono and Neri the previous night. The newcomer, a man roughly the size of a gate tower, had Dumond wrapped in his arms. Blood smeared our partner's face and shirt.

"You fellow with the pigsticker, back down that ladder lest we send your friend here down to join the rest of you—head first." His gravel voice grated on the quiet evening.

Worse, a companion appeared and dragged his own dagger's point across Dumond's cheek.

Worse yet, their black capes, tunics, and hoods were blazoned with white skulls.

19

One by one, like crows landing on a rooftop, five more of the Cavalieri Teschio appeared around the rim. The last one—of slighter build, but greater swagger than the rest—squatted at the top of the ladder, as close to our shady corner as the rugged landscape allowed. None of them should be able to see Neri crouched between Donato and Livia and the wall.

"Look who we have here, good comrades. I do believe our luck has changed." A woman, then. And one with a bitter edge. She jerked her thumb at the helpless Dumond. "Bind this one securely, whilst we disarm the little piggies down in the sty."

Placidio dropped from the ladder and joined us. His back to the center of the cellar, he spread his arms slightly, his cloak and body hiding us from the observers. He nodded when he spotted Neri. "Be ready to walk, lad," he whispered. "I'll shield you."

Neri's magic could get him out of the damnable pit, but he had to be walking to trigger it.

"Who are these new people?" said Livia through clenched teeth. She stood at my shoulder. "Haven't we played your game long enough?"

"I'm not at all sure this woman sees hostages as valuable in their present situation," said Placidio quietly.

"You down there," called the woman. "Swordsman. Gather your party's weapons and tie them to this rope. Overlook even one, and your friend up here will be rolled over the side."

She cast our bucket rope over the rim.

Placidio collected my puny sword and my boot knife and added them to his dagger, his main gauche, boot knife, and the dull, elderly war sword he had carried here for show.

We needed a story, a plan. Of all things to be caught in our own prison. And Dumond . . .

A grim Placidio glanced up to the rim where Dumond's muffled struggle to avoid their ropes had come to naught. Our friend lay on his belly, his hands bound at his back. They shoved his balding head, his wide shoulders, and torso out beyond the rim, and a hooded cavalieré planted a foot on his backside.

Fear constricted my heart and breath. The pressure of that foot was the only thing that kept Dumond from plummeting, head-first, to the broken paving.

"This is madness," said Livia. "You're telling me *these* are the real—"

"The true Cavalieri Teschio," said Donato softly. "Vile. Despicable . . ." His arms wrapped his chest as if to keep his organs from flying out of it. His eyes were closed, but he did not sink to the ground.

"As if you would recognize vile and despicable," snapped Livia.

"Soft," I said, "else they'll hear everything you say."

We could not have these two fighting between themselves or persuading the real Cavalieri that they could collect our six-thousand silver solets if they just killed us and returned Dono and his bride to the Villa Giusti.

Placidio had returned to the ladder. He slowly twined a series of loops in the dangling ropes and inserted our weapons one by one. "Do you wish me to include the lady's hairpins, dama?" he yelled. "Or my bootnails? Scum like you might be taken down with the feather in my hat."

"Send up your blades, piggy," she said. "Then I'll come down and teach you who's scum. A jongleur's monkey, you are, imitating your betters."

"Ah, you're scared to face an impostor in a fair fight, then. Feared you might find the imitation better than the original?"

While they exchanged more boisterous insults, I pushed the seething Livia and trembling Donato deeper into the corner, to prevent the gathering Cavalieri from spotting Neri.

"Listen, quickly and carefully. We brought the two of you here to find some way to stop your marriage. This particular union creates a dangerous imbalance of power between the Confraternity and the city—and raises a risk to Livia's future."

I snapped a finger at Donato, whose mouth twisted, ready to contradict.

"Don't! I'll not debate this with either one of you until we have you safely away."

At the cavalieré's first jerk on the rope, all Placidio's knots came undone and dropped the weapons on the ground.

"All right, all right," he yelled, as the capo yelled and Dumond moaned. "I'll tie better knots."

I took advantage of the distraction. "Understand this: We contrived to make it seem as if your abductors were aided by sorcery. If the Cavalieri suffer for our contrivance, they fully deserve it. But in doing so, we've brought you two into a danger we did not intend." I had to make certain they understood. "Donato, if your director enforcer deems the Cavalieri tainted by sorcery, will the snatch-crew who returns you for ransom live to enjoy it?"

"No." His voice was scarce audible, but it displayed no uncertainty. "No one will survive that, except—"

"Except you!" Livia spat on his bare feet. "So I was right. About Marsilia. About your family's bloody intentions."

"Honestly, damize—L-Livia. On my word, worthless though you may deem it, I do not know. Never did I imagine— But I should have." He stumbled onward. "I just cannot— But there are good reasons. By wisdom's flame, let me—" His eyelids drooped.

"No!" I snapped. "You cannot *leave*, Dono. When these people try to persuade you that *they* are your salvation, you must not believe them. Yes, this is our fault, but *we* can get both of you out of this safely."

I hoped they were persuaded. My time was up.

The woman shouted orders.

One cavalieré started cautiously down the rope ladder; another hauled up the rope containing the last of our weapons.

Placidio hurried back to our corner. "Time to get the boy away."

He crowded up behind Livia and Donato, and then, billowing his cloak, he took off along the wall away from us and away from the Cavalieri gathered atop the ladder. From my vantage, Neri's bare feet were just visible below the hem of his cloak. No one above would see him. Walking, Neri could invoke his magic. . . .

I glanced at the other two. Livia was watching the big man with the graveled voice half climb, half slide down the ladder. He jumped off when little more than halfway down. Donato's eyes were closed, but his trembling had quieted and his fevered cheeks were pale again. Discipline. *Spirits.* I needed to learn that from him.

Placidio's cloak swirled as he reversed course and returned to us, wearing a smirk between his mask and his beard. Neri had vanished.

I laid my palm on my breast in thanks. One weight lifted, though I knew my brother was far from safe. I hoped Placidio had given him some kind of direction. He was one man alone with at least eight up top. Certain, there was Teo . . . yet Teo had warned me that he could no longer participate in our business. Of course I'd assumed that mortal danger would prove an exception to that, as it had earlier. Clearly not this time. He'd not rescued Dumond.

Something broke inside me at that realization. It was not my heart. I didn't love Teo, though I deemed him a friend. What fractured was my sense of Teo's place in the universe—a noble beauty that lay beyond the dirt and hardships of ordinary life. I had never believed in anything like that . . . until the first time he'd spoken in my head. *Not lead. Not dead. Name's Teo.* But he'd been told not to interfere, and he had obeyed.

Meanwhile Dumond kept lifting his head as if to look on friends, instead of his death waiting so far below, but clearly it was getting more difficult every time. If his captor moved his foot, even slightly, Dumond would die.

"Show yourselves, captives." The woman had slithered down the ladder to join the gravel-voiced man and the weedy third, whose exposed chin was riddled with the pustules of unwashed youth. She sauntered toward us. "Bagi, bring them out where we can get a look."

"Step out here, you two. Off with the hoods and masks." The gravel-voiced man yanked me from the sheltered corner and sent me stumbling toward the woman. Placidio followed before the man could touch him.

Bagi glared at Livia and Dono. "Where's the other one?"

"What other one?" I said. I hoped our captives understood their safety might depend on Neri staying free.

"There were five in the hole," Bagi snarled, stepping forward. "These two impostors. Three . . . guests."

Livia edged backward, startled to discover no one between her and the wall. Donato glanced around as well, casual as one might when looking for evidence one didn't expect to find, until, for a brief moment, his eyes met mine. Hard. Cold. He knew.

I should have taken on Nis or some other impersonation in our meetings, though even then Placidio and Dumond, now stripped of their disguises, and Neri would remain recognizable. How in the great universe were we to get free? Placidio trusted me to design a story.

"On the ground, you two, or I'll put you there." The gravel-voiced man was angry, and his sword waved tantalizingly out of Placidio's reach. "Where is he—the bloody one without a shirt? Any of you dogs up there see where the other fellow went?"

A few negatives. A few shrugs. No one else had noticed a fifth. Placidio and I exchanged looks of resignation, then got down on the ground.

"I know there was another when I first stepped out." Bagi's moustache was twitching with anger. "Check the walls, Moro. There must be a hole. Or a way to climb—"

"Which of you is capo of this crew?" It was Donato asking—and with startling sharpness.

"What do you care?" The brute plowed his boot into Placidio's ribs, then moved to examine the crumbling corner for himself.

Only I, lying two handspans away, could have heard Placidio's painful grunt. Only Dumond's situation, moments from death, kept Placidio from taking Bagi to the ground.

Dono halted Bagi with a firm hand. "Look at me, cavalieré, and answer my question. Which of you is the capo?"

Bagi's sneering gaze raked Donato. "What are you, boy, this bully's ass licker?"

Dono did not rise to the insult. "Have you not guessed who I am? Are you so ignorant as to misunderstand the respect due me? That's why you're not capo and likely never will be." He gave a knowing nod toward the woman.

"I *am* capo," said the woman. "But my *tenente* does nothing without my orders. You will answer him and obey."

"I speak with no one but the capo, and I will not be touched by hirelings. Nor shall my bride." One might imagine Dono wearing the red robe already instead of a filthy shirt that scarce reached his knees.

Bagi snickered, curling his lip. "Stick like her might not be much—"

"I have a word for your master, Capo." The brute might not have existed.

"My *master*? Why do you think I have a—? Ah, never mind," said the woman with a steely laugh. "I know exactly who you are and who this red-haired wench is. Every cavalieré still breathing in Cantagna knows—and that's not so many as of this evening. I doubt there's any word a soft boy like you could say would interest me lest it was accompanied by a thousand solets. I've heard you're an idiot afflicted by fits when anyone looks at him. If I scare you enough, will you show us one?"

"You would not care for my fits," said Donato, unruffled. "If you'll not heed my warnings, let me say the word aloud for all your crew to hear. Tell Giorgio the Hand—for no other capo's crews would have been sent on this search—*incrocio.* Tell him that, as of tomorrow, I shall hold his life in *my* hand. Your life will be there right beside his, Capo, assuming he doesn't cut your throat first for forcing me to speak what no hireling should hear."

Livia's eyes could not have been fixed tighter to Donato di Bastianni were a wire stretched between them. She appeared very near fainting from astonishment. I felt a bit light-headed myself to hear so many words—and such focused composure—from the strange young man.

But then the woman broke the spell, laughing with the manic ferocity of one being led to the gallows. "Oh, Segno di Bastianni, how the world has changed since you were snatched from it! As of *tomorrow,* Giorgio the Hand will be no more alive than he is on this night. The praetorians hanged and gutted him in the Piazza Livello this noonday for arranging the snatch of a Confraternity director's son and the daughter of Cantagna's steward. No sorcery was proved."

A Cavalieri capo had been executed for the abduction, but with no magic proved? That meant the philosophists simply wanted this Giorgio dead. Silenced. Yet they had shared a code word . . . why?

The capo stepped forward. Donato held his ground.

"Giorgio did not send us on any search before his guts spewed, boy child. The Cavalieri Teschio are no more. Our little cadre managed to escape the scouring and chose to wait out its spread in this cursed place. Though now it seems Lady Fortune's generous hand has tossed us a pip to make us grow again. I hear there's a reward of two thousand silver solets for capturing the crew that pulled off the snatch of the director's son."

Eyes glinting through her mask, the capo smiled down at me and stepped on my hand.

Pain shrieked through my arm.

"Atladu's divine balls, I'd like to know how you people did it— breaking into the Villa Giusti itself. Your father, young segno, put out that the two of you were out in the town when you were taken, so no one would imagine the Villa Giusti vulnerable to the likes of the Skull Knights. But Giorgio the Hand—when he sent word for us all to make a run for 'it—said he knew better. Street folks said 'twas magic done, while soldiers blame everyone but themselves for their failures. As I said, no sorcery was *proved*."

I forced myself not to upend her at just the proper angle as to break her ankle. *Oh, Dumond . . .*

The capo waved her hand around and nudged my mouth with her filthy boot. "Myself, I doubt the sorcery. What sorcerer would bring anyone to this cursed desolation? What sorcerer would have need of shackles or the broke-down horses we spied below? How the pesky philosophists found Giorgio, I've no notion. Old fool thought he was well hid and had the goods that would keep him alive. Clearly he wasn't and didn't."

I spat at her feet.

"Giorgio the Hand dead." Donato spoke the words as if he were examining them for subtle meanings. "Interesting. Are you certain of that?"

"I didn't witness it, but 'twas reliable sources. . . ." It was the first doubt I'd heard from the woman. And it was short-lived. "Someone else must interpret your code word—if it even has meaning any longer. I'm only questioning whether I might profit more by killing you and your bride and turning these three over to your father, or killing all five of you and saying we stumbled on you too late, thus saving him the trouble of gutting the impostors. Which would be better worth a free passage to Mercediare or Tibernia, do you think?"

Donato folded his arms across his chest, easy and proud as if

he'd never in the world had a shaking fit. "I will likely be looking for a replacement for Giorgio the Hand, if ever I get shed of
these villains. Capo, if you are so clever as to get yourself out of a
city that must surely be locked down tight . . . and to survive and
laugh at these inept players . . . you must have excellent skills. If
you were to get me, my bride, and my prisoners back to my home
in good health, I might be able to provide a future far more profit-
able than those you propose."

The woman tilted her head, doubt and suspicion sculpting her
face. "That sounds very convenient—for you. What if you decide
I've too little experience or my crew is too big or too small or too
stupid or too dirty to serve your needs? How easy it would be to
turn on us once you're comfortable again."

Dono dipped his head slightly. "I acknowledge the risk you
would take and am prepared to reward it with the ransom my
family is preparing to pay these imbeciles. Certain, I would be
placing my clear trust in you by putting my person and that of this
most valued lady in your hands. Thus"—he extended his hand—
"on my honor as a loyal son of the Philosophic Confraternity, if
we come to no permanent agreement, I shall provide free and safe
passage to the port of your choice for you and your crew, along
with the wherewithal to enjoy your travels."

Livia stepped forward, her complexion flared as red as her hair.

I hissed and pinched her foot. No doubt she wanted some say
before having her person placed in the hands of thugs, but Dono's
play might be her only way to safety.

Neither Donato nor the capo looked anywhere but at each other
as the woman considered his offer.

The last remnants of sunlight flared red through a breach in
the heavy clouds. With the same dramatic brilliance, Giorgio's silencing exposed a pattern linking the other bits and pieces. Dono
had wanted to send a message to this Giorgio the Hand. He had
also expected to gain responsibility over Giorgio and his under-
lings on his wedding day—when he assumed his new post in the
Confraternity. Giorgio had commanded the rest of the Cavalieri
to run, thus Giorgio had been one of its topmost leaders—and
the very one whom Dono believed would have dispatched this
woman's crew to search for us.

This strange young man, who had no skill with words or people, who had contorted his life to create a refuge from paralyzing fear, had evidenced a truth as astonishing as if the citizens of Cantagna had begun walking on their heads: The Confraternity and the Cavalieri Teschio were working together.

Were *the goods* Giorgio thought might keep him alive this very intersection—a crime of child-snatching that could indelibly taint the Confraternity? The selling of children. *Innocents,* Donato had said.

And then did full horror fall on me like the rivers of sewage that drained from the villa Giusti cesspool. Sniffers had always seemed to outnumber the arrests of sorcerers fit for future as a slave. What if the Cavalieri Teschio had been supplying youths—some stolen or perhaps bribed with a silver coin—to the Confraternity, and the Confraternity sorted through them, finding ones they could make into sniffers? Children with hidden magic, perhaps. Or maybe whatever gave sniffers abilities beyond ordinary magic could also make a sniffer from an innocent.

My every bone, every sinew, every droplet of my blood revolted, so that I almost missed the completion of Dono's pact with the remnants of the Cavalieri.

"You don't want these impostors dead?" said the capo. "Want to deal with them yourself, do you?" The capo's sly smile, grown throughout their exchange, now broke into a grin, as if the light of the world had not darkened to pitch.

"It will be a *great* pleasure," said Donato. "Have we an agreement, Capo . . . ?"

"Mannia," said the capo, clasping his wrist. "Sure we do. I'll gladly join in rites of vengeance. I've a great hunger for it just now. We flourished under Giorgio, till these folk interfered and set praetorian blades at our throats. What a fortunate meeting, this. Beyond every expectation."

"Capo Mannia." Dono's fingers closed around her wrist to seal the agreement. "You can start by binding these two and leaving them and their dangling third shackled to these walls while we share out their supplies and strategize our return to Cantagna. There's a storm rising, I've had no decent sleep in three days, and I've no wish to drag this lady onto the road on a stormy night. I shall dream tonight of exquisite revenge."

Mannia's humorless laugh bounced from every rock and tree.

"A fine plan. My cadre have been on the run three days now, scarce a moment for a bite or a sip. With the stores we've found here, we can have a proper celebration. One that's fitting for a fine-looking, privileged young gentleman of the Confraternity and his virgin bride. My people have need for some fun."

"Don't trust—" The brute kicked me in the side, silencing my warning.

Dono didn't even turn his head. Spirits, how could the young fool trust this Mannia? Her every word oozed with spite.

As the bearish *tenente* and his pustule-afflicted henchman fetched the coil of rope a comrade threw down, Donato took Livia's hand and bowed. "Gentle lady, will you accompany me to this celebration and a sleep in whatever comfort these rogues have allotted themselves while we were thrown into mole dens? Tomorrow I shall welcome you and your good father back to my house that we may fulfill his wish for our future."

"Anything to get out of here, segno," Livia said with a sickening sweetness. "We shall negotiate our *private* destiny later."

Only when Placidio and I were securely bound and shackled to the spikes in the wall did they at last drag Dumond back from the brink. Scarce able to squirm, my mouth full of dirt and filth, I twisted around to watch as they tied his hands to the bucket rope, and lowered that gentle man toward the floor. Before his feet could touch, they cut the rope. He dropped to the ground and the rope fell on his head. Not once did Dumond move on his own.

"Old man," I called. "Old man, are you all right? Let us know you breathe."

"Silence, impostors!" At least we knew exactly where Bagi, the gravel-voiced giant, was posted up on the rim. His blotchy companion dragged Dumond to the spike across the cellar from us and tied the bucket rope to it, then climbed back out and pulled up the rope ladder.

Dumond didn't answer. Didn't move.

Tears welled in my eyes with a vision of four clever, dark-eyed girls and their dear mother lost in grieving. If that vision came to pass, I would never forgive Teo. Somewhere between the marvels of his magic and the strength and quickness of his body, he surely could have found a way to save Dumond without compromising . . . whatever he was concerned about. Especially if he and

Neri worked together. Even injured, my brother was clever and skilled, and he would never let Dumond die if only he had a bit of help.

As darkness slid over the cellar, I felt movement from behind. The quiet rattle of a chain. A great deal of soft cursing, which roused more annoyance from above.

When all fell quiet again, a finger touched mine behind my back. Then came the whisper. "Think carefully, lady scribe. He didn't give up Neri."

He. Donato. What in the Night Eternal was he doing? Easy to imagine that he was, himself, an agent. But I knew that was a wishing dream. There had been no compromise when he met my gaze after Neri vanished. He knew we had used magic. He believed magic was the taint of Dragonis. And no believer was ever going to set us free.

20

An hour passed. Another. Neri would come—unless they'd caught him. It made sense for him to wait and let our captors fall into carelessness or sleep, but it was wretchedly difficult to be patient. And Teo was somewhere up there, too. Not interfering.

Under cover of the pitch-black night, Placidio picked at the ropes binding my hands, and I his, but the Cavalieri were clearly expert with ropes and knots. I dared not speak. Someone could be listening. Placidio must have felt the same.

For a brief time, the sky cleared enough to allow moonlight into the pit. Dumond must have put up a hard fight while we played interrogators. He had not moved, nor was there any other sign that he yet lived. Then clouds boiled over the moon and released the promised rain.

Rest became impossible. The repeated cycling of deluge, respite, and brief bursts of moonlight until thunder signaled another onslaught brought the chill that came with being soaked to the skin on an autumn night. Meanwhile, the mystery of Donato di Bastianni plagued me. I tried twisting the bits of the mosaic into different relationships, different meanings. But no matter how I tried to reinterpret what he'd said, the result came down to the same.

An alliance that no one in the Costa Drago would accept: a respected institution had conspired with a gang of street rats to enslave innocent children.

A possibility that no one in the Costa Drago would believe: Sniffers were not always condemned sorcerers.

And a young man, one who professed a sincere belief in the strictest dictates of his family, had exposed that family's horrific crime in front of us.

Was Donato so certain we would die with that secret? Though

he had most assuredly saved our lives for the moment, his agreement with Capo Mannia might raise the Cavelieri from the grave under another name and restart their unholy business.

Left in my hand was the piece that did not fit. Donato and Neri. Donato had distracted Placidio, leaving the supposedly starving Neri a bucket of food, and, knowing that sorcery was the only true explanation for Neri's disappearance, he'd not exposed us as sorcerers to the Cavalieri.

Certain, there remained his personal oddities that my speculations could not quite explain. His difficulty with people and words. The personal discipline that had started so young. The shaking fits that appeared to drive him to it. Was it dreams of innocents being mutilated, inked with red mouths, and sheathed in silk that plagued him? Certain, that was fodder enough for nightmares if one had a remnant of a conscience.

I believed he did. He'd told Neri that his father was wicked. And when he claimed to know nothing of the bookbinder's murder, I had found him credible. He believed Livia naive.

Sandro had provided me books of natural philosophy and introduced me to several men and women who studied the movements of the heavens, the behavior of moving objects in relation to each other, and the marvels of systematic alchemy. All intelligent, rational people. All fervently searching for answers. It was the echoes of such fervor I had recognized both in Livia's writing and in the woman herself. She wasn't afraid of being wrong. Only of not looking deep enough.

Of course, if Teo was to be believed—if my dreams were what he said—then Livia was indeed wrong and Donato correct. *There are truths,* Donato had said, implying universal horrors ordinary people could not imagine. So what did Donato know? And how? Neri believed Donato's strange habits were how he kept his frights from making him into a lunatic. Dreams . . .

"Ssst."

I lifted my head from the wet dirt. Had the sound come from above the rim or inside our prison?

My fingers felt like sausages, my hands half numb from the tight, wet ropes. But I drew up my knees and dug my feet into the muddy paving and eased backward. The sodden bulk that was Placidio was still only a finger's breadth behind me. That was reassuring. Even more so when he bumped my back with his elbow—apurpose. So he wasn't asleep either.

The hiss was not Placidio's. I squinted into the pitchy black and blinked when I glimpsed a pale blur and a spark of blue fire inside a cavern of night.

My pulse raced and I struggled to sitting, nudging Placidio. I dared not name my hopes until the pale blur whisked my way, bringing the stink of overripe male and soft, raspy breathing. In moments my arms and hands were free and a familiar shape pressed into my fingers. A moment for the blood to return and I could feel my dagger's defining boundaries of pearl and sharpened steel. As the ghostly figure hovered over Placidio, I cut the ropes from my feet and knees, taking care not to rattle the chain. Had Neri remembered the shackles?

Even as my mind voiced the question, a hand pressed a key to my shoulder. I retrieved and used it without jangling, and passed it on to Placidio as soon as my foot slipped out. Free of aught that might make noise, I scurried toward the spot where I had seen the blue flame . . . and found a whiff of burnt rope and the cold, wet shape of a square-shouldered man. Sitting up.

No matter the necessity for speed and silence, I flung my arms around Dumond, pressing my head to his and fumbling around until I felt his cheek. He blew a long breath on my wrist, knowing exactly what I was asking, then gripped my hand and moved me away just far enough that I could give him leverage to stand. He held on to me for a moment, and then freed himself and patted my arm.

Soon Neri was back and guiding Dumond and me to the ladder he'd lowered for us. Even in the rain, my brother's hand felt dry and hot. Feverish? Or perhaps only my imagining of the fiery magic coursing through his veins. He pressed my hand to the rope, but held it still for a moment, hinting I should wait. Soon Placidio joined us. With a last squeeze of my hand, Neri's pale form vanished, his magic taking him back to wherever he'd come from.

Then it was Placidio's turn to use hand signals. He took one of my fingers and put it on his own forehead. Then he pressed two of my fingers on Dumond's cold cheek. Then three fingers on my own. In the ensuing pause, I assumed he did the same for Dumond. The order of our going.

Yet Placidio didn't ascend right away. Instead, as we stood at the base of the ladder in a steady drizzle, his finger tapped a regular, rhythmic pattern on my wrist. Counting, I thought. Perhaps he and Neri had set some timing interval. After a small eternity, the rain came down harder and he released my hand.

Ah, he'd been waiting for more noise to cover him. His dark bulk vanished upward into the timely downpour.

I might have actually heard Placidio's grab-the-spike-and-roll-over-the-rim-move or I might only have imagined it once a reasonable time had expired. But that's when I urged Dumond onto the ladder. I stayed close behind, unsure as to his condition. I encouraged but did not push. With the both of us on the ladder, I hoped his spikes were still well seated.

Someone gave Dumond a hand over the rim. I could feel the change in speed and weight ahead of me, but just as I reached the top, finding stone instead of another rope rung, something heavy crashed into the nearby brush. A body? Sticks broke; branches—cedar branches—scraped each other. I could smell them.

A storm of silent grunts, muffled yells, and pounding blows followed. A moan. One more blow. And then silence, save for hard breathing and the patter of the rain.

I grabbed for one of the spikes and did a less artful scramble over the rim than what Placidio had tried to teach me so many times. And less successful. One foot yet dangled over blackness, and my right hand could find no sure grip on slick stone.

My stomach lurched into my throat as my foot scrabbled for purchase.

When a hand grabbed my arm and hauled me over and up, my terror did not dissipate. It took a wet, bare, reassuring arm around my shoulder to soothe me. Evidently it had rained enough to clean my brother up a bit. His fevered hand had cooled.

After clinging to him longer than was necessary or appropriate for an elder sister who aspired to be mother, friend, partner, and sibling all at once, I let him go and followed the path into the trees until I found Dumond.

"To the keep," he whispered.

I squeezed his hand to reply, and then reached for Neri, but he was gone again.

Dumond and I crept onward as quickly as we could manage, using the lightning flickers and our extended hands to keep from running into sharp-edged rocks or impaling ourselves on dead tree limbs.

Another silent skirmish from the left paralyzed us with our backs to a scabby oak. An ugly gurgle ended the fight. We stumbled onward and were soon joined by Placidio. I felt almost whole again.

Patchy light ahead halted our steps. A flash of lightning gave us an instant's view. The keep, the chimney stack of the newer ruin that pointed skyward like a dead man's finger, the broken archways that led to the courtyard behind the keep. From that courtyard the stone stair descended to the grotto of the spring and Dumond's painted doorway. Escape.

The mottled light came from the inside the ancient keep. Torches burned inside the tower, the dancing light an invitation to good cheer. Though I couldn't make out the words, the walls rang with bouts of raucous laughter, bawdy singing, and the kind of boasting banter one might expect after a successful venture. The riot suggested the snatch-crew had brought a great deal of spirits to add to our flask of mead and short cask of ale. Some drunkards sounded jovial, some angry or belligerent.

Outside those bright openings in the walls, beyond the raucous noise, lay inky shadows that could harbor sentinels. A moment's stillness, listening through the patter of rain, and Placidio—who had the best hearing of us all—drew us away, back behind a standing wall. We crouched low so our voices wouldn't carry.

"Danger awaits at the keep. Don't know that I've ever felt the sense so strong or lasting," whispered Placidio. "It's more than just the capo. More than rowdy drunks. So we've decisions to make. Are you well, smith?"

"Can't run. Left fingers don't work right. Head will take some work to fix," said Dumond in a hoarse whisper. "But let me get to the grotto; I can get us out."

"Lady scribe?"

"My head is all my own," I said. "And you, swordsman?"

"Killed two vermin between the ladder and here. No choice in it." He was in no way apologetic.

"I want the Cavalieri dead," I said. "Every one of them. And every philosophist working with them. Though—"

"—we have yet to decipher our bridegroom," said Placidio. "He knows what we are, but didn't give Neri away. He's found himself and the girl a way home, but I'd not trust that Cavalieri vixen were she buried in a stone vault."

"I agree," I said. "So we need to get Dono and Livia away with us."

"Where's Neri?" said Dumond. "Would be nice to send him into the keep for a glimpse of what's doing there."

"He ran off as soon as he had me over the rim," I said.

Placidio hissed displeasure. "He'd best not be haring about. Before he came to us, the fool moved our weapons stash from the keep. They're stacked near one of the dead fellows under a fallen branch. Wouldn't have found them even then if he'd not left his luck charm on top of the stack where I couldn't miss it. By the time he set us loose, he felt fevered, so I told him to get back to the grotto and wait."

"So how do we fetch our bride and groom from yon beehive?" I said.

"We've plenty of arms, and you and me fit to wield them. But it sounds like more than three Cavalieri are left."

The rain had stopped and the moon sailed through the retreating clouds. I hated the rain, but the light had me nervy and imagining sentinels.

"There was at least ten of 'em to begin," said Dumond, grunting as he shifted position. "Two came up the path like they were lost . . . got me distracted . . . and then they pounced from everywhere at once, like a frenzy of scorpions. Maybe I damaged one. The world went blurry pretty fast. I know they posted watchers at the path so none of us would get away."

So at least seven left and we weren't sure how many were in the keep and how many lurking in the dark like we were. "So we need to wait until they all fall down drunk before we attack," I said.

"Dumond, you should get to the grotto," said Placidio. "See to Neri. Get a drink. Be rested and ready as they're like to be hot on our tail when we join you."

"Hate to desert my partners," he said. "Feel like the old man you named me. Would be nice if Teo could lend a hand."

"'Tis a difficult road Teo walks," said Placidio. "We must respect it."

"I look forward to hearing about that road someday," I said. "For now I'll do my best not to walk off any cliffs." I nudged Dumond. "Go on to the grotto. None can do what you can, and we want you seeing straight when you do it. After all, there's only seven give or take a few: one for me, the rest for Placidio. I think we'll do fine."

Dumond laid a hand on each of us. "Thank you for behaving yourselves for the Skull Knights. Knew you would . . . but after that hour, I can tell you exactly how deep is the Great Abyss, and I could draw the likenesses of each of the *daemoni discordia*. I'll get you out of here. If they've left the horses alive, we'll be home before morning."

Placidio and I retreated to visit the arms cache he'd found. Clever of Neri to get them out before the Cavalieri got their hands on them. Yet it left me curious. Down in the pit Neri had brought us the same poor-quality blades the Cavalieri had stripped off us.

"If Neri had already carried *all* of our weapons out here, why didn't he bring one of these better swords to you in the pit instead of this relic you've got on?" I said. "Here's your *spada de lato*, your poignard, and Livia's Lhampuri recurve dagger, all better for fighting and hiding."

"Sometimes there's no understanding how the lad's mind works," said Placidio. "Though it's generally in the right direction, the steps are no better ordered than the path of a water beetle."

At least he'd brought belts and sheaths, too. I'd just buckled on the Lhampuri dagger when a woman's shrill scream split the night, quickly followed by a man's. A whip cracked, releasing a round of whoops and jeers.

But the jeers were quickly silenced by a ferocious, exultant bellowing. Loud enough to crumble the stone, its brazen malice scraping my bones.

"Damnation," breathed Placidio. "Who is that?"

We raced through the skeletal wood, dropping any weapons we could not wield immediately. New shouts and screaming grew into pandemonium.

Two Cavalieri darted through the open ruin toward the keep just as we arrived. They halted abruptly when they spotted us in the mottled moonlight. Placidio, sword in one hand, main gauche in the other, never slowed, engaging the larger man at full speed.

The force of his rush pushed the skull knight back two body lengths. My own swordwork was still that of a beginner, thus my primary duty was to taunt, engage, break off, and delay until someone better could take on my opponent. That I did.

The lanky young cavalieré must have had fewer hours of practice than I'd suffered in my first month with Placidio. I gave him a lesson in feint high, strike low, and was going in for a second strike when Placidio slammed his fist into his opponent's jaw and laid him out flat. Almost without pause, he kicked my fellow's backside, staggering him so I could bring my sword hilt to his temple. The scrawny Skull Knight collapsed.

"Round to the courtyard," Placidio whispered. "I'll finish these two."

I did not ask if he planned to kill them. My conscience had no room for Cavalieri.

The din from the keep had lessened in volume, but was no less horrific. Wails of madness, groans of agony, growls of fury. One cry might have been Livia's but I couldn't swear to it.

I raced around through the courtyard, seeing no signs that the mayhem had spread down the grotto stair. Instead, the mayhem was in the yard itself. Gravel-voiced Bagi and his youthful assistant sprawled on the broken flagstones, almost floating in a lake of dark blood. Both bodies were riddled with deep gashes. Entrails floated loose beside each slashed belly. Their positions . . . the fouled weapons . . . the absence of any bloody footprints beyond them testified that they had slaughtered each other.

As I throttled my urge to vomit, Placidio rejoined me.

Abruptly, a last shout from the keep broke off.

In the sudden quiet, Placidio pressed me to a broken column, then crept to the doorway and peeked inside. Pulling back quickly, he beckoned me to his side.

The display of blood and hacked limbs beyond that doorway was straight out of my nightmares. Six lay dead inside, the count only possible because human bodies possessed only a single head. Livia, her body rigid with terror, stood with her back to a wall, fists clutched to her ears. Remnants of rope dangled from her neck and wrists. Her bedgown was missing; her chemise splattered with blood. Impossible to say if it was hers.

Donato stood in the middle of the room, arms extended to either side, fingers spread, as he glared at the only two living Cavalieri. Each of them—the capo, Mannia, and a craggy woman whose jawbone could have sliced bread—held a sword at the ready. Both faces were twisted in hatred, yet neither of them moved until Dono twitched one finger of each hand. They screamed in mindless rage as they attacked—not Dono, but each other. Viciously, crudely, in wild madness, rather than anger or calculation or mastery.

"Stop this," shouted Placidio. "Lay down your weapons. Donato, what's going on here?"

The women paid no heed. As they destroyed each other, our one-time captive pivoted to look at us. A knife gash creased one of his cheeks, but even as we watched, the trickle of blood slowed and the skin knit itself together.

"I am sorting," said Donato, his voice lower and smoother than his usual, as if he were commenting on a display of shoes. "The one there"—he pointed to Livia without looking at her—"shines. She does not bear the flame of eternity, and her physical being is unexceptional. Yet her every word shimmers like the stars of the Wain in the long night. She could amuse me for a generation. These other creatures sanctioned brutish cruelty aimed at her. Even so, I offered forgiveness to those who erred, telling them that one of their number might prove worthy of my favor. But you see what they've done? Turned on each other, as is so often the way of humans."

"This is not Donato," I whispered into Placidio's shoulder, choked with fear. I recognized that voice and knew, at last, why Donato di Bastianni feared his dreams, and his anger, and his life.

Donato leaned sidewise to peer around Placidio, and when he spotted me his pleasant face, so often expressionless, was transformed by a radiant smile. Gold fire sparked in his dark eyes. "Oh, my lovely! How is it we meet here on this plane?"

How in all understanding had Donato encountered the Enemy? And what were we to do? Knock him senseless? Chain him? Then again . . .

For the first time since the rain had begun, I felt warm inside. We oughtn't harm Donato . . . or the one devouring me with Donato's eyes. Mayhap I could persuade him to leave the dull, incurious human. He treasured me.

"Come, my lovely," he said, extending a bloody hand in my

direction. "Shall we take our pleasure in these forms? A prelude to the music we can make as our true beings? We can explore this world . . . and other worlds . . . together."

No Moon House instructor could have prepared me for the heat that bathed every part of me. How sweet those lips would be. Those wondrous hands. Somewhere behind that mask of ordinary flesh was the one who had touched my hair. What was it I'd thought to beg of him?

Hands gripped my shoulders from behind. Not the hands I wanted. I tried to brush them off, but I might as well have swatted brick or stone. They drew me away from the doorway and into the courtyard.

"Friend Romy, turn around and look at me," said the voice at my ear. Not Placidio's voice. "Do not give him your hand. Do not invite that voice inside you. We need all the water we can bring to cool young Donato. Can you help with that?"

I dragged my eyes from the extraordinary Donato and the charnel pit at his feet. The hands of stone released my shoulders so I could turn around, but they didn't move far.

I squinted. "Teo?"

21

Ssshh. I beg you don't speak that name so near him. Nor say nor think anything about me. If you must have a name, call me visitor."

"Visitor." I blinked, fighting to see in the darkness behind me. I couldn't make out anything. The gold in those eyes had been so bright, far brighter than the flickering torchlight in the keep.

"It's so hard to see in the dark," I said. Hard to think, too. Curses, cries, and the clash of steel spilled from the keep doorway. Placidio blocked the doorway behind me, sword drawn.

"Certain, that's true. But only for the moment. Remember what we spoke of earlier. Feel only what your own senses tell you. Keep aware of—"

"—my true surroundings," I said, parroting the echo of a distant conversation. "My own voice must command my actions." Mine, not that teasing, tempting sweetness.

"Feel the moisture in the air, Romy. Hear the roll of thunder, the lingering drops from the trees and bricks. Smell the wet cedars. See the moon that, for the moment, has triumphed over the clouds."

I did exactly that . . . and shuddered at how easily I'd been lured away from myself. I'd not been using magic at all!

"Spirits . . . visitor! What do we do about Donato?" And Livia, trapped inside the keep with that monster.

Teo drew me farther from the doorway and pointed to the grotto stair. "Earlier today, we moved all your extra buckets and waterskins, flasks and pots down to the grotto. Fill them. Bring them. To keep your charge alive and whole, we must cool him down with flowing water. Alas that the rain has stopped."

Blinking again, I met Teo's gaze—swimming with blues and greens and all those hues I could not name. "Water. Yes. How is this possible? By the Mother, did I do this to him?"

"His state is naught to do with you. Now go. If we're fortunate, cooling him will force the Enemy to retreat. If not—" The bleakness in his voice left no question.

"You'll kill him."

Teo's complexion was paler than the moon. "I see no other choice."

"No!"

That was not acceptable. *We* had brought Donato to this cursed place. Put him in a position that somehow led to this horror. What we had gleaned of his story—about Guillam and nightmares and sitting up to sleep and keeping himself apart—told me that this was rooted in his childhood. He had twisted his life to stay in control of himself. I couldn't explain how or why, but something dreadful had happened to him, and he did not deserve to be put down like a mad dog before he could explain.

I pushed at Teo's chest. "You told me once you were not meant for killing. When you strangled the three bargemen who beat you and left you for dead in the river, you said it was a sign of weakness. A failure."

"I did not understand myself back then. We cannot loose the Enemy upon the world, and if this man's body is dead, the Enemy cannot work his will through him. I am not rea—"

"You're not ready for whatever your role in history is to be. Your safety is imperative, so you must not become entangled in human concerns. I can accept those things. But you also told me those months ago that you believed your duty was to protect the world from monsters. I don't know why Donato di Bastianni is afflicted, but he is a part of this world, too. Isn't it your duty, as a student of these matters, to understand what's happened to him?"

"Ah, my friend, certain, you are right, but you just—"

"You could have killed the assassin last spring—a soul-dead man who wanted me dead—but you chose mercy. Yes, he was human, but so is Donato." Teo could fight with strength and speed his slender frame did not suggest. His magic was beyond anything we knew. Surely he had knowledge to guide him.

He averted his gaze. "You don't know what you ask."

And then I drew my last weapon, unfair as it was. "You swore to me. I saved your life, and you swore to do whatever I ask of you until the end of days."

He blew a soft breath. "So I did."

He scanned the clearing skies above us. Held out his hand as if to feel the air. Closed his eyes and wrestled with himself.

"There might be a way, though it would not be without consequence. Just . . . be armed and prepared, both of you." He glanced
at Placidio, who was listening from a few steps away—between
me and the doorway to the keep. "Macheon must not move into
any other person."

"I'll keep the fiend distracted." Placidio patted his swordbelt.

"Now, my friend," said Teo to me, "fetch water, as much and as
fast as you can."

A last glance through the keep doorway showed that Donato's attention had reverted to Capo Mannia. The cavaliera, fallen
to her knees, stared at the slash in her thigh where her remaining
life gushed onto the floor. As the light in Mannia's face dimmed
and she toppled, her steel-jawed opponent collapsed as well. Dono
knelt beside them and laid a gentle hand on each head. "Alas for
such sturdy, capable women. I asked only that they prove themselves worthy to remain in this beauteous world. This was all they
could think to do."

I backed toward the stair, my body sluggish, my feet leaden.
The fingers of desire teased at my breast.

No, no, no. Turning away, I blocked the sound of him, focusing
instead on the paving under my feet, the black hole of the stair
across the courtyard, and Teo's quiet commentary behind me.

"Swordsman, you must force him to take up a sword. It will
connect him with the physical world which is Donato's. Don't fear
to wound him, but don't get too close. If you can, draw him outdoors. Just occupy him while Romy brings the water, and I prepare. I am still so very slow. She must pour it or throw it on him as
we did with her. As much as they can bring . . ."

Every step toward the stair cleared my head, and soon I was
running.

Donato laughed and called after me. "Come, my lovely, don't
make me settle for the shining clot of clay. Your spirit longs for me."

I was halfway down the stair, feeling my way in the dark, en-
visioning the turns I had climbed half a day ago. Macheon the
Enemy—Dragonis—was here inside Donato di Bastianni. And
Teo had said he was not ready to face it. And I had forced Teo's
hand. . . .

Another turn and light gleamed from below. "We need water,"

I shouted, shoving aside insidious doubt. "Fill everything. Hurry. Hurry."

In moments, I joined Neri and Dumond, who began gathering and filling vessels scattered beside the spring.

"What's going? A fire?" Neri, his color much too high, worked with one hand fetching vessels. Dumond knelt at the verge of the deep clear pool, dipping each one and thrusting in stoppers or tying closures with fingers that were as much impediments as useful appendages.

"Something like," I said.

I hung straps over my shoulders, bales over my arms, and gathered flasks to my breast until I could carry no more. "Dono is possessed. The Enemy has him. Dragonis . . . Macheon. Teo says we need to douse him like they did me."

Too slow, too slow, I staggered upward. Around a bend. Into the darkness. I squeezed my eyes shut to force them to adjust. Onward through moonlight and shadow, past the dead men in their clotting lake. Just outside the keep, Teo had stripped off his shirt and slops and stood naked, face upturned to the boiling clouds that were once again swallowing the moon. His marks—many more than before—gleamed silver, almost like . . . scales.

From inside the keep, swords crashed.

"Again, Donato," yelled my swordmaster, exertion clear in his speaking. "Try that sequence a little slower to feel how the positions flow one to the other." A clash of weapons followed by a heavy grunt. "I know Confraternity youths are trained in swordplay. I was." Another clash. Another grunt. "It was my Academie years that proved I was unteachable in many areas. But the sword . . . that was my calling."

I paused in the doorway.

The steel rang out yet again. "You are"—Donato snarled and spun with a quick feint and slash—"a nothing."

Placidio blocked the move and darted to one side. They circled, stepping clear of bags, crates, and corpses. Livia huddled to the wall, arms covering her head.

"I've other things to be about," spat Donato. "Pick up a sword, young woman of the shining intellect. *You* can fight this annoying gentleman. Men don't understand how much you disdain them."

Placidio attacked, keeping Donato's attention on himself.

"Come to me. For Marsilia," I yelled, choosing a name Livia might heed. "For your father. For all of us. Help me put an end to this."

I set down the flasks, buckets, and skins, ready to fetch her and force her to act, but after a shuddering breath, she clambered round the perimeter of the tower. She climbed over the chests and bags rather than taking a shorter route through the splashed blood or nearer the duelists.

Placidio taunted and darted away from the doorway where I waited for her.

Indeed, to get in the way of the battle, defenseless, would be a mortal mistake. Placidio was clearly the more accomplished duelist, but Donato's strength—the Enemy's strength—was wearing on him. Few of Donato's blows landed, but those that did were punishing.

"We need to cool down Dono," I said softly, when Livia reached my side. "Get as close as you dare and throw water on him, as if he were a blaze destroying your home. It's the only way to weaken him just now. Do it and don't ask why." Not that I could tell her.

It was a measure of the fracturing this night had wrought on Livia's certainties that she did not argue or question such mad instruction. She simply grabbed a bucket.

It was a pitiful battle we fought. No more than half the drops we dispensed reached Donato's body. The rest just made life more miserable for Placidio as the drying blood became puddles that muddled dismembered corpses with the supplies we'd left in the keep—blankets, bandages, linked sausages, bunches of grapes. In moments our buckets and flasks were empty.

"Another round," I said, and we gathered the emptied vessels. Livia followed me out of the keep. Fog drifted through the courtyard, hiding Teo and the carnage. Not daring to linger, we hurried down the stair.

Neri and Dumond had filled the remaining containers. Even Dumond's shirt had become a water bag, albeit a leaky one.

"I'll take these," I said to Livia. "You help them fill the rest, and then bring all you can carry. Flowing water is anathema to the thing that has Donato in thrall." Mages of fire, mages of water, as in Teo's story. "These actions, the words, the horrors . . . they're not of Donato's doing."

"He saved me," she said, her long face stricken with shame and guilt and terror. "How is that? All was well. He was playing *tartaruga,* as always. But as the brigands got drunker, they surrounded us, brandishing weapons, calling us fools and pigs, screaming that my father and the Confraternity were the very ones who had murdered their leaders and comrades and forced them to run. Then the woman captain, drunk as the rest, ordered them to tie us to the wall, lash us, and cut off our hands and ears. She would deliver them to our families herself as proper revenge."

A sob did not slow her tale. "They cheered and bound me, but Dono fought—throwing things at them. He moved impossibly fast. Weapons, flasks, stones, flew about the keep, but then this sorcery fell over him. He got loose of them and began . . . taunting . . . the Cavalieri to fight each other." Her voice trembled, teetering between lecturing and lunacy.

"Don't think of it now, Livia. His body is burning from the inside, and we're cooling him off. That's all."

Neri hunched over, coughing and clutching his shoulder. "I'll come . . . soon's I get over—" He broke into more horrid hacking.

"Nay, I need you here with me, lad, so's my door will be right ready when they come," said Dumond, laying a hand on Neri's heaving shoulder. "With only one working leg, half a hand, and eyes that see two of everything, I would be far more hindrance than help up there. And I need you to tell me which is the true and which the double of anything."

Neri couldn't get a breath to argue.

Grateful beyond words, I ran.

Placidio's back was pressed to the broken stair. Donato thrust, slashed, and whipped his blade with little precision, but the quickness of the blows required Placidio's every skill to counter, and their power shivered Placidio's arms.

"Look here. Confraternity boy!" he yelled. Every word grated as if passed through crushed glass. "Will you—allow—a pitiful drunk like me—to take you?" A few more blows and he'd be dead.

With a bucket and an uncorked waterskin, I crept up behind Donato and sluiced his back.

Snarling, he flailed at Placidio.

I doused his leg with the contents of the waterskin. Ducking, I snatched the poignard from my boot.

Donato spun to see where the water was coming from, ready
to swat me like a mosquito, I guessed. But I stayed low, moving
with him. I needed to slow him down. When the next attack from
Placidio drew his attention, I jabbed the well-honed poignard into
the back of his thigh.

With a growl of rage, Donato twisted around and raised
his sword. Livia flung Dumond's dripping shirt over his sword
hand and hurled an uncorked stone flask straight into his face. He
stumbled. Bellowing in pain and fury, he dropped the sword and
grabbed for the dagger in his thigh.

I scuttled away from his thrashing and grabbed more of Livia's
pots and botas, emptying them on his foot and ankle, anywhere I
could reach and escape before his fist could smack my head. Was it
imagining that his skin began to steam? Recalling what my friends
had done for me, I decided not.

Placidio retreated up the stair and raised his beloved *spada de
lato*, only to behold a jagged stub.

With a triumphant yowl, Donato yanked out the bloody poignard and launched it at him.

The stub was enough to bat the dagger aside.

"Swordmaster!" I yelled.

When Placidio's eyes flicked to me, I tossed him the arming
sword I'd drawn from my belt.

He grabbed it just in time to counter Donato's next hacking
blow.

Vessels empty, Livia and I backed toward the doorway. At
the same moment, Teo climbed through the broken south wall
of the keep. Changed.

His ink markings had blended together, gleaming as if he were
armored in a skin of engraved silver, even to the twining ring
about one eye. He seemed taller, slimmer, his fine-boned features
even more spare than those so familiar. His fair hair had become
a floating tangle of silver.

"*Paré*, Macheon! Begone! Leave this soul to its own life and return to your rightful dwelling." His voice thundered like the Falls
of Rodhlann, the birthplace of the Venia high in the mountains of
Argento.

Not only his voice recalled the wonder of Rodhlann. When Sandro took me to the falls to see the roots of his beloved city, I had never imagined anything so powerful or so lovely. The stepped cascades gleamed silver, blue, palest green, colors that shifted in the light of sun or moon or stars. But that luminous cataract would pale beside the radiance of a thousand hues that shone from Teo—masking the bloody horror of the keep with glory.

Donato peered closely, his forehead creased. Puzzled. "A Vodai Guardian! Here? But what *kind* are you . . . an initiate? Has the caste of the Great Fish become so degenerate it must send its roe into battle?"

"This is no battle, prisoner," said Teo. "You stand not on your own feet, but on those of stolen flesh. No Guardian would desert the Timeless Watch to shoo a fly. I've come only to cleanse the ground poisoned by your foul burning."

Teo . . . or whoever he was . . . spread his legs and raised his spread arms skyward, as he had done those months ago on the docks of Cantagna. *"Me to dóro pou mou édose, Theíko Patéra, kathariste aftó to dilitiriasméno chóma."*

The words rang like Cantagna's bells in times of celebration, when their tuning and sequence and joyous exuberance could swell the heart. As to their meaning: I recognized the initial phrase, *by the gift granted me,* as it was the beginning of every signature on Typhonese artwork—a humble acknowledgment that talent was the gift of the gods or the universe and not the artist's own doing. And Teo had long acknowledged that *Theíko Patéra,* the divine father invoked in his first cry for help those months ago, was the Lord of Sea and Sky we named Atladu. Of the rest—well, he had already spoken his objective. Cleansing.

Bellowing in rage, Donato slashed at Teo. Sparks glanced off the silver armor once and then again. But as Donato kept up his attack, dancing around the motionless Teo, one strike and then another that could dismember a human body left thin lines of blood in the silver. The next left a deeper stripe across Teo's back.

Teo did not falter.

Donato laughed and slashed again. Only this time, his sword met steel—the Tibernian arming sword in Placidio's hand. The moment's respite had given my swordmaster new legs . . . or perhaps it was the rising wind or the first rain shower of a new storm that blew through every hole in the old keep's thick walls—no matter whether it faced east or west, north or south. A freshet poured through the broken roof.

The duel shifted away from Teo and then close again. Still he held position. The rain washed his blood from a dozen cuts.

A drenched Donato howled and charged at Teo, but Placidio sloshed into his path and took the blow.

Livia tugged my arm, pulling me away from the courtyard doorway, for the drainage from the courtyard had become an ankle-deep river gushing through the keep—blood-red murk that cleared as we watched.

Soon the deluge from every side made swordplay impossible. Neither Placidio nor Donato could land a blow. Shielding his eyes with one arm, a heaving Placidio sheathed his sword and slogged through the rising water toward Donato. Before he could get there, a wooden shutter tore away from its rusty mounting, flew through the air, and glanced off Donato's brow.

With a cry of pain and terror—human pain and terror—Donato staggered. A thundering blow from Placidio's fist . . . and then another . . . and he collapsed, face down, in the flood.

"Help us, Livia," I said as I sloshed through the knee-deep water. "You and the swordsman bring Dono; I'll get this one." For Teo, too, had expended everything.

Bleeding from multiple wounds and—Mother's grace—his flesh cold as death, our friend stood motionless, scarce breathing. His arms had collapsed; his pale, soaked hair hung down over his face and shoulders. His brilliant armor had returned to ink marks of pale gray. I caught him under the arms just before he toppled.

"The lady's hand would be most appreciated over here," said Placidio. He squatted in the knee-deep water, supporting Donato's head while trying to extract him from under floating chests and sodden blankets.

Livia placed her hands on her slim hips and said, "Are you a lunatic? Why aren't you putting that sword right through the devil's heart?"

"Because he is *not* a devil," I said. "I'm not sure why or how, but he's been holding that particular devil off since he was a child. That's why he would *leave*, I think. And if you heard his last cry . . ."

"A human cry," Livia said, yielding.

"Aye. So get over here and help me get him on my back," said

Placidio. "I'll carry him down to the grotto, assuming it's not washed away. Find some of that rope's been tangling my feet, and we'll make sure of him before we let him wake up."

Livia sloshed and stumbled through the flood.

"*Síko páno*," I said to Teo, grabbing him as he slumped. *Stand up.*

I knew only a little Typhonese, and had no idea if I pronounced it correctly. A thousand years had passed since it was spoken in the Costa Drago.

"Remember when I pulled you from the river last spring?" I said, draping his arm over my shoulder. My arm went around his waist. "You were just like this. Cold and limp as a . . . dead fish. And as on that night, I cannot bear your full weight. You have to help. One foot . . ."

I waited and slowly he moved one forward.

". . . and the next," I said, exultant. With so much water dripping from my hair, I could scarce see anything . . . nor could anyone accuse me of letting tears fall. I refused to be a weeping ninny.

His other foot moved forward.

"I'll get you out of the wet, though it's clear that water is where you flourish. But I certainly can't bear any more of it myself. And I know that if I get you warm and feed you my swordmaster's salt tea—which if Lady Fortune is kind, will have survived this storm of your making—you'll be able to heal yourself."

I hoped.

22

We had no choice but to shelter in the grotto of the spring long enough to rest, dry out a bit, and make a plan. Neri was feverish; Dumond battered, broken, and asleep; Teo and Donato insensible. All of us were at the edge of exhaustion.

Quick and careful, I drew the Lhampuri dagger down a cedar limb, shaving bark we could dry for tinder and hoping to find some burnable kindling underneath. Neri sat beside me, huddled tight about his knees.

"Will you be able to help me get this soggy mess to stay lit?"

Neri had worked all summer on using his magic directly for fire or light and not solely for his *walk-anywhere* talent. Only one torch yet burned and it was flickering wanly toward its doom.

"I'll try," said Neri. "I'm just cold. Can't stop the shivers." I had applied Vashti's salve to his hot, swollen wound and left it open.

Earlier, while Placidio guarded the sleepers, Livia and I had retrieved a heap of the driest wood we could find, Vashti's wound salve, and a few other oddments that had somehow escaped the bloody floodwaters. But we found no dry shirts, blankets, cloaks, or gloves. No dry bandages. Worrisome. We needed the fire.

I had rinsed the blood out of Teo's shirt, slops, and eye patch and put them on him for modesty's sake—and privacy's—to hide his marks. He couldn't be any colder than he was, lying on the cool stone in his deathlike stupor. The gashes in his flesh yet gaped and bled. His ink marks were all a dead gray; the silvery one about his eye had lost its glint, no different now from the others.

Donato had not stirred, either. We'd bound him and sat him against the wall. He appeared unwounded, save for the split lip and swollen jaw from Placidio's last blows—and whatever damage the Enemy left behind after occupying a soul. Would he ever open his eyes again?

Livia had refused to touch Teo or Donato, either one. I didn't blame her. Her life was grounded in a view of the world drawn from reason, logic, and experience. The events of the night had proved that view a lie.

Now, Placidio had gone off to salvage our scattered weapons and anything else useful from the dead, and to make sure no Cavalieri had escaped. Livia had gone with him, claiming she couldn't bear to sit still. We'd given her to think we were a full day's walk from the city, fearing she might take off on her own just to be shed of us. That must not happen until we had convinced her not to speak of what she'd seen. It was only hours, if even that much, until her wedding day.

My knife released another curl. Neri piled the thready cedar inside a raised stone ring and laid out what twigs and slivers I'd thought might be coaxed to burn.

"I hate to think of you running around in the rain all night while you were fevered," I said, "though a hand was never so welcome as when you pulled me off that cursed rope ladder."

"Didn't run around, and wasn't me p-pulled you off the ladder. It was all I could do to get the shackles unlocked. If those keys hadn't been dropped an arm's length from your head, you'd still be there. On my way b-back here after getting you loose, I near passed out. Got to asking myself what would happen if I did that when I was neither here nor there? Scared me shitless. Once I got back here, I wasn't going anywheres. Sorry. D-damned useless."

"Clearly not useless," I said. "We're all alive. And that was no certain thing."

So it must have been Teo. I should have known by the coolness of his hands and his lack of stink. Why had he not spoken? So I wouldn't expect more from him?

"Try it now," I said, tossing the shredded branch aside and starting on another.

After a few moments' concentration, Neri held his quivering hand over the tangle of tinder. My knife paused. . . .

Nothing. Not a flicker. "Cripes! I'm so cursed feeble, I can't hold my hand still. It's got to be steady."

"Maybe together." I laid the knife aside, knelt up, and cupped my hand beneath his wrist and hand. When my fingers sensed the molten silver flow of magic that was distinctly Neri's, I reached for the pool of magic that lay waiting in me. With will and intent, I focused on the cedar strips and their tendency to burn when dry, and on the need for warmth to soothe Neri's feverish trembling, Dumond's aching body, and Teo's depletion. . . .

"Oh!" Neri jumped. A small green-and-orange flame sat atop his hand.

I used a twig to pick up the tinder clump as if it were a bit of meat to roast, exposing its underside and then its edges to the flame above Neri's hand. We needed spark, not smoke. *Patience. Patience.*

When the tips of the threads began to darken, I set the clump back in the fire ring. We let his little flame lick the edges of the clump as I laid a few of the twigs across it. A trail of smoke rose straight up. The tips of the cedar curls glowed orange. Neri blew on them gently, while still holding his green flame close, and in moments the little heap of bark and twigs burned. One by one, I fed twigs to the flame. Eventually the blaze was hot enough to sustain itself. The last torch winked out and we still had light.

"Let it go," I said. "Rest if you can. We can't stay here long."

He didn't need me to tell him. He curled up as close as he dared to the snapping flames and was asleep in an instant.

As warmth crept around us, I moved to Teo's side. His hand was stone-cold and heavy as lead. His breathing was undetectable. I blamed the snap of flames and wet branches for my inability to hear a heartbeat. I thought I detected a slight gleam of silver in the lacework about his eye, but a few drops of water dripped on his lips and down his cheek, inciting no movement.

I cut off the tail of my shirt, rinsed it out, and tied it around his middle. The wound in his flank was deep.

"Heal, my friend," I said quietly. "Fortune grant I did not force you beyond the boundaries of recovery. Forgive me for calling in your oath. But the young man lives—as himself, I think. He may yet prove to bring answers for you as well as the Chimera."

The Enemy's reference to the *caste of the Great Fish*, spoken in disdain, led me exactly to where I'd gone before . . . into the mythic stories of Leviathan and Dragonis. If *Dragoni* were the mages of the fire, then *Vodai* must be the mages who took their power from water, those who had imprisoned the Enemy and offered their future to guard it. Everything Teo had told me—of his intense preparation, of his need for secrecy, for safety, of how his people were not flourishing—and even the dreams of a crumbling city he had shared before I understood his power, suggested that the Vodai defenses were failing. Was Teo the only one capable of controlling the Enemy? Please the universe that was not so.

I oughtn't even think of Teo. Now that the Enemy shared my dreams at will, how long might it be until my waking knowledge was exposed as well? Was that why I had such difficulty seeing in the dark of late . . . because the Enemy was using my eyes? I should ask Donato to teach me how to play turtle. The Enemy had focused on me because of my particular magic—and perhaps my connection with Teo. But how had Donato, a son of the Confraternity, a believer in its mission, been exposed to the monster?

My fingers stilled. Logic set the answer right in front of me. Unexpected, because it was unthinkable.

Neri had found the keys to the shackles on the ground beside me. If Teo had brought them, he would have unlocked us. Bagi had been a brute, but not stupid enough to drop the keys at his prisoner's feet.

"You didn't move the weapons from the keep either, did you, little brother?" I said softly. Spirits, I'd been blind.

"Neri!" I scrambled across the cavern floor and shook him. "Where's your luck charm?"

"Lost in the pit," he mumbled without opening his eyes. "D'mond said . . . make me 'nother."

"Not lost," I said. "Snatched straight from your pocket. By the same person who fetched the key to the shackles and placed them where we'd find them. The same person who loosened the ladder spike on our first day here. And it wasn't the wind that blew the ladder off the rim the night I rode to Cantagna." That's what I'd not been able to recapture in my memory of that moonlit glimpse of Donato's prison. "It was a bit of errant magic. If it hadn't been tangled, our captive might have escaped that very night."

It was Donato di Bastianni had moved the weapons from the keep so that *we*, not the Cavalieri, would have use of them. But he hadn't used his hands and feet.

"How many times did your fellow prisoner take out his little charm, Dono? You were curious, so you took it, even though it was well out of your reach. When you shifted the weapons outside the keep so we could use them and not the Cavalieri, you left the charm there to make us believe Neri had done it. Because you have a secret that is your death for anyone to know."

He yet sat unmoving, his back to the cavern wall, strands of wet hair dangling over his face. He looked not at all like a beast who had caused eight brigands to slaughter each other.

I squatted in front of him. "When you were fourteen, you brought down that shelf to stop Guillam di Fere from tormenting you. Without touching it. Sometime after, you began dreaming of a man . . . sometimes a woman . . . sometimes a monster. By the Mother's heart, a son of the Philosophic Confraternity was born with magic."

Maybe the kind of magic that eroded the Singular Wall.

Donato inhaled a fragile breath. "Since I can remember, the monster has violated me—used me—when I get angry or afraid or even overly curious." His words were quiet. Every syllable controlled. "Most especially when I'm in danger. It wants me living. I've never known why, because I work so hard to fight it. I do what the Confraternity asks of me. What's necessary. Dreadful things to protect us all. Never before has the monster taken me over so completely as on this night, and if you people had not been there . . . By the Night Eternal, woman, hang one of your chains about my neck and throw me into that pool. Please. If you truly mean what you say about stopping it, that might be the only way."

"I won't," I snapped. "I just coerced a friend into saving your life, and I don't know whether he'll survive it or not."

He threw his head back. A bitter laugh, filled with pain and despair, rolled out of him. "But *why*? What do you want of me? You've seen what I am. You despise my family and our work. The one who shared the pit with me—your brother?—is a sorcerer like me. Surely you see now why he cannot be allowed to use the taint. Why we cannot allow people like Livia, clever and otherwise worthy as she may be, to lull the world into complacency about his kind. I would not have her dead; I would only have her silent."

He thought silence was a mercy.

"There are other ways of living with sorcery," I said, but he wasn't listening.

"While the monster had me, I saw things . . . a being . . . a vision I've seen only as a drawing in a book. I—the monster—feared that being more than anything that I've encountered through all these years. I hated him with a fervor that even now throttles my breath and grinds my teeth, yet I cannot explain why he rouses these feelings in me. I came very near destroying him." His bound hands, shaking, pointed at Teo. "If that being of my vision is your friend who lies here, then I am most certainly your enemy. Why would you not kill me?"

I didn't have to imagine Dono's childhood—born to magic inside the Confraternity, believing himself evil so young. But at the least my father had refused to drown me or Neri. And even my mother, who rued my father's choice and sold me to the Moon House, had let Neri live. By the time I saw the face of the Enemy, I had Teo to tell me what was happening. Dono had been granted no such mercies.

"No. We're not going to murder you. We'd rather help, if you'll allow it. Prevent the monster from using you. You're not a lunatic; you're just ignorant. That you recognize the truth of the monster's manipulation and have tried so hard to keep from falling into its snares, tells me you are worthy of our—"

A clattering on the stair interrupted me. I rose, dagger at the ready.

Placidio burst into the firelight from the stair, Livia on his heels. "Wake the smith. We've got to go—now. The two men I dropped out near the steeps carried ropes and spikes and grappling hooks. They carried these, which look to me intended for signaling, and were wearing these other under their jerkins."

In one hand he held a wad of red-dyed cloth with a length of twine attached and a palm-sized mirror glass, and in the other a yellow badge stitched with a scarlet lance.

"Praetorian scouts," I whispered, horrified. "They're coming up the steeps."

23

How long do we have?"

"They'll top the steeps at dawn; maybe sooner when they realize their scouts are not coming back," said Placidio.

All our concern for defensibility was exposed as idiocy. Not even with magic could we defend against a force of praetorians who could swarm up the steeps. And in no wise would they fail to leave a party at the base of the downward path, ready to pick us off one by one as we descended the narrow way. Our only hope was Dumond's portal.

"I can carry Donato," said Placidio. "But I don't know how we'll manage Teo. Mayhap you and the young lady can get him moving?"

Livia, scratched and sodden, had stopped at the last step on the courtyard stair. She looked uncertainly from one of us to the next.

"Our captive can walk," I said as I shook Neri awake. "He's got nowhere to go but with us, am I right, Dono?"

The young man's eyes were closed again. His hands trembled. But he nodded agreement.

"You can't think to let him loose," Livia blurted, shuddering. "Leave him here for his own people to deal with, or better yet, trade him for our lives. And where can you possibly think to hide? The smoke from this fire will lead right here to us."

"We have another way out," I said, crouching beside Donato.

Placidio helped Dumond shoulder his paint satchel and hobble to the painted wall. "Does the artwork need improvement?"

"Shouldn't," said Dumond, shaking off sleep. "I'll wait till everyone's ready to go. Wouldn't want to rouse any sniffers might be about."

"Are you fully in control of yourself, Segno di Bastianni?" I said.

A whisper. "For now."

My knife sawed at the ropes about his ankles. "So tell this young woman what happened in the keep. The truth. Briefly. She deserves that."

As I freed his knees, he spoke quietly. "I am demon-tainted. When I am angry enough, it rouses the demon monster that lives inside me. I am also naive and stupid. My family . . . has had dealings with the Cavalieri, thus I believed my bargain with Capo Mannia would keep us safe. Not so. When they turned on us so despicably, it . . . infuriated . . . me. Until now, I've always been able to control the monster."

Livia spluttered in disbelief. "Do you think I'm a fool? A prattling son of the Confraternity demon-tainted? He's a madman, not a sorcerer."

"It's true," I said. "Whether you will or no." Though I certainly wanted to learn more of his family's dealings with the Cavalieri.

"Then you're mad, too."

"Time to go." Dumond stood in front of the painted wall, his palms open. Bright blue flames popped into life above them.

"*Cédéré.*" As he spoke the word, he pressed his hands to the painted door, extinguishing the flames. In an instant, the door took on its full dimension, and he reached for the handle.

"Where did that—? What did you—?" Livia's expression shifted so quickly from outrage to puzzlement to astonishment to *horrified* astonishment, I could not but smile.

"If you've a hand to lend to a hobbling fool who means you no harm, damizella, I would appreciate the loan of it," said Dumond, gruffly, wagging his hand at Livia. Only one who knew him well could see the spark in his eye at her examination of his unburnt palm. "Well, come on then. You're an adventurous woman. Not going to eat you. Not escorting you to the Great Abyss. I've just opened a tunnel will get us down the hill to where our horses graze. With luck, the praetorians will think to find us up here, rather than down there."

A moment to assess . . . and judge . . . and a hard swallow, and Livia took his arm. A soft ivory light shone from his hand into the dark tunnel ahead of them. More magic.

"Happens I've got girls will grow up like you," said Dumond. "Smart. Thinkers . . ."

"Our turn now. Get up." The toe of my boot nudged Donato's freed legs sharply. His eyes flicked open and he scrambled to his feet. The new opening in the wall caused him a momentary puzzlement. His glance flicked from me to Placidio to Neri, but he said nothing.

I wrapped the cut end of the rope that yet bound his arms to his body around my left hand. "Follow the light," I said. "I'll be just behind you. We risked a great deal to save you, but know that this prize of a dagger can slice through your spine should you twitch a muscle out of turn."

Placidio hoisted Teo's dead weight across his shoulders.

"Go on," said Neri. "I'll close the door behind."

The narrow passage through the heart of the bluff was smooth and steep. Dumond had often speculated about the possibility of devising steps in one of his magical passages, but had never discovered a way to do it. At least it was stone and not loose dirt or gravel underfoot. That was marvel enough.

The door behind us closed, cutting off the smoky gold light at our backs. The echoing boom would be Neri dropping the heavy bar Dumond often built into his painted doors. The door would exist until Dumond banished the matching one he had painted in a rocky niche at the bottom of the bluff.

The distance through the bluff had already stretched Dumond's talent, yet I could not but wish it might open to my house in the city. How fine it would be to be home, worrying about my next tedious client, instead of what might lie beyond the end of this passage.

Neri's bare feet slapped on the stone as he ran to catch up. We'd never found his boots.

We slogged on. No one spoke. Keeping our footing—and keeping focus on Dumond's handlight ahead of us—required all my concentration. I tried to banish the image of a cadre of praetorians waiting in the sheltered meadow outside the painted door.

The journey seemed interminable.

When the ivory light swelled, clarifying Donato's silhouette, it took me a moment to realize that Dumond had stopped and we'd caught up with him. "Everyone here?" he said.

"Aye," said Neri and I together.

"Aye," said Placidio, with a hint of strain. "Lady scribe, would you help get our friend safely to the ground? Long enough for me to spy what we're walking into."

His mind had been the same place as mine. Everyone's had. This could be a brief and bloody end.

I unwound the leash from my hand and tucked it into Donato's cold fingers bound behind his back. Once Placidio and I got Teo to the ground, Dumond dimmed his light. Placidio's sword slipped quietly from its sheath. I drew mine as well.

"Damizella, a hand with the bar?" whispered Dumond.

Quiet movements in the pitchy dark and a soft thud signaled the door's wooden bar was set aside. A clink of a latch, a grunt of effort, and a brief, ponderous movement on well-oiled hinges opened the stone-dry tunnel to a sliver of moonlight. The cool night air was redolent of damp dirt and scrub . . . and horse. A soft whinny brought a smile to my face. Quicksilver.

"It's quiet out there," whispered Dumond, face pressed to the narrow opening. "I can see all three beasts. If the cart's still there, as well . . ."

"Might as well open up. No use to go back into certain ambush," said Placidio. "I doubt I have the reserves to make the climb—not carrying a man who seems to weigh five times what he ought."

The slab of oak and iron matched the upper door in every detail. We dragged it open.

Clouds scudded past the setting moon as Placidio and I stepped from the tunnel. Three horses grazed in the mottled light. The cart was as we had left it, the tack safely tucked under a damp canvas in the bed.

"Let's go home," I said, my breath shaking more than I would like.

When we all were out, Dumond pressed his palms to the door and pronounced, *"Sigillaré."* The door, the paint, all evidence of Dumond's wondrous talent vanished.

Dono's head snapped up and his gaze followed Dumond as he limped toward the cart.

While Livia and one-handed Neri fetched the horses, Placidio and I laid Teo beneath an overhang a short distance from the cart, out of the way of frisky horses or sudden rainstorms.

Urgency robbed us of speech beyond terse necessity. Placidio,

Livia, and I saddled Quicksilver and hitched the cart horses. Livia might have been sleepwalking for all her expression, but her experience with the needed tasks was apparent and welcome. I had Donato climb into the cart bed and tied his leash to the lantern post. Certain, he could undo it if he worked at it hard enough, but he did not seem inclined to rebellion. His armor was firmly in place. I ordered Neri into the cart beside him. When all was ready, Dumond levered himself and his game leg onto the driver's seat.

Placidio and I headed off to fetch Teo. We had to feel our way. The bluff blocked the moonlight so close to the rocks.

"I'll take guard and nurse duty in the back," I said softly. "Livia can ride pillion."

Placidio's only answer was an explosive stream of cursing that far surpassed anything of Neri's. Sword in hand, he reversed course and bolted for the cart and horses. Though dread turned my legs to lead, I drew my own blade and followed. His magic . . .

We were too late.

One attacker had control of the horses. Another took a struggling Livia in hand, while a third dragged Dumond from his seat and shoved him to the dirt. Two more closed in on our flanks.

"Toss those blades and any others you have," snapped a tall figure standing apart from the others. An officer, by the keen edge of his voice and manner. "Plant your faces in the dirt."

Another person unshrouded a lantern and raised it on a pole. Its swinging illumination left me nauseated—as did the dome-shaped steel caps, the yellow-and-scarlet badges, and the swords that bristled like deadly porcupine quills from the newcomers closing in on us. Praetorians.

"Best do," mumbled Placidio. "Bide."

He cast his sword and other weapons into the dry grass in front of us. Not so far he couldn't reach them in a scramble. But he dropped quickly to the ground, his hands flat beside his head where the soldiers could see them. Praetorian commanders were no easy-to-play street rats.

I wanted to scream. But even if Placidio and I could hold eight fighters—eight *praetorians*—at bay after the fight we'd endured this night, Dumond couldn't run. Teo lay insensible. And there could be another twenty damnable praetorians hidden out in the hills with good horses. Yes, Neri could walk away with magic . . . but likely only back to the ruin atop the bluff, which would get us no-where but accused of sorcery.

So I did the same as my swordmaster, though I kept the pearl-handled dagger strapped to my thigh underneath my trousers. *Bide.* Wait for opportunity.

"Get your cursed hands off me, praetorian," said Livia, wrench-ing her arm from the soldier. "I am Livia di Nardo, daughter of the steward of Cantagna."

I snarled approval into the dirt. *Yes, Livia, show them your fire.*

"The steward's daughter?" said the officer, who strolled up to her, the bobbing lantern moving alongside him. "I sorely doubt that. All know we search for the scholarly young lady—but you, sweeting, are no scholarly young lady, wandering the night in your netherstocks. Bloody ones, too. If the young lady's dead, you'll hang for it."

The praetorian officer was fit and trim, only his thin lips out of order. They seemed too wide for his bony face, and thus were never still—pursing, drooping, curling, advancing, and retreating within a ring of close-barbered beard.

Livia was not intimidated. "I'll not have you hanged, you inso-lent pig. A public flogging would be more humiliating. I wear my undergarments because I was stolen from my bed by fiends of the Cavalieri Teschio—whom you, for all these months, have been un-able to control. In the cart you will find Segno Donato di Bastianni, my affianced husband, who has been direly ill this day past, and a third victim of the Cavalieri. Now, bring horses, cloaks, bandages and drink for us, lest my father and Director Bastianni have the hide off you."

"Silence this squawking crow, Zagno," snapped the officer. "I want everyone here bound, gagged, and dragged into a heap. As far as I can see, these are all murderers, proven to consort with sorcerers."

Horror throttled my breath. Certain, the officer knew Livia had been abducted from her bed. But he didn't care. He'd just provided himself an excuse for killing her—for killing all of us. Livia had been right all along.

But the astonishments were not over. Donato, free of his bind-ings, stood beside the cart in a prideful dignity at odds with his lank hair, stained shirt, and bare legs. "Attention, Captain. You will apologize to the lady immediately. *No one* addresses a guest of my house with such contemptible disrespect. And no honorable praetorian could be so ignorant of the circumstances of her captivity. Between now and the moment we return to Villa Giusti, you will prove to me that you are worthy of your command or you will lose it."

By the Night Eternal, who was *this* Donato?

"Who might you be, boy? Mayhap a catamite for rogues who prefer their pleasures out the other side of the bed."

"You know very well who I am, Captain Legamo. You've been my father's liaison to Giorgio the Hand for two and a half years. Do you imagine that the director advocate's eldest son has no eyes or ears? And the rest of you—Praetorians Lippo, Mazzato, Diedi, Racce, Monte, Zagno, and our young Lantérne Nozzo—I know you are not Captain Legamo's usual cohort. But I know your parents' and wives' and children's names. I know the oaths you've sworn and the day you offered them."

I was confounded. An hour previous, Donato di Bastianni had begged us to kill him. An hour before that, he had been possessed by a monstrous creature left from the Creation Wars. And evidently for his entire life, he had spent every moment trying to control a most well-founded terror. Was this a masterful performance or had he been playing us all along?

Donato surveyed the positioning of Legamo and his men and glanced briefly at the sky. "The moon's position tells me it is well past midnight. No matter what orders you've been given heretofore, Captain, you know well that all of that changes as of this day, our brotherhood's most solemn feast. Though my formal induction is yet to take place, I am now Protector of the Seal of the Philosophic Confraternity and First Defender of Truth. Your future is bound to my word."

No, he was neither pandering nor playacting. This was discipline. Now, apparently, fortified by authority.

The praetorians stiffened and presented their swords in salute. The captain did not. Arms folded about his chest, his wide lips working at double speed, Legamo was the very portrait of a man who had just received legitimate orders that exactly countered the last ones he'd been given.

Was Donato now considered too dangerous to the Confraternity? That was easy enough to imagine if Dono's father had the least suspicion that his son bore the taint of magic or that he was engaged in an intimate struggle with the very Enemy the Confraternity was dedicated to contain. Or was this the director's way of eliminating any hint of corrupt connection between the Confraternity and the Cavalieri Teschio? Certain, this captain—Director Bastianni's liaison to the Cavalieri leader—had been planning to murder us all.

Placidio must have deduced something like. He had wormed his way forward so that his weapons were but an easy lunge from his hand. I echoed his move.

After a few most uncomfortable moments, the captain threw his hands up in surrender.

"Segno Donato! It *is* you, indeed so. All grace to the universe to find you living. In this poor light, this strange place . . . and as we have never actually conversed . . . Everyone in the city assumed the vile Cavalieri had done for you and your bride. They made terrible threats in the ransom demands, and as so many hours had elapsed . . ." His shoulders lifted to the vicinity of his ears as if the weight of the universe had been wrapped up in his decision.

My heart resumed its tenuous beating.

The captain swiveled sharply toward Livia and jerked his head at the soldier holding her. "Release the lady, Zagno, and give her your cloak with my sincerest apologies. As to these others, Excellency, what is your wish as to *their* disposition? Your father insisted we grant your captors no quarter and no opportunity to spread lies or confusion."

Dono glanced coolly from Dumond to Placidio and me. "These three are a rogue gang who found us where the Cavelieri snatch-crew hid us. They overwhelmed the thugs, and then led the lady and myself out here, supposedly to return us to Cantagna. Whether they are innocents to be trusted or but another cadre of the Cavalieri Teschio I have yet to determine. But I, and I alone, will do so. Bind them and bring them along. The youth in the cart was another victim brutalized by the snatch-crew. He has a wound growing septic. If your cadre has a leech, tend him. No binding is needed, but keep a close watch. I *expect* him to arrive at our destination no worse off than he is now."

The captain whipped his hand into a salute. "You heard His

Excellency. Snap to. Nozzo, fetch our horses. Racce, restrain the driver. Lippo, Mazzati, Diedi, bind these two on the ground. Monte, collect their weapons and make sure we've all of them."

Not sure whether to be relieved or dismayed, I glanced over at Placidio. As the skinny Nozzo planted the lantern pole, dropped a coil of rope, and trotted off, my swordmaster's lips formed one word. "Bide."

I didn't like being patient. The praetorians were brutally efficient, and now they were under a philosophist's eye, they remained disciplined. I didn't like Dono's story, either. If he meant well, he could have contrived something that would allow us to go free or, at the least, remain unbound. Perhaps he thought leniency would push Captain Legamo too far to the wrong side of his decision. Or was he not wholly convinced of the trustworthiness of anyone who knew his deadly secrets?

Lantérne Nozzo darted back into the light almost immediately. "Cap'n, there's a dead man over there!" Damnation, he'd spotted Teo.

"You're sure he's dead?" said Legamo.

"Dead as these boulders. Should we plant him?"

"Bring the horses as you were told. Master Bastianni can dispose of the corpus as he will."

"Yes, sir."

Donato had indeed wandered off to where Teo lay and crouched beside him. I couldn't see what he did there—checked for signs of life, I assumed. Looked under his eye patch or at his skin under his damp clothing. I'd babbled foolishly when in the grotto. He could have heard my apology to Teo. Please the universe that even if he understood that Teo was the one who had brought the storm—the one who was the focus of the Enemy's lingering anger—he would leave him unburied.

When Donato returned, he paused beside me, where one of his minions was binding my hands behind my back. "Fetch a cloak and cover the dead man, Diedi. Weight it with stones. Do it now; then finish this."

The praetorian scurried away.

Donato looked down at me, expressionless. "I regret your friend's passing. He was clearly extraordinary. I'll send someone to fetch his body. At that time, you could tell me what death rites he would prefer."

He moved on without waiting for any response. Had he detected Teo's laggard heartbeat? Perhaps he knew something more of Teo's kind from his studies. He'd mentioned a drawing in a book—was it a drawing of Dragonis or Leviathan? Or was his offer some pretense of honor from one who also happened to believe my brother and Dumond should die for their talents?

Donato returned to the horses. "Captain Legamo, I would not have these prisoners hearing passwords or spying out our defenses as we return to the villa. See to it."

I pressed my head to the dirt, filled with dread. No matter the hints that Donato di Bastianni was wholly different than I could ever expected, he was taking my friends and me into the heart of the Confraternity. His choice to leave Neri unbound was no relief. If Neri vanished in plain view, Donato would have inarguable evidence that my brother was a sorcerer.

One small mercy—they hadn't chosen to bury Teo. I would not believe him dead. Maybe whatever power was infused into this cursed ground would sustain him while his magic worked a healing.

Stay alive, Teo. Heal. The Enemy is waiting.

24

W here is Nis? Stars and stones, wake up and answer me."
The noisy visitor's bony fingers threatened to rattle
my bones so hard they crumbled. I ignored her summons. Waking
meant moving. Moving was just going to remind me of everything
in my body that ached . . . my head, in particular. Hours of jounc-
ing while thrown over the back of a praetorian's horse like a bundle of old sacking, blindfolded and my ears stoppered, had left me
a headache for the ages. And then they had deposited me here—
wherever here was. At least had prevented any sort of dreaming.
I could do with a year of dreamless sleep.

"Is she dead?" The fingers poked again.

As is the way of the world, once such thoughts were racing
around in my head, waking would have its due.

"Nis is not dead. Just . . . hiding," I said. But Neri, Dumond,
and Placidio . . . where were they?

I did not open my sticky eyelids, having determined upon arrival that there was nothing in this cramped little room with an
iron door that I wanted to see. Four stone walls. A wooden bench.
No window but a slot near the stone ceiling that allowed no illumination to speak of and only a wisp of outside air to battle centuries of damp, oceans of piss, and worse. The solid iron door was
centered with a small grate of thumb-thick bars and a hinged plate
to cover it, through which various obnoxious people had peered,
blinded me with a sun-fired lamp, and yelled at me to go back to
the sleep from which they had just wakened me. I concluded that
the whole purpose of the exercise was just so they could slam and
latch the hinged plate again and make my head burst.

"But where *is* she?"

I swatted the bony fingers away. They were, indeed, human
fingers. Throwing off the threadbare blanket, I swung my legs off

the bench and allowed the blood to return to all the bruised spots whence it had fled. My temples pounded like Dumond's foundry hammer, and my stomach threatened to unleash a river of bile.

Livia sat beside me on the wooden bench, lit by a glaring lantern. She was much cleaner than I was. Much better dressed in a modest, embroidered gown of pale green that went well with her clean red curls, but did nothing at all for her sun-browned complexion. Yet she appeared no better rested.

"It is gratifying that you're alive, damizella," I said, more equably than I felt. "Are you my cellmate?"

"No. I'm not a prisoner . . . well, I'm stuck in this place and told I cannot leave until the *master says.* But my accommodations are more comfortable than this. I sneaked down here. Now where—?"

"Have you seen my partners?"

"They were perfectly fine when we arrived. There are other cells down here. They're likely in those. The maidservant, a village girl who scarce knows her own name, knew only where *you* were, as she brought you the blanket."

"What do you want of Nis?"

"I wanted to hear what she had to say of you and your companions. I'd thought of her as brave to succor me. And honest. But then none of you were who I thought, so what was she? A shill?" She peered closely at me. "She looked nothing at all like you, and yet . . . Aaagh."

She scrubbed at her damp curls in exasperation, releasing the scent of lavender soap. She'd had a bath to celebrate her return. Spirits, what I would give for a bath—

Celebrate.

My mind woke with a jolt. "Mothers' heart, Livia, you've not married him!"

Surely this was still the feast day. The wedding day. The day *before* Livia's birthday, so she could not yet call a challenge to the marriage contract and persuade Donato to forgo it.

"Certainly not. We're not even back to the city as yet. We've stopped at a private villa I'm told lies somewhere near the village of Nieves. I'm just not sure what to think—and I don't like that." Exasperated, she threw her hands in the air. "Dono was his usual odd, mannerly self before we left that horrid place—not a murdering lunatic. He even promised I'd get to see my father today, but that hasn't happened either, of course. I just don't know what to do . . . and I've never had that problem before. I don't like it."

A villa outside the city? Trying to make sense of what was going on, I caught one of her flailing hands before it smacked my head. "So you've not spoken with Dono since we arrived?"

She yanked her hand away. "No. He raced ahead of us, after threatening to rack Legamo if he didn't get us here before dawn. Certain, I *intend* to speak with him. But first, I want to know who in this cursed world are you and these others, and what more you can tell me about Dono's *condition*."

Fully awake now, I pressed my hands on her bony shoulders so she could not bolt. "Before we are interrupted, let me tell you this one thing. You do not have to marry this man. After midnight tonight—the hour when the law says you come of age—you can challenge the marriage contract and refuse it. If Dono does the same, the contract is void. It's the *only* way you can stop the marriage without burdening your father with the penalties—or the risks to his honor—that a broken contract will bring down on him. And after what we saw . . ."

She grimaced. "Well, of course that was awful, but . . ."

"Livia what we witnessed in that keep is near unfathomable, even to someone like me, who knows something of such matters. Think. Using that secret, you can surely convince him to agree."

"So that's truly what this abduction was about? Stopping the marriage? You said so, but we were still in that cellar and no one had yet gone berserk." She was astonishingly calm, considering what had happened over these past three days.

"It was. We hoped to protect your ability to study, investigate, and write about natural philosophy as you see fit. Even more important, we hoped to protect your good father's independence and that of the city he serves. The Confraternity holds far too much influence already."

She narrowed her pale eyes. "That's why you took Dono as well. To convince him he didn't want me. But what you found instead . . ." She pressed her fingers to her mouth as if she saw the horror yet again.

"Never did we imagine what we witnessed yestereve, Livia. Never. Somehow"—I did not want to introduce the word *magic* to this discussion, at least not until she did so—"Dono's got caught up in something beyond our knowledge, and what dreadful deeds he's done in service to that experience, I don't know. A few things he's said and done these few days—like getting us all this far alive—lead me to believe he wants to be his own man, not solely his father's parrot and not solely the monster we saw. He begged us to *drown* him. We must persuade him to let us help him instead. But you mustn't bind yourself to him."

"He's no monster," she said as if stating that the sun rose in the east. "He's mad. Somehow he can use his madness to force others into madness, too. But you're telling me I should *blackmail* him into setting me free of the contract? What if he gets angry and infests me with his disease? If we don't understand the disease, we cannot understand how it passes from one person to another."

"Sssst, damizella." The hissing came through the door grate. A girl's voice. "They're looking for you."

"One moment," she said, then turned back to me. "Dono's family must have some way of controlling his illness. They could never risk letting him walk around the Academie if he were going to set people to gutting each other. I'm thinking they must give him draughts to make him so dull and empty, but then you people stole him away for this ridiculous purpose . . . and he was without his medicaments. You terrorized him, starved him, made him think you were going to murder us if our families didn't pay . . ."

Appalled, I blurted, "Livia, you can't be thinking to do this."

She wasn't listening to me. "I'm sorry about your friend. What he did—raising the storm and then drawing it inside the keep—what a wonder that was. I saw it, felt it. He must have had tools or mechanisms in the armor he wore. Lodestones or some variant of quicksilver to create the *virtu elektric*. Was it the mechanism killed him or the wounding?"

Near speechless, I stared at her, trying to understand a mind so determined to shape the world to her image. "Who could say?"

She tilted her head and wrinkled her sharp features into a ponderous knot. "You see, I have to believe there are natural principles at work here. Principles the Confraternity would call *magic*, just as they would name Dono's fits demon possession. Just as they name earthquakes and volcanoes *a demon's raging*. Back there, for a moment before I put my mind to it, I myself called Dono a sorcerer, and your partner who opened the tunnel as well.

But *sorcery* is just a made-up word for all the things in the world
we don't understand yet. If I marry Dono, I'll have full access to
the Atheneaum; he assured me of that. There I can learn the wisdom of ancient peoples, natural philosophy that does not support
Confraternity teaching, mysteries of nature that have been lost
or hidden. I might even learn something about illnesses of the
mind like his. Someday the world will know both the truth of
nature and the harm the philosophists have done by keeping us
in ignorance."

She had me halfway convinced. Yet the danger was so clear.
"But, meanwhile, they murdered your friend Marsilia. And that
Captain Legamo came a hair's breadth from killing us all—Dono
included. The Confraternity is corrupt, Livia. Marry Dono and
you would be fortunate to live out the year. And that's assuming
he can get back in control of . . . his illness."

"Damizella. Now!" The hinged plate slammed shut and the cell
door opened.

"I'll think on it." And she was gone.

I believed magic was a part of nature—but not in the way
Livia did. Physicians were learning how our bodies worked. As-
tronomers could calculate the motion of the moon. But I had felt
the flow of extraordinary power in myself, my brother, and my
friends and used it to work impossibilities. And what Teo had
done—what he was—was no such particular magic as we of the
Chimera had. And certainly no lodestones or quicksilver. Though
applauding Livia's determination to seek truth, I was terribly
afraid for her—and for the four of us, who had yet to face our
captor. Afraid for that captor, too, who battled an enemy none of
us understood.

I pushed on the hinged metal plate that covered the little grate
in the door. It was dented and ill fitting; I was not the only prisoner to want it out of the way so I could see into the corridor. I
untwisted my trousers and fumbled through the slit pocket until
I found the soft leather strap around my thigh. Tucked away in its
sheath was my pearl-handled dagger. Careless praetorians.

Forcing patience and concentration, I slipped the slim blade
through the bars and picked at the latch, considering the possible
varieties of closure it might be. Neri would have it open in three
heartbeats. It took me a little longer.

The view through the grate told me exactly nothing. Across the passage was another iron door. Its view plate hung from one hinge as mine now did.

"Partner," I whispered through the bars. "Sssst. Partner."

Silence soon returned me to the bench. I pulled the coarse blanket around my shoulders. *So make a story. Make a plan.* But that was difficult when I didn't know what Dono was up to or who was in control at the moment. My head ached so dreadfully.

The door burst open. "Up with you!"

A praetorian stood in the open cell doorway. He was a short, sober-looking man with wide-set eyes and a cap of tightly curled, steel-gray hair. Not Captain Legamo, and not a regular praetorian. On his clean green tabard was pinned a yellow badge embroidered in black, proclaiming him a Defender of Truth—a nullifier or one who worked with them. My stomach churned.

As soon as I was on my feet, he stepped back and opened his hand, inviting me to come out and precede him down the passage.

Yet even after the wave of cold sweat passed, I didn't move. "Where are my companions?"

"Elsewhere. As healthy as when they arrived."

"I want to see them."

"Come, and all will be answered." The hand motioned yet again. "If you please . . ."

Stubbornness did not seem a productive option. So I followed him.

The passage was shorter than I imagined. My cell was one of a block of four iron doors that took up half of the corridor's length. As we walked toward the opposite end, we passed between two larger cells closed off with barred, not solid, doors. One was deserted. In the other, five men lay on the floor, sleeping. None of them were my partners. Others—two or three—occupied benches in the dark corners of the cell. I would swear—

Glancing over my shoulder, I peered into the dimness. Surely the one sleeping nearest the barred door was young Nozzo, the lantérne of Captain Legamo's cadre.

My feet stumbled on the uneven stone floor. My escort stepped up and caught my elbow, blocking my view of the cell before I could be sure. Nothing about this place made sense.

Around the corner and up a short, narrow flight of worn steps, and we crossed a cramped stone yard. Though the hour was something near midday, there was no sign of activity. Empty barrows, casks, baskets, and poultry crates littered the space bordered by a modest main house, sheds, and kitchen. Though a tendril of smoke rose from the main house, the kitchen-house chimney stood cold and smokeless. A hatchet rusted in a splintered chopping block. A water trough was half full of sludge after the night's rain. Clearly this yard had seen more weather than use in recent years. As Livia had said, a country house. Seldom visited. Private.

Country houses were often used for private executions. Perhaps Dono had decided it was too dangerous for anyone involved in the night's activities to live. And yet Livia was not confined. . . .

Under a short roof and through an arched wood door, we entered the main house. My escort whisked me through a short hallway flanked by a flower room, a lamp room, and a dish room. We emerged into a spacious foyer flanked by salons with shuttered windows, covered furnishings, and sheeted artworks. A wide stair led from the foyer to an upper gallery. The house was modest in size compared to Villa Collina, *il Padroné*'s country home, but likely no easier to escape.

At the top of the staircase, one of a pair of double doors stood open, leading into a study. Its clean plastered walls were devoid of artworks or other decoration; a brick hearth staved off the autumn chill with a snappish fire. Paned window glass shone the afternoon light on Donato di Bastianni, writing at a cherrywood desk, a most ordinary setting for a man I'd seen only in highly unusual circumstances.

Surprisingly, we bypassed that and two shuttered rooms before my shepherd opened a door. "You'll find refreshment and washing things inside. I'll wait out here. Please be quick. Time is of the essence."

That we could agree on, though perhaps to different ends.

He closed the door behind me.

The chamber must once have been quite comfortable. The shuttered windows were wide and tall; the walls were covered halfway up with expensive fabric. But the fabric's narrow stripes were sorely faded, and most of the furnishings had been removed. A washing stand held a basin, pitcher, and towel. A small, ugly table was set with a cup of wine, a carafe of water, and a plate of cheese and apples. Below a wall-mounted lamp hung a clean, well-worn linen shirt and gown.

Wine first. Then water. I was parched. Then a wash of face and hands. Leaving the dungeons behind had done nothing for my throbbing head or unhappy stomach, so I pocketed an apple and yanked open the door. Donato had not returned to the Academie in triumph, his foes vanquished by his partisans, sorcerers captured to display and execute. I was impatient to learn what that meant—and where were my brother and my partners.

My unnamed escort seemed unsurprised at my speed. More likely he just didn't register expressions any more than his master did. He led me back down the gallery. When he tapped on the open door, Donato glanced up and waved me in. "One moment, if you please."

He folded the page, dripped wax on it, and sealed it with a signet pulled from a string around his neck. So that's what Neri had noticed. We'd never had a chance to check.

Donato rose and passed the sealed message to my escort. "Dispatch this immediately. When the acceptance comes, as I expect, disperse the cadre as we discussed, no matter whether I've returned here or not."

"It shall be done, Excellency."

"And the other errand?"

"The situation is yet unchanged."

"Very well."

The man made a crisp bow and departed.

Donato then shifted his attention to me, just as I was digesting *disperse the cadre* alongside my glimpse of the sleeping men in the dungeon cell. Did *disperse* mean scatter, as usual, or was it a code word for murder?

"Sit, if you like," he said, while rising from his stool. "Gaspar will bring the others."

Relief softened my knees. Only for a moment. He might mean *bring the others in chains* or *bring the others so I can torment them to squeeze answers from you.*

"I'll stand for now," I said. I would not pretend to comfort when I felt so powerless.

He acknowledged my preference with a glance and retreated to the hearth. He had washed and changed into loose breeches, a clean shirt the color of eggplant, and a dark gray doublet, simply stitched in black, entirely appropriate to a gentleman in the country. His hair appeared damp and clean, but the three day's growth on his face had not been barbered.

His slender hand rested on the polished wood mantelpiece. Though he directed his attention to the fire, his eyelids closed and his breathing smoothed. Even here he enforced his personal discipline.

"Look at me, segno," I said. "Straight on, if you please."

He did so for a moment. Set deep under black brows, his eyes displayed no golden glints, no echoes of that other face. Haunts, most assuredly, but this man was not the being who had forced the Cavalieri to slaughter each other with the twitch of his finger.

He returned his attention to the fire.

"Why am I here, offered food and dry clothing after being bound, manhandled, and thrown into a dungeon?"

Only as I said it did I realize how easily he could respond, *to return the favor.*

But he didn't. "I will explain when your . . . partners . . . join us," he said, without shifting his attention from the fire. "You seem to be the leader of this group. But I've no wish to disrupt whatever accommodation you make with each other that enables you to do such things as breach the defenses of Villa Giusti and steal its residents away. There is wine on the sideboard. Coffee if you prefer, though it has cooled since it was brought. I've no household staff here, only Gaspar and his brother."

Thus Livia's village-girl maidservant was explained. Had Donato raced ahead of our party to make household arrangements? Or was it to set up an ambush for Captain Legamo's cadre?

"Will Damizella di Nardo be joining us?"

For this he glanced up. "Later."

"I hope she arrived here in better state than I did. Or perhaps she was returned to her own home in the city?"

He tilted his head, brows raised, as if to decide if I was making a jest. "Did she not tell you of her condition when she visited you an hour since?"

I was a fuddle-head! Of course Livia had been *allowed* to find me.

My fumbling response was interrupted by Placidio's arrival. A massive bruise on his forehead and a split on his cheekbone spoke to the force needed to render him docile—and his hands were bound tightly at his back. His expression was thunderous until he saw me . . . and then Dumond, who hobbled in shortly after him with the aid of a walking stick. Dumond's left arm, sprained in his ordeal at the cellar, was bound up in a sling.

No matter what it might or might not reveal to Donato, I could not but lay a hand on each man's shoulder as I blinked away more evidence of sentimental foolishness. When Neri arrived on their heels, clear-eyed and wearing a clean shirt, I felt as if I had the strength of ten.

I whirled on Donato. "Now may we have your explanations as to"—my gesture encompassed the state of my companions, as well as the house in which we stood—"all this."

"Sit, if you wish. And if the swordsman agrees to a truce, you may remove the binding on his hands with your cleverly concealed dagger."

All those times we'd thought Donato oblivious, he'd been observing and listening, as well as detaching himself from dangerous emotions. I'd best remember that from now on.

Taking Placidio's grudging *harrumph* as agreement, I tossed my dagger to Neri, who cut Placidio's hands free. I didn't want to take my eyes from Donato's face. None of us sat, not even Dumond.

Donato's gaze shifted from the fire to our feet to the empty doorway and back to the snapping flames, lingering only briefly on our faces. "You told me a few hours ago that you judged me neither monster nor lunatic, but only ignorant. Knowing what I did . . . what I was . . . I find that judgment unfathomable. But then you four are at least as much of a mystery to me as I am to you. By your own admission, you are also entangled with Dragonis—or whatever name you call the monster. You also said I should trust you, and that you would help me if I allowed it. Was that true? Is it still?"

"I meant it when I said it," I said. "Events since have not entirely encouraged my belief as to your state. What say you, my friends?"

"I say that he is a hypocrite—a sorcerer who has spent his life maiming and enslaving sorcerers," said Placidio, rubbing his rope-burned wrists. "I would hear why the Confraternity allows him to live. And why he has allowed himself to live, if he believes as he professes. He is a servant of the Enemy."

"I say that he is alone in fighting a battle he does not fully understand," said Dumond. "I would hear how it began, how he has managed it, and what he thinks to do to prevent himself from committing savage murder yet again."

"He didn't rat me out to the Cavalieri," said Neri. "Had a leech in from the village to take care of my arm. And if ignorance was a crime, I'd have been dead a thousand times already. So I'll listen—and help if I can."

Ah, to be so young and so able to get to the heart of things.

My turn. "I believe he prevented Captain Legamo from killing us all, including himself. And I would like to think our actions in that dreadful hour at Perdition's Brink have granted us a modicum of trust. Donato, have you retrieved the body of our friend?"

"Yes. Hours ago. You heard Adjutant Gaspar report a situation unchanged, meaning that your friend is yet living, though one would think it scarce possible. Then again, my ideas of possibility have been altered of late."

A gesture acknowledged Neri and Dumond. He'd witnessed their magic.

His brow creased and clouded. "Before we move forward, I'll offer . . . I had naught to do with the bookbinder's murder. Nor do I have any knowledge that my father or any other Confraternity Director was involved in it. Nor do I have any knowledge that my marriage contract might have been falsified. However, grievous as it is to confess, neither of these things would astonish me."

He paused, and glanced from one of us to the other, assessing our reactions. The effort his speaking entailed was visible. Though his voice was steady and clear, I had the sense that every word was shaped as a child draws her first letters with pen and ink.

Seemingly assured we weren't about to slice his throat or pounce on him all at once, he closed his eyes long enough to take a few calming breaths. Then he began again, perfectly composed. "Your recent conversation with Damizella di Nardo clarified a few matters. This marriage—" He shook his head. "I have never desired to bring *any* person into *any* sort of relationship with me, and certainly not a woman I believe to be sorely misguided and a danger to this world. I, obviously, am a much greater danger. More even than I knew."

He required another few moments to still the tremors in his hands. We waited for more.

"To hear that I can refuse the contract was a revelation, though the reasons to see it through are compelling. But I have a proposition for you four—which I will extend to the lady if you agree to your part."

I was fascinated. Such brutal honesty . . . and a proposition?

"Go on," said Placidio.

"I offer you a pledge that when Damizella di Nardo and I are returned to Villa Giusti, I will join her in a challenge and refusal of the marriage contract if she so desires, pending an agreement between the two of us to keep up certain formalities—courtesies between our families that I deem necessary for her safety and my own."

"And in return?" I said.

"I have spent my life trying to make amends for the abomination that I am. It seemed enough that, unlike what I was taught about sorcerers, I never felt any desire or urge to unlock the monster's dungeon and set it free. Personal discipline has enabled me to continue in my duties and suppress the monster's allurements. Even as I've come to understand the corruption and hypocrisy that permeate the service the Confraternity renders to protect the world, I've seen no alternatives. But every time I perform what I have believed to be my duty, the grasp of the monster grows stronger. After what happened last night . . . I realize that there is no prison cell to be unlocked. No *desire* involved. The way Dragonis walks free is through me. Help me stop that from happening."

"Why not run?" I said. "Hide for a while . . . become someone new. We know people learned in these matters. Build trust and they can help."

"Were I to run and somehow stay free of the monster and of praetorians hunting me, my father would find someone else to take on my duties. Someone without the understanding I've gained. Someone not so experienced at personal discipline, who could fall victim to the monster's wiles. You cannot fully understand without seeing what my duties entail. This situation is my responsibility to repair, but I cannot—I am clearly not able to change the course of events on my own."

Donato moved away from the fire, sat on the edge of his writing desk, opened a plain wood box that lay there, and pulled out a dagger. Simple. Unadorned. He turned it so the lamplight caught its blade and then scraped the cutting edge slowly across his palm.

I stiffened, glancing at Placidio, who stood at my shoulder, to see if he sensed any extraordinary danger. He shook his head.

"You wanted to know why I've not ended my perverse life with a dagger." Dono met Placidio's hard gaze and raised the weapon in his hand. "I've tried with this one. Fifty times I've tried. A hundred. Slitting my wrists, my neck, the great vein in my thigh. I tried poison as well, and smothering. Drowning oneself is difficult at any time, but impossible when one has watchers every waking hour. And I'm not sure even that would succeed."

His trembling grew fierce until he put the knife back in the box and slammed the lid.

"The monster will not allow it," he said. "The moment I feel the blessed night descend, the whispers begin. Then come the visions. I fight them, I deny them, yet I wake up healed. Her words slip into my mind until I can hear nothing but that I am her instrument. His voice plucks at my basest desires, saying I'll be his lover . . . his consort . . . stars, what does that even mean? Sometimes it comes as a woman . . . sometimes a man . . . sometimes as a winged monster of fire, but . . ."

". . . but they are only the one being," I said, "and you can neither unsee their eyes nor deny the desires roused by their voices."

Donato's trembling slowed and his gaze locked to mine as if he were seeing me for the first time. As he was, in a way. He nodded.

"What would you have us do?" asked Dumond.

"As soon as it is dark tonight, help me enter the Villa Giusti without being seen. You seem quite good at that. Once there, I will show you the source of my connection with the monster, a place where we use its own power to fight it. If you could discover the mechanism of what goes on in there and help me find some way to subvert it, then I might be able to hold on to myself long enough to root out the corruption that makes such horrors possible. My father's corruption."

Intriguing. Perhaps this was the battleground where Macheon's growing power could be weakened, and Teo's people given more time. That would be worth a risk or two.

"Once we are out again without anyone in the villa the wiser," Donato continued, "you must then enforce your demands on my family, that is, deliver me—and Livia, if she consents—back to them in whatever fashion your ransom message demanded."

"The ransom exchange?" said Dumond. "Why in the name of sense? Much safer if you walk up the Academie steps."

"Absolutely not. We must maintain the fiction that this has been a true abduction. I cannot appear to be complicit in any fashion—or anything but a restrained captive since the hour I was removed from the villa. If my father believes for an instant that I have cooperated with my captors, I will be given to the Executioner of the Demon Tainted, who will throw me, chained, into the sea as he does every sorcerer—only I will not die, but drown and be healed over and over. Forever, I fear, unless the monster sets me free."

He took a deep, shaking breath. "My father—and he alone—knows I bear the demon taint. It serves his purposes. He does *not* know about . . . the monster . . . or its influence over me. He just assumes I am weak and afraid, which, of course, is true."

Not weak, I thought. Not at all weak. I had heard that seductive voice only a few times and near walked off a cliff.

"You've just made a very dangerous admission," said Placidio. "You trust us that far? And what of afterward, when you are safe at home amongst your own people and praetorians are set on our trail? There is no guarantee that what you suggest is even possible."

Then he did look directly at us, bewildered. "I presumed—perhaps wrongly. You didn't attempt to drown me when I begged it. You imply that you see these same visions, yet you remain the people who saved me from madness, who risked your lives to prevent my father's attempt to corrupt Cantagna's steward. Certain, that was and is his plan. Though it's hardly credible, your friend who lies in this house is somehow also the mortal foe of my tormentor. You offered help, so I presumed you knew enough and were willing to exchange trust. But if not, you may leave and do as you will. My adjutant will see the lady and me returned to the city with the best story we can devise. . . ."

. . . and what would happen to Donato the next time anger or fear drove him out of control?

Placidio's gaze drilled into Donato as if trying to pry out all the things he was not telling us. "The praetorians who dragged us here know our faces."

"He hid them down below," Neri volunteered. "I heard him telling them that Cavalieri *sorcerers* had marked them and the only way to keep them safe was to lock them up behind bars of iron for the night and then send them away, each one to a different place—Invidia, Mercediare . . . all over. Forever, never to return."

"Dispersed," said Placidio. "With a fat purse and solid reasons to stay away. Clever. Still, you ask a great deal—for us to walk into that house using magic and to believe you won't call us out. And then we risk our lives again to send you back to a life devoted to our destruction? You believe we should be dead."

"Show me I've been wrong about sorcerers. I've heard their curses, their threats to unleash the monster. The danger is real. Even you don't dispute it. So show me a better way. You set me free of the monster last night. On this night, we could take a further step. My father has stripped the last honor from the Confraternity and will not stop until he controls Cantagna. Only a dutiful son, one he believes dedicated to the Confraternity, can stop him."

"I cannot walk away from this," I said, turning to the other three of the Chimera. "Speak now if you want out, and go with my blessings."

"And miss the excitement?" said Neri. "Pssh."

"We'll need our weapons," said Placidio. "The good ones, not the decoys. Not praetorian shite. Not sure how much we can help without our friend in the other room."

"I'll need my paint case," said Dumond. "It was in the cart. Where exactly inside Villa Giusti did you have a mind to go, segno?"

Donato took hold of himself and attempted a smile—with only momentary success. "The *pérasma*," he said hoarsely. "The chamber where we transform human men into sniffers."

25

Had Donato asked us to fly him into the sun, I could have been no more astounded. And what other bargain could address so many of our concerns: not simply the threat to Cantagna posed by the marriage contract, but the mystery of sniffers and the Confraternity's despicable connection with the Cavalieri? Understanding Donato's relationship to the Enemy could shed light on my own. And Teo . . . if Donato was right that the Enemy was growing stronger, Teo needed to hear it.

Livia heard him out and thought the bargain reasonable, but was not yet ready to declare what she might agree to. "You are all entirely mad to do all this sneaking in and out. I see no point in negotiating until we two are back in that house without anyone dead or having a murderous fit."

And so we prepared as best we could.

Donato insisted that the best opportunity to breach Villa Giusti would come just after sunset. "I've a way to bypass the city gates. If you can get us inside the villa, no one there will heed us."

I was instantly skeptical. "Why is that?"

"It's the feast day of the Lone Praetorian. From sunset till midnight, all but the gate guards will be in the main courtyard. There are rites and ceremonies to honor both living and dead. Readings from history. Songs. Everyone who lives at the villa or the Academie—praetorians, administrators, proctors, students, servants—will be there and well occupied. All others will be sent home or posted to duties in the city."

"Aye," said Placidio. "I've heard of the custom."

I was little familiar with Confraternity history and customs. My interactions with philsophists had been limited to individual tutors Sandro brought to his house for me and his occasional social evenings with Bastianni. I'd had no desire to spend more time with anyone who might uncover my secret.

Dumond persisted. "What of sniffers? Are they allowed a holiday?"

"They'll be deployed in the city or outside the villa gates. Their presence would . . . defile . . . the rites."

Dono sketched out our route. His way to bypass the city gates was promising, but he needed us to breach the villa walls. He knew a relatively secure section of the villa wall that would fulfill Dumond's requirements both during his work and after our passage.

"Inside the *pérasma* are two chambers. The upper is a workroom. The lower holds a pool . . . a hot spring," he'd said. "That's the heart of the matter."

Only when he tried to explain what he wished to show us in the *pérasma* did he falter. "You must experience the place for yourselves. To describe the rite and what I perceive as it unfolds, I—I don't have the words. I know trust is difficult. It is for me as well. But I've no recourse."

I believed him. My partners did too.

While the others began hurried preparations for our journey, Neri and I looked in on Teo. Neri took it hard when I told him he couldn't come with us right away, griping that his fever was gone and his arm almost useful.

"If we didn't need Dumond to paint us into the villa, I'd leave him as well," I said as Gaspar vanished down the stair, leaving us outside the chamber where Teo slept. "You must see to Teo."

"Nursemaid, then?"

"More than that," I said. We closed the bedchamber door behind us. "You've got to protect him. I've no idea how safe this house will be with Donato gone. Gaspar seems stout enough, and loyal to Donato, but who knows?"

They had laid Teo on a sling bed, and someone had covered his face with a linen sheet. I pulled it back. His eye patch had been twisted out of place, revealing the mark around his eye. The lacework twists were a dull gray. The gleam of silver I had spied at Perdition's Brink must have been my own wishing. Either that or it had faded again. Bindings of fear tightened about my chest.

I untangled the patch and settled it in place, then examined his arm. His ink marks might have been streaks and blotches of ash.

Neri touched one of them. "Atladu's balls, he still feels dead."

"He felt like this the first time," I snapped, though the cold surged through my blood and I knew this was different. Indeed, his stillness was profound. I could detect no breath at his mouth, and a seeming eternity of listening at his chest produced but a single weak heartbeat that could have been my own.

"Go after Gaspar," I said, struggling to stay calm. "Get him or the maidservant to make up the salt-and-ginger tea. See that they taste it first, but bring it quickly. And send Placidio up here."

While Neri hurried off, I whispered in Teo's ear, telling him of Donato's confession and our bargain with him. "Whatever Donato shows us, we're going to need you to solve it," I said. "Hold on, my friend. Live. The world needs you."

Placidio burst into the room. "What's happened?"

My fear spurted out of me like lifeblood. "He's dying."

"Boundless Night."

Kneeling at the bedside, Placidio did as I had done. Examined the marks. Checked for breath and heart, pressed his fingers at Teo's neck . . . his wrists . . . his ankles. He pressed Teo's hand to his own brow for a very long time, as if he might read the pulse of life there. Then he lowered it and tucked the soft blanket around our friend's arm.

His eyes remained closed; his face grim.

"I've sent Neri to make salt-and-ginger tea," I said, as if my babbling might reverse the report of his stony silence. "It helped before. Certain, you know more of his people than you've told us. You must know something else we can do."

My swordmaster's long exhale was the sound of vanishing hope. He would not look at me. "There's naught I know of to help. It's up to him."

"Spirits, what have we done? This is my fault." My fear and guilt had grown so huge, it spilled out on its own.

"Nay. You know better. We'd be dead or worse without what he did for us at the Brink. He knew that. He chose. His duty is to contain the Enemy, but when he said he was unready, he meant that, too. He was vulnerable. Couldn't replenish—couldn't protect his human state, while using the other. We must ready ourselves to go on without him." He glanced up at me at last, bleak and weary. "And we need to go now. They've food for us down to the kitchen. You must eat something. I'll wait here for Neri."

"No, no, no . . ." Cracks spidered through what strength I had left.

"Maybe he can yet find a way." But my swordmaster didn't believe his own words. "Before you leave here, you should tell him whatever you want to say, and that . . . it's all right to let go. To hold himself this way so long—to keep trying—is a torment. I do know that."

"I'll be back as quick as I can." I was not at all ready to tell Teo goodbye. I'd think of something.

Though it seemed impossible, I was ravenous. It didn't take long to devour my portion of Gaspar's bread, figs, olives, and roasted fowl, and join in the other preparations. Half an hour and all was ready. Placidio had joined Donato in the stable, but I returned to Teo's room. Neri had propped him up with pillows and was trying to get him to drink. To no avail.

"Spoon it down him," I said, "a few drops at a time. If it's like before, he'll relish the taste and swallow, even while he's insensible."

But that didn't work either. As at Perdition's Brink, the droplets dribbled out of his mouth. My eyes prickled. His marks were unrecognizable. Some had completely vanished.

"What do I do?" Neri's grief echoed mine.

Denial did no good. This must not be for nothing.

"Give him a little time. Try again. But after a while—a couple of hours—you should take him back to the city. Not through the gates, but to the woolhouse—whether he's better or no. We need you with us, but I won't leave him here to die among strangers."

There, I'd said it. How in the Night Eternal could we unravel any mystery of the Enemy without Teo's advising? Yet we had to be prepared to do just that. We were on our own.

"Donato's left the cart and cart horses for you. Even if Teo's awake, I'm not at all sure he knows how to ride a horse. But Livia does, and she's agreed to help. Don't let her drive Teo crazy with questions." My voice was near breaking. "If you get to the woolhouse and he's not yet speaking, and the marks are still gray . . ."

I didn't know what to tell him.

"Swordmaster said if the marks all fade, I should give him to the river."

"Give him— What?"

But I answered my own protest. Though I'd near forgotten it, on the way back to Cantagna two nights past I'd dreamed of plunging into the sea, into a forest of color and life and darting creatures. Sure enough, Teo had been waiting for me. That exemplified the connecting thread I'd felt between us all summer.

"The sea is Teo's home," I whispered. "He dreams of it." But to put him in the river . . . My chest near seized to consider it.

"Only if he's truly dead, Neri. Only if you're sure. Otherwise, if we're not at the woolhouse when you get there, make him comfortable and then get yourself into the villa. Dono says Dumond can hide in the loft of the praetorian stables while we do whatever we're going to do with him. That's where we'll meet you."

"I can do that."

The responsibilities seemed to encourage him, the prospect of using his magic even more so. But his bleak face when he turned back to Teo told me what he believed.

And so I knelt at Teo's side, held his cold hand to my forehead, and told him to let go when he could fight no longer. "It's all right, my friend. I'll hear your voice forever, and heed your teachings."

I touched Neri's cheek before I left. I hoped I'd see them both again. Trust was hard, but giving up was unthinkable.

Four of us—Dumond, Placidio, Donato, and I—rode out within the hour, fed, armed, and dressed in dark-colored clothes that had no white skulls sewn on them. Dumond's paint case was looped over his shoulder. Fortunately, Gaspar had brought Teo from Perdition's Brink in the cart where Dumond had stashed the case.

"Live, my friend," I whispered, as we threaded the golden hills north of the city. "Heal."

Though I poured all my will into the wish and opened the reservoir of magic inside me as if to give it wings, I felt no answer, no warmth. The thread between Teo and me had vanished.

In half an hour from Via Solitor, the sun had set, our horses were tethered, and we were creeping through a graveyard outside the city's north wall. A Confraternity graveyard.

"The Bastiannis have always believed themselves above the law," said Donato as we picked our way through increasingly monumental gravestones. "My great-grandsire disliked submitting to searches or questioning at the city gates, so he built himself a mausoleum long before he died. And inside it, he dug himself a tunnel."

The white marble mausoleum gleamed in sunset's afterglow. It was a magnificent little edifice, octagonal, with a graceful column at each of the eight corners to support its bronze dome. Seven of its walls were adorned with life-sized sculptures of scholarly men and women. A bronze door, etched with the book, flame, and lance of the Confraternity, opened from the eighth. Donato retrieved a key from the mouth of a carved frog lost somewhere in a sculptor's vision of nature's abundance, unlocked the door, and showed us inside.

The place smelled of dry leaves, dust, and incense. A lantern hung ready for any Bastianni who wished to bypass the city gates. As Donato fumbled with flint and steel, Dumond lit the lantern with a dollop of flame from his hand.

Donato took a sharp inbreath. "By the Night Lords, you do these things so casually. Have you never—? The monster . . ."

"Not every sorcerer has the kind of magic that lures the Enemy," I said. "Evidently Dumond's does not."

In the open space beyond four marble catafalques, Donato moved a woven mat aside and hauled open a trapdoor. As we descended a ladder into a narrow tunnel lined with stone and timber and waited for Placidio to help Dumond down, I gave him Teo's description of the Singular Wall and the kinds of magic that might or might not create a breach in it.

"You move things without carrying them, yes? When the magical act is done, it doesn't rebound. The world is different. You make the lie into truth." Unlike Dumond's passages that were always closed. And Neri, who was back where he started.

Donato dragged open an age-blackened door. "When I was small, I thought a demon must live in our house, moving things at random. Then I realized the demon lived inside me, and that it moved things when I was angry or fearful or overly curious, so I taught myself to be none of those things. When the Cavalieri attacked us—such a disgusting, brutish assault after I so stupidly thought I'd outwitted them—a cyclone of anger rose inside me. Then the cyclone was outside, too, everything in the keep spinning, flying. I didn't—couldn't—make it stop. I didn't *want* to make it stop."

Placidio held the door as Donato and I passed through into a chokingly narrow tunnel.

Dumond hobbled after us, using the walking stick Adjutant Gaspar had found at Villa Solitor.

"That's what happened with the other boy and the shelf," I said. "You were angry."

"The demon in me wanted to hurt a person I hated. Instead I killed an innocent."

"It was never a demon, but only your inborn talent. The monster—the Enemy—is something else. The monster comes through your dreams."

"The monster devoured the demon in me and took its place, feeding on my evil. I should have been sent to the Executioner long before that. Drowned while it was still possible."

"You were very young."

"I was half grown! I committed murder, violated the First Law of Creation, lied. I cowardly accused Guillam, and so my father— Night's daughters!" Donato flattened his back to the wall, eyes closed, breathing rapidly. In the shifting light, I felt as cold as if what warmth existed so deep in the earth had fled.

Pressing a finger to his mouth, Placidio waved Dumond and me backward—away from Donato. Then he raised the lantern high, spreading the light.

"Where exactly do we come out of this passage?" he said. "Beggars Ring for certain. Then we've got to climb to the Heights, and our friend here with the twisted ankle is going to be slow. We need to have a plan."

"We come out—?" Dono's eyelids twitched. His breathing slowed. "Near. Piggery. Owner has a mule."

"Ottone's pigs. I know where that is," said Dumond, understanding Placidio's strategy—get Dono's mind to fix on the mundane. On present action. On the ground under his feet. "A mule will help. You said you knew a sheltered spot for me to work our entry. It will take me half an hour to prepare. But we've only five hours or thereabouts until we need to have you and the lady to the Avanci Bridge. Is that enough?"

"To get there, yes. To devise some way to stop all this? I hope."

"Good," I said. "Onward then."

Moments later, we left the mausoleum tunnel for a pitch-dark alley. Placidio dimmed the lantern and asked if he should leave it before we closed the door.

"Take it. None will miss it tonight," Donato said and walked down the alley into the Beggars Ring.

We nudged a boy awake at the piggery barn and gave him three coppers for a half-day's use of the ass. The child was asleep again before Dumond was mounted. Our route took us around the Ring Road to the Serpentine—the backside road that threaded the secondary gates through Cantagna's rings.

I'd thought to use the climb through the city to find out exactly how Donato had become entangled with the Enemy, but after our experience in the tunnel, I hesitated to press. It was no longer a mystery why he traveled so little and kept his rooms plain. He had chosen to live without feeling or stimulation, because any emotion could lead to magic and to the monster who would not let him die. Think about *that* too much, and I would be the one with my back to the wall, shaking.

The Serpentine took another twist and led us into the Asylum Ring. Here and there, light flickered from an alley or a window. Faint music piped from a tavern. A cart of wine casks lumbered through the streets. The city was stretching, not quite asleep as yet.

Onward. Upward. Watch for sniffers in every corner, every alley.

Stay safe, little brother. Wake healed, my guardian.

Though heart and ears were open, as before, I felt nothing.

• • •

The city bells rang eight strikes as Dumond dabbed the last color on his painted door. I held the lantern for him, trying to stay balanced on the steep, rutted ground.

Placidio, sword drawn, stood guard in the gap between two buttresses, built to reinforce this section of Villa Giusti's north wall. The land beneath the massive wall had slumped over the years—earthquakes . . . landslides . . . drainage—and the wall had developed cracks. The massive piers built to reinforce it were joined at the top by a broad cornice which prevented the rain from doing more damage and any patrolling guards atop the wall from noticing us or our light.

Donato stood to the side, watching Dumond intently.

"That should do it," said Dumond, wiping his brush as he surveyed the finished work. "You say there's shelter on the other side at this spot where I can paint an exit door?"

"The stables," said Donato. "The minders sleep there, but they're all praetorian initiates, thus will be at the ceremonies. The loft would be the safest place for you to wait, lest a messenger ride in. Can you do this . . . work . . . from there?"

"I can. And safest is always my preference."

"We'd best go," said Placidio. "Night's passing."

Dumond packed his paints and called up his magic.

"Night Eternal . . ." whispered Donato as the small, narrow door became its truth and Dumond's blue fire winked out.

Placidio pulled it open. The odors of horse and hay mingled with those of mud and stone as he ducked and squeezed cautiously through. A sharp snort and rustling movement greeted him. "Hey there, beastie," he whispered. "Sh-sh-sh. Just passin'. All's good."

The rest of us followed at his word as he continued his soothing murmurs to the occupant of the stall.

Dumond quickly vanished the door. "I'll find the loft and ready our exit. Have a care, my friends."

Donato, Placidio, and I ghosted through a small yard, keeping to the shadows through a torchlit warren of outbuildings. A sniff told their tales. A reek of coal and iron bespoke a smithy; the sweet scent of leather and the dry grass smell of rope a saddlery. A blockish, windowless stone structure, sealed by massive locks, was surely an armory.

Donato did not speak or pause until the hard-packed dirt of the service yards yielded to an open expanse of cobblestones. Halting at the corner of the last work shed, he glanced in all directions, across the remnants of walls and abandoned fonts. Alone beyond the cobbled waste stood the stone-and-rubble structure Neri had described—a dome built atop four square walls the height of a tall man. Torches set to either side of a low doorway darted in the night breeze.

Neri hadn't known the words that would tell me exactly what this structure was. But I'd seen several very like when traveling

through the northern wildlands of Invidia with *il Padroné*. Sandro had said they were shrines so ancient none knew what gods
they honored. Invidian folktales named them gateways to the
Great Abyss. Certain, that was where I'd heard the word *pérasma*.
Pérasma meant passage or gateway.

Unease riffled my spirit. The Great Abyss was where the *daemoni discordia* waited to torment the unvirtuous. Demons existed
in the bowels of the earth, so Teo had told me, but after an earthquake or volcanic eruption could drift into occupied lands and
linger wherever they felt warmth. The maw of volcanoes. Hot
springs. *Demons . . .*

A trumpet fanfare sounded in the distance, its brilliance muffled by the bulk of the great house that rose to the south beyond a
jumble of kitchens and laundries.

Donato released a great exhale. "Come," he said. "No one will
be inside."

"Sniffers don't . . . sleep . . . there?" I said. Neri had seen them
being led inside.

"No one sleeps there."

We sprinted across the cobbles. Dono lifted a narrow plank
leaned against one of the broken walls. "If you would assist,
swordsman; I usually have attendants when I come."

Placidio helped Donato carry the heavy plank to the edge of
the sleugh. As Neri had reported, the iron trench surrounded the
entire building, and was very deep and very wide. A year's supply
of oil for ten villages must be required to make up the traditional
proportion for its filling. Water dribbled into the trough from the
mouth of a bronze fish just inside the trough—no doubt a connection to the city's pipes from the natural springs deep inside
Cantagna's hill.

Though no sound came from inside, Neri had been right about
the foul stench. The natural hot pools of the Costa Drago often
smelled of sulfur.

The men laid the plank in a bracket alongside the iron trench
and shoved it across the oily surface of the water through fittings
atop four iron supports until it reached another bracket on the far
side. Donato led us across.

A plain door—much newer than the stone and rubble wall—
was not locked. I followed the men inside. Donato turned up a

lamp. One might think the *pérasma* a crofter's home. The domed ceiling was lost in darkness, but the square walls were the same stone and rubble as the outside. Hooks and rings had been hammered into the walls to hold coiled ropes, lengths of cloth, and tools. Plain wood furnishings were set in useful groupings: a long table with a high stool beside it, a wooden chair with wide flat arms alongside a small table. Shelves holding a variety of cups, bowls, jars, flasks, and vials sat atop a standing workbench. "How ordinary."

Placidio stared at the workbench. "Not so much ordinary."

A closer look set my skin shriveling. The lengths of chain hanging from the hooks had neck collars attached. A bolt of green silk lay atop the scrubbed table, surrounded by a litter of thread spools and scraps, a needle case, and a fine pair of scissors. The wide-armed chair was festooned with straps, and the small table beside it held a tray of razors, knives, and large needles and a ceramic bowl stained with blood . . . or red ink. And what vile alchemy was done in the bowls and flasks on the workbench? This was where human men were transformed into howling beasts.

"Do either of you have open wounds?" asked Donato, giving us each a glance. "Bleeding?"

"Tied off," said Placidio. "Your man provided a roll of bandage along with the clothes."

"No," I said. "Why?"

"Blood attracts attention you'll not want. Bring that, if you would." Donato motioned toward the lamp. He picked a few things from the workbench shelves, slipped them into a small bag he'd hung from his shoulder, and started down a narrow stair off to my right. I'd not even noticed the stair.

My skin slithered across my bones. I reminded myself of the knowledge I believed was waiting here . . . and of this man's despair when he begged us to drown him. Reason claimed we were fools to follow him into the dark. Instinct told me to go.

At the foot of the stair was a stout iron door. At Donato's nod, Placidio pushed it open. Close, steamy air, redolent with the stench of rotted eggs, bathed us as we entered a natural cave of black rock. To either side of us was a bed-sized shelf of rock. A wall of iron bars, with a locking gate, masked the rest of the chamber.

Donato folded his arms across his chest. "My father brought

me down here for the first time two days after they dragged Guillam away. He told me to close the outer door. At fourteen I could scarce move it. We'll need to do that."

The door would shut off the stairs—and the outside world—for I saw no window slot or ventilation hole. A nervous quip about monsters and dungeons came to mind.

"What of our weapons?"

Placidio's question startled Dono, as much as it did me. "Weapons?"

"Should we bring them or leave them on the stair? On one hand, I've little faith in any Confraternity man—especially one who invites us to trust him as he leads us into a cellar, especially a man who was possessed by a murderous monster not a full turn of the sun ago. On the other hand, when he was possessed by that monster, weapons were more dangerous than helpful in the case of his perceived enemies."

"I won't— Down here, I have more control over myself. More experience than out in the world. I've no reason to believe matters should go so wrong, but then . . . Bring them or leave them as you feel is best. I swear to tell you everything and protect you as best I can."

Donato's mien was so open . . . so horrifyingly sober . . . I could not doubt his sincerity. I needed to know why the Enemy would not let him die. Placidio answered by shoving the door closed. We kept our weapons.

"Two others were here that night." Donato picked up his story without looking at us. "Zattiglia was an elderly man I'd seen in my father's company numerous times. I knew him only as an aide to the director enforcer. He lived in the east wing of the villa. But on that night he wore the yellow badge of the Defenders of Truth on his red gown. My father introduced him as the Protector of the Seal . . ."

". . . and First Defender of Truth," I said. The titles Dono was to assume.

"Yes. Father told Zattiglia that he might have found him an apprentice from his own house. He wished me 'tested' in the night's events."

"Was Guillam bound to one of these slabs?"

"No. He already lay beyond this next gate. I could hear him mewling like a wounded animal."

Dono's pale hand snapped a latch and drew open a narrow door in the barred wall. Before us the murky, green-black water of the font burbled, steamed, and whispered in a nest of jagged rock, crusted with black, green, and yellow. To the left of the pool was a low table—or bed—of polished basalt. Facing it from the opposite side of the pool was a high-backed, thronelike chair of the same black stone, carved and smoothed. Both bed and chair were fixed with enough leather straps to immobilize a man. Or a boy. *Spirits* . . .

Donato moved quickly to the far side of the pool, where a stone table held a wide iron bowl. He set out the pottery flasks and small jars he'd brought, then busied himself making a fire in the bowl.

"Guillam, was, of course, bound to that table," he said as he worked. "He had already been prepared. A part of the preparation is to ensure the candidate is weak. *In extremis,* so it was described to me, and left with open wounds."

The fire in the bowl blazed high, scented with incense and other rarities, Donato glanced up, his eyes bleak as winter in the flickering light. "I confessed then, as my father knew I would. I dropped to my knees and babbled that I was demon tainted, and that it was I who had brought down the shelf and killed the boy, and would they please just drown me in this pool and let Guillam go."

"But he already knew," I said and brushed my hand before my face as a cobweb or stray hair teased my eyelashes.

"Indeed so." Donato drank from a red-painted flask and replaced its stopper. "Father assumed that fear, strictly focused education, and encouragement in the personal discipline I already displayed would allow me to become his most effective ally in reforming the city. My public fit had sorely disrupted his plans. Thus he must turn my breach of discipline into a lesson, assuring me that I would understand the consequences of such insupportable weakness. He wished me to watch Zattiglia make Guillam into a sniffer. The conversion would not really be effective, of course, as sniffers must possess the taint of magic in order to be useful. But who would ever know?"

"Arrogant bastard!" spat Placidio.

I shared his revulsion. "Such stonehearted cruelty to use a boy so. *Two* boys."

"I am not searching for sympathy you've no reason to offer," snapped Donato. "The nature of—"

A tremulous chill swept over and through me despite the blaze and the steaming pool. At the same moment, Placidio hunched his cloak about his shoulders.

Donato shuddered. "Our bargain stands? You agree that I should demonstrate my problem, yes?"

"Yes." Placidio and I replied together.

Moving quickly, Donato thrust a blue-painted flask into my hands. Then he sat in the black stone chair and slipped his feet through the leather straps, pulling the buckles tight around his ankles, hips, and chest. "One of you should lock both the outer door and the inner. The other, if you would, please fasten these last two. . . ." He slipped his clenched fists through the straps across the chair's arms.

Placidio saw to the locks. I yanked the wrist straps tight.

Stepping back, I brushed my face again, realizing even as I did so that there were no cobwebs in this place and that no stray hairs had escaped my braid. Another tease at my neck, like wisps of storm cloud. But the blood on Donato shook me more.

"Dono, what have you done?" I said. "Your hands . . ."

He had unclenched his fists. His palms were bleeding . . . and trembling more violently with each passing moment.

"I'll be all right. As will you, I promise. You feel them, don't you? They're already roused. The smell of blood is a promise."

The mounting heat of the chamber neither soothed my shivers nor dismissed the cobweb sensations on my face and hands, and now through my clothing as well. "A promise of what?"

"Warmth. And purpose," he said. "Please cover the lamp and keep silent."

Darkness enveloped us, the only light the fire in the bowl across the pool. Reflections of the orange and green flames glinted in the bubbling water and illumined Dono's face. His eyes were closed and sweat beaded his temples.

"They bound me in this chair that night," he said, "and Father watched as Zattiglia ignited the summoning fire. Though I fought them, they forced me to drink from the red-painted flask, saying it was the same they'd given to Guillam to prevent his will resisting what was to come. Not to sleep, though. Never let the subjects sleep. They didn't cut me; Guillam was bleeding enough for the summoning. But something happened they didn't expect."

He laughed . . . despairing.

"Never thought I would do this voluntarily. Listen. Observe. As soon as you've seen enough to understand, force me to drink from the blue flask. Be sure I *will* fight you."

Dread infused every part of me. "Dono, what are you—?"

He began to sing in a clear, strong baritone. Eerie. The words were no language I recognized. The slow, complex melody, composed in a scale that grated on the ear and on the soul, could have been a rising storm wind or the rising dead. Three times he repeated it. By the end his tongue had grown thick and his head drooped. The only sounds remaining were the burbling water and the whisper of worms creeping across the ancient stone.

My hand found its way into Placidio's. I clung to his icy fingers as terror's own fist squeezed my heart ever tighter.

Of a sudden Donato's head lifted, slamming against the high back of his stone chair, and his eyelids opened. The firelight that bathed his face did not reach his eyes. His pupils had grown huge—wells of blackness.

"Sssssummoner, I answer. And I. And I. Ssssooo deliciously warm, this place offered . . ." Not one voice but many. Though they all spoke with Dono's lips, there were many timbres—smooth, sharp, harsh, hopeful, dull, brilliant, all of them filled with hunger . . . desire. "Mine own. Nay . . . *mine* own. A furnace burns in this one; sssuch pleasures await. . . ."

As the voices argued, Dono strained against the thick leather. His fingers twitched. His head thrashed. His eyes blinked. The toes of his boots wriggled. He fought for breath as if he were buried alive. Suffocating.

Demons. Enthralled and horrified, I now understood why sniffers possessed perceptions ordinary sorcerers lacked. Donato's reference to sniffers as demons back at Perdition's Brink had been no lazy metaphor.

How had Teo described them? Faulty scraps of human souls, formed for obedience, beings who longed for warmth and found it in the hot bowels of the earth. Beings who longed for purpose, though *of themselves* they had no ability to cross the barrier of flesh. But the Confraternity had discovered this barbaric way to instill them in a living person. No wonder that sniffers howled in pain and madness, when the freedom their spirits—their demons—

hungered for was no freedom at all, but sightless, wordless enslavement at the end of a chain.

As Dono writhed, the pool bubbled and steamed. Chill dampness wafted across my face. The floor and walls were native stone, shaped by flood and fire a millennium past. Livia could tell me of its metamorphoses. But in this hour it seemed to waver . . . fluid in the shifting light.

A fleeting streak of red. Glass shattered against the iron bars. The great iron bowl where the fire yet burned rocked alarmingly. A small jar flew off the black table and bounced on the uneven rock. Dono's magic . . . triggered by his terror . . . and the chaos inside him.

Still the yammering from Dono's mouth continued. "Sssssummoner, choose this being! No me. No me. Let me live. Thy will shall rule . . . mine own being is thine to command."

Dono's shaking threatened to bring down the rocks around us. His arms twisted in the wrist bindings, leaving thin bracelets of blood on his skin. His fingers curled into open cups.

My own tremors mimed his. Surely we should stop it now, before he burst.

"*Vieni vicino,*" he said, before I could move. "*Avvisami.*"

Spoken in the oldest dialect of the Costa Drago, it was a request for counsel. Companionship. Intimacy.

The world sighed as if the winds of summer had thawed the ice rivers of the northern mountains, releasing a blast to cool its sweating brow.

Sweet servant, so weary you are. . . . A woman's voice whispered through the heavy air. Heated. Sultry. Not inside me, but very near. The chamber had grown so chill, I shivered, as even the billowing flames rose high from the iron bowl.

As ever, you hold yourself too much prisoned in this human garb. Let me comfort you and set you free to wreak your will on those who think to master you. How dare they? Taste these sweetmeats you've brought me. I'll gladly share. We've no Vodai Guardian to torment us here . . . and yet someone else is near, a presence I yearn for. . . .

In the moment she paused, a great emptiness gaped inside me. I hungered for her touch on my hair, for her warmth to fill my veins. "Choose *me*," I murmured.

A huge, cold paw clamped over my mouth before I could utter another sound. Another hand squeezed my fingers, pinching, distracting, even as a gleaming knife whizzed past my head and clanked on the iron bars. A sharp crack, and a jagged chunk of yellow rock broke from the pool's rim and skittered across the floor.

My captor pressed his mouth close to my ear. "You're afire," he whispered, forcing my quivering fingers before my eyes. "They must not see you. Time to stop this."

They . . . Dono and Macheon the Enemy, who now looked out of Dono's eyes.

Even as fear and desire twisted my gut into a knot, I knew he was right. I nodded and Placidio released me. I unstoppered the blue flask and shoved it into his hand. He crept along the lattice wall through the shadows. For a moment, he crouched behind the black throne, then darted around the chair. Securing Donato's head in the crook of his arm, he pressed the flask to the young man's lips.

Donato roared and jerked. His shoulders writhed; his feet drummed; his arms yanked on the straps until the buckles rattled. Face down, I threw my body across Dono's lap to keep him still, so Placidio could get the liquid down him. A spray wet the back of my neck. Placidio's weight, smelling of wine and horse and sweat, pressed down on me as he tightened his grip.

A snarling gurgle above my head. Surely Dono would die choking.

Placidio's weight lifted, and he drew me back into the shadows as Donato gasped and coughed.

Water. Was there cool water anywhere in this hellish place? The boiling water from the pool would flay a man. I scuttled around to the tall stone table where the fire had dwindled. Indeed an urn sat underneath it. It stank of the pool, but was cool to my touch.

Ready to empty the urn onto Donato, I peeked around the table.

He was no longer fighting his bonds, only snapping out words. *"Vattene, spiriti rotti. Ritorna al fuoco. Ritorno. Ritorno."* Over and over. And then he added, *"La tua vera padrona ti aspetta. La tua vera padroné ti aspetta."*

Begone, broken spirits, he'd commanded. *Return to the fire. Return.* And then, *Your true mistress awaits. Your true master awaits.*

One expression after another—wonder, hilarity, rage, madness— glanced across his features. But his stone-hard commands erased every one. One surge of satisfied lust—not my own—and then my spirit hollowed.

The rattling litany ended abruptly, and Dono's head fell back against the chair. He breathed deep. Then again and exhaled long, slow, tremulous. A very human exercise.

The Enemy was no longer with us. That I felt bereft nauseated me.

"To my father's astonishment and Zattigllia's," he said, soft and hoarse, continuing as if nothing had interrupted his tale of horror, "the demons fought over *me*, not Guillam, even though it was his blood and weakness had drawn them here. Only when Zattiglia gave me the antidote, allowing me to assert my own will, and taught me the words of dismissal and sending would they leave me. Zattiglia had me dispatch one demon to Guillam and the rest of them back to the pool and the earth fires that make it boil. Once he'd cauterized Guillam's wounds and locked the iron collar about Guillam's neck, he brought in the inker and the sheather. Thus the boy who had tormented me had a demon prisoned inside him, while I was confined to my bedchamber to contemplate my future. A few days later, my father came to me, gleeful. They had tested Guillam, and, to his amazement and delight, Guillam was able to detect magic on certain artifacts kept for that purpose."

"Even though the boy was not truly a sorcerer," said Placidio.

"Even though. They had tried many times to find a rite to put a demon into an untainted subject. There are references to such a practice in old journals in the Athenaeum. But in five hundred years no one had managed it." Dono's fists clenched. "So you see why my father considers me valuable and will not suffer me to slip from his control."

"Because you enable them to use anyone—like Guillam, like youths your father bought from the Cavalieri Teschio." Disgust and loathing filled my arid emptiness.

"Yes. He's out there somewhere. Guillam. Maybe in Cantagna . . . maybe in some other independency. Once disciplined to the leash, they're sent where they're needed most. I once thought that, if ever I was free and sane, I'd try to find him . . . what's left of him. But I doubt that could ever happen. They burn out quickly, sniffers, especially those without the taint of magic. Some can be revived here, but most not. This corruption, my father's and my own, must be ended."

Placidio and I unbuckled the bindings. Donato sat for a moment, rubbing his forehead tiredly. Then he rose and began methodically to clean up the room—the broken glass, the fire bowl, the other items his magic had scattered.

"Father and Zattiglia surmised that it was my innate desire to cleanse myself of the taint made it happen, and that the demon had somehow carried the power of my magic into Guillam. They believed me to be the instrument the universe designed to rid itself of sorcery. I wanted to believe that, too—that my perversion had purpose in our great work. But then came the dreams, and eventually the voices of the dream took form. At first I thought they were gods, approving my work, but the dreams taught me elsewise. As the monster took deeper hold of me, I studied in the Athenaeum, trying to understand what I was. I worked even harder on self-discipline until I could control my magic. Until I could *control* the dreams and visitations."

He glanced up, questioning.

Everything I thought I understood about him shifted yet again. This time my quivering was a powerful, growing fury. "You're telling me that last night was no uncontrollable accident. You *purposefully* invited the monster so you could destroy the Cavalieri. You risked setting the beast free to savage the world only to discover you could not pull back. What kind of stupid, arrogant—?"

"And here tonight, you did it again," snapped Placidio. "You summoned the Enemy apurpose. What if you'd lost control again?"

"You are exactly correct." Dono paused in his work. "I was an arrogant fool last night, consumed by anger, humiliation, and the fear that has not left me since I first understood I held the taint. I assumed that because I had learned to control my . . . partnership . . . with the monster down here, I could wield it as a tool of vengeance. And that I might be able to save *one* life . . . do *one* decent deed after all these years. Clearly I was wrong. And yes, tonight I should have been more forthright. But would you have come here if you knew what I had done? And how could you believe all this, understand the risks of my father's plans, if you didn't experience it for yourself? Tonight I was the only one bleeding for the summoning rite, and I used the red flask to ensure

I could hold no barrier to the demons. Blood and weakness lure them. Once I drink from the blue flask—the antidote to the red—I can issue the words of sending and dismissal. But over the years, it has become more and more difficult to get the demons out of me. Zattiglia always dispatched the rest of the demons back to the spring—heated by the earth's fires. If some refused to go, he would lock a bleeding victim inside here, and after a few days, the victim would be dead and the demons would have returned to the hottest place they knew—the pool. One will always take the offer of a living body of its own. But now they know that I can provide an even better destination."

"Better?" said Placidio.

"More and more of them refuse to leave me unless I send them on to their maker."

"To Macheon," I said, despairing in a moment when I thought I could feel nothing more.

"I think that's why the monster won't let me die. Because I send it companions. For now, I send the monster a few of the demons and I'm able to force the pathway closed, as I just did. But clearly I cannot hold forever. Soon it will be impossible to send the demons elsewhere or to close myself to the monster, even in this place where I'm most capable. You see the problem."

Donato's problem—the world's problem—was imminently clear. Teo had told me that the Enemy's prison prevented Macheon from devouring his demon servants and thus making himself stronger. *Impermeable*, he'd said. *The demons cannot find their way back to their creator. . . .* Only they had.

26

Fanfares and exuberant cheers filled the night from the Confraternity celebration as Placidio, Donato, and I slipped into the dark stables. After a few moments' listening, Donato had told us the feast day ceremonies still had some three hours to run. Events would continue after that, but guards and servants would start drifting back to their posts.

Placidio whistled a round of a favorite drinking song as several of the horses nickered a soft greeting.

"It's about time." Dumond's words dropped from the top of the loft stairs like old boots. "Between the cheering and the trumpets, I had all sorts of visions of you three being paraded up to a lopsman's block to finish off the ceremonies."

As I topped the stairs, Dumond was leaning against a roof support, shining his pale handlight on a hay door in one corner of the loft—or rather the painted image of one that would look perfectly natural to any ordinary observer. "Are we ready to leave this benighted place?"

"Not yet," I said. "We have to decide what to do."

"This gentleman's problem is most definitely problematical," said Placidio, sitting at the head of the loft ladder. "We've a nest of demons—true demons, not human ones—being fed to the Enemy, which is why he's getting strong enough to rattle the earth. We've a nest of vipers—human ones—who believe it's righteous to infest anyone they please, even non-sorcerers, with said demons, and enslave them as sniffers. These vipers are so obtuse, they have no idea this little ritual is going to bring on the very calamity they claim to be avoiding. And this young fellow here has more secrets than our friend from the Isles of Lesh, and I wish I had leave to beat the last of them out of him."

"You've heard them all," said Donato, who did not sit. Rather he looked as if he could wish no better fate than to become one of the boards in the plank wall. "Ask me what you will, and tell me how to unravel this tangle. I'm willing to fight. I'm willing to die if you can figure out how to accomplish that . . . but only if I can be sure that doesn't leave matters worse."

"I would dearly love to ask our friend from the Isles of Lesh—" Placidio stopped abruptly and leapt to his feet, sword drawn, a hand upheld to hush us all.

Dumond held his hand steady lest a sudden movement of his handlight attract attention. My hand rested on my dagger.

From the darkness below, amid the grunts and whuffles of the stable's residents, rose a clear tenor, singing softly.

> *"Damizella, damizella, come and have a feast with me.*
> *No fish nor fowl nor pig will tell the landlord what they see.*
> *We can roast them in the firepit, while we wrestle in the*
>   *hay. . . ."*

Neri. A knot in my chest that I didn't even know was there loosened.

Dumond grinned; his ivory light even revealed the ghost of a smile on Donato's stony face.

Placidio lowered his sword and completed the round. "With bellies full and pleasure sate, we'll laugh the night away."

Neri bounded up the ladder and glanced around, bedraggled and uncharacteristically solemn. "I'm not dead. You four are not dead. Guess that's good news."

"What of your charges?" I said, the moment's relief vanished. Neri was no good at hiding distress.

"The lady is ready to play the ransomed bride, but she's nigh on to bursting with wanting to know what's doing with him." Neri waved his hand at Dono. "I told her some that seemed safe enough to say. But it wasn't enough. She swears that she'll march straight through that burial place and knock on every tomb, if I don't come back to fetch her to the rest of us."

"And Teo?"

Neri's mouth worked . . . but for a moment nothing came out. He didn't look at me. "By the time we got to the city, his marks were gone. His lips blue. He'd never blinked, Romy. Never moved. So I told him . . . to do what needed done. That we wished him at peace. He took one breath, but there was a hard rattle to it. I'd only heard such breathing twice—both when Mam birthed a babe didn't live past a day. The lady agreed he was surely dying, though she came near knifing me when I told her what I was going to do. But I . . . did like swordmaster said."

No, no, no. Teo was the promise . . . the hope of some grace beyond the tawdry world. I'd been so sure his capacity for healing would revive him, and yet he'd warned me over and again that he was not ready to confront the Enemy.

"You put him in the river." Placidio voiced what I could not.

"I sat there in the shallows with him. He never moved of his own, else I'd have pulled him out. Never breathed again, never twitched when the water washed over his face or when the current took him. Romy, I tried— I hoped I might *hear* something from him like you did. But I didn't. I just believed what—I told myself he'd want to go home."

Guilt and grief drove me to my knees. Teo had warned me of the risk, and I had forced him, not considering whether wielding a weapon too early could mean losing it for the coming war. In a cruel irony, my last plea had been that I needed him. And at the end, I'd not been there to beg his forgiveness. Even now, I was consumed by selfish doubt: How in the Night Eternal were we going to solve this problem without him?

"You did right, lad." Placidio laid his big hand on Neri's shoulder. "The river will take him wherever he needs to go. We have to do this without him."

For once, I didn't question Placidio's uncanny certainty, nor did it annoy me. For once, I just willed him to be right, no matter where Teo's destination might be.

"Your friend dead?" said Donato. "I am so sor—"

"Do not speak that word. Don't even think it." I could not stem the rush of murderous resentment. "You have no idea what you and I, in our thoughtless arrogance, have done."

He fell silent, eyes closed.

But we had no time to spend on resentment or sorrow, even though stars, sun, and moon must surely be dimmer from this night forward.

"All right," I said. "As Placido says, we must solve this problem on our own."

"Shouldn't we get out of here?" said Neri, looking round uneasily. "That's a sizeable crowd of hostile folk out to the fountain court."

"Not yet," I said. "Donato's difficulty is worse than we imagined, too. We might need to return to the *pérasma*."

"Let me tell you what we're dealing with here," said Placidio, and in an unembellished narrative described the events in the *pérasma* for Neri and Dumond.

As he told the story, I fingered my luck charm . . . and its graven symbol of Teo's family—the Vodai, mages who took their power from water. We had thought the charms might protect us from a sniffer's magic. More likely they shielded us in some way from the sniffer's demon.

As Placidio's narrative ended, Dumond ruffled his thinning hair. "By the Great Anvil," he whispered. "What a nasty stew."

Neri's brow had wrinkled tighter with every word Placidio spoke, and as soon as the narrative was complete, he could no longer contain himself. "So, Dono, you can't simply refuse to make sniffers, because you'll die *or worse*. Then your da'll find some other sorcerer to take up your job, and *that* sorcerer might not be able to prevent the Enemy walking right into his body and slaughtering whoever steps in his way, because you've worked at keeping the monster out of you for a very long time and are damned good at that part of it—when you don't let the villain have you on purpose."

"Yes."

"But if you keep on doing your nasty job, you'll have to feed the monster, else you'll get stuck with a thousand demons in your head who won't leave. Then you go crazy *or worse*, and perhaps the Enemy walks right back into you like it did yesternight, and you can't do anything about it."

"Yes."

"Yet you would like to be able to stay on in the Confraternity—in good grace, as to say—because it gives you the chance to clean up the wickedness your da has played, like buying young folk from the Cavalieri and murdering bookbinders. And because you are his loyal son, you think you could get the goods on him and stop it."

"Exactly so."

I was awestruck. So clear. Right to the point. Enough that it told me what question had to come next. "Why do you have to send some of the demons to Macheon and some go willing to the pool? You said the other man, Zattiglia, would always send them back to the pool."

"The entities are not"—Dono searched for the word—"raindrops or leaves. They are individuals. Without name or memory of themselves or the world, but distinct from each other. They know the words of summoning give them a chance for a new life of their own. They recognize the ritual: the fire, the blood, the presence of a warm body that will not fight them and could give them a chance to live and breathe. That is a lure that is irresistible. They knew Zattiglia, the man I replaced, and they know I am different from him. From the moment I entered the *pérasma* to watch Guillam transformed, they recognized that I was bound to the one you name Macheon—the Enemy—Dragonis. To be with their maker is their uttermost desire. Some—more each time—refuse to return to the pool or anywhere but their maker. They learn."

"Spirits," I said, understanding. Macheon, the Dragoni mage, stripped the spirits from living humans, then cut and trimmed and twisted them to loyalty and obedience. Teo had even said that demons were not purposeful evildoers. They yearned only for warmth and purpose. "So, Dono, do you . . . experience . . . the same individuals every time?"

Donato's eyes fell shut in that now familiar retreat. But his body did not sag. "I've been doing this since I was fourteen. Rare is the day I feel a new entity. There are thousands of them. Tens of thousands. So even that rarity could just be one I've not noticed before."

"So all of them are particular to this hot spring." Demons drift, Teo had told us, but once they found a good place they had no motive to leave but for a better one. "When you've summoned them as you did tonight, are *all* of them inside you?"

"It's impossible to know. I make the summoning as brief as possible . . . to prevent that. They are so very many . . . so very hungry . . ."

Unimaginable. And yet it—and the cool bronze of my luck charm—led me onward. "How long can you hold them before sending them on to a victim or to Macheon or back to the pool?"

I'd never seen his lids pop open so fast or so wide. "How *long*? I never—why would you *ask* that?"

"Because I have an idea. Neri laid out your problem quite succinctly. We have to separate those demons from that spring."

I'd not thought Donato's complexion could pale any further. "You want me to summon them . . . all of them, and then hold . . . carry them with me." The words could scarce squeeze past his horror. "To where?"

A plan was forming. Desperate, but perhaps just possible. "There's a place that might work. I know it would be terrible for you. Dreadful. But you've shown us your strength and your control, and we would help in every way we could. Could you do it? An hour? Two, maybe?"

"Two *hours* . . ." He might well have said *eternity*. "And at the end of that . . . what?"

No need to say what we all knew. At the end of that, the Enemy would be waiting for his feeding and for Dono, too, and what strength would Dono have left to resist?

"I have an idea about that, as well," I said. Teo had told me—in things he said, and things he did not say. Unless I was entirely wrong. This would be a wicked gamble, but the only way I could see to accomplish the most important things. "A way to lure them out and eliminate them."

I didn't force an answer. Dono hadn't said no, so I continued.

"That would leave you intact and returned to your family and your . . . position. The demons would be gone from the *pérasma* and only you would know. Perhaps, we could even find a way to render this spring unwelcoming to demons in the future—the drifters, those dispersed by earthquakes or volcanoes."

"Easiest to just bring down the damnable place to start with," said Dumond. "The structure was well-built—in perfect equilibrium— but some sapping and a careful application of nitre powder and it's a ruin. Without anyone having to carry demons around."

"No good if the demons are still in residence," said Placidio. "The Confraternity would rebuild the structure. Begin the cursed practice again. Am I right?"

Donato acknowledged it.

"And it would be awfully suspicious to do it right when Dono returns home," I said. "But perhaps we could pour or drop something in to sour it so no passing demons would settle there."

"We know someone might be able to help with that," said Neri. "When I told Livia you were going to a place smelled like rotted eggs, she was surprised. Said no one told her there was a hot spring at the villa. I guess she's seen lots of them on her travels. Seemed to think they were fine for bathing and good for the skin and all manner of hurts unless they were too cold or too hot, in which case something had to be done."

His recitation was a perfect rendition of Livia. Worth a laugh on any other day.

"Colder might do it," I said. "So maybe she knows what that might be. Fetch her, Neri. Bring her through the graveyard like Dono showed us and up to the villa wall. Do you remember the place? Dumond can meet you there. Dono says we have at most two hours until people start leaving the ceremonies." This could be our only chance for Livia and Dumond to see the pool.

"I'll meet them at the piggery and get the girl up here," said Dumond. "Ottone's genial little ass should be right where I left him outside the wall. You three sort out the demons. We'll figure out how to make their nest unwelcome."

Neri was gone in an instant. Dumond glared at me from under his scrub-brush brows as if he had guessed the terrifying notion that had come to me. "You won't decide anything . . . final . . . until we're back, yes?"

Must reading thoughts be added to Dumond's growing list of extraordinary skills?

"We have to think it out," I said. "But I'll need you to— We need a change of clothes and some extra weapons cached. And I believe we're going to need a boat under the bridge. It would allow one of us to keep watch for praetorians readying an ambush." And other possibilities.

"I can see to the boat and Vash to the supplies." Dumond fired his new doorway that should take him back to the matching one between the buttresses of the Villa Giusti wall. A few moments and both had vanished.

"You're certain no sniffers are inside the villa walls, Donato?" I said, imagining the steady rumbling of Dumond's power, and the darts of bright magic that had brought my brother inside and taken him out again.

Donato yet stood with his back to the wall, arms wrapped tightly about himself. But his shoulders and his head drooped with every appearance of sleep. "No sniffers within the walls as yet," he whispered. "I always know when they're near. Their demons . . . call out to me."

"Mother Gione's heart!" Those threads . . . those voices. Dono paid harshly for his power. "So sniffers that are made in other places are seeded with demons, too."

"This is the only place in the Costa Drago where we do this work. So, in essence, yes."

"Aye. And therein lies a difficulty, young Dono." Placidio yet stood beside the ladder, back slumped against a roof support. His powerful hands fingered his unsheathed dagger. An idle pose by appearance, but I'd not have challenged him on any matter at that moment. "You want to continue in your work to give you time to expose your father's crimes. But what of the Confraternity's crimes? Is our young friend who just departed, a youth who can draw a smile even from you who has likely not smiled ten times in his life, ever going to lie on that stone table of yours *in extremis*?"

"If there are no demons left—"

"The Confraternity made sniffers long before they understood why those made here were more effective than those made elsewhere." The dagger had fallen still.

Dono raised his head, allowing us to see the trouble in his face. "That's true. If I can return here uncompromised in my father's eyes, I will hold the office of the First Defender of Truth. If the demons are gone, I will have the use of my mind, as well as time and authority to investigate. In any case, my position gives me final say over any candidate. Even my father must yield to my judgment. He raised me apurpose for this work and has no doubt of my loyalty. He believes me too cowardly and weak to choose any course he would oppose."

"So you might save Neri, but you would still condemn other young sorcerers to mutilation and slavery or send them on to the Executioner," I said.

I could not be entirely surprised at that. I no longer thought

Donato at all weak or cowardly, but precepts of a lifetime, loyalties so deeply ingrained, could not change instantly.

For me, it made no difference to this plan. I did not take this risk for Donato alone, but for our city and the world that would suffer if the Enemy was unleashed. For Livia, and my oath to her friend Marsilia that I would keep the girl alive. And for Teo's people, who must groom someone to replace him in duties beyond understanding. Teo had thought the danger at Perdition's Brink worth risking his own safety. His life. *Spirits* . . .

Grief threatened to shroud my every thought and word—like a sheath of green silk that separated one from the living world. How could he be dead?

"Please understand." Dono looked at each of us in turn, his dark brows knit tight. "I've never encountered any sorcerers like your vanishing brother, and that quiet man who paints magic, and the two of you. Despite what you may think, not all of your kind— *our* kind—are so thoughtful about their workings. I've witnessed horrors beyond my own. Heard testimony of others. And even if I trust your word that this Enemy does not have power over *all* sorcerers, how can you deny that there is danger in what we are? All I can promise is that I will look deeper. Be more careful, more thoughtful. Assuming I have eyes or mind by the end of this night."

"Forcing a man to live as a sniffer is evil and inhuman, whether or not you put a demon in him. Our position on that will not change," I said, "assuming we have minds to judge with by the end of this night."

"Just thought we should have matters clear," said Placidio. "Shall we hear out my partner's plan?"

27

The Feast of the Lone Praetorian celebrated a victory over a sorcerers' uprising three centuries past—the last such rebellion. Whatever magics those sorcerers possessed had not saved them from their fate; even the dead ones were bound in chains so that the Executioner of the Demon Tainted could throw them from his cliff into the sea—the only ending considered certain for our kind. Only Teo had made me believe a dead sorcerer might not be *entirely* dead. But as I gazed from the North Tower parapet out over Cantagna and its great river, bathed in the light of the full moon, and willed my friend to speak to me, the world remained silent, its colors reduced to gray and every shade of black.

He was truly dead.

There would be time later to mourn, if the night went well. Even so, I could not shed the loss; the gamble I planned was grounded in logic, but no one could tell me if it was possible. Teo could have. Teo could have made it work. But his teaching would have to carry me through. That and my partners. *The four of you,* he'd said, *bearing each other upon your shoulders . . .*

I yanked at the ropes binding the bridge warden I had blind-sided with a risqué song, a sloppy kiss, and a flask of wine thoroughly laced with Vashti's sleeping drops. The knots held tight; the warden slept peacefully.

The sleeping drops and rope were only two of the treasures Vashti had left for us on the stair hidden inside one of the bridge's mold-blackened abutments. The Shadow Lord had shown me that stairway, one of his many private byways through the city he loved, when I was fifteen and still terrified of him. It had been a moonlit night like this one when we had first strolled across the Avanci Bridge. From this vantage, the graceful footbridge appeared like a ribbon of starless midnight stretched tight across the sparkling water.

Tonight Sandro's stairway held changes of clothes for all of us, more ropes, two flasks of ale, wound dressings, blankets, spare weapons. Vashti's six sand-filled bags, their type and weight a match for those I'd specified for the ransom had been there. They now sat waiting a few steps away from me.

Donato was tucked away down in that hidden stairwell, too, the chaos of the frenzied demon horde inside him contained from bursting through his skin by naught but a few loops of rope and his iron discipline. He had cut his forehead to ensure he had plenty of blood to entice them, and he had sung his ritual summoning for half an hour to be sure to get them all.

Placidio and Livia kept watch on him. I had volunteered to take the tower post, as I could no longer bear to see his agony—expecting his face to shatter like an overripe carcass at any moment to reveal the horror within. Please the universe and every being within it, the night's result would be worth that pain.

Livia fidgeted, believing she could sour the *pérasma* with time and the right materials. Tonight we had neither. If we failed, it might not matter.

A sharp rap on the thick wood door in the tower's center turret sent me across the short radius of the rooftop. I pressed my back to the curved wall beside the door. Two more raps . . . a delay . . . and a third. Breathing again, I responded with a double rap of my own, then returned to my watchpost.

Neri joined me, his black hood raised. He stood carefully close so we would appear to be the same shadow to any observer. "Nothing yet?"

"No movement at all," I said. No ransom had been deposited on the bridge. That left me—and my partners who lurked in the secret stairway or bobbed in the little dinghy tied up in the deep shadows under the bridge—stalled breathless at the brink of the Abyss after two frantic hours racing to get there.

"Dono's in a bad way."

"But still holding?" I said.

"Don't know how."

I knew how. He had refused to ingest any herb or potion that could dull his mind or sap his will. He believed full control of himself would be the only way to prevent yielding to the Enemy's allurements. But by the time we got here his flesh was already too hot to touch. While Livia sponged his brow and whispered encouragement, Placidio stood guard, his attention riveted on Donato rather than any threat from the Confraternity. That watch was left to me here atop the tower and to Dumond far below in a borrowed dinghy, from which he could see the water and the river path as he pretended to fish. And to Neri, who was everywhere.

"What if the Confraternity bastards—?" I silenced Neri with a touch.

A shadow . . . three shadows . . . topped the steps that ascended from the riverside path and entered the tunnel under the Tower that led onto the bridge. Three figures emerged onto the bridge. Good. They had not left one behind to obstruct our path.

I tapped Neri's hand three times to call attention and felt him nod in acknowledgment.

The bridge lamps had not been lit tonight—no coincidence— but not a circumstance to prevent our moving forward. The full moonlight silhouetted the newcomers against the dark bridgework. Dark-colored ankle-length gowns—Confraternity gowns?— swirled as they hurried to the exact center of the span and deposited several pale objects the right size for a miller's standard small portion of flour. Number, position, and kind were exactly as my message had specified. But as two of the three hurried onward to the far side of the river, one remained with the bags.

I cursed under my breath and scoured my memory for the exact words I'd written. No praetorians, wardens, or constables on the river path, in boats, in the Bottoms, on the bridge *tower*. Had I truly not specified the damnable bridge itself? As I'd held a dagger at his throat, the overwhelmed tower warden had whimpered that he was just finishing his supper before vacating his watch as ordered. The small basket with the remains of bread and sausage had testified in his behalf. So I'd assumed our adversaries were complying with our terms. Now I was not so sure.

No tower, but two lampposts marked the far-side terminus of the Avanci. It was too far to judge if the other two persons remained between the lampposts. But I'd best assume so. Steps descended steeply from the terminus into the crowded jumble of shanties, stables, and warehouses called the Bottoms. We had always assumed the Confraternity would hide praetorians or Gardia near the stair, ready to swarm the bridge as soon as we tried to leave with the money bags.

Given Donato's state—and all we hoped to accomplish by it—one man's presence and a possible two more could not deter us. The Confraternity had gambled and won a slight advantage.

"You can work around him, yes?" I whispered over my shoulder.

"Certain."

I squeezed his hand. "Go. And be careful of your shoulder."

"Shoulder's fine. Don't even feel it."

The door did not move, but when I glanced over my shoulder next, my brother and two of Vashti's bags were gone.

Fighting not to blink, I trained my eyes a few steps from his destination, the lamppost that marked the exact center of the span. The gowned person—height and stride suggested a man—paced and swiveled, clearly watching both approaches. Occasionally he glanced over one stone railing or the other. The long climb from the river was possible, but very exposed, and the winds that gusted through the three great spans made any attempt even more perilous.

I blinked and there was Neri, two bags in hand. The man was at the apogee of his path, facing the far-side end, and spun sharply, but Neri had already vanished. The fellow leaned over the upriver railing and studied the great piers to either side of the center span and the sharp-nosed footers that protected them from the floods that could roar down the Venia.

In an eternal few moments, a heaving Neri was walking toward me from the vicinity of the turret.

"The fellow's Confraternity for sure. No weapons in his hands." He dropped two bags that chinked instead of thudded, and picked up two of our false ones. "Coin sounds real enough."

We cared little for the ransom money, but everything for the appearance of truth in this exchange. The knotted cord came loose at my picking. I pulled out a handful of silver solets, pitching one to Neri. "So far, so good."

Neri grinned, pocketed the coin, and was off again before I could return the rest of them to the bag.

This time, I never glimpsed Neri on the bridge, just noted two bags in a slightly different position. The pacing Confraternity fellow didn't seem aware, and, on his return, Neri didn't even pause. Soft, quick steps. A chink of bagged coins, a moment's glimpse of his black-clad figure, and the air shifted at his turn and departure.

The third time the man on the bridge heard him, too, and spun just before Neri took form. I near choked until I realized that the fellow had spun the wrong direction. Close.

"Two helmets by the lampposts on the Bottoms end of the bridge." Neri's whispered words reached me before he was entirely visible. "Praetorian helmets."

He set the bags down carefully and sagged against the turret wall, shoving his hood and his lank black curls backward. The grin was gone. "Still none below us here that I could see. But, Romy, the man on the bridge. It's Dono's da."

Bastianni! A man who knew me as the Shadow Lord's longtime mistress. Never did I imagine a director would risk himself in an exchange with a snatch-crew, even if he believed the danger slight. Every lingering fear for Livia . . . and Dono himself . . . came to the fore. Was the director here to murder them? This could change everything, yet we could afford to change nothing.

I glanced over the parapet. Bastianni was walking slowly along the bridge toward the Bottoms, arms folded, head bowed as if in contemplation—or as if hunting the source of the noise that had startled him.

"How did you get him to look the other way?"

"Tossed that coin over his head. Tried to bounce it through the railing. Gave me a chance to look at his face, but kept him distracted so he wouldn't see mine."

"Clever." But I glanced back and Bastianni was crouched down. Had he found the coin? "Come," I said. "Leave the treasure here. We're out of time."

If Bastianni discovered the bags were filled with sand beforetime, he might call off the ransom exchange and call up a hunt instead. We had no intention of staying around to haul the bags off the bridge after the exchange, but we wanted them to discover the crew had taken the money. For Donato's safety, this had to feel like a play by a legitimate snatch-crew. They already believed us sorcerers.

Wordless, we sped down the gate tower's left-side stair. The stair ended in an alcove off the gate tunnel below. Inside the alcove, behind the last twist of the stair, was another door, a boarded-up relic of an older structure. A hidden latch opened that door onto a short passage and yet another downward stair inside the bridge abutment—the Shadow Lord's private stair that led down to the riverside.

Neri stood watch in the tunnel alcove while I raced down the hidden stair toward the glow of lamplight.

"It's me," I called, as the same tableau I'd left behind came into view. Placidio armed and alert beside the outer door. Livia chewing her nails as she watched Donato. The young man himself shaking in pent-up madness, face ravaged, hands contorted, lips bitten bloody—the absolute argument that we could not stop now. He had trusted us beyond measure.

"Stars and stones, tell me we're ready to go," said Livia. "He'll have no mind left."

"We go now. But there's a wicked complication. His father is waiting for us on the bridge."

Livia paled. "I want a weapon."

"You can't," I said. "Not if we're to preserve the lie of the snatch as long as possible. If matters turn sour—and yes, I'm worried about that, too—grab my boot knife." I patted my left boot. Certain, there could be a problem with that, too, if her need came too late.

Placidio sheathed his sword. "Gods' breath . . . I'll take point. You keep your hood on and stay behind me."

"No," I said. "Neri spied at least two praetorians hanging about the far-side approach. You're our only defense."

Placidio had to wait in the tunnel, ready to fend off any attack from the two waiting praetorians or others who might rush in behind us. Neri had to join Dumond in the boat for the event's final play. I was counting on them. I had no Vodai Guardian to watch over me.

"I'll just have to use my magic earlier than I planned," I said. "If Dono can contain a thousand demons for nigh on two hours, I can play out the prisoner exchange while not entirely myself. I shall recall my late tutor's lessons about grounding my senses and I'll survive it all . . ."

. . . assuming Livia and Donato did their part as we planned, and Neri and Dumond were in the right place at the right time. Assuming I had not misjudged Teo's implications about demons or my own skills at survival. So many pieces to a most imprecise gambit.

Placidio's gray eyes spoke his beliefs. "Are you sure of this, Romy? Did you speak to Neri about what you plan? I thought you should be the one to tell him."

"Yes, I'm sure, and absolutely not. Neri's still too fond of going his own way without thinking. I've the skills. The Enemy values me. And any other plan leaves Livia and Dono—the two *we* pulled into this benighted scheme—at even greater risk. If the outcome is what we want, my fate won't matter."

Before he could argue, I turned to Livia. "So, one thing is going to change. Nis will lead you out to the ransom exchange."

"Nis?" She looked around wildly, as if discovering she'd failed in the vigilance we'd impressed upon her. "Is she . . . capable . . . of pulling this off? You said she was in hiding, though I'd come to think she was actually—" The girl recovered herself and squinted at me in that way she had that made you feel like you were an insect under her opticum lens. "Ah no, I was right. Nis *is* you. What a *player* you are, to be so convincing! How—?"

"Let me tell you this one thing about Nis," I said. "If she begins to act very un-Nis-like—as if she's afflicted with Donato's madness—run away from her as fast as you can."

"Well, certain, I would, but how could that happen so quickly? And why? I insist on hearing about this—"

"Explanations must come later. For now, we go. Remember that if Donato should falter or collapse from the weight of this illness, it is safe to help him. You'll recognize if the other takes him over as before?"

"As when people start gutting each other? Yes. I do see clearly that something different is going on with him tonight, and I look forward to a *complete* explanation of that as well. But I shall play the rescued victim, dutifully concerned about her husband-to-be and wishing to strangle the vile felons who snatched us."

"Exactly that," I said, a smile working its way out from a place I thought was barren of them just now. I bound her wrists for show, as we had agreed, leaving the ties loose enough she could assist Dono or grab a weapon to defend herself.

"Donato, we are ready to begin our exercise." Placidio released the bindings on Donato's ankles and got him to his feet. The young man, forlorn in his filthy nightshirt, could stand alone, though shaking and hunched over his bound hands as if he had aged sixty years. "Do you understand me? Let me know that you comprehend."

A determined jerk of Dono's head was clear agreement, despite his wordless trembling.

"We will climb a few stairs and walk out onto the bridge. Livia and another woman—a stranger—will accompany you. No matter who else is there, no matter what is said, your strength and your resolve will carry you onward. You recall the words of dismissal and sending, yes? And you recall their destination, yes? Spoken at the right time, they will set you free. And perhaps, at the same time, illuminate your conscience."

Another assent. And one more.

I pulled up my hood and joined them.

And so we climbed to the bridge. Donato and Placidio. Then Livia, her shoulders square as she marched into the unknown wearing naught but her soiled chemise. And then Romy, who must risk a leap of faith while looking square into the face of her Enemy. Failure or miscalculation meant death or, as Neri had put it, *worse*. Best put that prospect aside for now.

First, I had to become Nis, with all the risks that implied for our long, slow walk to the middle of the bridge. Nis had to be wary of the other voice that would intrude. She had to focus on her important mission, and put that voice off until the snatch-crew business was done. She knew the words she had to say no matter what else was happening.

I spat in my hand, scraped a dusty corner of the stair, and dirtied my face. Nis was not so great at cleanliness. But she was stalwart. And trustworthy. These snatchers trusted her to redeem their captives. Livia, the rich girl, had taught her how to be brave. To speak her mind. Her mam would be so proud of her to have such a responsibility. . . .

The young man's father was to be the contact. A wicked man, by all accounts, though his silver tongue spoke of virtue and honor. A man who might be armed. Who might have a mind to murder me and the clever rich girl and even his son, the shy rich boy who had survived his captivity and this strange illness so bravely. My new capo was not beholden to the old Cavalieri, but only to these clever bandits. They had taken me in and were allowing me to prove my worth because I was the only one who had been with the two since the beginning. . . .

Capo, a big man in a black hood, yielded the sickly young man's arm to the rich girl as we walked out of the tunnel. I walked proudly beside the two. The moonlight showed our way—and showed us the tall man who stood waiting beside the ransom bags. I knew a secret about the bags that made me smile.

"Who goes there?" Anyone could recognize the tall man as an important personage by his bearing, even if his red gown, shifted by the river wind, were not so fine. His garments were sewn with real gold, so Capo had told me. But I must not be brought low by the man's clothing. I must do proud duty for this new crew who had faith in me.

Our progress was slow, as the young man was shaking near hard enough to tremble the bridge. And the rich girl helping him walk kept glaring at me like I was a spectre. I could hear Mam advising that I must stay in control of this dangerous meeting. Mam had died young, but she was very wise. Her voice told me that this event was far more important even than I knew. So I didn't answer the imposing man until we were within twenty paces or so and could halt with dignity.

"Get down, you." I pointed to the ground, and the young man dropped to his knees, trembling like a drunkard in the last throes. My hand was steady, my dagger perfectly still.

"I am Nis, come to complete the ransom bargain and deliver these two young persons to those who have deemed them valuable."

"Who is your crewmaster, Nis? I understood the Cavalieri Teschio were no more." An arrogant man in red and gold. The bones of his face were long and fine like his son's, but sharper. Fiercer. He thought I was dirt.

. . . and his first question was about you, *not his own boy.* Mam's indignation fired mine.

He stepped closer and my blade pricked the son's throat. The son hissed and moaned, shaking so hard his bones rattled.

"Stay at a proper distance, segno. And tell me who you are that claims these two. Perhaps you are a deceiver. Perhaps these bags are full of grit."

"I'll vouch for the gentleman's identity," said my rich girl, bold as ever. She had taught me how to hold myself proud. "He is Dono's father, Director Advocate Bastianni of the Philosophic Confraternity. My gratitude, Director, for seeing to our rescue."

The young man lifted his head. Blood streaked his chin. His eyes were black and hollow. His face reminded me of famine season.

"Are you ill, Donato, or ill-treated, or merely overwhelmed by a few days' uncertainty and rough living?" asked the father. A cold man, certain. No wonder the rich girl despised him.

"These brigands pretended to be the Cavalieri," said the rich girl. "When Dono dealt with them as a gentleman, they starved and beat him, as you see. My father will ever be grateful for the completion of this bargain."

As she spoke another voice slithered into my head like an eel. *What is this, my lovely? Your power . . . this sweet fire that brings you so close to me . . . blossoms so beautifully. Take my hand and walk with me in this realm.* A finger brushed my face, rousing heat I had not felt since I was thirteen and loved a Cavalieri boy.

This was not Mam, but the wicked spirit Mam had warned of. I must not listen.

Business first. For so long, my word had been the only thing of worth that I owned. So I'd complete this task, and only then seek my pleasures where and when I chose.

The red-gowned man had bared his teeth, inspecting the rich girl. "You seem well and strong, Damizella di Nardo. Somehow that does not surprise me. You might be a good influence on my boy after all—show him how to grow a backbone. I'll summon my men to haul him home. Then you will walk with me and tell me of these ruffians who violated my house and my heir. A prize of one dowdy girl with a rat-sticker, and the retrieval of our payment, will not satisfy my desire to punish them."

"You'll do nothing until we close the contract, segno," I said, speaking up clear as Capo had taught me. "Only then will I set your son and this woman free—alive. My crew honors our word."

Daggers and blood, pleasures we share. That hidden voice again and another touch from somewhere. My breath hitched at the pleasurable heat of it. Smooth, but firm, dry, and so very clean. I longed to live clean, away from rats and dirt. Surely I must split in two—this seducer tempter inside me, and the wicked philosophist outside.

The philosophist laughed. "Certain, we shall complete this bargain, Nis." He hissed my name like an adder. "Have you someone planning to come haul these bags away? All six together are both heavy and cumbersome. Or did you bring a barrow? You seem sturdy enough, the kind of girl who has experience with barrows. Certain, my men could carry them for you, but then why would we do that. Your masters were a bit foolish to send a girl alone."

He wanted me to blurt out that I had crew close by. But I ignored all the temptations. Like evil spirits, men in red-and-gold robes were tricksters who used girls like me. Certain, I didn't want them to pick up the money bags. Not yet.

Chin up, I held out my hand, inviting the contract bond. "No need to carry the bags or inspect them. We accept an honorable man's payment."

He mocked me with a bow. "I accept the return of my son and his affianced bride."

He clasped wrists with me as if I were a proper business partner, though he sneered and wiped his hand on a kerchief when he was done, even polishing a golden ring on one hand as if I had somehow tarnished it.

"All right, then," I said and cut the rich girl's wrists loose. She rubbed them and watched the arrogant man turn his back on us.

I'd thought a rich father might care more for a son than my da had cared for me. But this one was busy waving to someone at the far side of the bridge, while his boy knelt sick and shaking, hands and arms still tightly bound with our ropes.

Kneeling before the trembling young man, I cut the bindings.

Remember the greeting you were to give him, daughter, Mam reminded me. The old-language words that will sooth his ills. Just be wary of what comes after.

The words she'd given me seemed a strange comfort for a man so sick. *"Vieni vicino. Avvisami,"* I said as I pulled the ropes away. They meant, *Come close. Counsel me.*

A thrill of triumph rushed through me, like nothing I'd ever felt. Fire kissed my skin, threaded my veins. I tasted blood—warm and salty and so, so sweet. *Oh, my beauty!*

This was the tempter!

Let us dream together, my darling one. Let us fly. Let us conquer and find perfect vengeance on the Vodai jailers, perfect harmony of earth and sea and sky that is our birthright. You are the doorway. Uncountable generations have I waited for one bold enough to stand in two worlds at once. . . .

The wicked spirit might have been sitting on my shoulder, his breath hot and sweet on my ear. The moonlight dimmed to gray, and lust knotted me so hard I near spilled over with it. From the corner of my eye, I glimpsed a chamber painted with forests and vineyards. A great bed laid with fat pillows and blankets of fur and silk. Clean. Warm. Beckoning me through the door I had just thrown open.

But I did not turn to look at it full on. Not yet. I must not walk through that door. The young man yet knelt in front of me, scarce visible in the graying light. Tears dribbled down his face as he laid gentle, trembling hands on my own cheeks. *"Vattene, spiriti rotti; la tua vera padrona ti aspetta."* His damp forehead touched my own as he whispered, "Thank you. Romy."

The world went black. Howls of obscene joy rose in the distance. I had time enough to know who I truly was.

To comprehend Donato's words of dismissal and sending: *Begone, broken spirits; your true mistress awaits.*

Time enough to feel Dono grasp me in his arms and drag me up and sidewise. To understand what was to come and beg Dumond to be ready with the boat—

My mind dissolved in voices. *Choose this one. Hold me; keep me; send me. So warm . . . so living . . . hot, hot. So near the maker. The source. He wants us . . . needs us . . . wants you. Twist this body . . . break it. Reach for the maker. The walls be thin here, push, squeeze, rip . . . Let us through.*

Demons crowded into my lungs, crushed my heart, my gut, clawed my spine, tore at my hands. Howls and screams hammered on the back of my eyeballs. I thrashed, fought, wrestling the living body who held me. I needed to get away. But where? I couldn't see; the moon and stars had winked out. I couldn't breathe. . . .

"Uff." Someone dragged the one holding me away. I staggered and fell into chaos.

This one is mine own, the doorway to the maker . . . No me. No me. The wailing shredded my spirit.

And then the temptress whispered, *You know what they want, beloved. Send them to me; let them bring me solace for lost companions. Come with them and bring me delight for a new era. We shall talk of stars and music, of mysteries those beneath us shall never know, of truth and gods and lightning. Take my hand and pain will vanish forever.* The woman stood before me in her diaphanous gown. Exquisite. So luminous my heart ached for her beauty. Her lips parted, revealing pointed teeth. She was so hungry. . . .

I blinked. It was the man now. He had the most beautiful hands. Graceful, strong. If I dared touch them, yield to his will, they would be deliciously warm as they swept away this heaviness in my heart, the grieving. . . .

Romy. My name was Romy. Dono had said it before chaos fell, before he was ripped away. *What are your true surroundings, Romy? You are not blind or deaf. What do you hear? Let your senses bring you back to where you are. They'll protect you.*

I heard countless beings crying for help, every one of them different. . . . No, no that was *in*side.

I crouched to the hard surface of the bridge, patting the rough stone as I struggled to get my bearings amidst the noise and chaos. Hard fingers dug into my arms of flesh.

"Stay still, little filth. Sagano, fetch one of your praetorians to bind this wench before she runs away. If she won't tell us who employs her, tear out her hair, her fingernails. What's holding up Bieneto?"

"They found two men in a boat. Think they might be more of the snatch-crew. What of your son, Director? Looked like he was about to kill this one! These snatchers must have brutalized him."

Men in a boat? Cold fear sliced through the din . . . and was quickly drowned before I could consider it. *Push, squeeze, hurt, and this one will let us go. The maker beckons . . . so near the fire . . .*

Touch my hand, lovely one . . . yield to me and all will be right with the world.

Silence, spirits, I pleaded. *Silence, beckoner.* I needed to listen. To attend my senses. To understand.

". . . turtle shell. When Bieneto returns, we'll get the dullard to his feet. Fetch him a cloak. My son is the First Defender of the Confraternity, beaten by sorcerer-brigands. Who knows? They might very well have poisoned him."

Poison! No, no, no. I told myself to keep aware. In control. My knees and chin grated on the paving. My foot was caught between narrow uprights. My arm felt like to be yanked out of its socket as the arrogant speaker tried to drag me away. *Bastianni.*

Let me set you free of pain, beloved. You invited me, now take my hand. Do not toy with me. This time my own hand brushed my face. Pressed on my eyes, grinding in mud and grit from the paving. Why would I do that? Why couldn't I stop?

"Let me go, brute! You've no right to hold me!"

That was Livia, angry. Good. My hand fell away from my eyes.

"Dono, wake up!" she yelled. "Time for vengeance!"

The names glared through the storm like lightning bolts, amidst the thunder of lust, the battering wind of hunger and loneliness, the floodwaters filled with broken bits and jagged pieces. My lungs filled with the debris. . . .

I commanded myself to fix on the names and to breathe. *Force air in and out.*

The cruel hand dropped me on the paving. But his cold body crouched beside me and that hard hand gripped my chin, trying to force my head up. *No.* I alone controlled my thoughts and my actions, and this man must not see my face. Focus on surroundings. Sensations. *Think.*

The fingers were long. Well-manicured. His heavy gold ring bore the engraving of a book, a flame of tiny rubies, and a sharp gold pin, the Confraternity lance—extended outward. Poison . . .

"Look up here, girl. Let me see the devil sorceress who dares challenge the Philosophic Confraternity. There is something so familiar about you."

In a moment of clarity, I reached for the Lhampuri dagger and slashed it across his curled fingers, scraping off a few rubies, the poisoned gold pin, and the skin of his knuckles.

He yelled in pained fury and leapt to his feet, clenched fist dripping blood. Quivering, I scrambled backward, away from him. My back met stone posts, a railing, just as his boot slammed into my side. All breath left me.

Movement and pain drew down the curtain of blackness again. Writhing, weeping, snarling beings squeezed my lungs as I strained for breath. Hundreds more, raw with hunger, churned my stomach. My skull was cracking with their pleas, their bargains, demands, but I had to push back. I could not let them go; the only way out was through the door gaping open in my soul. That's what they wanted. *Please, please, please, send us . . . we are so cold . . . so hungry . . .*

Stay present, Romy. You have to do this. There is no one else.

Steel clashed in the distance. A sharp yell was followed by pounding boots.

A scrambling body took my arm gently, but was wrenched aside.

"Get out the way, young master, damizella. This witch cut the director." Someone grabbed my hair. "Who might you be, girlie? One of these snatchers?"

"She's one of them," said a woman—Livia. "She's the one who tormented Dono and me."

The boots arrived. "Get away from her."

Steel crashed right beside me. "Move aside, young master. This is no time to cower, else you'll get cut with these accursed snatchers."

I buried my head in my arms, unable to care. The harrowing inside was what would kill me.

"We come for our own," bellowed the newcomer between breaths and grunts of effort.

As crashing swords, sliding boots, and angry growls sketched the bloody fight, a woman's quiet voice said, "Now. Together." Icy hands grasped me, wrists and feet. Lifted me.

My back rested on a stone rail.

Then the hands let go with a gentle push, and the bottom fell out of the world.

Surprised rage howled from the dark . . .

Wailing, crushing terror bursting my head . . .

A glimpse of starry ripples below . . . No boat.

My own terror joined the madness, but I remembered to hold open the way. *Master . . . Mistress . . . I bring you these servants . . .* But not yet.

A flash of silver moonlight and the icy water closed over my head, yet still I plunged, down and down, faster and faster. I needed to go up. Swim . . .

Water rushed past my face, tugging at my hair, at my heavy clothes. It snagged my boots and swooshed them away and made my arms' flailing useless. My chest burned. Panic demanded air. Which way was up?

Faster still through the torrent, and soon all I could think of was the cool flood. Rage faded into the depths. The mad wailing inside dissolved into gurgling. The heated voice faded, the open doorway washed clear. Then the world fell quiet save for an occasional muffled slurp.

So deep. The weight of the river comforted and soothed, holding me as I plunged. My lungs no longer burned, though my mind claimed they should, nor did I feel the need to gasp in the airless dark. Had time stopped? Stretched? Or was I drowned already? The rushing water felt so lifelike on my skin. Speculations rippled through my mind . . . unobstructed. My head . . . my soul . . . emptied.

The darkness gave me pause, but this was no heated vision. No seductive voice teased my ears; no exploring finger violated my skin. No begging, threatening mob clouded my senses. The door to that other place, washed clean, was firmly shut. I was Romy, and this formless, watery darkness . . .

The cool water rushed past, faster than any current. How could I still be falling?

Keep all of your senses well-grounded in the place where you are.

My eyes were closed, of course. I squeezed them tighter, then opened them a little. A sting of rushing water and I closed them again. I had seen enough. This was magic, and the silver brilliance that surrounded me, bore me up, and propelled me through the Venia's heart, washing me clean of demons, could be none but Teo.

28

He nudged me gently onto the embankment nearest the city-side abutment of the bridge, steps away from the path to the secret stair. By the time I'd wiped the streaming water from my eyes, he was gone, so I never saw his shape. Nor was I sure if the silvery streak upstream was him or the moonlight.

Not dead. Need fed. Name's Teo . . . for now.

I laughed and wept when the whimsical phrase whispered through my head, miming the first words of comfort he had given me all those months ago.

"Thank you, whatever-your-name-is-to-be," I whispered in return, though I had no notion he could hear. "Come back when you can."

Grim truth quickly overtook that magical moment. I'd no idea where my brother or partners were. Dumond had promised to be waiting close by when I fell from the bridge, with Neri along to help fish me from the river. But in that instant of chaos and terror, they were not there. Certain, there was no sign of Dumond's dinghy upstream of the bridge right now. Gardia wardens with torches patrolled both banks. A flotilla of small boats downstream of the bridge appeared like a bobbing field of fallen stars between the bridge and the flickering lights of the docks in the distance. Which left me with the praetorian's worrisome report of detaining two men in a boat.

Shoeless and dripping, I scrambled over the false buttress to the hidden door. Disappointment struck again when I found none of the Chimera in the hidden stair. But I wished Fortune's blessings on dear Vashti, as I rummaged through her supply of dry clothes. Shapeless tunic and trousers of nondescript brown, a short, ragged cape of fir-needle green, boots I recognized as belonging to her daughter Cittina. An oversize brown wool toque contained my tangle of wet hair. Once I belted a short sword at my waist, I charged up Sandro's stair to the bridge level.

Muffled voices snapping orders outside the stair alcove kept me moving upward, taking the tower steps two at a time. The turret door stood open, and a careful survey showed the roof deserted. The sleepy warden was gone, the ropes left in a heap. The ransom remained, but a loose coin in the corner and a knot that was not my own in all six bag closures told me he had taken a share from each before a hasty exit, thinking no one would notice what was missing. Fair enough; Vashti's drops left a wicked headache. He had likely not summoned a replacement, hoping to come back for the rest.

The view from the parapet was astonishing. The hunt was up. As always, even in the middle of the night, such doings had drawn a noisy mob. Onlookers crowded the bridge, shouting and pointing at the water. Illumination spread slowly across the river as lamplighters fired the dead lamps. Small boats with running lamps crisscrossed the river and trolled the banks, occupants poking the shallows with sticks. Searching for me? Perhaps someone had glimpsed something in the river far more wondrous than a woman thrown off the bridge.

At the far-side end of the bridge, a circle of blazing torches and gleaming helmets surrounded a small knot of people. Livia and Dono? Director Bastianni? Let it not be my brother and Dumond in chains. Or Placidio dead or prisoner. He had been dueling praetorians when I fell.

Other helmed praetorians and Gardia wardens strode through the crowd on the bridge, accosting onlookers here and there. No doubt they were alert for white-skull-marked clothing or perhaps a sodden woman crawling back up the bridge piers.

Like the current of the Venia when a barge approached the docks, the crowd parted to let a sniffer pass, dragging his nullifier. Did the Enemy or his creatures leave traces of magic behind as sorcerers supposedly did?

Nauseating memory near dropped me to my knees. I shook my head and rubbed my arms, as if the sudden movement might dislodge a squirming being left behind by the rushing water. A deep breath in and out and moment of contemplation revealed naught but my own self occupying my skin. Reassuring, though worry for the others still rattled me.

Not daring to stay long atop the tower, I scanned the crowd

once more, frustrated until I spotted a tall fellow with broad, slouching shoulders and an old-fashioned, wide-brimmed hat plodding slowly along the railing. The sight might not have been quite so compelling had the hat's overlarge feather not been so bedraggled as to hang down over his face in just such fashion as might hide an old dueling scar. I knew that hat.

I raced down the stair and out of the alcove, dashing past whatever guards lurked in the tunnel. Once deep into the boisterous melee, I slowed my steps and kept my head low, making as if I were attached to one party of chattering gawkers or another. It might have been noonday, rather than the first hour past midnight.

The big man with the drooping feather leaned his elbows on the downstream railing. He bore every aspect of a curious observer, except for the tight knot of his huge hands as he stared at the rippling water.

He moved on, reluctantly, it seemed. Assuring myself that no one else was paying him any mind, I quickened my steps.

"What news, swordmaster?" I murmured, as I came alongside and matched his long strides.

He kept his head down. "Atladu's holy, everlasting balls, woman," he mumbled. "You are the damnedest."

"For a while, I *felt* like the damned or the drowned, but then . . . oh gods . . ."

A quick glance my way. "He was there. Our friend."

"You *knew* he wasn't dead," I said, forcing my head down and my feet to keep walking rather than shaking my swordmaster until his hair fell out. "I thought—"

I'd thought I was going to die with a thousand demons in my head—or worse, not die, and remain in thrall to the Enemy.

"He wasn't sure he could recover; Romy, he was so low there back at Villa Solitor. We dared not let you think it."

Of course they couldn't tell me that a Vodai Guardian might be waiting to catch me when I fell and ensure I was washed clean of demons. I was planning to open myself to the Enemy and would need every scrap of my own discipline and strength to accomplish my task. Still, I hated that they hadn't told me.

"We *will* talk about this," I said. But at the moment, only one issue truly mattered. "Dumond and Neri? I heard—"

"Last I saw they were drenched and bloody and being dragged

into a crowd of about fifty praetorians and at least three sniffers. Too many for me to take on." His fists and jaw hardened at the admission. "I've not seen 'em hauled off. Not this direction at least. Now the crowd's thinned a bit, I was headed over to see what's what."

"Let's go then."

We squeezed our way through the gawkers, louder and more numerous at this end of the bridge. A few steps on, progress became even more difficult. Armored praetorians leveled their spears, shoving the crowding citizens to the railings and yelling, "Move aside, move aside, let them through! Make way for your betters!"

Standing on tiptoe, I watched the small clot of scarlet-robed philosophists as they passed. Livia's limp red curls peeped out from under a voluminous gray cloak. At her side shambled Donato, cloaked in red, hollow-eyed, but otherwise without expression. On the other side of him strode his father, the director, one hand wrapped in a swathe of stained linen, the other gripping his son's shoulder. Protectively. Possessively.

The posture made my skin crawl.

Placidio nodded. "Both still living and unbound. I think we've carried off this part of our bargain at the least."

"And one villain wounded," I said, willing the damage to Bastianni's knuckles to be painful. "Virtue's Hand, let those two be wary. Bastianni was ready to poison one or both of them."

There were no prisoners in the group. But two sniffers trailed along behind, their featureless faces turning from side to side, silk-clad hands held high as if to grasp magic from the air. Slaves. Demons. Could Dono hear them—those silent wails and moans that had clogged my veins and choked my breath? *Spirits* . . .

At least they didn't turn our way.

Once the party had passed, we pushed our way through the milling onlookers. Gardia wardens tried to disperse the crowd. "Get to your homes. Naught to see here."

Three rowdy sots hurled pebbles and mud clots at a kneeling praetorian who was sifting through a heap of sand. A warden bawled at them, "Move along or we'll have ye on charges."

A praetorian leaned over the parapet, shouting to someone below. "*Tonight,* fool, not a month ago! Nothing newer afloat?"

The reply was indistinct, but elicited no excitement from the soldier.

By the time we reached the steps that led from the brightly lit bridge down to the inky lanes of the Bottoms, we'd seen no sign of Dumond or Neri, no evidence of any arrest or execution. But then, *summary* justice would be rendered down in the dark, not under the blazing lamps.

Grim and wordless, we sped down the steps, past the bundled beggars preparing to occupy the wide stair until the Gardia chased them off at sunrise.

There was no tidy common riverside path on this side of the river. Between the crumbling backsides of old warehouses and tenements and the slopping eddies of the Venia lay a dark, muddy embankment of slimy weeds, unrecognizable refuse, and frequent, dangerous entanglements of mysenthe sellers, smugglers, thugs, and rats.

"You search left; I'll go right," said Placidio as we reached the bottom and drew our blades.

"Need help for that search?" mumbled one of the bundled beggars from the bottom step.

"Three coppers'll get you decent help for sneaking," said the one next to him. "If you're wanting assistance on the water, you needs must look elsewhere."

I spun to see, not daring to believe . . .

"Aye," said Placidio, throwing his head back in a silent crow. "Come along, you two brutes. We'll test your skills right enough."

• • •

We sat on empty casks at the end of a plank table at the Goblin Bait, far from listening ears. In that hour the Goblin Bait's ale tasted like the Shadow Lord's wine, no matter that it looked like something scooped from the puddles in the lane—and might have been. The partners of the Chimera were together in the Bottoms of Cantagna.

Certain, Bottoms was entirely appropriate. The air of the seedy alehouse was so dense with grease and smoke we could hardly see each other. Not that any of us were much to see. Neri and Dumond were miserably wet, though they insisted that the blood in the puddles underneath them was not their own.

"So it worked." Neri's question popped out first. "Dono sent the demons into you and then threw you in the river?"

"The two of them—Dono and Livia—gave me the toss." The acrid aftertaste of the ale had me coughing out my affirmation. And then I sneezed. A great deal of water had gone up my nose. "I saw there was no boat. Went half crazy. Came near drowning. It didn't seem so far to fall when I was thinking about it, but I'll swear I grazed my head on the riverbed."

Neri leaned forward, disappointment crushing his eagerness to rubble. "So Teo wasn't—?"

"So *you* knew the truth, like this one!" I said, jabbing an elbow into Placidio.

Neri blew an ale-soaked exhale. "Couldn't believe it when Swordmaster told me it was possible. Almost couldn't do what needed done down by the river, neither. I wasn't lying about how bad he was."

"You were stronger than me," I said. "I could never have let the river take him. Yes, he was there. I don't know that my plan would have worked without. Certain, I could never have stayed under so long, so deep, or swum so fast. . . ." The powerful sensation of the rushing water flooding around and through me came back for a moment, forcing me to a breathless pause. "I never actually saw him, nor even heard him until he left me. But what of you three? What happened?"

"Thought Papa Dumond and I were done for," said Neri. "After we left the tower, a sniffer caught my trail on the riverside path and hauled us out of the boat. The nullifier smacked us around some, then dragged us up where all the philosophists and praetorians were."

"Saw that," said Placidio. "Couldn't get to you."

"Dono and Livia vowed we weren't the snatchers," said Dumond, as if the marvel of it was still new. "And—"

"Livia said the snatch-crew were pale-skinned Invidians," Neri burst in, "and that must be why they sent Nis to do the talking. And then she went on and on about how dreadful the place was—though she couldn't describe it—and how the 'scurrilous villains only wanted the money' and were so devious as to take advantage of all the hullaballoo about the Cavalieri. I thought old Bastianni was going to toss *her* into the river."

Neri gulped another half mug of ale. "And then somehow the sniffer changed its mind about me, like it lost the trace. Brought in two more, and they didn't mark us neither. The nullifiers wanted to chain us up anyways, but Dono said they had to let us go, as he'd 'not see the integrity of the Defenders of Truth besmirched' out of vengeance over his own abduction. *Besmirched* . . . can't you just imagine it? What a prig he is . . . and yet, gods' truth, what he went through for those hours!"

Neri's effusive tale telling was amusing, but the meat of the story wasn't lost on me. "A sniffer changed its *mind* after pinpointing a sorcerer," I said. "How is that possible?"

"The luck charms?" said Dumond. "It's what we've hoped."

Or maybe Dono could not only *hear* the demons inside sniffers . . . but respond or suppress or divert. I wasn't sure that skill would be worth the plague of hearing them.

"They didn't even get around to ferreting out our real names," said Neri, his enthusiasm undamped. "It was as near as I ever want to get to getting caught. Dono and Livia saved us."

"We should keep our stories for Vash," said Dumond, rising from his splintery stool. "Doubt if she's slept in four days, and how she got all the goods to that stair has got to be a story of its own. Can't say I want to venture city gates right now, but I'm thinking we could go around outside the walls and meander through that Bastianni mausoleum again. For me, that's not so far from home."

Certain, we had some thinking to do. Our relief at being free, relatively unscathed, and—on my part—of relatively sound mind could not mitigate our uncertainty about what we had accomplished. Was the Villa Giusti *pérasma* spring truly free of demons? Would Livia's scheme to sour the pool prevent more of them roosting should any come drifting by? And our two marks . . . what would become of them? Would Dono truly challenge his father? And what would we do about Director Bastianni who had now seen Dumond and Neri, false names or no? If I had a spymaster to whom I must report, I'd have no idea what to tell him of our mission.

"Go home, Dumond. Certain, you should spend time with Vashti and the girls," I said. "We should all get some sleep. Stay apart until things cool down a bit, as we've done before. Maybe then we can make some sense of what we've done."

We agreed to meet at Dumond's the next evening at the Hour of Contemplation if all seemed well.

Avoiding the Avanci Bridge, we took the long way around through the Bottoms to its partner, the Vinci. Once we were back cityside, Dumond split off, taking the main road that led around to the north side of the city. Placidio, Neri, and I took the riverside path upriver, a shorter route for the three of us to get home. Neri and I walked together; Placidio followed well behind. Gardia patrols were thick along the river path.

We decided it was too risky to fetch what might be left of the ransom atop the Avanci Tower, but we did take a few careful moments to clear the hidden stair. Vashti's two large canvas bags crammed with rope and bandages, sponges, ale flasks, and our wet and bloody clothing would provide us a good cover as scavengers, and *il Padroné* would find nothing untoward should he care to stroll the bridge privately any time soon.

Neri left us at the South Gate. He wanted to stop by the Duck's Bone and meet up with a friend. Food and ale, I guessed. Maybe the friend was a bed partner. With difficulty I refrained from any and all sisterly warnings.

I was happy to walk on with Placidio. He planned to sleep at the woolhouse. He was always cautious at reentering his life after a mission, concerned that someone who had seen him fight might make a connection with Placidio di Vasil, the duelist.

The closer I got to the River Gate that would take me home, the slower I walked. When it came time for me to turn, Placidio paused, but I walked straight onward. The night was cool, but not unnaturally chilly. The moon was setting, abandoning the sky to brilliant stars. I needed no light to find the familiar track to the woolhouse.

"You're not wanting to sleep, I'm thinking," said my companion, rejoining me.

"Don't want to dream."

"'Twas a brave thing you did tonight," he said.

"All of us—"

"We did our parts, but you risked your life, your mind, everything. If those two children have any sort of sane, honorable life ahead of them, it's you they've to thank. And here—" He dug in his waist pocket and laid a slip of metal in my hand. "Told you I'd give it back when you were back safe."

I needed no light to recognize my luck charm either. I had decided that if our theories were correct that the luck charm protected us from sniffers because they somehow shielded us from the demon inside that sniffer, then I'd best not have it on me when Donato sent a horde of demons my way. The scheme had worked, so perhaps we were right.

Placidio hadn't argued with the logic. He had been quiet over these past days . . . standing stalwart to the side, guarding our backs, unsurprised as we unraveled the mysteries of demons and myth.

"You knew about the triangle symbol, didn't you?" I said. "You knew about it long before Dumond gave you a charm."

We walked a little farther before he answered, guarded as ever, when we drew near the mysteries of his own past.

"I'd seen it. Didn't know its meaning, or whether it bore any power of its own, only that it was the sign of the Vodai—the mages of the water—the Timeless Watch."

What had Teo said when telling the story of his family? They had *offered the world their own future to maintain* Macheon's prison. "The Watch . . . They guard the Enemy, maintain the protections that confine him."

"Aye."

"That means, if Teo came here last spring to find the Antigonean Bronze—the statue of Atladu and Dragonis—as we surmised, then it must play a part in those protections."

"That would be a logical conclusion. I know naught of what that might be."

Placidio had told me that he once lived near the sea and knew a woman from the Isles of Lesh. He'd said she had the skin markings and skills similar to Teo's.

"The woman you knew from Lesh, she was a Guardian like Teo."

"She was a Guardian, but not like Teo. He is . . . more."

"And she?"

"She was my mother."

I inhaled sharply, but did not press. He had given me a gift that he knew would distract me from the lowering clouds of my dreams. My best thanks for that gift would be waiting until he was ready to give more.

"We have to see Donato and Livia again," I said, after a while. "I need to remove their memory of Teo. Nothing we've done tonight will undo Dono's link to Macheon. And who knows what Livia believes or will write or say when she is ready? We can't have them remembering anything about Vodai Guardians."

"I think that would be very wise. Tomorrow night—well, tonight it would be—after the day to let things settle a bit in the Villa Giusti, we could have Neri pay Dono a visit and arrange a meeting. By that time Dono should know his situation better and perhaps the status of the *pérasma*."

We walked a little farther, past the old docks where I'd first pulled Teo from the water. I slowed, hesitating. "I should head for home."

"If you would sleep better with a body nearby, come along to the woolhouse. Go home in the morning."

Though I felt a bit foolish, I did exactly that.

29

By the time I woke, afternoon sunlight poured through the woolhouse doorway and Placidio was gone. He'd laid his ugly robe over me. A filled mug of salt-and-ginger tea and a decent dagger lay where I could not miss them when I woke. Livia's fine Lhampuri blade had been lost after my attack on Bastianni.

I'd had no dreams that I could recall, and the air felt cool and the sunbeams pleasantly warm—good signs that the Enemy had not snuck into my sleep and raised the fire in my blood. I had felt a door close between Malcheon and me as Teo propelled me through the river. I wouldn't fool myself that it would stay closed forever, especially when I used my magic. But my friend the Vodai's lessons had stood me well and I would practice them every day of my life.

Holding my nose, I downed the awful lukewarm tea; though I'd never admit the fact to Placidio or Neri, it did return a bit of stamina after a rough stint of activity. Only when I'd drained the cup and wiped it out did I notice a fold of parchment tucked under the knife sheath. My scribe's eye identified it as fine parchment.

I snatched it up. Evidently Placidio or Neri had checked message box number six while I slept. It was admirable restraint that they'd not broken the plain red seal, but they certainly should have waked me to do so. They knew who'd likely sent it. One glance at the familiar script affirmed my guess.

To the Chimera: I was notified in the dark hours of the successful ransom exchange for my vicino-figlia *and the young man to whom she is contracted in marriage. I was gratified that they are seemingly unharmed. I was also told that the villains who snatched them from their beds by such extraordinary means were not apprehended. One, a woman, fell from the bridge. This outcome concerns me greatly.*

Although I've as yet had no chance to speak to the two young victims since their return, I have it on good authority that discrep-

*ancies have arisen concerning the marriage contract and that the
nuptials are indefinitely postponed. Perhaps not forever, though,
as the young woman has accepted the gracious offer of protection
by the gentleman and his family.*

*I would very much like to discuss these matters with you. I will
be taking coffee at a favorite Garden spot this evening at the Hour
of Contemplation.*

So, one question answered. They weren't married. Yet.

I believed Dono would keep to his bargain if his position was
secure as he had hoped. But we didn't know that for certain. The
discrepancies Sandro mentioned could result from a challenge or
from the questions I'd raised about the contract's timing. Which
meant I had no idea if Livia had *chosen* to stay on. Her continued
residence at Villa Giusti might be a result of the family courtesies
Donato specified as necessary for their safety or simply because
Director Bastianni had decreed it so.

We needed to speak to Donato and Livia in person.

Pocketing the note, I leapt to my feet, strapped on the dagger,
and headed for the city and home. I would rid myself of the river
stink, find out where everyone was, and dispatch Neri to contact
Dono. At sometime after the Hour of Contemplation, I would meet
Sandro at his favorite bench in the Ucelli Gardens. Not so much
to ease his concerns about my welfare. He needed to hear what I
had to tell.

• • •

I'd scarcely had time to wash and dress when Neri burst through
our door. "You've got to come now, slugabed! It's Donato and
Livia!"

"What? What's happened?" Every sort of vision cascaded
through my head, from a forced wedding processional through
the Heights to the two being paraded in chains to the ship that
would take them to the Executioner of the Demon Tainted.

"I paid Dono a visit. Swordmaster said you'd talked about it."

"What? In the middle of the afternoon? How stupid—" I bit my
tongue. "Go on."

"I figured he'd be sleeping late, like all the rest of us. And he
was. I fixed on his signet, the one he wears around his neck, and

Cate Glass

sure enough I was able to walk right into his bedchamber." He rolled his eyes. "And yes, I made sure no one was in there watching over him."

"So he's all right. Not chained up or—"

"Nah. He says they are both all right. He's being watched close, but he thinks his da believes the snatch and the exchange. I told him we wanted a parlay, and he said the two of them—and lots more people—would be in the Ucelli Gardens at the Hour of Gathering. Then someone tapped on the door and I had to get out."

"The Ucelli Gardens!"

"Aye. *Il Padroné* is honoring Livia with a birthday celebration. Evidently no one at the villa wanted it—not even Livia, who's never even met him—but of course, it's *il Padroné* . . ."

". . . and even Director Bastianni daren't say no. You didn't—"

Neri's glare spoke clearly. He knew what I was going to say.

"Certain, you knew better than to mention *il Padroné*'s role in all this," I said, swallowing my question. "I do trust you, little brother. You are the spark that makes the Chimera work. You have leave to glare at me and roll your eyes anytime I forget that. Old habits are hard to shake."

Neri brayed like a donkey and proceeded to devour all the sausage in our larder while I gave thought to how to work this plan. I couldn't use a true impersonation; they would have sniffers everywhere about the gardens. Two episodes of memory-replacement magic would be quite risky enough for one evening. Besides, I wasn't sure I was ready to breach the Singular Wall so blatantly as yet. Another requirement, I had to go alone to the celebration. Director Bastianni had seen Placidio last spring when we played archaeology scholars in front of the Public Arts Commission, and he'd seen both Dumond and Neri on the bridge. So I couldn't bring any of them safely.

"Tell the others I'm doing this one myself. And with no magic save for the memory adjustments. They'll know why. I'll make it quick, but it would be well if I had reinforcements available. The Gardens have three gates."

"Got it," said Neri. "And I won't tell you to be careful and don't do anything loony, even though I feel the need to get in the habit of it."

I shoved him out the door so I wouldn't see his smirk.

So, what to wear? I'd believed I was done with intrigue for a while. But this venture could provide answers to our most important questions about Livia and Dono and the *pérasma*. And then I could stroll across the lawn to a very particular secluded bench and have a conversation with the Shadow Lord. I did not explore my sense of relief to know that the birthday celebration made his choice of the Ucelli Gardens for our assignation a logical convenience. Better a reasoned choice than some pointed reminder of us two drinking coffee on that particular bench.

• • •

The Hour of Gathering. The time for fortunate families to light the lamps at home . . . to make food . . . drink wine. The time to end arguments. To make music. The time when day markets closed and night markets opened, and when the destitute could stand quietly in the lanes where sellers might discard withered fruit or meat that could not last through a warm night.

In the Ucelli Gardens all was celebration. The white pavilion appeared as an island of light floating in a darkening sea of grassy swales, groves, and autumn flowers. Lanterns were hung from the branches of autumn-hued trees like the stars I'd seen reflected in the river on the previous night. The music of vielles and flutes floated on the cool air alongside laughter and conversation.

I pulled the voluminous gray cloak around my shoulders. Made sure the folds of my plum-colored underskirt showed stylishly through slits in my plain black skirt. Adjusted the fat, plushy toque that covered my hair and tugged at the filmy veil that would float in front of my face. A Beggars Ring seamstress had been delighted to press the wrinkles from a costume I had used when impersonating a wealthy young matron. I'd had no time to seek help from Vashti.

From what I could see, some seventy or eighty guests had obeyed *il Padroné*'s request to honor his *vicino-figlia*'s coming of age. I watched from a grove of birch trees atop a soft knoll about halfway between the pavilion and the Ucelli's south gate, where a gardener was packing up his barrow of tools after a hard day's work. Only it was Placidio, who had paid the gardener a fair sum to borrow his barrow and tools for the evening. Neri and Dumond manned the other two gates.

I held back until the evening waned a bit more, allowing the paths through the groves outside the party ring to be a little darker. A pause in the music yielded to unintelligible speeches followed by cheers and applause. The birthday well-wishes. When the music resumed, the guests scattered a bit, strolling about the gardens. Time to go.

A short sprint across a darkening meadow brought me up behind a small party who had taken a turn around a small pond. They were speaking of ducks and swans and whether it was fair to hunt them in such a lovely place. An older woman stopped to adjust her shoe, waving the others on. I offered to hold her steady and then took up the conversation as if I'd been there all the while.

Talking of gravel paths, and cobblestones, and shoes, we drifted back toward the pavilion where food and drink enough for half the city had been laid out.

"Such a pleasure, damizella," said the elderly lady with the uncomfortable shoe. "I shall certainly give your cobbler a try. I would as soon wear peasant clogs as these miserable pattens."

I wished her more comfortable feet and scanned the crowd. Directly across the pavilion, Livia's exuberant hair stood out like a beacon. She stood beside her father, the city's steward, speaking to several ladies. I did not see Sandro, though I guessed him to be the center of a boisterous group off to my left.

My costume would not bear scrutiny under the bright lamps underneath the canopy. Nor would my face, even veiled, bear scrutiny from many of the guests. Thus I snatched a cup of wine from a side table and meandered along the peripheries until I found where the servants were refilling the wine pitchers.

"Young man," I said to one. "These lights are sorely bothersome to my poor eyes—I have a condition, you see—but I *must* offer my felicitations to Damizella di Nardo. Would you take her a message for me? What is your name?"

"Certain, segna. One moment." He wiped his hands and bowed. "My name is Oswilio. What message?"

"Tell her that her friend is waiting by the swan pool, wanting to know how she got to be so very brave." I lifted my veil and winked at him in my best Moon House fashion. "Don't fail me, Oswilio. It's a jest between us."

"Right-right away, segn—damizella. Certain."

I retired to a stone bench by the swan pool. Livia arrived before I could drain my wine cup.

"Romy?" she said, keeping a few steps away. By speaking my name, she demonstrated exactly why I had to do what I'd come to do.

"Indeed so. Alive and possessed of my own mind."

The very air moved aside for her, she rushed so quickly to my side. "I'm so glad. I've felt so awful throwing you in like that. And I need to ask you more about what you experienced last night. . . ."

"Shh. I daren't stay but a few moments, and you need to get back before you're missed. I just have know to how things have fallen out here. Are you free?"

She took my hands in hers. "We challenged the contract. His father balked, but Dono held firm. He told his father that he could not dishonor his office by accepting a marriage contract the woman was not prepared for. As his duties kept him so preoccupied, it was necessary that his wife be 'comfortably left on her own.'"

"So you *chose* to stay?"

"I did. I told his father I wished to study both Confraternity history and . . . diseases of the mind. But we are not betrothed or otherwise committed to stay together. I made that clear and Dono agreed. We will talk and dine and perhaps travel—if something can be done about his illness. And if I can help him bring down the villain who murdered Marsilia, my stay will be doubly worthwhile."

"I'm glad it's your choice. About your friend the bookbinder, I found her before she died. . . ." I told of Marsilia's bravery and her clever hiding place.

"Oh, stars." Her bright spirit had turned ragged. "She died for me."

"She believed in you. At some time, when you think it safe, I'll return your papers and the book. Until then, they'll be well-protected."

"I can't say when," she said. "Dono and I will have to be so careful."

"That's very true. And you must persuade Dono to tell you the truth of his . . . condition. It should be a part of your getting to know each other."

"That is most certainly true. Thank you, Romy. I do like being alive. Which means I should go."

"I need to speak to Dono as well."

"I'll send him."

"Just one more thing, Livia. I want to tell you how I recall a few things about our adventure . . ." As I spoke, I reached deep for magic.

I had rehearsed the story I would tell her, and the variant I would tell Donato, not only replacing Teo with a wandering soldier of amazing strength who had died in the river, but also replacing Romy, Placidio, Neri, and Dumond with four people who looked nothing like us. I made the least possible changes needed to protect our identities.

"If you ever need help, send a message to the box I told you and someone will answer."

"Message box six, yes, in the Beggars Ring Road. All right . . . thank you . . . uh . . . dama. Tell Nis she was a great comfort and I'm sorry we threw her in the river. We were just so angry. . . ."

The uncertainty in her voice grieved me. As ever, I hated the breakage this magic left behind, fragments that could never be resolved no matter how hard she puzzled. And I could not help but regret removing the chance to know her better. But this was for her safety and Dono's, as well as ours and Teo's.

"You'll send Dono here, yes?"

"Of course. Fortune's benefice, segna."

"Virtue's hand uplift thee always, Livia."

She took a last puzzled look at me and vanished into the dark.

So Donato had kept his word. Certain, it was the lure of the Athenaeum—and perhaps the chance at understanding the events she had witnessed—kept Livia at his side. Perhaps something else, as well. I entertained the notion that an attachment had developed between the two over those last few hours. Foolish perhaps. Or an echo of the romantic streak I had developed in my years with Sandro, and excised so bitterly on the day he discarded me. But shared hardships could create interesting friendships. Livia had stayed solid and true to her beliefs through unbelievable and horrific events, but her curiosity would lead her forward, not hold her back. Her concern for Donato at the end had been generous. And he . . . what a sad, strange, brave young man who had done so much that was reprehensible . . . and yet desired so deeply to do better. Maybe a dose of intelligent, acerbic Livia would help him on his path.

"Romy?"

I sighed at the reminder of necessity, yet again. "Indeed so."

"Strange. Livia couldn't recall your name." Dono, too, sat beside me as if we'd been friends for a lifetime. As if we did not stand at opposite compass points with regard to the moral foundations of magic.

"You're free of them," he said, knowing I wouldn't be sitting there if I yet had a horde of demons inside me. "I—I hoped I would hear news of you. So it was indeed the river, the flow of water took them . . . and the Enemy . . . away."

"It was magic," I said. "The demons were created by twisted, horrible magic, but restored by something marvelous, healthy, and beautiful."

"I'm guessing your friend, the . . . Vodai Guardian . . . lived after all."

"I will not speak of him again, and you must not either. We are all at risk. Thank you for seeing that my brother and our friend were not taken."

"How could I not after what you all did for me?"

"Livia says you kept your word about the contract. And yet she chose to stay."

"She seems agreeable to a term of courtship. Though truly I think the lure of our library outweighs her anxieties about me or my father. I swore to her and I will to you, that she will never be used to destroy her father."

"Even though—on the bridge, I saw your father yet believes you are his puppet."

"He does. For now. But he's not stupid, either. He will worry that I am out of his sight even for these few moments. My position must be secure before I move, but I *will* move. Thwart, undermine, expose his crimes. Likely it will not be this month."

"Good. I trust you, Dono, but you've chosen a very hard road. I've lived— Well, you've already come through a great deal, so I have faith you can do this, too. Watch your back. Your father wore a poison ring on the bridge."

"That is not a new threat," he said.

"Well, keep your mind open. And though the Enemy will ever be a danger—as he is for me—remember that your soul houses no demon, only a powerful talent that is neither good nor evil in itself. Listen to Livia. Keep her safe."

"I'll do my best at all of those things."

"Have you gone back as yet?" He would know where.

"I have. This afternoon before coming here. All is quiet. I didn't do a summoning, but for years I've felt . . . I called them lingerers. Ones who did not go deep when sent back to the pool. It's as if they wish to be first in line to claim a life. Whenever I light a lamp or stir the ashes in the bowl, I feel them. But not today. I'm hopeful."

Which he had not been for a very long time. "I wouldn't want to do all this again," I said.

"Nor I. Livia believes she can clog the spring without anyone knowing. She might need your friend Dumond to acquire the material she needs and your brother to bring it."

As I gave him the message box number, I thought of one more thing. "One more favor. At some time, I wonder if my friends and I might perhaps borrow a book or two from the Athenaeum. We all should be learning our history. Would that be possible?"

"Yes, of course. Send me a message . . . best make it to Livia. Perhaps with a code word. How about *incrocio*?"

"Crossroad—the Cavalieri code word!"

"It'll not be used for that ever again," he said. "I swear it."

"Good." I laid my hand on his and reached for magic. "Before I go, I need to go over a few things about our story. . . ."

I told him his new truth and sent him away puzzled.

The bells of the Palazzo Segnori were ringing the Hour of Contemplation. The quiet hour after the bustle of dinners and birthday celebrations or putting children to bed. The time Vashti was expecting the four of us to return and celebrate the completion of our mission. I looked forward to that.

One more assignation first. Convenient that the man putting on the birthday celebration was the one I was to meet, so I didn't have far to go.

I strolled from the swan pond up the path to the highest point in the Gardens. Tucked into a grove of aged chestnut trees was a wooden bench. It had been installed there by Sandro's grandfather Giovanni some sixty years past. Giovanni would sit there of a morning with his beloved wife . . . and later with his beloved grandson . . . and drink coffee from a flask while watching the sunrise. Sandro said they rarely talked. Indeed the eastern prospect was glorious— orderly vineyards and fields of lavender, olive groves, and the far distant mountains of Riccia, and just a glimmer Sandro claimed was the sea, but was likely not.

Sandro had taken me there often, and though I hated rising so early, it had been a special place.

He was already there. He jumped up as my shoes crunched on the gravel path. Naught but a silhouette—but perfectly familiar. Even his profile was beautiful.

"Was it you?" he said, as if the question had already been spoken and was just waiting for ears to hear it. "When I heard . . ."

I halted at the top of the path, not quite sure what to do. My feet were tired; I wore ladies' slippers, not boots or pattens. They were scarce better than bare feet on the gravel. But I was not going to sit beside him on his grandfather's bench as if we were old friends, catching up on gossip. I unclipped my cloak and threw it on the grass, along with the toque and its veil that smelled of mildew. I sat on them.

"I didn't jump. I was thrown."

"Boundless Night! Why? I've heard such strange reports of the goings on. Donato was ill, and the Cavalieri woman who came to collect the ransom was strange . . . but not you. Yet when I heard she jumped . . . fell . . . I could not but get it out of my head that somehow it *was* you."

Sandro was a cool and dangerous man. I had not heard him speak with such urgency since well before I'd left his house.

"The fall was planned. I certainly wasn't going to let myself be arrested. I've discovered I am a very fine swimmer."

Clearly my sitting on the grass unsettled him. Standing was far too awkward. He sat on the bench fidgeting. Then, before I could get out another word, he sat himself on the ground in front of the bench.

I had to be careful with my questions and the information I wanted him to hear. We had never talked of sorcery, of course, while I lived with him, and I felt it best to keep the subject at a distance. He upheld the law.

"This was a lovely celebration of your near-daughter," I said. "Rinaldo is your friend and yet you were worried about his motives in forcing a marriage with her."

"Rinaldo's political motives are not always as agreeable as his company. I didn't like the potential for compromising our most

honorable steward. And I didn't like seeing those motives engulfing a promising young woman's intellectual pursuits. The Confraternity is not so welcoming of new ideas in natural philosophy."

"Your concern was and is well-founded," I said. "She is a
brilliant young woman and certainly forthright. I'm happy that
they've come to a reasonable agreement as to the contract. Livia
has chosen freely to stay, as long as no permanent commitment is
involved. She's discovered that she and Donato have some common interests. Though I disagree with him on many issues, he is
an extraordinary young man."

Sandro was up again, pacing short lengths in front of the bench.
After a few moments of stewing, he burst out, "How in the name
of reason did you convince Donato to challenge the contract? What
common interests could he possibly have with a young woman of
intellect? When Mantegna explained all he told you, I worried that
I had set an impossible task. And there was so little time . . ."

Of a sudden, I felt most uncomfortable. "Segnoré, I believe your
questions violate our agreement."

"Ah, damnation. Of course, you're right." His entire posture
stiffened. "I have overstepped. Please, forgive me. The task I set
has been amicably concluded. My *vicino-figlia* is satisfied that she
will be safe and free to pursue her studies."

It was uncanny to watch Sandro shift so smoothly between the
role of *il Padroné*—the benevolent guardian of a young scholar and
generous monitor of good order trying to maintain balance between all segments of the city—and a man who cared about Romy
of Lizard's Alley, whom he'd once known by another name. Now I
wanted to evoke his third persona.

"Livia is certainly not afraid to ask questions that the Confraternity and others deem unsuitable for conversation. As for her
safety, I'm wondering if you heard about a woman brutally murdered a few nights ago in the Street of the Bookbinders. Her name
was Marsilia di Bianchi. As it happens, she was a publisher of trea-
tises and a great friend of your *vicino-figlia*. Livia, in her current
situation, might be reluctant to broach the subject. The Confraternity has a long reach."

"I'll look into that." And there he was—the Shadow Lord, cold
and remote. Odd that I was more comfortable with him in that role
nowadays than in his other personae.

He drew a small bag from his cloak that was draped over the back of the bench and passed it to me. "The Chimera's fee, damizella."

I'd entirely forgotten that we were to get paid for this exercise.

"If you have a moment, there was one more matter I wanted to speak of," he said, seating himself on the bench and leaning forward as he dropped his voice. "Since the earthquake caused such a setback on the coliseum, we've had to cancel many art commissions. I've tried to find other works for the artists to keep them here, keep them fed, so I persuaded the Arts Commission to restore the old Palazzo Respighi into a cultural center. The work proceeds, but someone is damaging the artwork. No matter how many guards I set each night, by morning the work is drab and colorless. If we don't find out who's doing it, the Commission will withdraw their support. So I thought perhaps the Chimera . . ."

"Not tonight. Certain, they will be happy to hear your proposal, but I've . . . people waiting who will worry if I'm not there. The past few days have been difficult. If you'll forgive me . . ."

"Of course. Another time. I'll send a message."

"Fortune's benefice, *Padroné*. May your good works prosper."

"Virtue's hand, damizella."

I gathered my mantle and the ugly hat and left the most powerful man in Cantagna sitting alone on his grandfather's bench.

Every step down that hill, I felt lighter. I found Placidio outside the south gate, sitting in the gardener's barrow sipping on a flask of wine cadged from a serving girl. We collected Neri and Dumond and headed down the Serpentine.

"All's well," I said. "The young lady and young gentleman are amicably unmarried and have no memory of Teo or our names. We have an invitation to use the library. Dono seems to be in grace with his accursed father and senses no demons in the *pérasma*. And the Shadow Lord is properly confounded by our methods but has seen fit to pay us." I patted the bag suspended from my shoulder under my cloak. "I think we should buy at least a barrel of wine and share it out with whatever delectables Vashti has waiting."

"Oh, let it be that wonder she does with mussels and garlic and cream," said Neri. "A vat of it. I've been dreaming about it for a sevenday. Should we bring a cow? We could afford it. . . ."

He opened up his cloak to reveal a miller's bag hung from his shoulder. "Only one was left, and it's maybe half the weight, but it's not nothing."

We all commended his diligence and I said nothing of fool-hardy risks.

"There'll be pilchards, at the least," said Dumond. "We found a great crock of them outside our door this morning."

"Truly?" I said, my mind leaping to Teo.

"Those were from *me*," said Placidio. "This lady was snoring so loudly at the woolhouse, I hiked down to the docks to fetch some, as the last got lost in that bloody flood before I got a taste."

"That should be a new song to be presented at one of *il Padroné*'s fairs," said Neri. "'The Lay of the Lady, the Monster, and the Lost Pilchards.'"

We sang some other songs as we descended the Serpentine. I couldn't recall ever doing that, wandering through a Cantagnan night singing. The Enemy was still strong. I still feared my dreams—and knew why. But for tonight we were going home to our family where we would feast, and tell tales, and laugh at the dangers we had faced.

I envied Livia's talk of traveling the world. Surely celebrity could await me in a troupe of touring actors. But, certain, such celebrity would be short-lived. I would draw the notice of the philosophists, and end up in the hidden fortress of the Executioner of the Demon Tainted, who would bind me with chains and throw me into the sea. But Teo . . . I smiled. If Teo came again, perhaps I could persuade him to whisk me off to the Isles of Lesh for a while to introduce those who stood guard against the monster and show me the beauties of his watery home. Until then, I would be a diligent Beggars Ring law scribe and await our next adventure.

Acknowledgments

To name everyone who has supported me in my journey of words is quite impossible. Sometimes it is a singular encounter that carries me through a tough writing day—a few words from a newly returned soldier at a con, a shy hello email from a reader, a timely comment from a fellow writer. Sometimes it is another five-hour lunch with Linda the Muse, who was there at the beginning and has kept me honest at every step since. Or maybe a fortnight of walks, wine, and writing in beautiful British Colombia with Brenda. Sometimes it is my ever-faithful critiquing crew—Susan, Saytchyn, Curt, and the two most excellent Brians—who offer insight, enlightenment, or simply the poke that forces me to try harder and think deeper. Sometimes it is a long weekend with the Writers of the Hand and the generous welcoming of the Staff of the Hand that provides the focus and camaraderie to get moving on a new project or wrap up an old one. Membership in the community of writers is certainly one of the greatest rewards of this strange profession. I must also thank the Editors—Lindsey, Laura Anne, and Anne—and the one and only Agent Lucienne for their critical reading and professionalism over twenty years of publishing the tales that I want to write. And my love and gratitude, always and ever, goes to the Exceptional Spouse and our family for aiding, abetting, and understanding.

About the Author

Cate Glass is a writer of fantasy adventure novels. She also dabbles from time to time in epic fantasy and short fiction. For more information, check out categlass.com or follow her on Twitter @cbergwriter.